Truth

Nick Sabino

Contents

For my angel on earth and my angel in heaven

Prelude

If you're someone who lived through a divorce then I suspect you'll have a different experience reading this book.

Chapter 1

All's Well that Ends Well

A sliver of light poured in on the boy's dark room as he knelt, almost motionless, next to his door. He was a small boy, only about seven years old, with well combed straight black hair. His light brown eyes were twinkling from the buildup of tears. He relentlessly fought them back. He held his beagle, Rex, as tight as he could, the warmth of the dog's fur providing him little comfort. The posters of his favorite baseball players, his idols, taped to his dull, white walls brought him no solace. Going under the covers wouldn't help him escape either. He already learned that lesson on other nights like this. He knelt there alone, fear coursing through his veins, tears running down his face, and there was absolutely nothing he could do about it.

Time and time again he listened to the fighting, the screaming as his parents clashed with each other. The violence had become a normal activity, although it was one he still couldn't bear. Tonight was different. It was louder, more fierce than usual. The voices of his parents shot through him like knives, making him twinge in pain. Rex squirmed in his arms, trying to break free of his firm grasp, but the boy wouldn't let go. He placed his head down against the dog, still fighting back tears and praying it would just end already. His pressing tears sparked a rage deep inside, a rage he could feel surging through his body.

"We're leaving!" his mother screamed, the voice getting louder as she stormed towards his room. He jumped from the floor; Rex finally released from his grasp, and dove into his bed as his door was swung open. Time froze instantly. The next minute, the next sixty seconds, would play clearly in the boy's mind forever. A scar that would lie embedded deep in his heart,

to reopen frequently, to hide always, and to speak about with no one. The boy was a therapist's nightmare.

He saw his mother, Eileen, standing in his room looking destroyed, her beautiful face covered in fear, her eyes watery and red. Eileen was in her thirties. She had long dark brown hair and light hazel eyes. He loved his mother because she mirrored strength, certainty, and fairness. But none of that showed tonight. She trembled as she touched his hand. Her voice quivered and exposed her terror. She was wearing a pair of blue jeans and an old tank top. Ethan had never seen her looking so normal before. She usually had her makeup and hair done with something fashionable on. She was even lacking her signature Chanel N°5 perfume. Her smell scared Ethan. He wasn't used to her seeming so human and normal. She was always his superhero. With his mother's trembling hand loosely grasping his, he stumbled out of his room and saw him.

His name was Andrew Alosi, a New York City police detective who stood about 5'8'' with tanned skin and short, cropped dark hair. Andrew was the big man that should be called "father". The man small boys should respect and hope to resemble when they have children of their own. Ethan saw him sitting there on his couch, head shaking left to right in his hands. The man who coached his little league team, who taught him how to ride a two wheeler, who was supposed to show him how to tie a tie and fix a flat. He was giving up.

As Ethan crossed the living room, his father raised his head and their eyes met. He wanted to see a hint of remorse, a smile, or even a slight nod. Instead the man looked aggravated. Ethan was so confused. Why were they leaving? Where were they going? What's *wrong with dad? As they crossed the living room where he sat, no one had the slightest idea of*

what was really happening. A small, innocent boy was being destroyed inside. His heart ripped

slowly in half, a very faint spark of fury developing with every second. His father was staring at

a ticking time bomb, a force not to be reckoned with—a child whose face was blanketed in tears

and engrained with animosity. The two would never forget this second. As Ethan stared at his

father, he could feel his tears falling; however, he wasn't sad. He could feel this strange

emotion he had never felt before. A slight hint of this bubbling fire that he would desperately

try to extinguish for many years to come. Anger.

Chapter 2

Sex and Maseratis

What a gorgeous day. The sun shined brightly through the dark blue shades as Walter Veteri made his morning coffee. He skimmed through the New York Post, watched a little television, and brushed his teeth. He put on his jacket, smiled in the mirror, and then walked out the front door. Just another normal, pleasant morning in his perfect life. He smiled to himself as he adjusted his beautiful Maserati's rear view mirror. 'Life Is good,' he thought.

The man wasn't very attractive. He had a good amount of acne covering his pudgy face, and he stood about 5'5''. What Walter Veteri did have was a very attractive bank account. Stocks and Wall Street made sense to him. They made a lot of sense actually. He had found that despite his lack of good looks, money solved many problems.

Walter walked through his office, smiling and joking with his co-workers and building on his established strong reputation. The man glowed with power. They all smiled back at him. They loved the guy; they praised him like he was some sort of financial analysis God. He sat at his oversized desk, kicked his feet up, and did what he did best: he analyzed stocks. He made his phone calls, yelled at a few people, and before he knew it there was yet another day gone. Everybody in the office waved goodbye to the man they believed to be great. They waved at the man they believed was flawless, but everyone has their deep, dark secrets.

Walter marched down the marble staircase that led from his job to the parking lot, hopped into his car, and happily started the drive back to his luxurious home. Along the way he passed the Holiday Inn he frequented. Passing the hotel always made him smile, just seeing the building reminded him of some memorable experiences. His mouth watered as he smiled cynically. Walter slowly pulled into his driveway, parking his car behind his gorgeous girlfriend's blood red BMW.

Walter kept her around because she was a good house-wife. She took care of most of the chores, cooked him dinner, packed him a nice lunch, and she always smiled. She was a petite, happy machine. Walter couldn't care less if she knew about his excursions at the Holiday Inn. He knew he was a gift. Should she feel like getting smart, he would simply dump her and find a new toy.

Walter was greeted by the exhilarating aroma of a delicious home cooked meal of rigatoni with freshly made Bolognese sauce. Smiling widely, he dropped his briefcase by the door, hung his jacket up on the coat rack, and kicked his shoes off. He walked into the kitchen where he was attacked by a giant hug and kiss from his girlfriend, Naomi Menard. Walter sat back, embracing what he thought to be the good life.

This was the last normal day Walter would ever have. This was the last day he would cockily stroll through his office and embrace his success with such triumphant satisfaction. The last day he would admire a woman's elegance and beauty while he waited for a delicious meal. Walter wouldn't even make it to his job the next morning. Naomi wouldn't make it to hers. They'd both be brutally, savagely murdered.

Chapter 3

New York, New York

The bedroom was an ice box. The wide open windows gave way to the ice cold winter air and the loud Manhattan noises 19 floors below 729 7th Avenue. Wailing sirens and sharp honks bounced from wall to wall as the clock ticked silently next to a messy bed. At 3:20 a.m. these wouldn't be considered ideal sleeping conditions for an ordinary person, good thing this room's occupant rarely slept. The room was fairly empty with a full sized bed, a television, a pull-up bar latched on the doorway, and a small, wooden desk. The one bedroom apartment might have been bleak, but it served its purpose as far as Ethan was concerned.

Special Agent Ethan Carey sat reading a few files in bed, dressed in only a pair of pajama pants. Ethan was 31 years old, stood about six feet tall, and sported a clean shaven look. He was fit, it was easily visible he cared about his health and fitness, and his hair was black and messy. His body was chiseled from head to toe. The 189 pounds he stood at was almost completely solid and posed a very serious problem for anyone who wasn't a fan of the FBI. On his right arm he had a black tattoo stretching from his shoulder to a little above his elbow. The tattoo was a Celtic cross, whose vertical beam took the shape of a sword, surrounded by spiraling smoke.

Ethan got his tattoo before he entered the Bureau. Not many could see it but in the vertical beam of the cross were the words "mom" and "ma". The letters were camouflaged into the cross' design. These were the two most important women in Ethan's life. They had both battled cancers, his grandmother defeating colon cancer and his mother losing her battle with pancreatic cancer. The loss of his mother had almost caused Ethan to lose his job. The time after her death is a time he doesn't enjoy remembering. The mark on his arm is a constant reminder of the life long fight his mother had endured. Anytime something seemed too difficult, he would look down at his arm and remember all she had endured. This is why he carried his cross so unwaveringly.

Flashing on the TV in front of him was the only channel he ever really watched: ESPN. 'No point in even having a remote,' he thought. He inhaled deeply as he turned page after page, blankly staring at the folder's contents. The words weren't making sense anymore and a headache was developing. He tossed the folder to the ground and stared at his AM/FM alarm clock. Time just kept ticking by as he sat there wide awake. Next to the clock sat a picture of an older woman. He stared at her for a few seconds, taking in the picture's features as though this were his first time viewing it. A beautiful, smiling woman stared back at him, her dark hair falling across her shoulders. He laid down flat on his bed, still staring at the picture as he shut his TV off allowing the darkness to fall across his room.

The photo was of one of the few women Ethan loved. His mother, Eileen, was everything to him. Tears filled his eyes as he stared at her beautiful face. He shut them tight, imagining her touch and her warm words. Breathing deeply, he imagined her voice. She had such an amazing voice and always spoke so intelligently. Ethan picked his phone up and dialed her phone number as he did on most nights. His mother had passed away when he was twenty-four years old, but he continued to pay her cell-phone bill ever since. He knew if he stopped paying it he wouldn't be able to call her number and hear her voicemail. His mother's death created a wound so immeasurably deep—her passing left Ethan with an emptiness he battled regularly.

As Ethan reminisced, he heard a small knocking on his wall. An eerie, light tapping sound. 'This kid never sleeps,' Ethan thought.

"What was that?" The question came from the woman lying next to Ethan. She was a gorgeous, Spanish woman, about twenty-five years old, with long brunette hair and a curvy tanned physique. Ethan stared down at her trying to remember her name. He thought it was better not to remember. He figured that if he remembered these women's names that would mean he cared. He knew that if he cared he'd be making himself vulnerable to the inevitable: possibly losing another loved one.

"Nothing, gorgeous, go back to bed." Ethan had no idea how the little tapping could wake her up but the noisy traffic, ice cold temperature, and television didn't send her packing hours ago.

Ethan lived next door to a small, happy family of three. Dr. Luke Lianessa, who had a PhD in Psychiatry, lived with his wife Laura, his six year old son Robert Edward, who Ethan called Ed for short, and their little Schnauzer Roddick. Ed occasionally knocked on the wall separating Ethan's room and his. He recently started having trouble sleeping, and the thought of Ethan awake nearby made him feel a little more comfortable. The doctor loved tennis and named the dog after Andy Roddick, the famous American tennis player.

He had first met Luke when the family moved in about four years ago. He greatly appreciated the fact that the deaf, old woman who had previously resided there was gone. Despite the fact that Ethan never slept, and noise late at night didn't bother him, he still found it annoying trying to do pull-ups while listening to General Hospital. He enjoyed Luke's friendship as he always accepted an invite to dinner and loved destroying him in their occasional tennis match. The doctor and his family had grown fond of Ethan as well. Countless mornings Luke found himself bumping into one of Ethan's latest playmates on his way out the door. He constantly told Ethan, "I'm telling you, a few appointments with me and those commitment issues will disappear." Dr. Lianessa would probably throw his PhD out the window after just one session with Ethan.

Ethan loved what that family had, but, at the same time, he hated it. He tried hard to stay positive, to rid himself of all the hostility and jealousy, but sometimes it was hard. Luke was an amazing father. He scheduled his appointments around Ed's little league games and dropped everything to help Ed with homework. Not to take anything away from Laura, because God knows she did everything in the world for her son, but it was nice to see a father provide selflessly like that.

Ethan smiled as he rolled on to his side but grimaced as he read the clock's display: 3:58 AM. 'Jesus Christ,' he thought as he realized he had work in three hours. Ethan tapped on the wall lightly, letting Ed know he wasn't the only insomniac in the building, and let himself slip away to the distant, unfamiliar land of sleep. This was the world Ethan despised for all the hardships and demons it brought back to him.

Chapter 4

No Crying in Baseball

His Power Rangers wristwatch read 3:16 p.m. Ethan stood outside his apartment building on Mosholu Parkway, pacing back and forth, pounding a baseball into his glove. He could feel his hopes diminishing as he took a seat on a concrete step, the hot sun beaming down on him. 'Nothing can stop me today,' he thought. Today the coaches chose the starting lineups and everyone would give their all to earn their respective positions. Ethan felt his nerves creeping up as he realized it was getting late.

For months now he had thrown the baseball as hard as he could against his courtyard's wall, scooping up grounders like Cal Ripken himself. He practiced his batting stance, perfecting it to be just like Mattingly's. He was sometimes interrupted by neighborhood punks who came by saying, "Yo, let me see that ball," and then walked away with it. Even those punks couldn't hold him back today. Today the kid was unstoppable. Today he got to show it all on the field...at 3:30. His watch now read 3:24. Ethan took his glove off and placed it down at his feet. He stared up at the blue sky, noticing that the clouds seemed to move so fast. 'He's forgotten before', Ethan thought as he sighed heavily. This wouldn't be the first time, but today was just so important. 'This can't happen today,' Ethan thought as tears started to build up. He imagined the other kids running around on the field, their fathers watching them with the utmost pride. He could feel a small twinge of anger inside as he shook off the feelings of self-pity. He wasn't able to fight it off completely, though, and he put his face in his hands as he began to cry.

Tears trickled down onto his navy Yankee's t-shirt. He fought so hard to keep the tears bottled away, but he wasn't too good at that yet. That was a skill he'd perfect in years to come. He gritted his teeth together as he pulled at his black, messy hair. His head was hot from the beaming sun. 'What did I do?' he thought to himself. He couldn't understand why his father consistently let him down. He could see tear spots on his Yankee shirt through his watery eyes, the sight of which made him angry. He had laid that shirt out last night in anticipation of the big tryout today. He had fallen asleep with his glove in his hand and a giant smile across his tiny ten year old face. 'Why?' he repeated to himself.

The crying made him angry. He hated crying. What if someone noticed? He'd look like a big baby. Even knowing all of this couldn't stop the waterworks from flowing. 'God damn it, I practiced so long for this,' he cried, as the tears streamed through his fingers. Then he felt a hand touch his back. He looked up, startled, and saw his mother staring down at him, Rex was trotting close behind.

"Let's go Ethan, we're going to baseball."

This is exactly what he didn't want. His mother got so upset when she saw him cry. On top of that, he didn't want all the guys to see him with his mom. All the dads would be there, not moms. He got up from the step, grabbed his glove, and ran after his mother anyway. He knew his father would be disappointed if he didn't make it as a starter. As he got in the car he could see the anger all over his mother's face. He felt some comfort as Rex jumped onto his lap.

'Why did I have to cry?' he thought, holding Rex closely. 'Why am I always such a baby?'

Ethan didn't see, however, that as he sat on the step waiting for his father, his mother had been watching him from the apartment's window. She had been secretly crying with him the entire time. It broke her heart to see the love of her life so sad and down. She couldn't understand how a man could so easily give up his fatherly duties.

Eileen stood and watched her son as he played his heart out. He would go on to make the team. This would be just one accomplishment of many in his life. Ethan thanked her for bringing him to the tryout but the thank you wasn't sincere. Eileen understood that she'd be taken for granted, and despite knowing that she still fully loved her son. She still fully supported him in ever endeavor he chased. He would continue, even when he didn't realize it, to seek the approval of a man who ignored his existence. But he was just a boy, just a kid, and she knew that he would grow up and mature. He would eventually realize how many sacrifices she made for him.

Chapter 5

Secret Admirer

Ethan opened his eyes, feeling as though he had never slept, just in time to catch his beautiful play date storm out of his apartment. 'Wow, not even a goodbye,' he mused as he rolled out of bed and gripped his pull-up bar. The routine got easier over the years and was necessary as far as he was concerned. He wasn't like the other guys at the bureau, just an inconsistent slouch; he was ready for anyone and anything. He finished his morning workout and jumped into the shower.

The water poured over Ethan as he stood there letting it submerge his mind in the past. 'This is a curse, it has to be,' he thought to himself. Every morning the memories crossed his mind, hurting him and making him nauseous, and every night he was afraid to close his eyes. He had found notebooks that his mother kept during her long two year battle with cancer. He had them stashed away in his night stand drawer and from time to time he took them out to read Eileen's beautiful handwriting. The countless pages she had written dictating how scared she was of the cancer attacking her. How she was still needed alive. How she loved her baby boy more than life itself. How she regretted never finding a male role model for him to look up to. How she used the time he was out hanging with his friends to scream and cry because she never wanted him to see her vulnerable.

The steam dispersed through the room causing his mirrors to fog. Ethan stood still with his eyes closed, slowly unwinding under the steaming hot water. He recalled the day he made his little league team's starting line-up. He played third base for the Pirates and won the MVP award that season. He also earned the league award for most homeruns and runs batted in.

That was the last season he played baseball.

He bent over as a wave of pain overtook his body. He saw the same images every day

since his mother passed. The image of her lying in that hospital bed after she had passed. The

image of her at the wake, looking so beautiful and peaceful. The image of that last second that

he laid eyes on his hero. The very last second before the funeral director closed her casket.

With tears building in his eyes, Ethan roughly jerked the shower knob to off and quickly

jumped out. He put on a pair of jeans and a t-shirt, checked the barrel and chamber of his

Glock 23 and holstered it on his right hip. He picked up his single action .45 caliber pistol,

issued to him a year ago when he was assigned to a protection detail, and holstered it on his

left hip.

Ethan was known throughout the FBI to be a no-game, no-bullshit kind of guy. Most

found it surprising that he had never discharged a round while on duty. He excelled at

grappling while in the academy, a skill his co-workers and victims were well-aware of. What

most people didn't know was Ethan had been seriously practicing Krav Maga, a form of martial

arts centering on grappling and self-defense, Judo, and Ju-Jitsu since his first year in college

about thirteen years ago.

He tossed on his black leather jacket, locked his door, and hustled down the steps. He

barely ever took the elevator. Ethan wore his leather jacket in negative degree weather despite

the jabs he got from his co-workers. He had gotten the coat from his mother back in high school and absolutely loved it. It was stylish and he knew it looked good on him, so what if he

froze?

Many people believed an FBI special agent had to wear a suit. Ethan always found this

postulation comical and knew it to be absolutely false. Whenever he and his partner, Chris,

were out at a bar, he was scoffed at for his attire. "No chance you're a Fed my man," some

would say. "Nice try sweetheart, but you don't have to try that hard to get into these pants,"

was another retort he heard once. Ethan knew he didn't look like the valiant, knight in shining

armor type of guy, and he didn't really care that people mocked the idea of him fighting crime.

Ethan didn't have too long of a commute to work, thank God. He couldn't stand public

transportation, but, then again, who enjoyed it? He was sneezed on, stepped on, pushed,

shoved, and sometimes licked before he got off the train. This Wednesday wasn't too bad as

the train was fairly empty and the streets didn't seem as cluttered. Ethan had chosen the

perfect time to leave his house this morning.

He arrived at 26 Federal Plaza, better known as the Jacob K. Javits Federal Office

Building which housed New York's FBI field house and was also the largest federal building in

the United States almost a half hour earlier than he expected. The building's entrance was a

beautiful sight people never grew tired of seeing—honest, good people that is. A turnstile

entrance led to the building's vast reception area which was always shiny and alive with

commerce. Metallic pillars stretched up to the ceiling which had to be about 50 feet above the

ground, and elegant pictures of gorgeous landscapes adorned the walls. Directly in front of the

entrance was a marble desk that stretched from wall to wall.

"What's going on, Johnny?! Four days until the Jets smack the Pats!" Ethan said with a smile.

"Yeah, yeah, yeah buddy. We'll see what they can do in Foxborough. Pats don't lose at home in December, don't forget that!" Johnny yelled back.

Johnny Mendoza was a great kid. He was always smiling, never negative, and most importantly he was a good worker. Ethan couldn't recall the last time the guy had called out, in fact he didn't think there was a time. Johnny was born in the Dominican Republic and was constantly showing Ethan pictures of his "honeys" from back home. He was in his mid-twenties, stood about 5'6" with buzzed, dark hair and always wore a pair of suave designer glasses. Ethan had absolutely no idea why the Bronx resident was a Patriots fan nor did he ever bother asking.

Ethan might have been in pain every morning and night, but when he was at work or out with friends, he either felt great or did one hell of a job acting normal. He skipped through the stairwell's door and hustled up to the 26th floor. He nodded cheerfully at whoever he passed while he smiled to himself, pleased with how well his morning was going.

As Ethan walked through his floor he was shocked to see how many people were already at work. Nearly every cubicle and every desk was occupied. He looked around, waving and nodding at everyone as he strode down the hallway. Ethan liked that the room was always clean but was bothered by how there was hardly a single desk free of heaps of paperwork, pictures, and folders of all sizes. There was never a time his work area wasn't neat and tidy. Even at 8:00 am agents could be found running this way and that way, barking on the phone to this one, cursing at that one. All of the windows in the large room had their shades drawn,

giving way to a view of Foley Square and the city's busy life.

Ethan noticed that he was being stared at. He had gone unnoticed almost each time he

walked into this office, the exceptions being the days he brought coffee. This realization

occurred to him from the moment he opened the stairwell door, but he was having such a good

morning he refused to accept that something could be afoot. With a deep sigh he sat at his

desk, still pretending he noticed nothing.

Powering on his computer, Ethan leaned back and smiled at a few agents peering from a

nearby cubicle. 'What the hell's going on today,' he thought. Before he could begin to type his

username, a sharply dressed man approached and sat on the edge of his desk. Christian

Hawkins was an African American man in his late twenties. He was about Ethan's size;

however, he had a whole lot more style. He was never caught without his hair neatly trimmed,

a freshly pressed dress shirt on, and some slick designer dress shoes.   He had a menacing scar

on the left side of his face, right underneath his ear which he was highly self-conscious of. Chris

always took it personally if he caught someone staring. The injury came while chasing a suspect

during his first year on the job. While trying to hop a gate, a jagged edge caught him by

surprise. The surgeon who stitched his face claimed that he was very lucky to still be alive for

his jugular vein was nearly severed.

Christian Hawkins was Ethan's best friend, and had been his partner for about five years.

When assigned to cases, the agents would normally be placed individually but could choose to team up with another agent if they deemed it necessary. Chris always chose Ethan, Ethan always chose Chris.

"Good morning, sir...how was your date?" Chris asked, referring to Ethan's recent late night rendezvous. Ethan smiled but was well aware of the hesitation in his partner's voice. Something was definitely wrong here.

"She was great, I can definitely see we have a bright future ahead of us," Ethan said sarcastically. Chris always pushed for Ethan to settle down, so Ethan enjoyed messing with him when he could. "What's going on?" Before he could even finish the sentence, Chris had dropped an envelope and a manila folder in front of him. The envelope was addressed as the following:

Special Agent Ethan Carey

"No address? It was dropped off..." Chris cut Ethan off before he could finish.

"Johnny got it at the front desk. He gave it to Porter to give to you." Chris tried to mask the worry in his voice. Ethan was sometimes annoyed at how easily Chris resorted to hitting the panic button. Staring down at the envelope, Ethan slowly shook his head. 'Things just never stay good,' he thought.

Porter Hanoer was another agent in the field house. Ethan didn't really like him, but, then again, who did he really like? He thought Porter was too much of a wiseass, but the bad type—the type that could never figure out when to stop. The guy was smaller than Ethan, with long dark hair and tiny, beady eyes. He always had a snarky grin on his face which Ethan often dreamt of knocking off. He usually wore a pair of Aviator sunglasses which reminded Ethan of Tom Cruise in Top Gun.

Ethan immediately wondered why Johnny wouldn't just wait to hand it to him personally. Did Johnny get a name from the delivery person? Does he remember what this person looked like? He crossed his arms and took a deep breath, contemplating what he would do first.

"Maybe it's some sexy pictures from your boyfriend?" Porter said, smiling widely. He walked over to sit at the edge of a desk across from Ethan. "Didn't you go home with some guy last night? Definitely looked like a guy."

"It could just be more pictures from your wife," Chris shot back. Ethan was surprised at how personal Chris got. Porter nodded, puckering his lips out in a sarcastic manner before he slowly got up and walked back to his desk. "I guess that was a little too much," Chris said acknowledging his harsh words.

Ethan reached for the envelope, stopping abruptly, "Was this checked for prints?"

"No prints," Chris said, hopping off the desk and pulling up a chair next to Ethan.

The fact that there were no prints assured Ethan this wasn't an early Christmas card. He knew the fantastic morning was most definitely over. Granted it was chilly outside and whoever delivered this would have worn gloves, there should've still been some prints from when the contents were sealed inside. He picked up the light envelope and examined it. Nothing out of the ordinary, just a plain, regular envelope. He put it back on the desk and opened the manila folder, dumping out its' contents. Ethan stayed calm as pictures of bodies flowed out in front of him.

"Holy shit," Chris whispered. He shuddered and stood up, squinting down at the pictures and then up at Ethan.

This was the type of stuff he signed up for. Ethan calmly put everything back in the folder, picked up the envelope, and jumped up from his seat. Without speaking a word he motioned for Chris to follow him. They walked into a side conference room, shut all the blinds, and closed the door behind them. Ethan didn't need to try to stay calm; being rational and cool was his bread and butter. These most certainly weren't the first dead bodies he had seen; they weren't the first for Chris either.

Shit like this had happened before. Some sicko sends pictures and a letter to an agent, thinking he/she would be the next Zodiac or Ted Bundy or that they'd reenact something out of a Saw movie. There were always psychos trying to start up a game with the Bureau. Ethan and Chris sat down and stared at each other.

"Alright, let's see what we've got here," Ethan said, trying to get a handle on the situation. "Without looking at anything in this envelope, we have the security cameras in the lobby and Johnny's account of who dropped it off but we'll get to those later." Ethan reached for the envelope and in one fluid motion, dumped the contents on to the table. It all hit him at once; blood, bodies, bondage. It was horrible. "One at a time," Ethan said calmly.

They filtered through the bloody, despicable pictures one by one. There were three bodies shown, each in a different backdrop. Both agents whipped out pens and started to jot down notes as they observed.

"We have a middle aged woman bonded to a chair with her throat cut in what appears to be a complete circle," Ethan stated. He squinted closely at the picture, lifting the gruesome photo very close to his nose. "Based on the jagged skin I would say she wasn't cut with a knife. The skin's too loose and the cut is too wide to have been lacerated by something thin like a knife. She was cut with something blunt. I'm thinking like a meat cleaver or something similar to that." Ethan glanced up quickly at Chris. Their eyes met and although they didn't speak to each other, they both acknowledged that this was the worst they had ever seen. "Her hair is wet. Her eyes wide and pupils dilated. Fingernails clipped down to the skin. Clothing is torn away. Sternum and breasts exposed and the nipples are removed. Her arms are bruised, looks like she was manhandled a bit or possibly struck with a fist. The bruises aren't bad enough to have been created by a weapon. Her wrists are bloody and bound by rope. The rope looks old. Wait—there's no puddle under the body. Her hair's wet but there's no water under this body. She was tortured—submerged in water and then she was moved to this seat. She died on this chair, though. Look at the blood on the wood of the seat." Ethan lifted the picture close to Chris who nodded back. "Scratch marks on her arm indicate she had tried to escape. These scratch marks were made by long nails. They could be female nails, maybe her own nails?"

"I see the blood on the chair. Look closely-- you can see there's redness in her lips. That's lipstick. She has make-up on but if she's wet, the killer must've reapplied the makeup after the torture had begun," Chris added.

"Yeah but a woman's makeup wouldn't smudge under the water, her mascara would be running but the makeup would still be ok."

"I guess...I never really noticed that about Dana."

Dana Hawkins was Chris' wife and the soon to be mother of his child. Chris had excitedly told Ethan that Dana was 4 months pregnant a week ago.

"The next picture," Ethan said, tossing the picture of the first woman on the table. "Male in his late forties?" He paused for a few seconds as he took in the gruesome details. This was so much worse than anything he had ever seen. There were brief moments in his career where Ethan acknowledged that he was possibly afraid. He would never admit it to anyone but there were times he felt this way. This was one of those moments. Ethan did not want to meet whoever killed these people.

"No fingers and no toes," Chris chimed in noticing that his partner was speechless. "Eyelids are gone too. Obviously there's an ax in his skull." This was the most noticeable aspect of the picture. There was a medium sized ax, about two feet long, whose wooden handle was sticking out of the man's skull. "The ax is about three inches deep and I'd say based off the skin surrounding its penetration point it was probably hacked in there a few times. Based off the force I'd say it was a male assailant."

"I've seen some strong women."

"Yeah but...come on."

"I'm not ruling women out just because the ax is 3 inches in this man's head. Based on that penetration point, whoever did this could have been hacking away for a few minutes." Ethan rubbed his forehead as he observed a little more.

"It was a thought, Ethan. Calm down."

"The killer obviously didn't want us to see too much of the background. Can't really make out where these pictures are taking place."

He put the man's pictures to the side, partly because he didn't want to look at them anymore, and picked up the third picture. Another man. This man looked as though he had nothing done to him. He was laying down peacefully, his eyes staring blankly ahead. Ethan noticed, after examining it more thoroughly, that the man had small bruises near his neck and tiny scrapes and cuts across his face. Most likely choked to death by hand.

"Choked to death?" Ethan mused.

"I have no idea," Chris said reaching forward to get a better look at the picture. "A couple of scrapes by the throat region...maybe punctures done by fingernails? What the fuck, huh?" He shook his head and tossed the final picture onto the others.

Ethan put all the pictures together and placed them back in the folder. He swallowed, feeling a little light headed. These pictures were horrible, like something straight out of Hollywood.

"Can you pass me the letter?" Although he was lightheaded he wouldn't dare show his partner. This case, although it had only started a few minutes ago, was extremely disturbing. 'Why was this sent directly to me,' Ethan thought to himself.

He grabbed his letter as Chris stared in a concerned manner. The man's thin eyebrows rose as he looked into Ethan's light brown eyes. Ethan wondered if his fear was visible. Could Chris possibly see that Ethan was in fact very nervous about what was in this envelope? He dug his finger inside the corner of the white envelope and shimmied it across to the opposite end. Reaching inside he fished for the contents and pulled out a small piece of paper. He stared at the folded paper as thoughts of what it contained ran through his mind. 'Mom,' he thought to himself. He imagined her as he unfolded the loose-leaf.

My Dearest Ethan,

Good morning. I've sent you a few pictures I was hoping you could take a look at. Excuse me for the quality; I had an appointment I couldn't be late for. "Have no fear of change as such and, on the other hand, no liking for it merely for its own sake." Robert Moses wrote this believing exactly what I believe, you shouldn't fear change nor should you long for it merely for no purpose. I hope you can understand, Ethan, that I do not release these people from their hell because I wish to do so but because I have to. It's my job, what my life has been built around, why I'm right here on this great stage. I met these people and saw their life meant little. I saw the hell they inflicted on others, the carelessness they portrayed. There are many like this in this world, Ethan, I could use a hand. We can rip them apart; we can destroy them because that is what they have asked for. We'll make them pay for what their lives stood for. Clarence Day said it best, "We must make the best of those ills which cannot be avoided." Will you do me the honor? Will you help me?

Sincerely yours.

Ethan sat still as he stared down at the letter. He widened his eyes and leaned back, staring at the ceiling. 'This was a good day,' he though. 'A perfect morning.' His throat bulged as he swallowed hard.

"This psycho's asking you for help," Chris said, getting up to pace the room.

"The killer is saying 'I do not release' and 'I wish to do so'…" Ethan said pausing. "Whoever the killer is it plans on doing more."

"Well no shit. Whoever did this…damn." Chris shook his head as he stared down at the manila folder and letter.

The door slammed open and Assistant Director Illames stormed into the room. "What the fuck is going on in here!" he screamed. He looked furious; the veins in his forehead were bulging. "Who the fuck authorized you to take something like this into your own hands, not even having the fucking audacity to see me! Get in my office!"

Illames had been the Assistant Director for Ethan's entire career. His hair was entirely gray, probably from the stress of the job, and his face was covered in wrinkles. It appeared that the man had let himself go, but he was at the tail end of his career. He wasn't doing much field work anymore. He was shorter than most in the office, standing at only about 5'5", and his skin tone was almost a sickly pale. His thick mustache reminded Ethan of the Monopoly guy.

'How professional,' Ethan thought. He knew he slipped up. You can't just take evidence into a room and sort through it without going through proper procedure. The letter being addressed to him didn't make a difference; he still broke the rules. There were people in this office, one being Assistant Director Illames, who had been around a lot longer than he had, who knew how to handle stuff like this better than he did.

Illames' office was filled with Yankee memorabilia. He had a Yankee garbage can, Yankee post-it holder, Yankee everything. Outside of his window was a beautiful view of the city's streets, the pedestrians running to and from, no idea that shit like what Ethan had just looked at was going on twenty-six floors above them. No idea that this killer could be looking out at them just as Ethan was. The two agents took their seats across from the assistant director and sat silently as Illames studied the contents of the folder.

"Sir, I'm sorry I broke procedure, I..." Illames put a hand up, indicating Ethan should stop talking. Ethan took a quick glance at Chris who was sitting quietly awaiting Illames' input. The pictures were still so fresh in Ethan's mind. The fact that some lunatic was writing to him personally—it shook him. He rubbed his face and leaned forward in the chair wishing this was just a bad joke or nightmare.

"I want three copies made of all of these, three copies of the letter too, and I want the copies distributed between the three of us. The letter is addressed to you, Carey. Which makes it easy to assign this case to you."

"I'm fine with that," Ethan answered.

"I didn't ask you if you were fine with anything. I'm assigning you the case." Illames glared into Ethan's eyes. He did this sometime. He wanted everyone to know who the boss was. His bushy eyebrows and thick mustached didn't flinch as he peered through Ethan's soul. "We have one ruthless serial killer who thinks he or she is going to be the next big thing on the Daily News." Illames got up and stood in front of his window. "This will not reach the media. This spreads to the media and me and you will have issues. You two have trouble, you ask for help, none of that rogue bullshit. Don't get in over your heads. Give me ten minutes then meet me in the conference room. Send Cap and Marie in."

Cap's real name was Daniel O'Riley and Marie was Marie Hannon. Both had worked in the forensics department since Ethan had started. Ethan actually liked Cap; the guy was really laidback for the most part. Only problem was he liked the Mets. He was one of the few to really invite Ethan to the Bureau. He embraced Ethan as a newcomer rather than neglect him like most of the other employees on the twenty-sixth floor.

Ethan walked over to a desk occupied by a young, very beautiful young lady and tossed the folder and envelope in front of her. Wendy was one of the office's secretaries and a good one too. She didn't ask any questions, she was very trustworthy, and she worked fast. She was just out of college, settling here until she made her dreams in the fashion industry come true. Being that she was a pretty woman, Ethan had thought about inviting her out a few times, but he knew you shouldn't shit where you eat.

"Good morning, beautiful," Ethan said with a smile. He was often told that his smile was his best trait. He had one dimple on the left side of his face and his clef deepened as his face stretched. His smile was always his first weapon when trying to pick up a date. "I'd love it if you could make me three copies of everything here." Although his mind was still racing with thoughts of this lunatic killer, Ethan was pretty good at putting emotions aside.

"Uh-huh, I'll bring them over to you," Wendy said. She always gave him attitude. He watched her as she walked to the copy room, shaking her ass from side to side. Ethan shook his head, briefly wishing he could see that view in his own home, but then his mind wandered back to his newest case.

"So where do we start?" Chris said, sitting back on his chair by Ethan.

"We need to talk to Johnny and check those security tapes too. We should analyze the evidence, the letter, and the pictures again. These murders might have already been discovered. If they were, Captain will find them for us. Hopefully they have been. It would save us time and we'd learn a good deal from those scenes."

Ethan hoped he was right about the murders being discovered. If at least one of them was then they'd be a whole lot better off than they were now. There were times where a murder was picked up by the local precinct and passed over as an average homicide. It was very possible that could happen here.

Ethan graduated out of Fordham University with a very rare major/minor. He majored in cognitive psychology and psycholinguistics. His minor was in history. He also took enough classes in Russian to almost speak it fluently. Ethan studied the way people think, why people do the things they do, and he scrutinized hundreds of writing styles.

Wendy was back in less than ten minutes and dropped the copies on his desk without a word. He slowly pulled out the letter and skimmed it for details, anything that might be calling out to him. He particularly searched for any change in writing style, indicating a possible co-killer, or even a hidden message etched into the writing.

"Conference room," Illames demanded as he zipped past Ethan. The director startled him a bit as he was deep in thought.

Ethan and Chris jumped up and followed him inside. Cap and Marie joined them as well. "I just got off the phone with Detective Welch at the 52nd precinct. A homicide reported there over a month ago that matches one of the pictures. They'll be handing us all the information; it's our case now." Illames stressed those last two words, leaning in close to Ethan's face. "Cap and Marie will investigate whether or not these other two homicides have been discovered. They'll salvage all the reports for you. "

Neither of the agents responded. Cap and Marie sat in what appeared to be a pleasant manner. They had no emotional connection to this case. It didn't seem like that cared that Ethan did. They just sat there and jotted notes down as though it were just another case. This wasn't another case, though; it was a very serious, personal case.

"Ok then," Illames said with a deep sigh. He picked up his copies and walked out, Cap and Marie following him. They didn't even give Ethan a second look. They just walked right past him as though he wasn't being serenaded by a highly dangerous individual.

The conference room was a little chilly today, he thought as he looked around at the stark gray walls and black cushioned chairs. He had really hoped—prayed for a normal day, and that was obviously way out of the question.

Ethan hoped that Chris wouldn't say a word. At this moment he wanted nothing more than to be alone, but he knew that this wasn't possible.

"Well," Ethan said as he took a deep breath. "We're going to find this motherfucker." And just like that, the fear became what Ethan was most familiar with. Anger.

Chapter 6

Man in the Mirror

Ethan sat in the conference room, the contents of his envelope spread across the table.

He juggled through the pictures, making one observation at a time.

"See a pattern yet?" Chris asked as he walked over to the window.

Ethan shook his head.

"Let's go check out those security tapes."

He jumped out of his seat, scooped up all the evidence, and walked out of the

conference room. Chris followed closely, taking a quick glance back to make sure they hadn't

forgotten anything. This is why Ethan went into this line of work. This is why he put in so many

sleepless nights, so many excruciating workouts just so he could be a special agent. He wanted

to put these assholes away for good. He knew, for a fact, that he would have this psycho in less

than a week. The two agents made their way down the hall, stopping at Captain's desk before

heading out the door.

"What do you have for me, Cap?" Ethan said while grabbing a pad of paper and a pen.

"Three reports match these homicides, three different precincts too. The 52nd has an

investigation launched on one of them. I'm trying to get through to Detective Enchino over

there. I did find out that the 52 has a suspect in custody: The victims' ex-wife. I'll obviously get

the full info for you, just give me time." Cap looked up at Ethan, his face clouded with confusion. "Also, two of the victims were definitely divorced, one of them was separated. Maybe a pattern...serial killer by the look of it. Then again maybe it isn't a pattern; I mean who isn't divorced nowadays. That's the only constant right now. At least it's the only one I can see." Cap shook his hands in the air and shook his head. He was going bald on the top of his head and the little hair he did have he attempted to comb over the naked spot. He always wore a dress shirt with the sleeves rolled up and the top button unbuttoned. "Like I said...be patient *please*. I'll put it all together for you real nice." He made a shooing motion to the two and turned his chair away from them.

Ethan knew this was obviously a serial killer. The note, the pictures, and now this small connection between each victim—it could all be a coincidence but that was highly doubtful. Ethan already felt drained. Those pictures were killing him, haunting him, and it had only been an hour.

"The killer is writing to me and has killed three people in messed up marriages. Maybe I slept with his wife? I never go after a taken woman, but she could have lied to me." Ethan thought his idea over. It wasn't the most flattering theory, but why else would anyone target him?

"Well if we need to question all the women you've been sleeping with we are going to be interrogating for years." Ethan shot Chris a dissatisfied look.

"Yeah well my father left my mother when I was six. It could be tied to that too."

"What, you think your dad is involved?" Chris' question caused Ethan to laugh.

"Absolutely not. That guy is the weakest piece of shit I know not to mention a coward. I'll be right back. I need a bathroom break," Ethan said. He just needed to get away.

He walked down the hallway and entered the large, brightly lit bathroom. He opened a stall and sat down on top of the toilet, making an attempt to unwind, breathe in and out, and take a quick break from reality. 'Jesus Christ,' Ethan thought to himself. He brushed his hand through his hair and stood up. This guy, this girl, whatever this thing was, had reached out to him. He got angry at how repetitive he sounded, 'but seriously what the fuck am I supposed to do right now,' he thought. "Fuck," he muttered.

Ethan shook his head, walked out of the stall and stared at his reflection. He stared hard at himself; his light brown eyes staring back at him, judging him, criticizing how weak he was. No other case had ever gotten him this bad. He HATED when things got personal. This was his kryptonite. Had the killer been targeting Chris, he would have already analyzed the security tapes downstairs and been on his way to pick up the perp. Ethan slammed his fist down on the sink and looked back at himself. He saw *him* now, the man he hated. His father's devilish face stared back at him. He laughed at him, his stupid face glaring at him, mocking him, infuriating him. Ethan's fist tightened and as quickly as he could he raised his hand, poised to smash the mirror. His anger was pounding, driving him insane, his teeth were clenched together, and then he stopped. His beating heart had been slamming against his chest, but now he felt the hammering subside. He lowered his hand and squeezed his eyes shut. When he opened them, he was staring into his own light brown eyes. 'Calm down Ethan, it's time to work.' He quickly tossed some cold water on his face, took a few quick deep breaths, and marched out of the bathroom like nothing had happened.

"You ready to go?" Chris asked.

"Let's go down and see Johnny. We need those security tapes." Ethan grabbed his leather and stuffed his notepad into the back of his pants.

"You feeling ok?" Chris could see the pain in Ethan's face.

"I'm good."

The two walked side by side as the other agents stared at them. It was as though they were walking down death row with how eerily quiet the room had become. The word had most likely spread; everyone probably knew exactly what case they were assigned to. Ethan paid no attention to the annoying stares. He was set on a goal. All he saw was the end result. 'Just another day at work. Just another, normal day at work.'

Chapter 7

What's More Broken?

Ethan's body sat frigidly in the waiting room of Montefiore Hospital. He was in so much pain yet he was more scared than anything else. 'The dance is next week,' he kept repeating, 'God please no.' Ethan's mother was standing at the reception area, waving her arms around, probably arguing about how long the wait was. He cringed in pain; the sharp agony appeared sporadically and was worse when he tried to walk. He held his leg up, squeezing his thigh to ease the pain a little. He kept reaching into his mom's pocketbook, checking her mom-brand cell-phone quickly, hoping she wouldn't see him.

Only a few hours before, Ethan had been playing basketball with some friends. He loved playing basketball; he just didn't like playing while a big brute of a kid was standing on him. One of the bigger kids he had been playing with ran straight into Ethan, causing him to fall awkwardly, and then stood on Ethan's foot as he got up. "Sorry," the kid said as he ran down the court obliviously. 'SORRY!' Ethan thought. 'This kid just broke my foot, a week before I take Clarissa to the dance, and he's sorry.' Ethan's 8th grade dance was exactly a week away. Casts weren't exactly the style this year.

Eileen came walking back and took a seat. She looked fine now so Ethan figured everything must be alright. "They're coming with a wheel chair now. How does it feel?" she said giving Ethan's leg a concerned look. She reached to touch it but reconsidered, noting the painful look on Ethan's face, and checked her cell instead.

"It hurts a lot. I can't stand on it at all, Mom. Will I be okay for the dance?" He was probably more concerned about the dance than anything else. Clarissa was a prize. She was pretty, smart, and all the guys in school loved her. He didn't care if his foot, his arm, or his head were broken; he just wanted to John-Travolta-it-up on the dance floor. He could already see Clarissa wearing the corsage that he'd give her. Ethan glared out of the corner of his eye at his mother's pocketbook, checking to see if the microwave of a cellphone was buzzing. Nothing yet.

"Alright, let's go," Eileen said as the nurse pulled a wheel chair up. Ethan was helped into the chair and rolled towards the x-ray room. Eileen was speaking but he couldn't hear anything. He was too focused on hope and prayed that it would be fine. As they approached the x-ray room, he realized how hard he was squeezing the arm rests and let go. He was propped up on the table and laid back as he watched the room around him spin. 'Be strong Ethan, be strong, be strong, everything will be fine.'

He closed his eyes as the woman announced the x-ray was commencing. 'Where is he?' Ethan thought, 'I know he'll show up.'

The X-ray was finished quickly, and his mother was back in the room rolling him to the doctor's office. 'He's gotta be here by now.' Ethan jumped as he heard his mother's phone ring.

"Who is it?" he asked, barely able to hide his excitement.

"I told you not to bother calling," Eileen said as she answered the phone, walking away to the opposite corner of the office. She was speaking quietly, and although some of the words were muffled, he heard clearly for the most part. "Andrew, he's thirteen years old, thirteen

Andrew, why can you not understand this? We're sitting in the silver zone of Monte right now, he needs you here. Talk to your son." She walked back over and handed Ethan the phone. 'Thank God,' Ethan thought, although the look of rage in his mother's eyes wasn't too reassuring.

"Hey Dad, what's up? Are you here?" He did his absolute best to mask the thrill in his voice.

"Hey buddy, how's the foot?"

"It's fine, we're about to hear if it's broken or not. It doesn't hurt at all, though," Ethan lied, glancing at his mother and shrugging his shoulders. She crossed her arms and shook her head sarcastically. "Are you almost here?"

"What are you talking about buddy? I'm home."

"Oh," Ethan felt his voice quiver. He felt tears form in his eyes and then he felt the anger, a sharp horrible anger flash inside of him. "I thought you were coming though."

"Ethan, you know I live here in Yorktown now, you'll be fine though buddy."

"But I really wanted you to come Dad, the dance is next week, if it's broken I can't go."

"Ethan," his voice became sterner to reprimand Ethan now. "I cannot come down right now, I have work tomorrow and it is late. You can still go to the dance if you have a cast on; this isn't the end of the world. Come on now buddy, you have to be a man now and step up to the plate. Ok?"

"Yeah, I can," Ethan said as the pain in his foot crept up to his heart. He felt like an idiot for even thinking the guy might show.

The doctor walked into the room, his tiny glasses looked ridiculous behind his gigantic eyebrows. He looked up at Ethan and his mother and nodded his head, his impolite way of saying hello. Eileen reached over and took her phone, hanging it up and placing it back in her bag while giving her son a concerned look. Ethan had no idea what was said after this, all he knew was that he'd be wearing a cast for his 8th grade dance. He stared blankly at the doctor. 'Step up to the plate and be a man. Why can't I just be stronger,' he thought.

Ethan's foot was broken on that day, this he understood. However his pride was also shattered, his courage put into question, and his heart tampered with again. This wouldn't be the last time, oh absolutely not even close to the last time, but it was a pivotal moment in his life. A phrase he would always remember: 'Step up to the plate and be a man.' Sitting on that table, in that gloomy, unpleasant emergency room, Ethan completely forgot about Clarissa, about basketball, and about his foot. All he felt was anger...a burning inside. He couldn't wait to show his father exactly how much of a man he could be. 'Step up to the plate and be a man.'

Chapter 8

The Web We Weave

Ethan and Chris skipped the elevator and took the steps instead. Ethan hustled down, skimming through the ideas he had so far. 'This killer was obviously way too smart to deliver that envelope itself.' *20th floor.* 'The messenger would most likely be some random Joe who was desperate for a few bucks. Someone really desperate. Alcoholic, drug addict, sex addict.' *15th floor.* 'We have to find this person using limited resources. We've got the camera and what Johnny can tell us. We can check the criminal database as well, try and match a visual. If neither of those works, then all we have are the crime reports...that's not a bad thing.' *10th floor.* 'After we find this person, if we even can...no when we do...we would have to find out information on the one who originally made the envelope. This killer's too smart to leave its safety in the hands of some idiot junky, unless it really is stupid and delivered the package itself. I'm banking that's not the case. It's probably holding some sort of collateral. Half the pay or something like that.' *5th floor.* 'It's gunna take a lot of work but that's what we signed up for. And then, of course, there is that horrible, more obvious clue.' *Lobby.* 'We'd have to wait for it to strike again.'

Johnny sat behind his marble desk, slowly standing up as he saw Ethan and Chris strolling across the square lobby. Next to Johnny sat another man dressed in a janitor's uniform. He didn't get up as he saw the two agents coming towards him. Since it was already after nine there weren't many people around, just a few who were quickly passing through. Ethan took note of everything, he noticed Johnny's nervous expression and took note of the uneasy receptionist's neck as he gulped. 'Why so nervous?' Ethan thought. He saw Johnny

quickly moving his hands as he approached the desk; his eyes were shrouded in fear.

"What's up, Johnny, you mind if we step inside the monitor room for a second? We

have a few questions. Shouldn't take long." Ethan looked over at Johnny's co-worker, gave him

a slight nod and a grin, and then turned his attention back to Johnny.

"Yeah no problem...um...you mind keeping an eye on the lobby?" Johnny turned to his

co-worker who nodded back to him in agreement. "Come on in." Johnny opened the steel

door behind his desk and beckoned for Ethan and Chris to come in. The two walked around his

desk but Ethan stopped to scan Johnny's friend.

"How's it going?" He smiled lightly; something about this guy just rubbed him the

wrong way. He had seen him a bunch of times but never heard the guy speak a word. His

name tag read 'Danny' and by the look of his clean, navy blue jump suit Ethan guessed he was

just beginning his shift. His dark hair was combed neatly to the side and his brown eyes didn't

appear to be nervous at all.

"Not bad, just a normal Wednesday, you know?" The guy didn't sound nervous either.

Ethan also spotted the Cosmopolitan magazine that had been sloppily placed under a few other

books. Johnny must have tried to hide it when he saw them coming. Ethan had always had his

suspicions but now he realized they might be a little more concrete. He slowly realized that

Johnny and Danny could be more than just co-workers.

"You need anything just knock on the door a few times. We'll be out quick." Ethan followed Chris and Johnny inside and closed the door.

The miniscule locker room, or "monitor room", was packed with a small desk, computer screens, some cleaning supplies, a bench, and what must have been considered a bathroom. There was barely enough room for the three of them. Ethan, who was already getting frustrated with how slow he was moving, maneuvered over to the screens to get a better look. Should he somehow figure out who dropped off the package, he wanted to do it quickly and get a jump start on this case. "Who dropped the envelope off, Johnny?"

"I have no idea, I've never seen that dude before," Johnny said shaking his head and raising his eyebrows as he punched some button into his computer. "The guy came in, threw the envelope on the desk, and walked out...You *are* talking about the envelope addressed to you, right?"

"I believe you, Johnny; we're just trying to get somewhere. Can you tell us anything else we might be able to use?" Ethan asked calmly, praying the receptionist would tip them off to something. Chris shook his head slowly and moved to stand next to the computers, leaning his back against the wall.

"The guy was wearing a red Yankees hat; I know that for a fact...disgusting hat. His voice was croaky, you know, like he had a bad sore throat...he sounded like a frog. He said 'Deliver this' and he walked out. I can't even really remember what he was wearing, just that hat...wait, I think a black shirt too...that's it man, I'm sorry. I'm almost positive he was a pretty ugly dude but like I said, I didn't really see. It was early. I wasn't paying attention. We can check the tapes though."

Johnny's jitters were becoming annoying. Ethan watched him as he clicked and typed, rewinding the tape of the camera that oversaw his desk.

"He came in around 7:30. I was in the middle of eating my bagel. You're obviously not gunna tell me what's in the envelope right." Johnny looked up at Ethan and Chris who both stared back at him blankly. "Just asking. Alright, there he goes. See? I knew he was ugly." Johnny slowed the tape down as a man walked up to his desk. Ethan leaned in close as the man took out the envelope.

"Pause it!" He shouted, turning his head slowly to make out the picture. Johnny jumped and stared up at Ethan angrily and startled.

"You see something?" Chris said, squinting his eyes trying to find what Ethan was looking at.

"Rewind it back to where he was taking the envelope out. Play it slowly though, I want to see his hand." Johnny shook his head, still annoyed from Ethan yelling at him. As he played the tape a little more, the man started to extend his arm in front of the desk, moving to drop the envelope. His hand, now fully outstretched, revealed a web tattoo that stretched around his fingers. "Can you print this screen?"

"No problem, printer's right there." Johnny pointed to the far corner and Chris walked over to grab the picture. "Is that it?"

"Yeah, thank you." Ethan patted Johnny on the shoulder and nodded at Chris. As the two exited the room, Ethan gave a small wave to Danny, who nodded back at him suspiciously. He could tell the guy was curious as to what had just gone down.

He had seen that webbed tattoo before. A few years back he had put away some gang bangers who had that same tattoo around their fingers. Idiots tried to rob a bank in the Bronx and would have probably gotten away; problem was they lived down the street from the bank. Ethan was tipped off to them by the frantic teller. The gang, from what he remembered, was a classic, drug dealing, petty robbery type gang. They also happened to reside in his old neck of the woods.

Ethan and Chris walked out of the building and headed towards the parking garage. New York was bustling as usual, people running to and from, no clue of what was going on around them. Ethan was always aware of his surroundings, but today he was a little occupied. His mind was devoted to this case and only this case. He had made a step, yes it was a small one, but it was progress. The killer, or someone linked to the killer, had given that envelope to this Yankee fan, and now Ethan needed to speak with him. He reached into his coat pocket and pulled out his cell, scrolling to Cap in his contacts.

"I'm calling Cap to see if he has anything," Ethan said. He knew he hadn't said anything to Chris yet but his partner trusted him. Ethan glanced around, remembering how awesome this day had been about two hours ago and he shook his head in disbelief. Finally, Cap picked up.

"Nothing yet, Ethan. How about I just call you as soon as I get something?" Cap said, sounding agitated. He was probably annoyed that Ethan was pressuring him so early in the morning; Cap had only about 30 minutes so far.

"Thanks," Ethan said hanging up. He turned his head to his ill-informed partner.

"Ethan, you wanna let me in on some of this?" Chris asked, checking his pocket for the keys to their supped up Charger.

"I've seen this tattoo before," Ethan said pointing at the picture of the weasel-like messenger. "I put away a few guys with this same tattoo at the start of my career. They robbed a bank on 204th street in the Bronx; idiots lived right down the block."

"Ok, but like Illames said, none of the rogue bullshit this time...Ethan. We need to approach this smarter than how we're doing it right now. We go back upstairs, we get a visual match of the suspect, we get a print out of his rap sheet, mug shots, what he's allergic to, who his fucking baby sitter was when he was 4...Ethan, calm and steady wins the race." Chris might be against the course of action Ethan had in mind, but that didn't cause him to hesitate. The two approached the Charger and Chris tossed Ethan the keys. "This might be a different kind of case, yes this guy is after you in particular, but we're fucking up right now, Ethan. You're going to explain this to Dana after she drops my unemployed ass."

Ethan always liked Dana. Mrs. Hawkins was a model's height, with long, curly blonde hair and a slim, yet curvy physique. Chris had actually met her at the gym. He passed corny pickup lines for months before she had finally accepted a dinner invite. Chris and Dana made an incredible couple as far as Ethan was concerned, he also thought they were a very rare

couple. They were so happy together; they were perfect for one another. You just don't see

happiness like that often nowadays. Ethan knew that even if Chris were unemployed, Dana

would be there for him. Even despite the minor baby bump she was beginning to show.

Chris hopped in the passenger seat and shook his head as he buckled up. Ethan looked

over at him and smiled.

"You're always welcome to sleep on my floor," Ethan said jokingly as reached over to

touch Chris' hand. Chris quickly whipped his hand away.

"Drive the car, man. We do what we have to do, just don't leave me in the dark."

Chris reached forward and put the radio on, Jay-Z blasted from the speakers, and Ethan

put the car, and the manhunt, into drive.

Chapter 9

Bottom of the Totem Pole

"I really think you should come out with us tomorrow," Chris said, trying to convince

Ethan into another date night. "Sammy's a great girl… gorgeous, goal-oriented, has a great

career she isn't completely obsessed with," Ethan caught the slight jab in those last words and

looked over at Chris who winked at him wryly. "She actually has a personality…Ethan…a girl

who will kiss you and speak actual English with you! I'm just saying, I don't wanna go alone.

Dana's dying to go out and I told her you'd come already."

"What! I don't know why you'd say that, you knew I'd say no," Ethan said, he hated

when Chris volunteered him for things. "It's a Thursday night, who goes on a blind date on a

Thursday?"

Ethan immediately thought of the time Chris had conned him into meeting Janine.

Janine was supposed to be "perfect" for Ethan. She was a smoker, hated sports, and seemed to

only want to discuss *America's Next Top Model*. Ethan tried his best to engage her in

conversation, but it was like pulling teeth,

"What's wrong with Thursday? There isn't a special day for blind dates. Stop making

excuses and just come for ten minutes, I'll cover for you if it turns out bad."

Ethan noticed that Chris had finally started to look curious as to where they were going.

They were driving through Ethan's old stomping grounds and no, it wasn't good to be home.

This was the neighborhood that had partially driven Ethan to become an FBI agent. The Charger roared down Mosholu Parkway, the clock now reading 10:44 a.m.

"So you wanna set up Dana's friend with a guy who's getting love letters from an obsessed psychopath?" Ethan looked over at Chris and shook his head in disapproval. Chris made a face as though to say he hadn't thought about it that way.

Ethan knew the best thing for him would be to go out. It wouldn't help to think about this killer all day and night, he'd lose his mind. "Ten minutes and if she sucks, I'm gone." Chris smiled and nodded his head. He had already known Ethan would come.

"If she sucks, I'm sure you'll stay," Chris said, cracking up at his own joke. Ethan smiled and laughed back. "You used to live over here, right? So what do you know about these web guys?" He was looking down at the picture of the messenger. "Real ugly looking guy, huh? Like a mouse or a possum. I wonder how much he got to deliver this message."

"He probably got nothing," Ethan said, now staring up at the building he had lived in for twenty years. The tall, grotesque, horrible building that had housed him for so long. He wouldn't care if it crumbled to the ground that very second. "The killer, or whoever gave this guy that envelope, wouldn't have paid him in full yet, he's probably gunna head off to meet somewhere later. We need to find this guy before he goes anywhere." Ethan at least hoped this would be the case. So far in his career he had rarely been wrong, but there were a few times he was a little off. Hopefully this wasn't one of those times.

He parked the Charger in a spot right in front of an "Oval Park". Chris glanced out the window, then back at his partner. "What's in here?" Ethan got out and walked around the car towards the park's entrance.

"Drug dealers," he answered, looking back at Chris who stuffed the photo in the inside of his jacket. "We need to find this guy's kind, his competition, people who wouldn't mind him put away. They'll know where he is." Years of living in this neighborhood taught him where not to go. Now he had to go to all of those places.

The two partners walked into the park, looking as conspicuous as possible. Ethan spotted exactly what he was looking for right away. He could see a group of hoodlums, all menacing looking men with dark bandanas on, sitting on a few benches by the basketball courts. Ethan glanced at Chris, who stared back with a raised eyebrow.

"Those the drug dealers you wanted?" Chris said. "You sure about this?"

Ethan actually wasn't positive, but, like he had already said, he would have this killer in a week tops. "Yeah, I'm positive. Just let me talk."

As the two agents approached the men, the bandana group slowly got to their feet. A pudgy, scarred Spanish man walked to the front of the group, pulling his coat aside to reveal a semi-automatic handgun. Ethan raised his hands, Chris following, and shook his head from side to side.

"What you want bitch!" the small Spanish guy shouted. The little gangster waddled towards Ethan, his face scrunched into a tough, wrinkled heap of skin, eyes, and a nose.

Ethan's head started to buzz. He had always dreamed of this day. After the years and years of pain he had to endure because of these assholes, he'd love nothing more than to pull out both guns and pop each one of them. Obviously that wasn't a sensible option right now.

"Good morning. Me and my partner are special agents with the FBI." Chris looked over at Ethan, probably thinking he was out of his mind. "We have absolutely no problem with you."

Two of the group jumped off their bench and walked over to Chris, staring him down with their arms crossed. Chris stared back at them unflinchingly, knowing a wrong move would be the end of the case. "We're looking for someone, he's not a friend of yours. Us finding him might be good for both of us. We have a picture of him, can we show you?" Ethan realized this wasn't going how he had hoped. He was well aware of how a snitch was perceived but he had still hoped he could get some information.

"Mother fucker you talk a lot," the small Spanish guy said amused. He walked forward pulling his gun out of his pants. "My fucking brother's in jail right now. You know who put him there?" Ethan knew the answer was undoubtedly a fed. He smiled and looked at the little gangster.

"I don't care." Ethan's anger roared. He felt his hands pulsating; he was dying to pull a trigger. "I told you I'm here to help myself. It just so happens you might benefit too. I don't give a fuck about you, I have no beef with you, but you put a bullet in my head or my partner's head and I guarantee you'll realize how fucked up the U.S. government really is." Ethan realized this made absolutely no sense. "Rather than you and your boys taking a step up, we'll all be down six feet." Ethan still stared at the little guy, hoping these words triggered something. After a few moments of silence, the little Spanish man spoke.

"Show me the picture." The man put his gun back in his pants and gestured his hand at his friends.

"I have it inside my jacket, if you want you can reach in yourself and take it out," Chris said, turning his attention to the ringleader. The small Spanish man walked over and ripped the picture out of Chris' jacket. He glance at it once then handed it back.

"Lucky. They call him Lucky. He's with that faggot gang...Widows on Hull...W.O.H. You taking him in?" The guy walked back to his bench and sat down.

"We need to talk to him first, and then we'll take him in." Ethan kept his eyes set, paying close attention for any quick movements.

"29 Hull Ave. That's their home. If you don't take him in by tomorrow I'm putting a bullet in that mother fucker's head. Caught him dealing to kids for the last time."

"Thanks for your cooperation," Ethan said as he backed away. He and Chris both turned and walked back out of the park. As they exited the place Ethan had once played at, he took a moment to glance around. The park was rich with childhood memories. He found it sad that scum like these gangsters had to turn it into such a forbidden place.

"Fuck, man! That's luck...we got lucky! Why are you like this...why?" Chris said irately. Ethan did realize how fortunate they were and had no idea why he was like this.

"I don't regret doing it, Chris. I'm sorry. My life's *at* risk…If you want to drop this case its fine. I want you here, but leave if you have to." Chris eyed Ethan, then swiftly swung the door to the Charger open and jumped in staring up at the roof.

"I'm staying, you need me. Jesus Christ, Ethan. I'm down with crazy shit, but you're out of your mind. You need some serious help." Ethan wished Dr. Lianessa could hear that one.

Ethan realized they'd probably be in for a lot worse than what they just experienced. He turned the car onto Hull Avenue and looked for number 29. He maintained a normal speed as he and Chris skimmed the block. "Right there," Chris said. "Circle the block, I saw a good spot down by the corner…we can sit there for now."

Ethan drove the car around the block; it sickened him that he was back in this neighborhood. It was noon on a Wednesday and he was sitting in a parking spot, taking notes on who went in and out of a crack house on Hull. He had never dreamt of coming back here after that bank robbery, yet here he was, eating a sandwich and searching for a junkie. It was around 2 p.m. when they finally saw him.

"Thereeee he goes," Chris said relieved.

The little weasel like man walked up to the entrance of the house, smoking a cigarette and talking to another guy. Ethan watched him as he laughed and puffed on his cancer stick, such a pathetic looking man. He'd love to jump out right now and grab this guy, but he knew it would be more beneficial to wait it out and see what developed. Hopefully the killer would be revealed shortly. Ethan's phone began to ring and the caller i.d. read 'Cap'.

"What's up Cap?" he said as he switched to speaker phone. He hoped they had gotten something useful.

"Hey Ethan, I got the reports back from those homicides," Cap sounded less irritated, now, almost interested. "These scenes were clean. The investigating detectives reported absolutely no fingerprints, no significant markings on the bodies and we're still waiting for the coroner report…just gruesome acts of inhumanity. Now for the similarities between each of them, like I told you earlier, two of the victims are divorced and one is separated. Each victim was in fact tortured. One of the investigations revealed that this particular victim was exposed to a heavy amount of smoke…the guy's lungs were filled with it…and he was strangled, just a really cruel, slow way to murder someone. These are some weird murders, Ethan. I've never seen this before, an axe lodged inches deep into one guy's skull? That's some TV shit. I have it all here for you when you get back."

"Thanks a lot Cap, we probably won't be back in the office today. We're following a lead right now." Ethan kept staring at the little weasel man, Lucky, noticing his cigarette was finished. The man tossed his bud on the street and moved back inside the house. Ethan basically drew a mental picture, while also noting everything he saw on paper. Little did Lucky know there were four eyes glued to his every move.

"No problem, see you guys later. I'll call you should anything pop up."

The time rolled on and the sun started to go down, still no sign of Lucky. Ethan held on to his gut feeling, he knew he was right. He felt Chris' phone vibrate next to him and he watched his partner as he read a text message. Chris shook his head and put his phone back down. "It's unbelievable, man." He gave a heavy sigh and shook his head. "She's just oblivious." Chris laughed a little and shrugged his shoulders. He sighed again and looked out the passenger window. The sun was almost completely gone now; the shadows covering Hull Avenue gave it a ghastly feel.

"You ever think about answering?" Ethan asked, his eyes still glued to Lucky's criminal clubhouse. He always felt weird talking to Chris about his mother.

A while ago, after about a year of Ethan and Chris' partnership, Chris told Ethan the story of his mom. Chris lived with his mother, his father, his two brothers, and his two dogs in a beautiful house in Morris Park in the Bronx. "The model family," as many had labeled them. Chris was raised well by his family; everyone got together at Christmas and kissed each other on New Year's. He had believed in happiness, in marriage, in honesty and virtue as though it were all staples of the world he lived in.

The day finally came when his mother left. She explained to him that she was in love with someone else...that she no longer loved his father the way she used to. She made it sound normal, like it was a common thing that Chris should swallow, accept, and understand. Over the course of time, Chris was taught humility and experienced the harsh reality of what the world really was, he came to realize many people denounced honesty and virtue, trashed responsibility, and laughed at loyalty. His mother ran away with his godfather, the man who had once been his father's best friend. This is what seventeen year old Chris' mother had expected him to understand.

Chris recollected to Ethan about the countless times he had seen the two stare at each other. His father had sat there, sharing a table with his wife and his best friend; he could have never anticipated her doing what she did. The many holidays they had all shared a table together "happily" celebrating as a "family". Ethan remembered the pain in Chris' eyes, the way he clenched his teeth together and tightened his fist in anger.

"She'll never understand...they'll never get it. I guess it's just something we have to accept," Ethan said, he could barely even stand his own words. Chris had gone through years of torment, faced incredible hardships no child should ever have to face. Ethan had endured similar mental abuse, but here they were, sitting on Hull Avenue as federal agents.

The time slowly crept on and doubt began to form in Ethan's mind. He stayed focused, restlessly searching for any sign of life out of the house. Ethan and Chris were taking shifts, their usual routine during stakeouts, and Ethan had still not grown used to Chris' obnoxious snoring. He looked down at him for a quick second, shaking his head at his partner, whose mouth was hung wide open. Chris' light blue button down shirt was wrinkled where the seat belt hugged him. He looked back up at the house just in time to catch the front door slowly open. He reached over and woke Chris up quickly. Startled, he snapped out of his sleep and jolted upright, straining to adjust his eyes so he could see the figure through the dark.

The man walked out on to the porch, slowly closing the wooden door behind him. He was probably about 5'9", Caucasian, with short, buzzed hair. This definitely wasn't Lucky. Ethan leaned forward, trying to get a better look, and then sat back in his seat. "That's not him," Ethan said dejectedly. He was frustrated now, this whole stake-out could become a bust, and a pricey one too. He felt like he was wasting so much time sitting in this car when he could be out making some real progress. He was pretty sure Chris felt this way as well. Ethan stared out at the man on the porch, watching him closely as he mulled over certain thoughts.

Chris looked over at Ethan and let out a sigh. "Your turn," he said, the uncertainty vibrant in his tone. Ethan put the seat back and raised the steering wheel, turning on to his side to get more comfortable. He was starting to feel cold, the winter air finally getting to him, but the weather would definitely not put a halt on this case. Slowly he felt himself drift off to sleep.

Chapter 10

I'll Scratch Your Back...

Ethan couldn't believe he held a Super Nintendo controller in his hand. He stared at the glorious piece of machinery, the little box of heaven, and just shook his head. "Aiden...wow." The system had come out three years ago, but the two boys couldn't care less. He turned his head to his cousin who sat there with a smile from ear to ear.

"I couldn't believe it either. I have the new Mario game, too!" Aiden pulled out "Super Mario World" and both boys' eyes widened in amazement. Aiden was much smaller than Ethan. He had always been tiny and because of that, and the fact that Ethan was older, Ethan had always looked out for him. Ethan didn't see Aiden as much anymore, since his father had left, but Ethan's father brought him to hang out every other weekend when his visitation days rolled around. Today was the first time they were scheduled for a sleepover in a while.

Aiden opened the box slowly, like it was some kind of priceless artifact, and inserted the new game in the console as both boys quickly flopped down on to the floor, the controllers tight in their hands. As the tiny Mario came running onto the screen, they opened their mouths in amazement and gasped in awe at how incredible the graphics were. Aiden turned to Ethan and put up his fist which Ethan quickly pounded as he nodded his head in strong approval. The two played for hours upon hours.

Ethan woke up, startled as Aiden shook him violently. He looked around the room dazed; he realized he must have fallen asleep on the floor at some point. Aiden looked terrified, his face was covered in panic as he whispered quickly, *"Get in the closet, get in the closet."* Aiden helped Ethan get to his feet and then quickly pushed him towards the closet door. As the grogginess wore off, Ethan became alert to the screaming from outside the room.

"What's going on?" Ethan asked confused.

"Stay in the closet Ethan, don't come out no matter what, just stay in the closet," Aiden whispered nastily. He pushed Ethan inside and slammed the door closed. Ethan stood there, in the dark, motionlessly wondering what was going on. He slowly, quietly opened the door a crack and peered out into the room, he could see Aiden standing by the door, his ear pressed to it listening intently. The arguing was getting closer. Ethan shuddered, remembering all the times he had heard something so similar, and then the door to Aiden's room swung open. Ethan's aunt, Aiden's mom Nicole, came hobbling into the room, blood dripping from her mouth as she held both hands to her head. Her crying was deafening.

Ethan gasped and froze in fear as he saw Tommy, Nicole's husband and Aiden's stepfather, barge into the room. Tommy's face was red and distorted in anger, his fists and his teeth were clenched. Tommy was as massive as a UFC fighter; Nicole looked ridiculous standing next to this beast.

"You stupid bitch!" Tommy yelled. "You cheating on me? You fucking cunt!" Tommy grabbed Nicole by her hair and threw her across the room, her body crashing into the table Aiden's new Nintendo sat on. Ethan shook in horror and he could barely see through the tears in his eyes. Aiden's Nintendo fell to the ground, a piece of the machine breaking off. "Spend money on this piece of shit, right? Did your boyfriend buy it for you!" Tommy was screaming so

piercingly it was a wonder the cops hadn't been called.

He picked up the Super Nintendo and beamed the machine into the wall, shattering it.

Aiden let out a yelp, almost like a small dog, as he crouched cowering in the corner of the room.

Ethan could only watch as Tommy turned his attention to his cousin, advancing on him now.

Ethan, paralyzed by fear, felt the warmth on his leg as his urine streamed down to his feet. He

was still frozen as he watched Tommy beat Aiden. The monster raised his fist and came down

hard, over and over and over again, Nicole's body convulsing on the floor near Ethan's closet,

she was still crying as the blood seeped from her mouth on to the boy's white carpet.

The beating stopped suddenly. Tommy stood over his stepson for a few seconds,

blankly staring down at the boy's crippled body, and then he moved towards Nicole. The man's

expression dramatically changed, his face became softer now as his eyes were sad and he

started to cry. He knelt by Nicole, who was still writhing in pain, and took her head into his

gigantic hands. "Baby, I'm so sorry. I'm so, so sorry sweetheart." Tommy started to cry

heavily, his face broken and miscued. "I just love you so much baby. I need you in my life; I

never want to lose you. God, I love you baby." Ethan could still feel himself shaking as he

watched Aiden, the young boy's small body curled into a ball, clawing at the carpet, his arms

moving in strange, abstract ways. Ethan could see he was in a great deal of pain. Aiden kept

opening his mouth, trying to speak, but the words just wouldn't come.

Ethan felt his body convulse again. He felt the fear suddenly shift, the shaking suddenly

stop, the paralysis completely leave. He stared at Tommy, whose face was still veiled in tears.

He looked over the man's gargantuan body, flashes of the previous episode popping into his mind, flashes of his own father becoming clear now. His aunt lay in this monster's hands, still bleeding uncontrollably, still heavily crying. Her arm was bent awkwardly, broken from when she had hit the wall.

Nicole looked up at Tommy and raised her other, good hand. "I love you too baby, it's ok. I love you too." Ethan shuddered. Suddenly, a fire sparked somewhere deep inside his once stiff body. A strange, foreign ache overcame him, scaring him a little. He looked back at his cousin, the boy still clawing at the floor, blood sprayed around him and drenching his shirt. Aiden looked up and stared directly at the slit in the closet door. He couldn't speak a word but his face said hundreds. The boy dropped his head to the carpet, passing out, and Ethan lost it.

The anger overcame him finally. The war it had waged so long ago, had finally taken a turn. The tide shifting to anger's favor, the flame bursting inside of him, coursing through his veins. He could feel his eyes scorching, his hands tightening, his small, meager muscles toughen, and his teeth slamming into each other. He had never screamed so loud in his life. Tommy, even Nicole who was so damaged, jumped, startled by this peculiar noise. Their attentions turned to the closet as Ethan kicked open the door, bursting out and tearing for Tommy. He smashed his small fists into the man's enormous head, still screaming loudly as the man jumped to his feet to hold the boy back.

"Jesus Christ, Ethan!" Tommy screamed. He put his hand over the boy's mouth to muffle the screaming. Ethan could feel his new found strength slipping away. He grew weaker each second until he finally broke down and cried. Tommy stood above him, rubbing his head

where the boy had hit him, this time fear present in *his* eyes.

Chapter 11

Stomping Grounds

Ethan jumped up in his seat, sweat covering his forehead inside the freezing Charger, and swung his head towards the passenger side door, his hand ready on his pistol. Chris stared at him, leaning away, a confused look on his face. "You have a good dream?" he asked uneasily. "I got out to pee for a minute, I was right there, didn't take my eyes off the porch so don't worry." Chris shook his head and turned his attention back to 29 Hull Avenue.

Wiping his forehead Ethan caught his breath, rubbing his eyes to wipe away the drowsiness. He just wished he could go back a month. He would discover these murders for himself, investigate each crime scene with his own eyes, investigate each victim's background thoroughly and find each and every core piece of evidence…but he couldn't, so here he was, thrown into a hurricane of mystery. He sat there and looked up at the houses' front door, the door he had just watched Aiden Moore, his cousin whom he hadn't seen in so long, walk out of. Ethan might not have seen Aiden in about nine years, but he positively knew it was him. 'What the hell are you doing here Aiden?' he thought to himself.

Ethan's head was killing him; there was so much to process and so little time. Just as he was about to explain the situation to Chris, the front door opened again. The little weasel walked out onto the porch, standing there nervously, skimming the entire block. Ethan looked down at his watch, 2:45 a.m., and happily looked back up at Lucky. 'Thank God,' he thought to himself as he looked over at Chris and nodded his head at the man. He waited for Lucky to make a move, to jump into his car and speed away, but it didn't seem like he had any intention of doing so. The weasel walked straight up the block, right past Ethan and Chris who sat behind

their tinted windows and crossed the street quickly. Ethan watched him fumble with his box of

cigarettes, struggling to pull yet another cancer stick out. His jeans sagged off his ass and his

hoodie was a few sizes too big. The man was clearly a mess.

The two agents hopped out of the car and followed. They kept to the shadows, walking

slowly behind their prey. Lucky looked around every few seconds, fidgeting and turning in

circles as though he was fighting with himself. Ethan could see how reluctant the man was and

for good reason. The killer probably had no intention of reimbursing him for his services. It

was almost three in the morning, completely dark out, and they were in a neighborhood where

the occasional slaying of a crack head wasn't so exceptional. Ethan sadly didn't care about

Lucky's forthcoming; he just wanted the guy's employer, the lunatic serial killer. As Ethan

swiftly moved through the dark, he could feel the killer nearby; he could sense that he was on

the right track.

These streets were familiar. So many times he had walked these very blocks, scared he

would run into trouble. They passed a bunch of familiar places. A bodega that sold any fruit

you can think of, Sal's pizza shop that had been one of Ethan's favorite hang outs, and a dollar

store where you could find some of the best deals. He still couldn't figure out where the man

was going. He had guessed the Oval Park, but Lucky suddenly turned, walking towards Ethan's

grammar school, St. Brendan's. As they turned the corner, within sight of Lucky who was still

looking everywhere as he scuttled down the block timidly, an enormous black man emerged

from the shadows. Chris continued to pursue Lucky as the giant man reached for Ethan, a medium sized blade shining in the moonlight. "Give me your money…" The man stopped short as Ethan quickly grabbed his hand. It all took barely a second. He dislodged the knife from his attacker's hand and quickly smashed his palm into his nose, feeling the bones crack in his bare hand, as the man lost consciousness. He laid the thief on the ground and quickly, but quietly, met back up with Chris who had never taken his eyes off Lucky. Years and years of Krav Maga had been generous to Ethan.

Lucky stopped in front of St. Brendan's and stared in each direction before advancing to the school's side door. He pulled on what looked like a locked, alarm secured door, opening it slowly, and slipped inside the dark interior. Ethan and Chris looked at each other and Ethan reached for his phone.

"Hello?" assistant director Illames mumbled, sounding as though he had just woke up.

"Sir, Ethan Carey and Chris Hawkins in hot pursuit of a major suspect. St Brendan's School, located at Msgr. Patrick Boyle Street. Bronx, NY 10467. Please send backup and forensics," Ethan whispered.

"On the way, be careful," Illames said, sounding much more awake now.

Ethan signaled to Chris as the two quickly shifted to the side door, opening it and revealing the lock had been taped back. Ethan seized his gun, Chris doing the same, as the two agents, firearms ready, stared into the dark entrance. Together, they moved forward carefully, aware of the impending danger.

Chapter 12

Buckle Up

Ethan stared out the passenger side window, watching the rain drops streak down the glass. The rain was intense tonight as it slammed down on the street viciously…he could barely see outside. He looked over at his father; the man he saw wasn't the same as who he once knew. Ever since his parents had divorced, nothing had been the same. There were a few moments here and there where his father seemed like the super hero he once was, but this notion only lasted seconds.

Andrew Alosi was an NYPD Detective, a fact that made Ethan feel safe as the small Honda roared down side street after side street. The houses around them zipped by, the parked cars only came into view for a moment, as Ethan grew increasingly uncomfortable. The one thing he didn't want was for his father to see him scared. He sat there quietly, not saying a word, closing his eyes and praying he could just be home already.

The night had been terrible. They had gone over to his father's new apartment, his fully furnished one bedroom in Yonkers, where Ethan was supposed to spend the day doing homework and hanging out. This was all a part of the visitation schedule the judge had issued since his parents couldn't come to an agreement on their own. He had asked his father where he had gotten all the furniture, where he had gotten the big t.v., and where the brand new Honda had come from, but his father brushed all his questions off. "My friends, bud, and I leased the car so it's not really mine. What are you asking me all this for?" He watched his father walk away, his cellphone held up to his ear as he laughed with someone over the phone.

Ethan looked down at his homework; he was in sixth grade now and really didn't understand anything in front of him. "Dad, I really don't…" Ethan stopped as his father held up a finger and walked into his bedroom, closing the door behind him. Ethan finished his homework and turned the television on, laying on the couch thinking to himself. There was a time where he and his father did everything together. They went to movies, played catch, told jokes, watched sports, but now, it was all changing. His father came back into the room and sat on his recliner, giving Ethan a chance to come right out and ask him.

He asked a simple question, or at least what he thought was a simple question, and because of that here he was in the racing Honda Civic, tearing through a monsoon. His father had anger all over his face as they turned on to Mosholu Parkway. Ethan was finally almost home.

"I just want…" Ethan stopped short as his father reach across the car, grabbing Ethan by the arm and shaking him viciously. The car screeched and skidded as his father shook him yelling.

"Enough! Enough with the questions, you're gunna sit there quietly and not say a word! Do you hear me! Do you hear me?!" Saliva was swinging out of his mouth as he screamed the words at the eleven year old. Ethan was terrified, his arm hurt from where he had been grabbed…he just wanted to be home. The car pulled over and Ethan, without hesitation, jumped out and watched the Honda roar up the block.

He walked into the apartment building feeling horribly, knowing it had been his fault for the outburst. He felt disappointed as his mother buzzed him into the lobby, shaking his head as he walked across the hallway to his front door. His mother greeted him with a hug and a smile,

no idea of what had just happened.

Ethan was like a dog. He could be kicked and thrown around and he'd eventually just

come right back happily. He was swapped back and forth between parents, yelled at and

screamed at for asking too many questions, and forgotten on so many occasions. Andrew Alosi

knew he had a happy son who would let all of this just roll off his shoulders. He knew he helped

create a strong boy who could handle it all, one who was popular in school and who had a good

group of friends...but was he entirely right? Was he positive this wouldn't all build up, resulting

in an irrational explosion of hate...of anger? He had no idea, as so many don't, that each and

every word, each and every action and decision, would be remembered forever. Ethan's wrath,

his resentment, could have possibly been avoided had Andrew answered Ethan's one, tiny

question. "I just want to know...Why did you leave ME?"

Chapter 13

Secret Santa

The two stood in the entrance, the side door closed behind them, staring at the two

possible routes laid before them. Ethan knew the staircase leading downstairs headed to the

cafeteria and the other side of the school, while the other staircase led up towards the gym and

the classrooms. It had been a long time since Ethan walked these hallways, yet they were still

so familiar to him. As his eyes adjusted he could see the Christmas decorations covering the

walls, the tinsel wrapped around the banisters, the Santa Claus faces staring at him, smiling

creepily. He realized what would have to happen now, and although he knew it was risky and

unwise there was no way around it. Chris already suspected their next move as he nodded to

Ethan, proceeding, alone, down the stairs slowly. Ethan watched his partner move. Chris was

like a ghost, so quiet and quick as his form vanished into the dark. Ethan hoped he could be as

stealthy.

Ethan moved carefully, one foot in front of the other, his Glock pointed in front of him

as he advanced one step at a time. He strained his ears, desperately trying to hear some sort of

movement, but all he got was the disturbing creaking of the ancient building. He guessed he

had about ten, maybe twenty minutes before his Bureau brothers reached the school, and at

that point he hoped to already have this killer in cuffs.

Ethan reached the top of the steps and continued towards the school's gym. He

stopped to glance down a long hallway, staring to see if he could catch some form of life. The

hallway was so dark; all he could see at the end was some old desks and tables piled on top of each other. There was a side entrance which he assumed lead to the gym; he couldn't recall

ever seeing the doorway. He was uncomfortable with all the nooks creating an ample amount

of hiding spots but still he fearlessly pressed on.

He finally reached the opening to the gym, poking his head out slightly to review the

terrain. There was no sign of anyone, although his eyes were starting to play tricks on him. He

thought he had seen someone on the stage, but after adjusting his eyes a little, he realized he

was mistaken. Ethan was on high alert, it was pitch black in this place and his adrenaline was

pumping. He squinted, closing his eyes tightly and opening them again as he stared into the

gym. He could see himself standing there on the stage, receiving first honors for his academic

prowess throughout the semester, his father nowhere in sight amongst the audience, his

mother cheering loudly. He could see himself playing ball, running up and down the court with

his team, his mother and his uncle Joe beaming at him from the stands. He shook his head

quickly. 'Not the time for nostalgia, Ethan, get your shit together.' Sliding his feet to another

long hallway, he braced himself, looking forward at the doorways that lined the walls, a killer

possibly standing behind one of them, patiently waiting.

The silence suddenly broke as Ethan jumped, dropping to one knee, his eyes widening as

"We wish you a Merry Christmas" rang out loudly through the hall. He stared in front of him,

waiting for someone to pop out, but no one appeared. He rose back to his feet and moved

diligently, turning into each classroom as he made his way towards the noise, still no sign of

anyone. Each class he turned into was filled with desks, filled with hiding spots, filled with

darkness. Ethan swiveled his body, turning each way to make sure he wasn't tailed, to make sure this killer wouldn't sneak up on him. He reached the corner of the hall and quickly checked behind himself once more before diving out into the opening. He slid past the corner, propping himself up on to his knee, his gun pointed directly at St. Nick's forehead.

"You're fucking kidding me," he panted as he watched the miniature Santa Claus dance in circles, singing everyone's favorite holiday tune. He glanced around the intersection, no sign of anyone, and then he moved to the figurine to shut it off. The singing decoration was triggered by movement...someone had tripped it. Ethan put it back on the floor and looked around. It could have been a bug, wind, even a malfunction. On the other hand it could have been a psychotic, trespassing, serial killer. Ethan readied his weapon again, and continued to the stairs, still checking each room along the way.

Years of Krav Maga, years of being an agent, training and experience...how could that help him here? He was blindly walking through a maze. Sure, he was walking through the school that was once his, but the darkness caused him to feel like a stranger. The killer easily had the upper hand here; Ethan could barely see two feet in front of himself. Still, he kept his poise, breathed in and out calmly, slowed his heart rate as much as he could, and started to move up the steps.

He reached the second floor and slowly put his face in the square window pane on top of the door. Each floor was sectioned off by two metallic, swinging doors, with a square piece of glass revealing the other side. He looked down the dark hallway; the classroom doors were grim and uninviting. He reached forward to open the metal door when a loud bang sounded from upstairs. His body jolted as he quickly swung around, pointing his gun at the top of the steps. His heart pounded, tiny beads of sweat appeared on his forehead, and the hairs on the back of his neck stood erect. The sound was more of a thud, like something heavy falling. It didn't sound like a body or a gunshot Ethan thought. He moved to the steps again, looking up and down to make sure he wasn't being followed or watched, and quickly advanced to the top floor of the school.

He reached the next set of metal doors, keeping his body low under the windows, and tried to hear anything from inside. The whole school was deadly silent. He held his breath and listened closely, finally hearing a faint noise. It sounded like a high pitched scraping. Like metal scratching against another solid, that horrible screeching noise people made when they grinded their forks and knives.

Slowly he raised his head to the window and stared in, his eyes making out a figure at the far end, moving slowly in the dark. As he adjusted to the dim lighting he could see his partner pressed against the wall, signaling for Ethan to come in.

'This is it,' Ethan thought to himself. The killer was here, unsuspecting of the two agents as they closed in on its location. It was finished; there was a squad of agents on the way and it had no idea. Ethan moved into the hallway. He could easily hear someone walking now, only one pair of feet from the sound of it. He closed in on the noise until he and Chris were right on top of room 205. They stared at each other, Ethan feeling anxious, as he patted his chest indicating he would go in first. He took a deep breath, adjusted his grip, and swung into the room, his eyes wide and ready for anything.

"Freeze, get on the floor, get down on the floor!" Ethan shouted as he dashed forward to seize his target. Lucky stood in the room motionless, looking forward, not even noticing the agents as they hustled towards him. He dropped down to his knees and put his hands through his ratty hair as Ethan jumped on top of him, grabbing his arms and pushing him down onto the cold classroom floor. Chris ran to the doorway looking up and down the hall to make sure no one was making a run for it.

"You have the right to remain silent. Anything you say can and will be used against you in a court of law. You have the right to speak to an attorney and to have an attorney present…" Ethan stopped as he caught sight of what was in the room with them. He looked up at the blackboard, giant words were written across it, and then he realized that Lucky was crying. The man felt almost lifeless as Ethan lifted him off the floor.

All around Ethan were pictures, one on each desk, of children. Ethan slowly turned around; taking it all in at once as Chris also realized what was going on. There were sirens sounding outside now, police lights flashing in the windows, the lights bouncing off the room's dark walls. Chris flicked on the classroom's lights and took a deep breath. They could hear the sound of their fellow agents hurrying up the steps as they paced around the room, looking down at the children's pictures. Ethan looked up and read the message on the blackboard.

"Our death is not an end if we can live on in our children and the younger generation," Chris read out loud.

"Albert Einstein," Ethan said. He had heard this quotation while he studied at Fordham. "All these children, I think they're all dead." Ethan reached down and picked one of the pictures up, turning it around to reveal more writing. 'April 2nd, 2001 – May 21st, 2010.' "This boy was nine, according to this, when he died. No names on any of these pictures but some have dates." Ethan walked around the room, carefully lifting each picture to see the writing underneath. He was aware that he didn't want to tamper with evidence, but he was highly doubtful they would find any here. What Ethan was really searching for was some type of sign.

"What do you think it all means?" Chris asked, still staring up at the blackboard. Ethan stood in the middle of the classroom looking straight ahead and trying to concentrate.

"What's going on?" Assistant Director Illames said as he walked into the room. "Forensics, do something, just stop fucking standing there. Who locked the doors last night? Who set the alarm? Is there an alarm? I want some fucking names! Lock this school down. Hello! Wake the fuck up people! Who's this guy?" Illames walked over to Lucky, looking at him disgusted. Lucky was still crying. Ethan shook his head and rubbed his eyes. He was suddenly so tired and all of the yelling and cursing just added to his frustration.

"I've seen some of these kids before," Lucky squeaked, his words were hard to make out through the pathetic whimpering. "Lucy, acid, smack, dust, brownies, e…I sold that shit to them, it was just easy money." Lucky bawled like a baby, drooling on to the floor too as the agents watched despicably. "Some of these kids came to me to buy, they told me they wanted to sell but I saw them use. The money man…I needed the money, they woulda killed me." Lucky broke down, his knees hitting the floor again as he cried sloppily. Ethan looked over and saw the anger engulf Chris' face. He ran over just in time, grabbing his partner as he broke towards Lucky.

"You mother fucker!" Chris screamed as Ethan held him tightly. "You piece of shit, they're fucking children! They don't know better!" Ethan hauled Chris out of the classroom, ignoring the other agents who watched nearby. Illames still stood in front of Lucky, shaking his head in revulsion as he knelt down close to the drug dealer's ear.

"I can't imagine what they're gunna do to you in jail. You should start thinking up a better story." Illames whispered. "Take him to the station, get him processed."

Ethan let go of Chris, who had calmed down a little, and walked back into the classroom, scanning for a sign of something helpful. He stopped the two agents who were dragging Lucky out, holding one finger up to ask them for a second.

"You delivered a package to federal plaza yesterday morning. Who gave it to you?" Ethan stared down at the helpless drug dealer knowing there was little chance he'd actually know anything.

Lucky looked up at him, almost surprised that he was being addressed. "I have no idea, I don't ask questions. I just needed the cash, it was an easy job."

Ethan lowered himself, staring into the man's eyes. He knew the guy was telling the truth. Lucky was scum. He worked for the money and couldn't care less about the casualties caused by his actions. "You know who you are. You'll get what you deserve."

He stood back up, nodded at the two agents, and went back to reading the blackboard. He looked at each child's face, read each date frontwards, backwards, added the numbers together…nothing worked, nothing made sense. Standing still he could feel his brain freeze up, and then it hit him. He whipped out his letter, which he had stuffed in his back pocket, and unfolded the paper quickly, reading through it once more.

My dearest Ethan,

Good morning. I've sent you a few pictures I was hoping you could take a look at. Excuse me for the quality; I had an appointment I couldn't be late for. "Have no fear of change as such and, on the other hand, no liking for it merely for its own sake." Robert Moses wrote this believing exactly what I believe, you shouldn't fear change nor should you long for it merely for no purpose. I hope you can understand, Ethan, that I do not release these people from their hell because I wish to do so but because I have to. It's my job, what my life has been built around, why I'm right here on this great stage. I met these people and saw their life meant little. I saw the hell they inflicted on others, the carelessness they portrayed. There are many in this world, Ethan, I could use a hand. We can rip them apart; we can destroy them because that is what they have asked for. We'll make them pay for what their lives stood for. Clarence Day said it best, "We must make the best of those ills which cannot be avoided." Will you do me the honor? Will you help me?

Sincerely yours.

Ethan's breathing grew heavy as it all hit him at once. 'This great stage...do me the honor.' Ethan folded the letter and stuffed it back into his pocket as he bolted from the room, Chris chasing after him. He nearly jumped the entire flight of steps as he sprinted downstairs, speeding towards the gym, the same gym he had stood in for countless honor assemblies and countless basketball games. He burst into the gym spinning around in circles, searching for something out of place.

"Ethan what the hell are you doing?" Chris said confused.

"He told me he'd come here, he told me in the letter." Ethan looked everywhere, urgently trying to find something. "There's something in this gym, just look for something out of place. Hit the lights."

"Ethan I've never been here before, I don't know where the hell the lights are. Where's the light switch?" Chris asked as he joined Ethan in his hunt.

"Just look for something that isn't gym-like. I don't know. There has to be something here." Ethan jumped up on the stage, frantically looking everywhere. He knew he had to slow down; he was an erratic mess. There was still the chance that nothing was even here, maybe the letter held no clues, perhaps the words were just a coincidence. Ethan could barely see through the dark, but his eyes were slowly adjusting. His head pounded, the migraine he had developed growing worse. He put his hands to his burning hot forehead and did his best to focus, to see through his irritated eyes. 'Jesus Christ Ethan, snap out of it.' Then he saw it, a small object sat on top of the gym's scoreboard table. He jumped down and ran to the object, staring at it for a little until he finally realized what it was.

"A finger," Chris said, staring down at the human finger sitting on the table. Ethan didn't give himself anytime to register the shock; he quickly scanned the area and saw exactly what he had expected.

"Another finger," Ethan said walking over to where it was sitting on the gym floor. 'This thing killed again,' Ethan thought to himself. He looked up and saw another finger lying by the gym wall. "And another."

"Holy shit, Ethan!" Chris said loudly, standing at the opposite end of the gym. "There's an ear over here." Ethan looked over and saw Chris was crouched down staring at something. He noticed a few agents were now standing in the gym's doorways, watching the two as they called out body parts.

Ethan looked up from his third finger and continued to walk along the gym wall to the stage. He passed another finger, and another, as he reached the four little stairs leading up to the stage. On top of the third step sat exactly what he was looking for, an envelope. On top of the envelope, Ethan realized, sat a pair of eyeballs. It was addressed the same as the first:

Special Agent Ethan Carey

Ethan crouched down and reached for the letter, slowly rolling the two eyes off of it. He shook his head as he looked up onto the stage.

"This is a tongue! Ethan, there's a tongue here!" Chris called out. Ethan looked up at another small object sitting a few feet away from the steps. He got up and carefully walked over, crouching down to analyze it. He had no idea what it could be and the dark was definitely not helping. He reached down and moved it a little with his finger, moving his face a little

closer to get a better look. He jumped up as he realized what the object was. He felt unnerved;

he had just touched someone's lips. Ethan could feel vomit bubbling to the service, but he was

good at suppressing the nausea.

"There are eyes over by the steps and a set of lips on the stage. It ripped someone

apart." Ethan stopped as he said that, realizing the killer had told Ethan they could "rip" people

apart in its letter. "The psycho mentioned ripping someone apart in the letter. It's got this all

planned out." Ethan shook his head as the lights suddenly flashed on. He could see the body

parts easily now, scattered across the gym as well as some forensics specialists who were

scouring the room.

Chris joined Ethan on the stage as he fingered the envelope, ripping the letter out as he

tossed the rest to the floor. He read it out loud:

Dear Ethan,

He probably never knew his son played basketball. He was never

there to see him, never there to cheer him on, never there to hear him,

never there to hold him when he lost a close one. He sailed through life

disregarding his responsibilities. He fought his ex-wife when she "asked

for too much" and he broke his promises. He probably doesn't even know

his son is dead. Now Ethan, you're looking to put me away for life...but do

I really deserve it? Tell me you don't want this too. Tell me you don't find

it right. Do you think this man deserves to walk this earth like you and I?

I give a new meaning to 'deadbeat' Ethan. Duke Ellington said, "You've got to find some way of saying it without saying it." That's exactly what I'm doing.

Sincerely yours.

P.S. Apologize to the cleaning people for me

Ethan folded the letter and put it in his back pocket. He looked up, watching the forensics teams strip-search the entire gym, searching ever so fervently for a clue that they wouldn't find. This thing was too good, Ethan was starting to realize this now, but he didn't care how good this killer was. He had gone through a lot in his life, nothing like this, but never the less he had endured so much. Ethan reached into his pocket and whipped out his phone, opening a text from his mother which was sent at 9:47 pm. The text read, "I love you my beautiful, strong son." Ethan felt stone cold as he put the phone back in his pocket. He loved his mother more than anything in the world; she was his strength and what drove him forward.

"Trust me, Ethan, we'll find this thing," Chris said, reaching out and touching Ethan's shoulder. Ethan nodded in confirmation. He had the fire back in his eyes. He knew they'd get him, her, whoever it was. Ethan was a little startled as he walked out of the gym. As he walked down the hallways to exit the school, he realized something.

"Maybe he did deserve it," Ethan said, thinking about all the body parts lying in the gym.

"The guy in the gym!?" Chris exclaimed, hesitating for a minute. "No one deserves that," he replied, although not sounding too sure himself.

"Does Lucky deserve it?" Ethan asked, eyeing Chris curiously.

He didn't receive an answer.

Chapter 14

Real World

Chris sat at the dinner table playing with his food, thinking about what it must be like to

cry. How would he know? He could only remember crying once and he never forgot the beating

he got because of it. He looked up at his mother and father, the two latest additions to the

failed marriage category. Earlier in the day his mind had been on the difficult AP calculus

homework ahead of him, but now his mind was inundated with the confusion of what was

happening to his family.

"I'm so sorry Chris, I want you to go to college, more than anything baby, I really do,"

Lisa said to him, gingerly touching his hand as tears streamed over her face. Chris' father

lifelessly stood near the door. His face spelt distraught, he blankly stared out into space, lost in

his own home. Chris felt for his father and knew he couldn't fathom how horribly the man must

feel. If the love of his life left him for his best friend, he was sure he'd be dead inside too.

"So I can't go to college...because you are moving to Austin with your new boyfriend and

won't be able to pay my tuition?" Chris knew this was the real reason. He heard his mother's

side of the story, but he knew this was the truth. He sat there, staring at his mother, the woman

who was supposed to love him unconditionally, and watched as she gave up on him. He felt the

anger build inside as he smashed his fist down on the table.

"You fucking ruined this family, and now you're the one sitting here crying! You're

running away! Best part is you don't have your tail between your legs; you have your head held high like you're some sort of victim! Fucking pathetic!" Chris got up and stormed towards the door, knowing he had to leave the house.

"How dare you talk to your mother that way!" Lisa screamed back. She jumped out of her seat and followed him to the door, pointing her finger at her ex-husband. "This is your fault, he learned this from you. You need to look after your damn son, Marshall!"

Chris spun around, staring his mother in the eyes. He opened his mouth to speak, but he couldn't. He didn't see his mother anymore, he saw a stranger. This woman truly had no idea; she was oblivious to the reality around her. He shook his head, staring at this woman sadly.

"The fantasy world you live in…you're not alone there," Chris said shaking his head and smiling. "Go to Texas, forget your problems, forget your worries, forget the life you've already built…the three sons you bore, the husband you once "loved" who you left in exchange for his best friend, forget it all. You're great, you're the best, and never forget that. Have a nice life." Chris turned his back to her, knowing very well he would see this woman again one day, but sadly knowing he would never see his real mother again.

"Christian, you are so damn selfish. All you can think about is yourself!" Lisa screamed, watching her son get into his car. Chris turned the engine on and sped away, not glancing back once.

He drove until he forgot where he was. The words just replayed in his head over and over…he couldn't escape.

'I'm selfish,' he thought.

Chris whipped his car off the road and sat there staring out the windshield of his car, reminiscing all the times he had spent with his mother, until he finally exploded.

The tears came to his eyes slowly as he gripped the steering wheel tight, twisting his body left and right to try and ease the pain in his stomach. His mouth was open wide as his tears streamed out silently, he could barely catch his breath. Minutes went by as he rocked back and forth before he finally screamed in pain. He loved his mother, loved her more than anything in the world, but she was gone, she was dead now. Relentlessly he punched the steering wheel, the dashboard, screaming out in rage.

"Why! WHY!"

His crying didn't sound normal anymore as he touched the glass of his door's window, slowly curling up into a ball to try and ease the pain inside. His mother was gone, and he never even had the chance to say bye.

Chapter 15

Faceless

Ethan lay in his bed, obviously not sleeping, with both of his letters on top of him. He was finally home, he thought, looking around his room. Last time he had laid here he was so peaceful, so relaxed in his ways. Maybe not so relaxed, but he was at least free of an obsessed serial killer. He must have read those letters hundreds of times and still he just couldn't figure out a clue. He took the first letter of each sentence and put them together, tried mixing the two letters together, tried absolutely everything he could think of.

Ethan jumped up and walked over to the window, staring down at the city street and watching the cars fly by.

"It wasn't there, you know," said a strange voice behind him. Ethan spun around coming face to face with his father. "It was never there…you imagined it, Ethan. You have such a wild imagination."

Ethan opened his mouth to speak back, but the words just wouldn't come. He stared, wide-eyed, as the man he hadn't seen in nine years walked in his bedroom.

"I'll show you something," Andrew said with a smile drawing across his face. He tilted his head to the side, indicating Ethan to walk out of the apartment, and backed away, resting his arms on Ethan's desk. "Go ahead."

Ethan couldn't take his eyes off the man. He shook his head, closing his eyes tight and rubbing them with his hands. He reopened them to find himself standing alone in his room. He looked around, checking in his kitchen and the bathroom...no sign of anyone. "I'm seriously

losing it," Ethan said out loud, as he turned his head to see that his front door was opened a

crack. He froze for a second, trying to remember if he had locked it. He could see the light

from outside seeping into his apartment.

He slowly tiptoed to his counter, picked up his pistol, and moved over to his front door.

His apartment was so tiny, there was no way anyone could be hiding here, he thought to

himself. He quickly pulled his door open, staying behind it to peek out from the crack near the

hinges. 'What the hell,' Ethan thought.

He walked through his front door into a living room, a familiar living room; he just

couldn't remember where he had seen this place before. It was eerily quiet, not a single sound

could be heard despite the busy NYC traffic nineteen floors below. Ethan looked around the

bright, carpeted, elegant living room. He lowered his gun as he desperately tried to remember.

"Right there," a familiar voice sounded through the room. Ethan spun around, looking

everywhere for the source of the voice. Instead he noticed the awkward, wooden wall unit

towering in the corner of the room. Everything was so blurry now, the carpet, the couch, the

recliner...it was as though he stared from under water...all that was clear was the wall unit. He

moved towards the towering furniture, noticing the object sitting behind the glass. The object

was hazy, he couldn't make out what it was, but it illuminated the room, causing him to squint

as he reached for it. As his hand touched the ice cold glass, the room began to buzz. The

buzzing sounded like the final horn of a basketball game, just a long, loud screeching, and then

the glass shattered, hundreds of glass shards shooting all around Ethan.

He stumbled backwards, bumping into something solid as he spun around to see a faceless being kneeling in the room behind him. He fell back, hitting the floor as the screeching suddenly died. Backing away from the creature, he watched as it raised its hands to rest on its blank head. Ethan stared at it; breathing heavily, watching the creature as it rose…walking to what was once the wall unit. Slowly Ethan got back up, the confusion overwhelming him, as he inched his way back to the doorway.

"Your imagination, Ethan. You always had such a wild imagination." Ethan turned to see his father again, smiling back at him. The anger shot through Ethan's body.

"Fuck you!" Ethan screamed, surprised at the return of his voice, but never the less he grew more angry than confused. Andrew laughed, still staring into Ethan's eyes, as a loud scream erupted in the room. Ethan turned to see the faceless creature screaming in agony.

The noise completely stopped again, leaving the room in an awkward silence. Ethan stood there bewildered, staring at the two creatures before him, and then his father spoke.

"Grow up, son."

Ethan jumped out of his bed, sweat pouring over his face as he knocked his letters and files onto the floor. He dashed to his counter, putting his hands on his pistol as he panted, frantically catching his breath. "Fucking dream, God damn it."

The dreams were frequent. They weren't becoming easier to deal with, but what other choice did he have? He didn't want any sleeping pills.

.Ethan finally got his heart rate back to normal as he lay in bed, staring at his plain

ceiling. This dream wasn't foreign to him; he'd had this same one so many times. 'Just a part of

life. I can deal with it,' Ethan thought to himself, turning over to stare at his mother's picture.

Ethan picked up his phone, punched a few buttons, and placed it to his ear. He stared at

his beautiful mother as he waited for her to answer.

"Hi. You've reached the voicemail of Eileen Carey. Please leave a message after the

beep, and I will call you back as soon as I get a chance," his mother said. Her voice was enough

to distract him from his greatest problems.

Losing someone so close isn't easy. It took Ethan so long to come to terms with the fact

that she was gone. The woman he had spoken to every single day. The woman he had to

watch lose her energy. Whose vibrant life slowly dwindling over a long, excruciating period of

time.

Ethan threw the phone on to his bed as he stared out onto the city streets. 'Where are

you?' he thought, imagining the killer just roaming around outside. He heard a small knocking

sound on the wall; Ed was up, probably getting ready for school. He walked over and tapped

back, then sat down on the corner of his bed with his head in his hands. 'Time for work,' he

thought.

Ethan went through his morning routine as he normally would, not caring if he was late

today. He had the letters memorized now; he kept reading them over in his head as his body

bobbed up and down on his pull up bar. He knew there was something here; he just wasn't being thorough enough. This killer wanted to play a game. It didn't want Ethan to fail, it seemed like it wanted him to figure it out. He threw his leather jacket on and walked out of his apartment, fumbling with his keys as he tried to lock his door.

"Ethan, what's going on?" Luke greeted as he walked up to Ethan smiling. Luke looked exactly like what Ethan thought a psychiatrist should look like. He had a full beard, the nice glasses, and was always dressed professionally. Ethan smiled back; it felt refreshing to finally see someone new, someone who didn't know about all the bullshit.

"What's up Doc, how's it going?" Ethan said. The two shook hands and walked with each other to the elevator. Ethan thought about taking the stairs but he didn't want to be rude.

"Same old, when are you coming over for some dinner? You know the door's always open," Luke said as he pushed 'Lobby' in the elevator. Ethan loved eating with the Lianessa family; he just hated to feel like he was intruding. They were such a great family, always happy and laughing, he just didn't feel like he belonged. "Actually, I've been meaning to ask you something. What are you doing for New Years?"

"I actually haven't given it much thought yet, work's so crazy I don't even know if I'll have time," Ethan said, realizing how big of a loser he sounded. It was New Year's Eve, he had to go out with a hot date and party all night...not sit at home and waste away over two crazy letters written by some lunatic.

"Ethan, you're going out for New Year's. This is the one time I'll excuse your one night fornication tirades. Laura and I are going to a party on 48th hosted by some colleagues of mine.

You're more than welcome. Bring a date, bring a friend, it's always a great time. Let me know and I'll get you the tickets," Luke said as he exited the elevator.

"Yeah, I'll give you a call," Ethan said, waving goodbye. He knew he wasn't going but he'd rather not shoot the guy down so fast. The two walked their separate ways and Ethan realized it was time to put his mind back on what was important.

He thought about the case the whole way to work. 'I'm missing something; it's trying to deliver a message. Why was Aiden at that house? The killer had to have been planning this spree for some time; it has everything so perfectly picked out. It had obviously tailed Lucky, took pictures of all these children, found its way into St. Brendan's, but why pick me? It picked me for a reason, it obviously knows who I am…it's taking me back into my own childhood. If I were a betting man I'd say those first three victims also neglected their kids. This killer is targeting deadbeats, but this is all obvious stuff. Where's the clue? Where's it going next?' The train finally pulled up to Ethan's stop as he hopped off, still trying to make sense out of his limited information. He hoped forensics had made some progress while he attempted to get some sleep, but he doubted there was anything of use at the school.

"Johnny! What's up," Ethan said as he walked by the receptionist.

"Yo Ethan!" Johnny replied, raising his hand to say hello. Ethan wondered when Johnny would come out of the closet as he entered the elevator.

He arrived on his floor and walked straight to his desk, not paying any attention to all the stares. He dropped his jacket on his chair and took a seat, instantly getting to work.

"What up," Chris said sleepily. "You get much sleep last night?" Ethan could see Chris had probably gotten just as much sleep as he had.

"Oh yeah, I slept like a baby," Ethan said nodding his head. "No letters for me today?"

Chris smiled, "You obviously know Illames wants to talk to us." He sat down on Ethan's desk looking down at his feet. Ethan looked at him, lowering his head a little to look at Chris' face. Ethan could see that he wanted to say something. "I just wanted to talk to you for a minute." Chris looked around, nodding his head towards the conference room, and Ethan jumped up to follow him.

"What's going on?" Ethan asked. He had never really seen his partner like this before. They had gone through a lot of tough times together but right now the usually joyful Chris looked upset.

"I just wanted you to know that I'm here for you," Chris said. He looked so uncomfortable that it made Ethan laugh a little.

"I know you are, you don't have to tell me that. We've always been partners," Ethan said laughing and grabbing Chris' shoulder.

Chris shook his head and looked up at the ceiling, "No, I mean I'm here for you as your friend, as your brother. You've always been there for me, and…" he stopped and stared forward, glancing at Ethan a few times. "My brothers are never around, other than Dana, you're all I've got." He shook his head and moved towards the door. "I couldn't stop thinking last night...we'll figure this out." He walked out of the conference room heading towards Illames' office.

Ethan stayed back for a minute, contemplating what was just said. Chris' words meant a lot. He saw how hard it was for Chris to tell him this, and he knew it would be equally as hard for him to express his own feelings. There was a lot he would like to change, a lot he'd like to do over, but you just can't do that in the real world.

Ethan walked into Illames' office, sitting down next to Chris as he waited for chastising to commence. Illames tossed a newspaper down on his desk for Ethan and Chris to see. The headline read, "Body Found in Brendan's: School Closed for Investigation."

"Well fuck that right," Illames said, smiling. "Nothing we like more than some expert reporters helping us out. Thank God, because seriously, it's apparent you guys have no fucking chance. The news is involved, just so you know." Illames walked to his window, crossing his arms as he shook his head.

"We've had one full day, I wasn't really expecting a collar in a day," Ethan said, biting his tongue immediately. He wished he could retract that one. Illames turned his body just enough to see Ethan out of the corner of his eye. He made a face like he had just tasted something horrible.

"For real?" he asked. Ethan shook his head no. "Look, I know how this stuff goes, and yes...Ethan...I've seen agents targeted before. Guess how many got hurt? None of the agents personally targeted have ever been injured, let alone killed." Illames walked across his room, staring out of his office at all the agents running around. "This low-life will keep killing; it spread fucking body parts all over a grammar school gymnasium...that's pretty serious, right? We need him in a court room. We'll be ready for the full scale briefing in about an hour." Illames stared at the two agents, his eyes clean of emotion. Ethan felt as though there was something else, something more he had wanted to say but was now reconsidering. "I'll see you in the conference room," Illames said, sitting back behind his desk.

Ethan sat back down in front of his computer, staring at the two letters, trying to recall everything that had happened. He spread out the pictures of the first three victims, analyzing each and every fiber. Ethan tried, he tried hard to keep it together, but this case wasn't going the way he was accustomed to. He was still, very much, in the dark.

Chapter 16

Say it, Fight it, Cure it

He was twenty-five years old. *Ethan's car roared up the FDR, the scenery flying past him, as his glassy eyes remained on the street ahead. He had just received the call he dreaded, the call that had him on edge for weeks, and now his world was crashing around him. His mind was empty, blank, no emotion shown other than his watery eyes. His car skidded onto Van Cortlandt Ave., racing down the block towards his old home. He could see his Aunt on her cellphone standing on the corner, smiling at him as he whipped his car into a "spot," and jumped out, his Glock swinging wildly at his hip. He almost forgot to turn his car off.*

"Hey Ethan, how's it going buddy?" she said cheerfully, smiling at him lightly as he flew past her. Ethan knew something terrible happened; he didn't have to be a federal agent to know this. He could smell the fear, the terror, as he approached the front door to the building he once called home.

"Hey, what's going on?" Ethan said, opening his front door and flying inside, walking right past his uncles and some other people...there was only one person who mattered. He saw his mother...his beautiful, gorgeous mother sitting on the couch, a giant smile spreading across her face as he sat down next to her. "What's happening?" Ethan said, his heart ripping through his skin. She stared back at him, her smile beginning to quiver.

"I just want you to know..." her smile was now completely faded, her eyes swelling with water as the tears poured from both eyes. "I'm going to fight this and I will beat it. The doctor

told me I have pancreatic cancer, but it's going to be ok." Ethan's heart stopped beating. His mind blanked. The sound stopped.

His mother was all he had, the only one who had ever been there for him. When the asshole he called dad left, running to his fantasy life, she was always there. Everyone told Ethan, "You look so much like your father," and Ethan always responded the same way.

"I might look like an asshole, but I have the heart of an angel."

He stared at his mother, as she drew him in close, holding him tight. He sat there on that couch, feeling his heart break, his world crumbling around him.

"We'll beat this," Ethan said, holding his mother...his hero tight. Looking at Eileen you would never know that she was a woman who had just been given a death sentence. Her hair had been set in rollers that morning so her bangs were perfectly curled over her forehead. Her lipstick never smudged, she must have known some secret to keeping it on. The only thing slightly askew was the mascara at the corner of her eyes because of the tears she fought. Ethan had never been so petrified in his life, but he understood his purpose. He had to be there. He had to be strong for her. He rocked her in his arms, not shedding a single tear.

Chapter 17

Coincidence?

Ethan leaned forward at his desk, shaking his head as he thought about everything on his plate. So much weighed him down. He thought of his mother and all she had fought through. How could he let this stop him? 'She was a fighter...so am I.'

"You alright man?" Chris said, turning around to face Ethan who had just taken a seat in the back of the room. Ethan didn't want to burden Chris with his personal problems.

"I'm good, let's get started," Ethan said, looking up at Illames and Cap who were whispering to each other by the SmartBoard. Ethan saw the piles of paper all over the front desk and the multiple tabs opened on the computer screen, and he wondered to himself, 'Is the killer here in this room? Is the killer hidden behind these clues?' Could they really figure it out through the information they had here, or had the killer cleverly masked his/her identity and just added another leg to this ridiculous marathon? Ethan looked around, the only people sitting in the room were Cap, Lo, Chris, and himself.

Illames stood up straight, tapping the SmartBoard as he spoke to the room. "We have the autopsy reports on our four victims. Before we get to that, let me just say that Lucky was processed and will stand in court sometime in the next few weeks. I'm sure he'll be seeing a lot of court in the future, chances of him spending life behind bars seem pretty good as of right now. After a brief interrogation it was determined that the guy doesn't even know his full name let alone who gave him Ethan's package." Illames cleared his throat, shuffling through his stack of papers. "As you can see here, our first victim was severely tortured," Illames brought

up the picture of the woman who was tied down to an arm chair. Ethan still had the pictures

fresh in his mind as he stared at the enlarged photo on the smart board. "The forensics report

states that the woman, Simone Gardner, was indeed tortured. The knife wounds on her neck

show signs that the gash wasn't created with one movement. Her neck was cut open over a

period of time; reports indicate that the killer did his/her best to keep the victim alive." Illames

squinted and took a deep breath as he tapped the next tab on the board. "This man, Asandro

Jacopino, was also tortured as reports claim the man died of dramatic blood loss, and this death

was cited as happening prior to the ax being lodged in his skull. The killer murdered him slowly

before using the ax." Illames looked out at the four agents, his face showing signs of distress.

"This next body is Ryan Lakeland; his death was being named a suicide...obviously not." The

whole room sat up a little straighter. "Reports have it that the man choked himself...his cause

of death states respiratory complications...however we now know he didn't choke himself."

Illames laughed out loud as he shook his head. Ethan sat forward in his seat, he was

eager to hear about the next victim. "The next body, which was found in parts in St Brendan's

School, has been confirmed as the body of George Minnie. There's a report out stating that

George had gone missing a few weeks ago, we also have a report that his child support had

gone missing years ago. Our killer was on the money about that one."

Ethan sat still, staring at the different photos of George, as he started to laugh. "Ethan?

What's funny?" Illames asked, staring at him curiously. Ethan continued to laugh as everyone in the room turned to stare at him. Ethan stood up, whipping out the letter from the school and approached the front of the room.

"I'd like to speak for a minute, if that's alright," Ethan said, staring at Illames cautiously. Illames put out his hands indicating the floor was his and leaned back against the desk folding his arms.

"I understand how ridiculous this is all gunna sound but time seems to be of the essence here...I'm just gunna come right out with it. The killer is obviously targeting me, maybe trying to tell me something, send a message, maybe it loves me..."

Illames stuck out his hands as though to indicate they knew this already.

"The killer could also hate me and just be stringing me along before it springs an attack. I believe it might be relating itself to me. I was laughing before, because as crazy as it seems, I think it's giving me the next clue in the autopsy report. Its first clue was in handing the envelope to Lucky. It knew I'd check the security tapes and find him. It's obviously very smart, or just familiar with F.B.I. procedure, because it calculated that I'd wait for Lucky to move to a meeting point to collect the rest of the payment. The payment being for simply delivering the message." Ethan stopped, realizing how ridiculous he sounded.

"Keep going," Illames said, he looked intrigued and Ethan could see that he was diligently taking notes.

"It knew I'd follow Lucky up to the school, knew I'd find the body parts in the gym, and now I think it knew I'd see this connection. The man's name is...or was...George Minnie. The letter states he 'sailed' through life without responsibilities. Me and my family used to take trips up to Lake George every summer. We would go sailing on the 'Minnie-Ha-Ha' every time, I loved the place." Ethan smiled and shook his head. "I think it's obviously telling me to go there."

Everyone stared at Ethan as he stood awkwardly debating whether they thought he was completely insane or not. "Ethan," Chris said. "I think it would help if you told us anything about yourself that we don't already know."

Ethan knew this question would arise, and he wasn't prepared to answer it. One thing he was learning, though, was life was short…there was no time to hold things back. Whatever could help them solve this case, he'd have to comply with.

"I lost my mother to pancreatic cancer a while ago," Ethan said. Chris had actually met Ethan's mother, spent time with her. Every time Ethan tried to tell Chris, he ended up backing down. He felt like it was a burden on other people if he expressed his emotions. He thought about his mother all the time, but he never mentioned her out loud.

He thought about telling everyone about his cousin, but decided against it. "That's about it, I live in a studio apartment on the 19th floor, I graduated out of Fordham U., my father left when I was seven, and he left me and my mother with absolutely nothing. There's a lot to me you don't know but I don't think we have the time right now." Ethan walked back to his seat and sat down. He was furious; he never intended this to happen. He never wanted the meeting to turn into some documentary on his life.

"Let's break for a while. Ethan, hang back for a minute," Illames said, walking to the back of the room. "Are you sure you're ok with this assignment? We can take you off of it if you want. I'll assign someone else to the case."

"I want the case. Trust me. I'm fine," Ethan said shrugging. "Lake George is the next step. It's just another case. I'm treating it that way."

Illames stared back at Ethan, not saying a word. Ethan knew how ridiculous it all was, but the bottom line was that it was real. This was seriously happening and the longer they scoffed at it the worse it would get.

"Then get on it," Illames said, getting up and exiting the room.

The whole day went by excruciatingly slow. Ethan read through each letter another hundred times or so, stared at the dead bodies for hours, and re-read each report thoroughly.

"Ethan," Chris said. Ethan could tell he had been building up the courage to say something. "I know how much your mother meant to you. Lake George will probably be tough for you to revisit."

"Definitely don't worry about it; we have a lot to focus on here at work. What happened to my mother is completely separate from what we have going on here." Ethan couldn't hear anymore of Chris' words. They hurt too much.

"Listen, if you don't want to come meet that girl tonight that's completely fine," Chris said, changing the subject quickly. Ethan knew Chris was hopeful that he'd fall for this girl, that he'd happily spring into an exciting relationship by the end of the night.

"I'll be there. We need to talk about the case now. Each one of these people had their families questioned. Each family pretty much said the same thing…they hate these people. According to them they were all horrible, ran away from their responsibilities. There's little remorse in any of these statements." Ethan filtered through the papers, shaking his head. "I hope I'm never remembered this way."

"So the target's on irresponsible, immature people," Chris joked. "I don't know any of those."

Ethan laughed a little. "It's targeting people who neglect their responsibilities as parents. Not just targeting them but going to town on them. It's making sure they go through a great deal of pain…die slowly. This killer is most likely someone who was affected by this. Someone who grew up in a broken household…and of course someone who knows who I am." Ethan looked up at Chris and started to back away.

"Ha, ha, ha ok, Ethan," Chris said grabbing the papers out of his hands. "I do want to kill you sometimes, though." The two laughed as Illames walked up to them.

"Yeah your case is a load of laughs," Illames said sarcastically. "You're alright to go upstate tomorrow morning. I already notified the state police and the sheriff's department in Lake George." Ethan nodded his head in approval as Illames handed him a paper with the phone numbers. "Where are you going first?"

"I'm sure the killer will tell me where to go," Ethan said, realizing how badly that sounded. "I mean I'll check out the resort we always stayed at, I'm sure I'll find something there." Illames nodded back and walked away.

"So you guys always went to the same resort?" Chris asked.

"Every single summer from when I was eight until I was a junior in high school," Ethan said, remembering some of the happy memories he had there. All the times he spent with his mother, laughing and enjoying life. "It's a nice place; I'm not so sure about how nice it is in December though."

"Pack your winter coat, kid," Chris said, nodding his head and smiling. "We're catching this mother fucker and then we're taking a ride on the 'Minnie-Ha-Ha'!"

"Its winter, you're going to ride a tour boat in the winter?" Ethan joked.

Chris stared at him mockingly. "I knowwww but it sounded funny and you laughed. HAHA!"

Chapter 18

Table for One

Ethan stared in his closet wondering when he had last gone clothes shopping. He shook his head as he filtered through his shirts, trying to find something "proper and not hoodish," as Chris had warned him.

Ethan thought about how happy his mother would have been to hear that he had a date. She was always so critical of who he dated.

He looked down at his folder, filled with pictures of the four dead victims and all the rest of the case info. 'I should be staying home and studying, not going out on some ridiculous date,' he thought to himself. 'I don't even wanna go.'

Settling down would have made his mother so happy. He just couldn't bring himself to accept anyone into his life, though. Ethan picked out his outfit, lying it down on his bed, and jumped into the shower. He actually contemplated this for a little while. 'If I don't shower she might make a run for it, then I look like the good guy,' he thought to himself. Ethan raised his arm, the smell knocking his head back a little, and then he stared into his bathroom.

The shower was a quick one. 'If she likes me, she'll like me for who I am, not how I smell.' He put on his clothes, not too "hoodish" of course, and sprayed some of his better colognes. He stared at himself, contemplating if he had forgotten something, and then reached to grab his leather. He hesitated for a few seconds, staring at his leather and then at the pea coat his mother had bought him many Christmases ago. 'I hate this night,' he repeated as he threw on the uncomfortable, weird looking pea coat.

He stared at himself, feeling like some kind of monster...or Barbie doll, and just shook his head. 'What am I doing?' He grabbed his pistol, strapped it to his leg, grabbed his keys and his wallet, and with one nauseated look in the mirror, ran out the door.

As Ethan stood outside Rambling House, he realized this was the last chance he had to run back home. 'SportsCenter, a Hungry Man, and dead bodies,' Ethan thought smiling and nodding his head. He took a deep breath and walked in.

There he stood at his favorite bar, looking around for his friend and his lucky date while wearing the most ridiculous outfit he had ever put together in his life. His argyle sweater vest, poking out from his ridiculous pea coat, was tucked neatly into his slacks, which he quickly pulled out after seeing his reflection in the bar's mirror. He had his hair brushed nicely, his slacks were freshly pressed, and he even went as far as to wear a pair of dress shoes. This was a huge difference from his typical t-shirt, jeans, and leather jacket. Finally, he saw Chris come out of the bathroom and called out to him. Chris froze as he saw Ethan. He walked over to him slowly, Ethan watching closely to see if he'd laugh, and stood there in front of him, still just staring.

"What?" Ethan said. He started to laugh and Chris followed suit. Shaking his head, he turned around to leave but was quickly grabbed.

"Whoa whoa whoa, calm down," Chris said laughing. "Just give me a minute to digest." Chris stood there staring at him. "One more minute." He put his hand to his mouth, biting his finger. "Ok I'm good now...Was this your first time dressing yourself?" Chris exploded in laughter and Ethan, also laughing, turned to leave again.

"Oh come on that's it, that's it, I'm done." Chris said, grabbing Ethan and steering him towards the table. "My man, she is a hotttttttie!" Ethan wasn't sure if the big smile was about his outfit or to convey how beautiful his date was. "You hit the lotto; she's excited to meet you too."

Ethan could see that Chris was much more excited about this than he was. He knew he'd much rather rip his stupid sweater off, sit on one of the empty stools, and chug a beer.

"Ethan, this is Samantha. Samantha...Ethan," Chris said, sitting next to Dana who looked up at Ethan and choked on her drink. Ethan glanced at her but she played it off as though nothing had happened.

"Sammy," the gorgeous blonde said, smiling up at him. Ethan did think she was beautiful, no doubt about that, but that didn't change his mind in regards to commitment. He had met beautiful girls before. This was no different. He could see Chris and Dana out of the corner of his eye; they were like two vultures staring at their prey. He could see them gnawing at the straws in their glasses, staring at the two like they were some kind of aliens.

"Nice to meet you," Ethan said, giving her half a smile back and sitting down next to her. Ethan spent the next hour faking laughs, looking interested, and asking empty questions. Had it not been a date, he would have enjoyed the woman's company. The idea of a date put him way out of his comfort zone.

He stared at Sammy while envisioning the letters and bodies; even now he still studied the case. 'Could it really be Lake George?' he thought to himself. All Ethan knew was that it better be, because a five hour car ride yielding no collar would be destructive to his career. Ethan's head was starting to pound again, his mind drifting far away from the table and Sammy, all he really wanted was to lie down, put ESPN on, and go to bed for a few hours.

"I'm sorry, excuse me for one second, I need a cigarette," Ethan lied as he got up from the table, grabbing his coat. Sammy looked horrified. Ethan figured the girl was probably rarely, or even never, treated this way, but that didn't matter much to him. He hadn't said two words to her the whole night; he just stared at her as she endlessly spoke about her exciting career in make-up. Chris excused himself from the table also, following Ethan to the bathroom.

"You picked up smoking? You're not even trying, man," Chris said shaking his head. "Would it hurt to talk to the girl?"

Ethan didn't care what Chris thought at this point. He had so much on his plate. He didn't have time to deal with the petty bullshit that came along with a relationship. "Look, I'm sorry. I'm tired and we have a long ride tomorrow. I just don't have it in me right now…"

"No, Ethan, you can't hide forever." Chris stopped quickly; he looked like he realized he said the wrong thing. "You're hiding from shit, man, I know you are. I've been your partner for a long time Ethan, I know you better than anybody," Chris said lightly. Ethan stared back at

Chris; he knew this was all true. Chris knew a lot about him and he probably could see through him, but there was so much Ethan wasn't ready to let go of.

"Chris...She seems great, it's just a bad time. You're picking me up at seven right?" Ethan felt like shit. He knew Chris had hoped for a good night, but he couldn't bring himself to accept a possible relationship. Ethan put his hand out to his partner, hoping he'd understand.

"Yeah," Chris said sighing. He grabbed Ethan's hand tightly, and then turned to walk back to the table. "Can you just say good bye to her, please."

"Of course I'll say goodbye."

Ethan had gotten used to putting his emotions aside. It got so much easier over the course of time. He briefly said goodbye, citing a headache as the cause of his early exit, and headed toward the door. He put his pea coat on as he glanced back at the man he had fought crime with for so many years. There were thousands of things he wanted to tell Chris, enough words to fill months of time, but he'd rather keep It all bottled up in his mental vault. Ethan sighed deeply and continued to the exit.

As he was halfway out the door he stopped short.

Chapter 19

Unwanted

"Ethan!" a voice called from the bar. Ethan spun around looking for the source of the call. "Ethan Carey!" the voice called again. The voice belonged to a woman sitting at the edge of the bar.

Ethan's heart stopped beating, his eyes frozen on this unique, stunning human being. His eyes ran over her curvy, fit physique, her long brunette hair flowing over her bare, slightly tanned shoulders. Ethan could feel his stomach lighten and his eyes widen as the compressed, confused feeling in his head fizzled away, thoughts of any serial killer flying out the window.

She smiled at him, dimples perfectly creasing on her face, as her entrancing, big brown eyes glowed at him. "Hey," she mouthed as she waved him over. Ethan could feel an unusual smile spread across his face as his feet moved themselves towards his ex-girlfriend Rachel Serrano.

Rachel and Ethan had met when they were teenagers, both always in hot competition in academics throughout high school. They adamantly hated each other, even more so since Rachel was exposed to his cocky, egotistical mannerisms. She had the unfortunate job of interviewing Ethan after each of his tennis matches, which involved Ethan answering her questions while sweaty and shirtless, shamelessly hitting on her.

The hatred subsided over the course of many months as the two grew respectful of each other. The interviews grew longer and longer eventually turning into actual dates. Only weeks after they were both accepted to Fordham University did they officially venture into a relationship with each other, spending almost every day laughing, confiding in each other, and falling in love.

Rachel had been apprehensive at first. Ethan taught her how to play tennis. They would spend hours on the courts together, laughing and fooling around as she started to get better. Ethan could still remember her goofy face as she concentrated on her form. Rachel was an RA which meant she had her own room. Ethan spent a lot of his time there. They spent many weekends in the local bars, and on those nights he couldn't take his eyes off of her. She only wore a bit of make-up, but it made her eyes pop. However, they also grew comfortable together, and there were many lazy afternoons in Rachel's dorm room watching old TV re-runs, and she looked just as beautiful in her Fordham sweatshirt with her hair in a bun. One of the funniest memories was the first time Rachel accidentally farted when he was around. She was so embarrassed, but oddly enough it just showed him how there was no side of Rachel that he didn't like.

After a while, Ethan grew angrier as Rachel sought to grow closer to him. She always asked about his father, why he was never around, why Ethan never mentioned him. Her questions were harmless, things a girlfriend had a right to ask after a certain amount of time, but Ethan wasn't ready to let her in. He saw the beautiful gift he had, the incredible friend he could trust, but still he just couldn't let his memories go, and, in turn, Rachel became the one who slipped away.

Ethan couldn't believe she was here, sitting right in front of him at Rambling House of all places, waving and smiling in his direction. The last time he had seen her was about seven years ago during his mother's wake and funeral. Before that, he had last seen her in college. He instantly thought back to the day when he had to watch as she hysterically cried, barely able to breathe as she told him she couldn't do it anymore. She needed someone who could open up; who could let her in. Ethan had no chance. It ended.

"Rachel?" Ethan said as he reached the girl.

"Ethan Carey." Rachel laughed as she said his name. "Wow, how are you doing?"

"I'm great...this is so weird, do you live near here or..." Ethan just couldn't stop staring. Rachel was much sexier than he could recall. Her light brown eyes burned through him, her smile made him feel like they were back at Fordham.

"I'm actually here on a "date" but now I'm trying to escape," Rachel said as she stared past Ethan. "I'm using this new dating app on my iPad and it sucks!" Ethan turned his head to see a small man darting towards them. He looked as though he had never dressed himself in his life. Ethan quickly realized he had no business judging. The man was short with shaggy, brown hair. He was wearing skinny jeans and a Lacoste button down. Ethan looked back at Rachel who made a face and smiled. Ethan knew this wasn't her type. "He does not match his description."

"You mean he didn't say that he was a metrosexual pop star?" Before Rachel could answer her date was upon them.

"Is there a problem here?" the man probed, staring Ethan down. Ethan couldn't get past the guy's peculiar outfit. His voice indicated he was of Latino descent; it reminded Ethan of Enrique Iglesias.

"Julio, this is my brother Rob, he actually came here to bring me home...we have a little family emergency," Rachel said staring back and forth between Ethan and Julio. Ethan shook his head a little. 'What a lame excuse,' he thought. They looked nothing alike.

Julio's face lit up and his mouth dropped.

"Oh my, I'm sooo sorry Rob, what a pleasure to meet you," Julio said, extending his hand excitedly to shake Ethan's. "You have such a darling sister and don't worry because Julio is going to take so much care of this wild, *sensual* flower." Ethan held in his laughter as he glanced at Rachel shocked.

"Julio...thank you," Ethan said, breaking off the handshake and walking towards the bar exit.

"Rachel, I hope all goes well and remember, Julio is always here for you. Just call me," Julio said sincerely, taking Rachel's hand and kissing it softly.

Rachel shuddered and nodded back, getting up to follow Ethan to the exit.

"Oh my God!" Rachel screamed as soon as they made it to fresh air. "Are you kidding me!"

"Anyone who refers to themselves in third person is a definite no go. Get with it Serrano," Ethan said laughing.

"That was just ridiculous. I swear he sounds nothing like that online," Rachel said laughing also. Ethan had almost forgotten that he hadn't seen Rachel in over eight years. Talking to her again after all this time just made everything feel normal. It was like nothing ever changed. "So what were you doing here?"

"Same as you actually, mine was a blind date though. A friend set us up."

"Horror story?"

"Actually she was beautiful and nice, just the wrong time I guess," Ethan said as he started to walk to his car.

"It's never the right time for you, is it?" Ethan didn't say anything back. He was a little surprised she brought it up so quickly. Rachel ignored his affronted look and continued, "I live about a ten minute walk from here; do you wanna walk me home? We can catch up a little."

Ethan hesitated for a few seconds. He once had heavy feelings for Rachel; he didn't want anything like that sparking up again. As happy as he was to see her, he kind of wished he hadn't. He thought about Chris, how badly he wanted Ethan to break out of his comfort zone, and his mother who had just wanted him to meet a nice girl. 'How bad could a ten minute walk be?' he thought.

The two strode down 1st Avenue, all the yuppies stammering around them in their fashionable scarves and winter vests.

"So what are you doing now, you ever make it to the F.B.I.?" Rachel asked.

"Actually," Ethan laughed as he pulled out his shield. Rachel's jaw dropped.

"Are you serious? Ethan, that's incredible, congratulations!" Rachel said as she threw her arms around him, hugging him tightly. The cold winter air brushed around the two and Ethan could feel the hair on the back of his neck prickle up. Suddenly there was a warmth inside, a feeling of certainty. He put his hands on Rachel's back and squeezed, bringing her in closer. It all felt right, like he was meant to be here with her. He could smell her perfume, feel her hair blow across his bare skin, feel her breath on the back of his neck.

"I'm so proud of you Ethan," Rachel said backing away. Her face was straight, no emotion as she stared up at him. Ethan just wished they could hug some more, he didn't want to let her go. As incredible as it was, he knew he couldn't leave himself vulnerable.

"Thanks, I guess I forgot how badly I wanted you to succeed. I was always rooting for you back during our Fordham days." Rachel smiled up at him, making Ethan feel a little weird. He didn't like when people patted him on the back.

"By the way, I have to ask you. Since when did you start brushing your hair?" Rachel reached out, carefully touching Ethan's dark hair as though it might attack her.

"Today might have been my first time using a brush," Ethan answered laughing.

Rachel stared up at him, shaking her head as she examined him from neatly combed head to dress shoe toe.

"I always loved your smile," she said as she started to walk again. "You're not so ugly when you smile." The two laughed as they continued down the block. Ethan reminisced about how he used to smile to get himself out of trouble with Rachel.

"So what are you doing now?" Ethan asked, changing the subject.

"I *wanted* to be a top reporter...as you know...*but* things don't always work out the way we want them to," Rachel said shrugging. "Turns out I'm a mediocre, bottom shelf entertainment reporter for The Enquirer." Rachel laughed as she shook her head. "At least one of us followed his dream."

"From what I remember your dream was to *be* a reporter...from what I see we both made it," Ethan said. "I don't think you failed anything, I always loved your writing."

Rachel smiled, stopping to look at Ethan. "This is me," she said looking up at the building in front of them. "It was nice talking to you."

Ethan felt his stomach turning. This was the first time he had felt a connection with someone, and the only time he could remember actually wanting to talk more, however, there was Rachel running up the steps, fumbling with her keys without giving a look back.

"That's it?" Ethan exclaimed, looking up the steps surprised. He took a short step towards the stairs but stopped unsure of what to do.

She turned around, her hand on her hip as she stared confusedly back at him. "What were you expecting?"

Ethan felt stupid, embarrassed as he fumbled in his mind for words to say. He NEVER fumbled for words to say.

"I'm just joking, Ethan," Rachel said, laughing as she ran back down to him.

"It was nice bumping into you," Ethan said, moving into hug her. "I want to see you again, if it would be alright with you. I promise I won't speak in third person."

"I wouldn't mind at all," Rachel said smiling widely. "I'm free tomorrow night...is that ok for you?" She reached into her purse and pulled out her cellphone, handing it to Ethan.

"It should be...I'll give you a call if anything." Ethan said as he put his number into her phone. He felt his heart pounding against his chest. He knew why this time was different. Rachel wasn't the other girls, she was special. She was the only girl Ethan could relate to, who actually understood him because of their similar childhoods.

"Great," Rachel said, putting her phone away. "Then maybe I'll see you tomorrow." Rachel smiled as she turned around and trotted up the steps. Ethan stood there and watched her; he couldn't take his eyes away. She was so gorgeous. She made him feel incredible. At such a time like this, Ethan could never imagine he'd feel so great, but here he was goggling over her like some hormonal teenager.

Rachel opened her front door, stopping to turn around and wave. "You're not going to stand there all night are you?" she said laughing.

Ethan snapped out of his daydream, realizing he was standing in the middle of the street, grinning like a huge creep. "Good night *sensual flower*," he said sarcastically, waving back and walking away.

'What a night,' he thought. He laughed at how he almost didn't go out. How he stood outside of that bar and considered going home. Now here he was, about ten minutes away from his car, smiling like he hit the lotto. Rachel was still incredible. Ethan couldn't remember the last time he saw a girl that pretty, or the last time he smiled for so long. All he knew was he loved it.

Chapter 20

Evil

"Good afternoon! Is there anything I can help you with today?" the woman asked, smiling widely. Children were running everywhere, screaming, yelling, throwing things all over the place. It was like a human zoo. The music was happy, joyful as it screamed all around.

It glanced down at her Mickey Mouse name plate. The words The Disney Store glittered in big golden letters.

"Good afternoon, I'm actually looking for something in particular." The voice pierced the air, slithering like a deadly serpent to the unsuspecting ear of the customer service representative. The figure's smile portrayed trust, giving a sense of comfort to the innocent rep. The children ran rampant, laughing and jumping for joy, no idea of who stood in their midst. Nobody in the whole store knew, but the figure did, and that brought this beast great pleasure. The demon spoke its request to the woman, detailing exactly what was wanted. What was needed.

"Ok, we actually have one in stock, follow me," the woman said, still smiling widely. "Is this a birthday gift?" The figure stared back at the woman pleasantly as they walked through the store, filtering through the crazy, wild children. It actually was stumped by this question. It had never thought about what this gift would actually constitute as.

"I guess it's more of a sentimental gift," the demon said, smiling at the thought of the object's meaning. "He's going to die when he sees it."

"Excellent! Would you like me to wrap it?"

"I would love that."

The figure smiled. Everything was just so perfect.

Chapter 21

Blizzard

Ethan lay awake, his mind racing faster than ever. The room was pitch black, he didn't want ESPN on right now, all he wanted was to let his mind delve into tonight's events. The cold air poured around his naked body, the goose bumps bounced off his skin, but still he felt warm. He hadn't seen Rachel in so long and seeing her again brought so many memories back. She was gorgeous. Her long hair flowed like how he believed angels' hair would. Her smile was all he needed, cleanly wiping away all his troubles. Even personalized letters from the biggest psycho in New York seemed obsolete next to her sweet, amazing features. He couldn't believe how much he was thinking about one girl.

Ethan turned over and stared at his mother's picture. She would have been so happy to hear about Rachel. All she wanted was for her boy to settle down, or at least just be happy, and according to his mother, happiness meant being in a meaningful relationship. She always liked Rachel; she had even taken the girl's side when they broke up years ago.

Ethan continued to stare at his mother's picture. 'Why her, God, of all the people why her?" His mother had suffered through almost two years of pancreatic cancer. She had received weekly doses of Gemcitabine and some special drug doctors had concocted to try to beat the cancer. Her prognosis had started to look hopeful. Her tumor had even decreased significantly, a much unexpected outcome. Ethan had never doubted her for a second. But he still lost her.

After over a year of hope there was a rapid decline. During her last week alive, she had been rushed to the hospital because her pain had become too excruciating. While Ethan visited her one day, her doctor pulled him outside and surprisingly told him that his mother had only two weeks to live. Ethan remembered standing in front of the doctor in shock. He sat back in his mother's room and hid the tears as she sat up in her bed. He didn't know how to talk to her about it. He didn't know what to do. So all he did was sit with her in bed and hold her. She told him that she was in so much pain, and he held her closer and cried. He walked out of the hospital room that night only an hour or so before his mother was pronounced dead.

Ethan smacked his alarm clock before it rang out, jumping to his feet feeling powerful and rejuvenated. He wouldn't let what happened to his mother bring him down. Ethan almost floated to the bathroom, doing a little spin as he jumped through the doorway. He was ready to face this day, to find this brutal psycho and he knew he'd need to stay positive if he was going to work efficiently. 'I know it wants me to go to Lake George. I know it's sending me over there, but what does it want? What's its angle, its motive? Where's it striking next, who's it striking next, what's the point?'

Ethan got dressed, cleaned his guns, strapped them on and headed out the door. He wasn't sure if Chris was downstairs yet, but he just couldn't sit still anymore. He sat on the outside steps and let the cold air hit him as it began to snow lightly. Tiny flakes sprinkled onto the street, barely sticking, but it gave the dark morning a more ominous feel. Ethan couldn't escape the thought that this road trip could be a bust. Very valuable time could be wasted by driving all the way up there, a trip that would take almost half a day, but Ethan had this gut feeling.

'It's in this killer's court right now. It's making the demands, dragging me along, but what else can I do? I'm doing everything possible right now; I don't care what anyone says.'

Ethan felt the soft snow touch his skin. He watched it slowly turn to liquid on the top of his hand as he sat there waiting for Chris. Ethan loved the snow; it reminded him of his dog, Rex. He and his Beagle used to play in the snow for hours until his mom called them in.

Ethan smiled as he reminisced, he still missed that dog. No one could ever understand why he was so upset when Rex passed; they all saw him as just another animal, a possession. Ethan knew it was more than just an animal; Rex was a part of the family. That dog helped him so much when his father packed up and hit the road. He had the memory of his best friend etched permanently into his arm, the ink blasted into his skin in memory of both his mother and his best friend, both to remain in his interior and on his exterior forever.

Ethan looked up as Chris' Charger screeched on to his block. They were right on schedule, set to go find this thing.

"Good morning!" Chris said as Ethan sat in the passenger's seat. "So Sammy can't wait for the second date." Ethan had completely forgotten about his real date from last night, the one he had blown off.

"Good morning! I'm really sorry about that, I just couldn't do it," Ethan said apologetically.

"Dude, I just want you to be good you know? You're a good guy Ethan…" Chris hesitated for a second. "Look man, you're my boy no matter what you do. You like girls, you like guys, you like animals, doesn't matter man, you're my boy."

"I have a date tonight," Ethan said smiling. The car jolted a bit as Chris stared at Ethan.

"What!" Chris said in shock.

"On my way out of Rambling last night I bumped into my ex. We seemed to hit it off. I guess in a way you did hook me up."

"Is it Lindsay?" Chris asked.

"No."

"Ryder?"

"No."

"Marissa?"

Ethan looked over at Chris and shook his head. "First of all, how do you even remember all of that? Second, those girls weren't serious. I never told you about Rachel. I'm thinking of inviting her to this party my friend told me about. You and Dana are invited too. We should all go."

Chris opened his mouth exaggerating how shocked he was. "Dude, what happened to Special Agent Ethan Carey?"

"Yeah, some fancy New Year's Eve party. Sounded horrible but I feel like going now. Luke and his wife said bring a date and a friend. Its Luke's colleague's party."

"Luke your psychiatrist friend?"

"Yes sir."

Chris quietly paid attention to the road for a few minutes before laughing out loud. "The love bug baby! You didn't get bit, you got chomped!" Chris continued to laugh as the two pulled on to I-87 North to begin their long stretch to Lake George.

As the car revved up the highway, Ethan started to think about Aiden. He still couldn't figure out why he had been on that porch, and he couldn't help but wonder if it was anything he should worry about.

"I need to tell you something," Ethan said, fighting with himself. He didn't really want to say anything but he didn't have a choice. "When we were at the stakeout, that first guy who walked on the porch was my cousin."

Chris looked confoundedly at Ethan. "What?"

Ethan sat still, showing no emotion. He knew exactly how weird it sounded; he didn't even know what to make of it himself.

"I didn't say anything at first because...I just didn't know what to say. I haven't seen my cousin in about thirteen years or so."

"Well then maybe that wasn't him," Chris said, still looking confused.

Ethan knew for a fact that man was his cousin. There was no question about it.

"It was him," he said.

Chris shook his head and rubbed his face. The snow was starting to fall harder. Ethan stared out the window watching the flakes blow by. He missed the simple days, the days when he could fight crime and not have to worry about all this bullshit. Ethan wondered how a weaker person would deal with all of this...all he knew was he'd come out on top.

"Do you have any idea how bad this sounds? You should've come out with that right away Ethan, what were you thinking? You're getting letters from someone who knows you and now your cousin pops outta nowhere?"

"Chris I've told you more than I've ever told anybody. I knew I'd end up telling you, I was just trying to piece everything together first." Ethan shook his head. "You're obviously the only one I told."

"This is really good, Ethan. Real great…What happened the last time you saw your cousin? Could you ever see him doing something like this?"

Ethan shook his head. He clearly remembered the last time they spoke. "I don't know. We used to be close but I don't know who he is anymore. His name's Aiden Moore. He's my cousin from my dad's side. He had a fucked up childhood like us. He never moved past it." Ethan closed his eyes trying to bring himself back to that day, the last time he and Aiden had seen each other.

"Aiden was always really close with my cousin John-David. That was his idol, the same way my uncle Joe was to me. Last time I saw Aiden was the last time I saw my father, at John-David's funeral."

Chapter 22

A Sweet Memory

It was ironically pouring outside. The dark sky loomed over the funeral home, clearly pointing out the disparity of this day compared to any other. Ethan stood on the corner of McLean Ave. and Kimball Ave., as the rain trickled over his dark suit, thinking about what awaited him inside that horrible building. Hudson & Son's Funeral Home had never stuck out to him before. Just another building on a block riddled with bars and pharmacies, but today it was a giant eye-sore, a mountainous dilemma, a congregation of misery and demise.

Ethan walked forward alone. His mother stood by his side but yet he felt so alone. In a few seconds, he would have to face the biggest disappointment in his life, his "father", and that was putting aside the fact his cousin had just passed away. His cousin who was only twenty-eight years old, who had just married a gorgeous woman a year ago, who had a new born baby boy. It was a horrible thing; terrible no matter how you looked at it. There was just no bright side to the story.

Ethan placed his hand on the funeral home door. The metal handle was ice cold. It was the middle of January and the temperature was frigid, however it wasn't the climate Ethan was feeling. The robust, gloomy door stood as representation of the tears, the torment, and the anguish that was sheltered within.

Ethan entered the hall to the hundreds of red, watery eyes. Everything seemed to move in slow motion, the prospects of seeing his old man forcing his legs to wobble. Feeling this touch of weakness evoked a hint of anger. As he moved through the crowd, strangers approached him, hugging and kissing him, telling him everything would be all right. His uncle who he barely recognized, his aunt who he had forgotten about, his cousins who he didn't even know existed. None of these people had even picked him up a birthday card over the past ten years, yet here they all were, kissing and hugging him like the giant, phony, pathetic people they were. Ethan felt the anger surge up from a drop to an outpouring, still boiling inside as he moved from one fake smile and insincere remark to the next.

In the middle of the main room sat the king of responsibility himself. Ethan felt his mother's hand touch his shoulder as the two entered the viewing room. His father sat there, one claw on his step-brother Ray's shoulder and the other over his adulteress, or as he liked to call her, his wife. The tears streamed down his cheek and his eyes were closed. Ethan looked on at his father, watching him as he sat with his new, "improved" life. The glamorous one he'd go home to that night with new cars, Jacuzzi bath tubs, the elegant, white picket fence and the cute little dog running around.

His father jumped up and ran over to him, grabbing him tightly as he cried even heavier on to Ethan's shoulder. He stood there, taking the embrace in, feeling or rather smelling the weasel in his personal space. Ethan was distraught that one of the best, if not the best, from the Alosi side was gone forever, but his father's phoniness still disturbed him.

"I'm so happy you're here, son," the man sobbed. Ethan laughed to himself. How funny that he, at only eighteen, could be there for his father when there were hundreds of times his father hadn't been there for him.

He could see Ray over his father's shoulder, sitting there with his mother, crying hysterically. Ethan glared at him; the guy had grown more attached to his family than he had.

He watched Ray hug those who used to be his family, the people he had once ate Thanksgiving dinner with and opened presents on Christmas with, and now he was just a stranger.

His father let go and moved aside, letting Ethan see his cousin, who was lying there lifeless. John-David was beautiful, incredible, and so loved. The man was awesome; Ethan had looked up to him when he was still a part of the family. Ethan hadn't seen his cousin in so long but he still looked the same, still had the same curly dark hair.

Ethan knelt down in front of the casket and made the sign of the cross but there was no prayer to be said. He just knelt there and stared while everything else in the room seemingly stopped. Time stood still, all the strangers frozen solid as he stared down at his cousin.

"He did ask about you," Aiden said as he knelt down next to Ethan. "He just never knew what to say. None of us did." Ethan turned his head to stare his cousin in the eyes. He didn't want to address his own personal situation at such an inopportune time. He came because his mother had told him it was the right thing to do and because he wanted to show his respects to his cousin.

"I'm not here for that, Aiden," Ethan said, turning his head back to the body. John-David had died during a tragic, very rare elevator malfunction in his apartment building. The car, containing only one occupant, had fallen 25 floors. This was the cause of Ethan's aversion to elevators.

"Why are you here then? I know you hate Uncle Andrew but why did you cut me off?" Aiden's voice trembled. Ethan could hear the animosity in his voice. He knew the kid looked up to him. He knew he had it hard and in all honesty Ethan did feel bad. He liked Aiden a lot, one of the few on that side of the family along with John-David, but unfortunately Aiden reminded him of all the horrible things his father had done.

"It's not about you Aiden, I'm sorry but I can't save you all the time," Ethan said, rising to his feet. He began to walk away before Aiden grabbed his arm.

Ethan stared into Aiden's eyes; he could see the hatred written all over the sixteen year old's pupils. Ethan knew how important John-David was to Aiden. He knew Aiden was hurt, and he knew he couldn't relate.

"You never saved me." Aiden let go of Ethan's arm and knelt back down, making the sign of the cross and putting his head into his hands. Ethan backed away, still staring at his cousin. He could still remember all the times he had to console him. All the times Aiden's parents had fought, forcing him to sleep over Ethan's house. He finally realized as he walked back to his mother.

'I really never helped him.'

Chapter 23

No Vacancy

"Why did you think you *ever* saved him?" Chris asked.

"His parents used to fight a lot…physical, violent fights. I thought I protected him. It's complicated." Ethan noticed the snow was picking up. There was almost no area untouched now.

"That's not your fight. You can't worry about everyone else. I know it sucks; I went through the same shit with my brothers. They couldn't handle the fighting so I always made it my priority to help them…never thought about myself."

Ethan had heard Chris' story before. As bad as it was, both he and Chris knew they were just two of millions. Millions of children who are born into this world and abandoned. Grown "adults" shaking responsibility. Hiding from their choices.

"I don't think Aiden would do something like this. He did look up to me, but I just can't see him doing this." Ethan tried to place Aiden in the killer's shoes, but it made him shudder. He couldn't imagine his cousin being the culprit behind those gruesome photographs.

"I know how you feel about it, that's your cousin no matter how distant you two might be, but him appearing on that porch just doesn't look good."

Chris shook his head as he strained his eyes, fighting to see through the fierce snow. It was coming down much harder now, a full-blown blizzard at this point, and the two agents were definitely not happy.

Hours went by and Ethan still couldn't make sense out of anything. He knew how bad Aiden's appearance was. Had that not been his cousin, he would automatically tag that guy as a suspect. He would order a full-on-inspection, request warrants, and go after the guy. Although his gut told him to stay on the current course, he couldn't help but wonder if his feelings were getting in the way.

Ethan couldn't remember the last time he had seen that sign: Route 9N Lake Shore Drive. It was a long trip but they were finally here at the beautiful Lake George. This time, however, it looked like a winter disaster. The snow was streaking through the sky, blasting the Charger as it rumbled up the dicey road. Visibility was shot even with the wipers moving as fast as possible.

"I can't see shit," Chris said, cursing under his breath. The ground was completely plagued by ice and snow; the Charger's tires could barely keep from sliding.

"Just focus on the road, we're coming up to the place now. Keep your eyes peeled; this guy could be watching us right now." Ethan knew how farfetched that sounded. There was barely anything to see, the snow was completely blinding them. "Twin Birches resort, it should be coming up on the left. They own a small part of the lake to the right also."

The sign, despite the horrific conditions, stood out clearly. The profound, bold letters were once inviting, a sign of good times but now they seemed cryptic and threatening. Twin Birches Resort looked like an abandoned town, not a single person could be seen and only a few lights here and there were visible.

Chris maneuvered the car up the small entrance, the tiny hill seemed like a wall in such weather, but they still managed to make it. "Jesus Christ, what a freaking day to do this. We made really good time though."

Ethan hadn't even noticed how quickly they made it, just a little under five hours. "Yeah that's pretty good," he said. He leaned forward in his seat, eager to see any sign of life. "That building there used to be where you check in. There has to be a grounds keeper here." Ethan's eyes scanned the resort; he couldn't see a damn thing. He had hoped for a giant sign or something pointing him in the right direction. Wishful thinking.

"You ready?" Chris said, looking at Ethan. "I can't see anything out there, man, we have our work cut out for us." Chris grabbed Ethan's shoulder. "We *will* find this guy, Ethan. I have a feeling there's something up here." Ethan had the same feeling. As he looked around the grounds he could sense something wasn't right.

The small check-in house was made entirely out of wood. It looked like a small out-house compared to the much larger log cabins surrounding it. The grounds themselves were beautiful had it not been for the blizzard. There was a miniature golf course, a few basketball courts, two swimming pools...the resort was incredible.

'Looks like something out of a Stephen King book,' Ethan thought to himself as he opened the door, letting the howling, vicious wind rip through the car. This was nothing like how he remembered it. He quickly jumped out and rushed towards the fragile looking check-in cabin. His face was already turning red from the cold as the snow slapped across it. He could barely make out where he was going as he stumbled through the deep snow, his knees almost sinking under. If it weren't for the howling wind there would be dead silence. Ethan observed that there were no lights on in any of the cabin windows. It seemed deserted.

"Right here!" Chris yelled as Ethan saw the wooden front door swing open to reveal a dimly lit room. He hustled inside, slamming the door behind him and allowing an eerie silence to consume the room. The howling was nonexistent; the room was obviously well insulated.

Ethan looked around taking everything in. There was a small wooden desk in the corner of the room, the same one he remembered from so many years ago. The walls were filled with different brochures advertising the many attractions in the area, and, through the one dark opening in the room, he remembered there was a meager game room. He tried to peer inside the room but could only make out a few arcade games and an antique pool table. He could still remember all the times he played in that room, all the fun he had with his family, but he knew this was no time to reminisce.

"Hello?" Chris called out. The cabin remained silent. Chris looked over at Ethan and placed one hand over his gun. Ethan walked forward carefully, trying to strain his eyes to see into the murky game room. He glanced down at the reception desk and saw the giant calendar with all the customers' reservations labeled on it. He rushed around the counter to get a clearer look.

"Hello!" Chris yelled out again. Still nothing sounded back. Ethan flipped through the calendar trying to find December. 'Something's gotta be here,' he thought to himself. The room's small, lone window showed the blistering conditions still ongoing outside. The snow whipped past the window pane as the two agents investigated the small reception area. A small thudding kept ringing out as the wind smashed the shutters into the buildings side. Chris upholstered his Glock and placed his finger softly on its trigger as he placed his face to the small window. He could barely even see the Charger.

Finally Ethan came upon December 28, 2011. As he looked down the list of available slots, he came upon one name.

"Can I help you sirs, can I?" A shaky, rattling voice creaked out through the dark. Ethan jumped up whipping out his gun and pointed it squarely at the dark opening. He couldn't see a thing as Chris moved in closer, his gun also held in front of him. Suddenly through the dark appeared a small, decrepit, elderly man. His grey hair was very thin and ratty, his clothes ragged and old. The man limped into the room and pointed at Ethan. "I'm sorry, sir, that is confidential material you be looking at right there. Please move away sir, move away please." Ethan walked back around the counter, bringing his gun down to his side.

"I'm sorry, we called out but nobody answered," Ethan said, scanning the man up and down. He knew this could very likely be the serial killer he was searching for. He knew not to judge a book by its cover.

"I heard you sirs, I was very busy, very busy doing a lot of stuff, actually. Quite busy this time of year…it is here quite busy. I'm sure you two would like a room then, correct? I'll see if we have available anything." The man's finger nails were long and curly as they ran along the top of the counter.

"Wait!" Chris yelled out. He was back at the window staring out into the storm. "Never mind." Chris squinted out the window as though he had seen something but shook his head and looked back at the old man.

Ethan hadn't moved his gun from his side. He kept his eyes squarely on the caretaker, not flinching or blinking at all. The man clearly had some bolts loose, Ethan thought to himself. He talked in circles and reeked of body odor. He was also checking the availability of the resort in the end of December while there was blatantly no one lodging here.

"I'm sorry, we're actually here on business...maybe you can help us," Ethan said steadily, still not blinking.

"Ohhhhhhh business, eh? Very good, business is very good here this time of year. I can set you up in a cabin right next to the pool area; you can swim...can't you?" The man stared up at Ethan.

"Sir, has anyone else been here recently, or is there anybody staying here right now?" Ethan was losing his patience.

The man continued to stare at Ethan. "Many stay here, sirs. Many."

"There's only one name down for this whole month...right there on your calendar," Ethan pointed down at the counter.

The old man slammed his hand down on the desk and jolted forward, grabbing Ethan's arms. Chris had brought his gun up instantly but Ethan waved him off.

"Familiar sir, have we met before?" the old man said sternly as he brought his face closer to Ethan. Ethan stared down at him confused. A noise sounded from inside the game room, like the sound of a heavy object falling from the wall. The two agents stared into the game room, waiting for something to move, but still nothing. A giant smile spread across the old man's face, his few teeth bearing. The stench of his foul breath disgusted Ethan. He let out a slight cackle, "The mice sirs…just those fucking mice."

Ethan moved back away from the man, now completely agitated. He wasn't afraid, no matter how strange this whole situation was, he was simply nervous that he had just traveled all this way to speak to some batty old lunatic.

"My name's Agent Carey and this is Agent Hawkins, we're with the F.B.I. and require your cooperation. Who's here with you?" Ethan said, walking towards the game room's entrance.

The old man let out another cackle. "I told you sirs, there are many here. Very, very busy this time of year. It be luck to find a room here." The old man's toothless smile irritated Ethan.

"There's one reservation on that calendar, who is it?" Ethan demanded. He knew every second was precious.

The old man glanced down at his calendar, bringing his pointy, crooked nose close to the writing. "Special Agent Ethan Carey…the couple here today is the Bosco family. Very nice couple, but it is very busy here today. I can set you up in Unit F, sirs; it's very, very busy."

Chris moved into the game room, his gun pointed out in front of him and Ethan close behind. "Turn the lights on!" Ethan called to the old man.

"Power's out sirs, the storm is here." The old man laughed loudly, the sound boomed through the empty game room.

"If you're not going to cooperate, I am going to arrest you," Ethan said.

"I can't get reception," Chris said holding his phone to his ear. The old man laughed loudly again.

Ethan was even more frustrated now. This case was horrible. It had to be the sloppiest one he had ever been a part of. He and Chris were respectable, honored agents, and now this psycho was going to tarnish their reputation. All Ethan knew was he was definitely in the right place. The killer was here or at least it was at some point recently.

"How did you know my full name?" Ethan said, taking a deep breath. The old man shuffled uncomfortably behind his desk. His eyes wandered the room, shifting back and forth between Ethan and Chris.

"You told me it! You told me! I'm busy!" the man screamed. Ethan didn't flinch but quickly jumped forward slamming his fist down on the man's counter.

"How do you know my name?" Ethan yelled back. Chris stayed by the window, still staring out into the storm. The old man whimpered and fell back into his swivel chair. "The lights work fine in here don't they? You sure that power's out? How do you know my name!"

The old man stared up at Ethan wide eyed. His hands shook slightly as he reached for one of his desk drawers.

"Don't touch it," Ethan said, throwing his hand in the way. The man jumped back to the corner of the room.

"I have a message for you, I was so busy, I have a message," the old man whimpered. Ethan froze, staring at the man. Chris walked over to the counter curiously.   "A message from who?" Ethan said. "Do you remember who gave it to you?" Ethan backed away and holstered his gun. He didn't feel threatened by the old man anymore.

"No," the man cried. "I didn't see. I was so busy, I was told you would be coming, but I'm so busy and so much to do. I can't keep track of one person!"

Ethan moved back around the counter and read the old man's calendar. The Bosco family supposedly checked into Unit G at 9AM and was scheduled to leave the following day. He immediately recognized the name Bosco.

Ethan opened the drawer the old man had reached for to find an envelope addressed to *Special Agent Ethan Carey* sitting there waiting for him. He slowly picked the envelope up and began to unseal it.

"Please sirs, if you are not staying you'll have to leave. I'm very busy and need to do many stuff," the old man said, seeming more relaxed now.

Chris reached around and picked up the phone sitting on the old man's desk. He nodded at Ethan and then punched in the phone number Illames had given them. Ethan ripped out his letter and began to read to himself.

Dear Ethan,

It's an injustice. It's a catastrophe. It's everywhere. Why do we just sit by idly watching the world around us implode in selfishness and irresponsibility? I won't sit by idly anymore, I'll unleash my retribution upon those unworthy of life. I'm growing impatient. This isn't a hostage situation, this isn't a plea for media attention, and this is not a jihad. Ethan, this is a revelation. This is a way of life. This is acting upon what some call an impulse, a ridiculous venture, but I call it justice. I call it right. I call it necessary. Why did I choose you? When will I stop?

Who's next? Who the fuck am I? I'm sure you've been asking yourself all of this. Deal with it, Ethan. I chose you because we are one in the same. I know you feel this way. I know you'll come around. Out of many, I am one. I wouldn't mind adding a two. I'll never stop, Ethan. The scum of the Earth will be next. And last but not least the question that is burning you the most, "Who am I?" Meet me at midnight on December 30th. Where will we end up?

I leave you with a quote, "To the last, I grapple with thee; From Hell's heart, I stab at thee; For hate's sake, I spit my last breath at thee."

Herman Melville.

Love,

J.A.

P.S. I left popcorn in the microwave.

Ethan stuffed the letter into the inside of his jacket. He stared ahead, blankly, completely dumbfounded.

"The Warren County Sheriff's Department's on the way. What did the letter say?" Chris asked, still staring out the window. The wind had picked up even more now. The shutters blasted the side of the wooden building making loud, shattering noises periodically.

"I know where unit G is, it's the unit I always used to stay in. There was a guy in high school, he was like a dad to me...Artie Bosco," Ethan said as he moved towards the door.

"Good luck agents!" the old man screamed. He smiled at them from his corner, still pressed against the wall.

Ethan had barely even turned the knob on the old, wooden door before the wind had knocked it wide open. The snow had already begun to build on the floor of the small room before Ethan and Chris had the chance to get outside. The wind viciously swarmed over the two agents as they trudged through the snow, Ethan in only his leather jacket, their bare skin being ripped at.

Ethan mulled over his new letter. He tried his best to keep his mind on the task at hand, but it was too hard not to try and solve this next puzzle, for all he knew it could help them with whatever waited at Unit G. This is exactly what the killer wanted, the whole goal here was to overwhelm. This killer was creating a smokescreen with its letters and puzzles to blind Ethan while in the background it was diligently working on the next step of this master plan. Ethan knew he and Chris—and the Bureau for that matter—had to rise to its level, jump forward from being a step behind.

Ethan winced in pain as the snow, which was now turning to hail, drilled him, making it almost impossible to see. Ethan waved to Chris as he made his way towards one of the larger cabins. The interior was barely visible through the ice-crusted windows as Ethan, finally making it to the porch, placed his back against the cabin's wall.

Chris pressed up against the opposite side, glaring through the window, still unable to see a thing. The two agents sandwiched the doorway, staring at each other as Ethan moved to stand directly in front. Chris inched in closer, crouching low with his gun in a ready position. With a quick nod Ethan leaned back, bringing his foot up to his waist, and then slammed his boot into the wooden door, knocking it open.

It all happened so fast. Chris rolled into the room as soon as Ethan's foot made contact. Ethan sprinted in after, his eyes scanning the dark cabin as quickly as he could seeing no sign of life as he crouched down against the living room's wall. He held his breath, desperately trying to hear through the sound of the howling wind. He strained his eyes, forcing himself to adjust to the lighting but still there was nothing to be found. The cabin was empty as far as he could hear or see.

The living room was fully furnished with a recliner, couch, and a television set. Attached to the living room was the small kitchen area which had a large fridge, a small table, and a small microwave and oven. Ethan saw the microwave and immediately remembered the reference to it in the killer's letter. In between the two rooms was a thin hallway leading down to what he remembered as the way to the bedrooms and bathroom.

Suddenly a small, sizzling noise sounded down the hallway. It was like the noise that sounds when someone opens a new soda. Up ahead, Ethan could now see a faint, flashing light illuminating the darkness.

"Come out with your hands on your head, this is the F.B.I.!" Chris yelled. He stood behind the wall in the kitchen, his gun poking out and aimed straight down the hallway. Ethan crouched opposite him also ready for whatever might be waiting.

Nothing happened as the agents waited, but the noise continued to sizzle through the cabin, adding into the howling of the wind that still whipped through the open front door. Ethan nodded to Chris as he stepped into the hallway, slowly moving one foot in front of the other and breathing slowly. Carefully floating down the hall, he readied his mind and body.

They came upon two openings facing each other on opposite sides of the hallway. The two agents looked at each other before they burst into their respective doorways, guns pointed ahead; eyes peeled skimming the room as fast as they could. Ethan swirled around, taking everything in as he spotted *him* out of the corner of his eye. He turned to see the barrel of a gun pointed straight at him. His heart stopped beating, his legs gave way, and out of instinct, he closed his finger on the trigger.

Chapter 24

Quiet

The glass shattered to the floor, pieces bouncing off the wooden dresser that lay beneath what used to be a mirror. Ethan knelt in the room, the smoke filtering from the tip of his gun as he stared up at the empty frame. Chris rushed in, swiveling his body to see each direction. He placed one hand on Ethan's back as he turned his head to the doorway, the sizzling noise sounded louder than ever now.

Ethan still stared at was once the mirror, at what was once the image of his father. The reflection wasn't himself, it was his father, he was certain of it. His father smiling back at him, pointing the gun at him as he sneered. Ethan panicked and shot at him. He felt unnerved at his rookie behavior but didn't have time to dwell on it. He'd have to worry about the problem another time.

He shook his head at Chris. "My reflection," he whispered. He glanced around the room, noticing that everything was still in perfect condition…like nothing had been touched in a while. He noticed the same thing in the living room and kitchen. There was always the possibility that the "Bosco" family was really clean, but Ethan was pretty positive that name was put down as another small jab from the killer. Just another message saying, "I'm still a step ahead and, yes, I know everything about you."

Ethan moved ahead of Chris, filtering back into the hallway. He checked the front of the cabin, making sure there was still no one there, and then continued moving towards the sizzling, which was now much louder and covering up the wind. The dark wasn't bothering

Ethan anymore since his eyes had fully adjusted. The only thing still bothering him was the constant flash of light from the end of the hallway.

A horrible smell hit Ethan's nostrils—the smell of burnt hair— followed by a horrible realization. The killer might not have been here now, but it had definitely struck already. Ethan glanced at Chris whose eyes told him he had just realized the same thing. He scuffled forward, coming upon the sizzling room and quickly dipped his head in and out of the doorway. He pressed his body against the wall, gasping for breath. It was by far the worst smell he had ever encountered.

"There's no one in there," Ethan said. He looked over at Chris who placed his arm over his nose and entered the room's doorway. He stumbled back, holstering his gun and putting his hands on his knees. Coughing heavily, he spit on the ground and gasped for breath.

"Holy shit," he mumbled.

Ethan holstered his gun, put his arm around his nose and walked into the room. His head became light instantly. He staggered forward; feeling the shock and horror hit him at once. He reached to the outlet, unplugging whatever was plugged in as he stared in repulsion at the bathtub. Not pictures, not movies, not in textbooks or even the internet had he ever seen such a gruesome act of inhumanity. A woman, or what was left of her, laid in the *full* bathtub, one leg and one arm hanging out, completely burned from head to toe. Ethan scanned the room, finding nothing else of importance, as he shook his head, still holding his arm to his nose. He could hear Chris still coughing outside.

The woman had a blow-dryer, what looked like a flat-iron, and a few other electronic devices in the water with her. It was hard for Ethan to make anything out, everything in that vicinity was burnt to the core. He wasn't completely positive if the body was definitely a woman being that he glanced at it quickly, but he couldn't bear to look anymore. The head was burnt so badly he mostly saw bone and one eyeball which had rolled out on to the bathroom floor. Ethan grimaced, shaking his head harder as he turned to leave the room.

"This is…" Ethan cut short as he looked to the front of the house. Chris was still bent over outside the bathroom, not paying attention, as Ethan spotted a figure in the doorway. The figure didn't hesitate, quickly bringing its arms up.

"Down!" Ethan screamed as he dove forward, one hand grabbing Chris and the other grabbing his gun. The figure fired one shot, just missing Chris as the two agents hit the ground, both of their guns drawn instantly. The shooter quickly dashed away, as Chris and Ethan jumped to their feet, sprinting down the hallway in hot pursuit.

The weather was still atrocious as the two agents burst out into the open, just barely spotting their target up ahead running across the resort's grounds. They bolted forward, running as fast as they could in all the snow, realizing it was futile to try their luck at sniping from so far in such conditions.

'Fucking snow,' Ethan yelled to himself as he stumbled, trying his best to maintain a visual. Out of the corner of his eye Ethan saw Chris fly into the air, falling face first into the snow. He stopped, waiting as Chris got back up. He knew better than to leave his partner. Just the few seconds proved to be enough time as they both stood staring into the blizzard, seeing absolutely nothing but snow and trees. They were beat again.

"Ethan!" Chris screamed over the wind. Ethan looked back at his partner who was running back to where he had fallen. "It's a body!"

He turned his head to stare at Chris, watching his partner as he dug relentlessly in the deep snow.

"Ethan!" Chris yelled.

'This is all on me,' Ethan thought to himself as he stared off into the winter wonderland, the snowy tundra he had just lost the shooter in. 'It's all involving me; these people are dying because of my failure.'

The body was a man, completely naked and frozen solid. As they dug his body out Ethan could easily see his legs and arms were broken. Either the killer had broken them and then dragged him outside to die in the blizzard, or the guy had made a run for it and gotten caught.

The sound of sirens blazed through the wind as the flashing of the police lights became visible through the snow and the hail. Chris jumped up, running out to the main road to wave the county police down, leaving Ethan standing over the dead body in disbelief.

"So which direction did he *exactly run off to*?" Sheriff McSweeney asked, squinting out of the small window in the check-in room. Ethan stared at the tiny sheriff; his short blonde hair looked like it hadn't seen shampoo or a brush in decades. He was dressed appropriately, wearing a neck warmer, gloves, a hat, and ear muffs. Ethan didn't respond but continued to stare at him, checking his watch quickly, surprised to see that it was only about one o'clock.

"Not positive it was a male but the shooter ran off down towards the lake," Chris said. "I couldn't catch a description, but we were shot at in Unit G. At least we can figure out what firearm was used."

Ethan looked over at Chris wondering how he knew there was a lake in that direction. The weather was so bad there was no way anybody could know what was over there. 'I told him the lake was on the right,' Ethan thought to himself.

This is what it had come down to. Now he was suspecting his own partner, he was falling right into the trap this killer laid out. He wanted to harvest uncertainty, to prong at everyone's disbelief, everyone's trust, until all hope had completely depleted.

"Did old man Giangrande see anything?" the sheriff asked. Ethan figured that must have been the loony caretaker, he had never bothered to get the man's name.

"Are you serious?" Ethan asked, turning around and walking out the front door. Chris followed behind, leaving the sheriff confused. Ethan took out the note from his inside pocket and passed it to Chris.

"The microwave!" Chris screamed over the wind. Ethan nodded his head, walking through the caution tape wrapped around the cabin's door. Inside were a few forensics workers, dusting the room and examining the bathroom. Ethan was impressed at how well they could stomach the gruesome sight.

"Good afternoon, sir. I understand you were shot at. Can you show us where the shot was fired from?" one of the forensics guys asked. Ethan pointed to the end of the hall.

"I came out of the bathroom and saw the person standing in the doorway, only fired one shot in our direction," Ethan said, picturing the incident as he spoke.

"Thank you sir," the man said, walking down the hall to examine where the bullet may have landed. Ethan walked straight into the kitchen, pulling open the microwave without hesitation. Inside the microwave sat another letter; this one however was accompanied by a VHS tape.

"He fucking filmed it," Chris said, reaching forward to pull out the tape and the letter. He handed the letter to Ethan and walked into the living room, crouching down to put the tape into the VCR. "He knew he had to film on a VHS tape, this was well planned. How many VCRs do you see nowadays?"

Ethan looked down at the paper, reading the only word written on it.

Enjoy

He crumpled the paper and tossed it on the floor as the TV lit up, showing the image of the living room, with two adults, a male and a female, sitting on the couch. Ethan crouched next to Chris, his eyes widening in anticipation.

The two stars sat still, staring straight ahead as a bright light shined on their terrified faces. Each person held what looked like a sheet of paper in their hands; the woman's shook slightly, tears streaming down her face. The man broke the silence, raising his paper as he began to read. There was nothing bonding the man's hands, nothing bonding his feet either. The killer had left them completely free.

My name is Walter Veteri. For the duration of my defenseless, innocent son's life, I refuged to support him and his mother. The man cursed loudly as he shook his head. Tears came running from his eyes, as he gritted his teeth. *My actions left my son without heat every winter and without air conditioning every summer. His mother worked three jobs…*the man froze for a second, closing his eyes tight as he lifted his head to the ceiling…*as I enjoyed my life with the irresponsible whore next to me.*

The woman next to Walter raised her paper, still crying heavily.

My name is Naomi Menard. I'm the mother of two gorgeous children who I haven't seen in over five years. I would much rather drive my BMW, plaster myself with makeup, and get my hair done constantly than worry about my real responsibilities, such as clothing, food, and a good education for my kids. Naomi could barely get the words out through all the crying. *I did enjoy frolicking around with Walter behind his wife's back.* Naomi burst out into heavier tears, shaking uncontrollably as Walter sat next to her with his face in his hands. She let out a scream for help. *Today my…*Naomi gasped; having trouble coming up with air….*pathetic life will thankfully come to a close.*

Walter spoke immediately after:

My miserable, unaccomplished life will also come to an end. You fucking…

The video cut out, leaving everyone in the room standing quietly, their eyes still focused on the small television set.

"I'm surprised he didn't show anything," Chris said, leaning forward to eject the tape. "We're going to take this into evidence, thank you gentlemen for all of your help. Please forward all your findings to 26 Federal Plaza." Chris handed his card to Sheriff McSweeney and walked out of the cabin.

"Giangrande believes your shooter was a male, just so you know," Sheriff McSweeney called.

"That caretaker also thinks the resort has no vacancies," Ethan responded.

"It's not trying to scare anyone," Ethan said as he sat in the Charger. Ethan wasn't surprised. He didn't expect the killer to show anything gruesome on film. "This is my theory on it. Number one…we have to focus; it's trying to blow smoke in our faces. Throwing a whole bunch of mumbo jumbo, sending us five hours upstate, filling the letters with riddles and shit, most of it's a diversion." Ethan sat still trying to collect his thoughts. The weather was still ridiculous outside as the Charger slid down towards the highway.

"So what's our next step then?" Chris asked sounding impatient. Ethan knew it was frustrating, and he realized the case would soon fall squarely on his own shoulders. The killer was using him to spread its' gospel. The quicker they understood Ethan better, the quicker they'd find this murderer.

"Our next step is to figure this letter out…the end," Ethan said unquestionably. "Other bullshit will pop up but we have to stick to this. Like I was saying before, my theory is this thing isn't trying to get on the news. It's not addicted to killing. My thought would be that whoever it is grew up in a broken household and just wants revenge. It sounds simple and you and I both know sometimes it's not as complicated as you'd think. Sometimes it really is that easy."

"We've been through…actually we haven't been through worse than this but I'm not worried. I can't wait to put an end to this. What do you think about the letter?" Chris asked, still straining his eyes to see through the storm.

"First thing that pops out to me is the 'Out of many, I am one. I wouldn't mind adding a two' line. Just a little weird, not its typical writing style. Then there are the initials J.A." Ethan said running through the letter quickly. "Right off the bat, I have no idea."

"Me neither. Do you know any J.A.'s?" Chris said. Ethan tried to recollect but he came up blank.

"I'm pretty sure I don't know any J.A.'s, but you're going in a good direction. It's gunna be personal to me, just have to outsmart it now," Ethan said, closing his eyes in an attempt to think harder. "We know the date and the time, neither have any significance to me...I don't think."

"Do you think that 'add a two' line is referring to you?" Chris asked.

"I literally have no idea," Ethan said laughing. "It's not funny, but damn this is sick." Chris nodded his head in consent as they made their way home, bound with just a letter to show for the whole trip.

Chapter 25

Twelve Years Old

Ethan lay awake, the excitement seethed through his body barely letting him close his eyes. He could hear his father snoring loudly next to him, but the noise wasn't the reason he couldn't sleep. He had been waiting for this vacation for months, and finally it was here. 'Disney Cruise! Disney Cruise!' Ethan repeated to himself, smiling from ear to ear. The clock said 5:58 AM, only one minute later than the last time he checked.

He tossed and turned in the pull out bed in his grandparent's living room. Finally, he just couldn't contain his excitement anymore.

"Dad! Dad, wake up!" he screamed. His father groggily opened his eyes, checking the time and turning back over.

"Dad, come on! It's time to go!" Ethan yelled, jumping out of the bed. The alarm clock started to buzz as he ran to the bathroom, flying past his grandmother who was laughing at his excitement.

Ethan was eight years old and this would be the first time he'd be going on a vacation with his father. His stepmother and stepbrother would be going also, but he didn't care as long as he was with his dad. Ever since his parents had split, Ethan barely had a second alone with his father. With all these court dates, arguments, fights, and visitation perimeters they had to adhere to, Ethan felt like he never saw his father anymore.

Ethan showered as the thoughts hit him again. He couldn't help it; these dark thoughts always bloomed no matter what was going on. His father left. He went all the way up to his palace in Yorktown Heights leaving him and his mother scrapping in the Bronx. The fighting revolved in his head, thoughts of his father cheating on his mother, thoughts of his father lying, fighting to gain as much ground as he could financially without considering Ethan. Ethan had absolutely no idea what any of this meant, he could barely even keep up with remembering his times tables let alone all of this. The weight was overwhelming for anybody, let alone an eight year old boy.

The water poured over Ethan as he stood in the shower crying. He couldn't even understand why he cried, but sometimes he just felt the urge. The anger built up inside, the thoughts still swirling and swirling and swirling in his head. He just wanted it all to go away. He wanted it to be the way it was before, when they all lived together happily.

"Ethan, you alright buddy!" his father called.

"I'm coming out now!" Ethan yelled back, rubbing his eyes to stop the tears. 'Just stop...just stop crying,' Ethan said to himself.

"Booka Man!" his father said, dancing into the room as Ethan finished getting ready. Ethan laughed as his father tickled him, knocking him back on to the bed.

"Stop! Stop!" Ethan yelled, laughing hysterically.

He picked up his heavy suitcase, hoping his father would recognize how strong he was, and hurried outside to meet his stepmother, Michelle, and his stepbrother Raymond. Michelle Xavier was no Jennifer Aniston, as far as Ethan could see. She looked much older than his father and was definitely not as pretty as his mother, he had no idea what his father saw in her. She had long brown hair that draped over her 5'4'' body, she wasn't skinny but she wasn't fat either.

Ray was only a year younger than Ethan. He was much smaller though, standing about six inches shorter with shaggy, Justin Bieber like blonde hair. The fact that Ethan's father lived with Ray was, unfortunately, reason enough for Ethan to despise him.

Michelle ran up to Ethan, giving him a huge hug and kiss. The phoniness nearly blew him off the sidewalk. Despite the fact that he hated her for taking his father away, Ethan was always civil, saying hello politely and giving her a hug back. All he cared about was that he was about to go on an awesome vacation with the man he looked up to...

The cruise ship was enormous. Ethan looked out the window of the shuttle bus as they drove to the dock. He could see the incredible piece of machinery, the majestic, beautiful boat sitting idly in the water, awaiting the thousands of eager passengers. Ethan had his face pressed against the bus' window, his mouth opened in surprise and excitement.

"It's huge, right?" his father noted, leaning over to get a better look.

Ethan nodded his head, sitting in shock, unable to come to terms with his astronomical excitement. He looked up at his father, beaming with happiness. Although he didn't know it then, there would be a day in the future where he would do anything for that moment. To feel like his old man cared about him, to actually feel like another human being in his eyes.

The group walked on to the boat, the elegant red carpet, lined with gold thread invited them on board as the sounds of trumpets blazed the air. Ethan had heard stories, he had seen all the 'Magical' Disney commercials, but at that moment, as his foot touched the ship's floor, he finally understood.

"And now, ladies and gentleman, The Alosi Family!" a tall man wearing a tuxedo and a top hat announced. Ethan laughed to himself at the thought of Michelle XAVIER and Ray

XAVIER being a part of the Alosi family. This would be a big factor in Ethan changing his last name to his mother's maiden name, Carey. He almost wanted to grab the microphone from the happy idiot and re-introduce the two families as separate entities.

Ethan tried to take it all in at once but it was way too much. The main hallway was like something straight out of a fairy tale. The cathedral ceilings were painted with pictures of Disney characters, the walls and balconies were all draped with elegant banners, bright colors, and a sparkly dust making it seem even more imaginary, and no matter where you looked, only smiles could be seen. It was magical.

"Wow, huh?" Ethan's father said, looking just as shocked as Ethan. Disney characters ran all over the giant room, taking pictures, giving hugs, and making funny gestures as the passengers boarded the "cruise ship". It looked more like a giant hotel to Ethan.

'This is so awesome,' he thought to himself.

The four made their way to their rooms with Ethan and his father staying in a separate room from Michelle and Ray. The small hallways were a lot less glamorous than the main hall but, none the less, it was still incredible. Paintings of famous Disney characters hung from the walls, some ancient memorabilia such as the original script from Fantasia also hung on display.

Ethan hadn't even noticed Michelle and Ray walk off to their room but he wasn't too worried about them. He hurried into his own room, his mouth dropping as he spun around seeing all the great features. The towels were arranged in the shape of Mickey Mouse ears. There were small mints decorating the two twin sized beds, both dressed with beautiful sheets and a colorful, Disney inspired comforter. The port hole, also in the shape of Mickey's ears, looked out on to the dock where all the non-passengers stood waving at the lucky people on board.

At thirty-one years old, Ethan could still remember the entire cruise; he could easily sit down, take a pen and paper, and write the entire cruise down word for word, second to second. It remained in his mind. Always remained in his mind, but he never wanted to sit down and recollect on that horrible, nightmare of a "vacation".

Ethan ran down the cartoonish hallway, seeing the words "gift shop" lit up ahead. His father followed behind, laughing at how energetic his son was.

"Who do you want to buy for?" he asked as they entered the massive gift shop.

"I just want to get for mom," Ethan said, distracted by the millions of gifts all around him. He walked the aisles, picking up a couple of picture frames and a few of the key chains but nothing caught his eye. His father tried to talk him into buying a postcard but Ethan didn't pay attention. He wanted to get his mother something incredible, something she would really love.

Ethan froze still as the object illuminated from on top of the shelf. It was a "Beauty and the Beast" snow globe, a combination of two of his mother's favorites, Christmas and Beauty and the Beast. It was incredible; he knew his mother would love it. The globe was surrounded by small statues of Belle and the Beast dressed in their ball dancing clothes, with all the other characters filling and surrounding the rest of the globe.

Ethan took it into his hands, staring down at the musical masterpiece in awe. He slowly cranked the lever, causing the snow globe to play the movie's famous song, 'Tale as Old as Time'.

"You like that one?" Ethan's father asked, picking up its box and checking for the price tag.

"Yeah, definitely, it's perfect," Ethan said, placing the snow globe back on the shelf. "Can we get it, dad?"

Ethan's dad found the price tag and leaned back surprised. The snow globe was surprisingly less expensive than he had thought, only a little more than fifty bucks.

"Yeah buddy, let's look around a little bit more," his father said, putting the box under his arm as he walked down the aisle still looking around. Ethan couldn't wait to see his mother's face.

He skipped up the ship's hallway, his father close behind holding the bag with the souvenirs.

"You wanna go to the game room?" his father asked.

"Yeah!" Ethan said, agreeing with his father's great idea. He couldn't remember the last time he had such a great time with his dad. He was always so preoccupied with his new life but right now Ethan saw the man he thought was lost for good. He just hoped his dad could see how much fun they had and this way when they got back to New York he wouldn't run away again.

"Look! They have the Star Wars arcade game!" Ethan exclaimed, seeing the entrance up ahead.

"Alright!" his father said, holding out his hand for a high five. As the two slapped hands, Ethan heard the shrill screech erupt, tarnishing his hopes. Michelle stormed towards them, Ray close behind her, the steam almost visible from her nose and ears.

"Andrew!" Michelle screamed, storming up to him and slapping the bag out of his hands. "Are you kidding me? Where the hell have you been?"

Ethan's heart stopped as he watched the bag hit the floor. There were probably about forty more of those snow globes on the boat, but that one in particular meant something. He picked it up quickly, opening it to check if it was damaged.

Andrew stared wide-eyed at Michelle; the hundreds of passengers in the near vicinity all stopped and stared.

"You left us alone Andrew, you left us alone! The floor is burning hot, what were we supposed to do Andrew!" Michelle screamed, putting her face right in front of his.

Ethan stared up at her, his face burning hot, his heart beating faster and his fingers drawing close to his palm as he squeezed his hands tight. Ray stood next to her, shaking his head at Andrew in disgust.

"I'm sorry honey, I went shopping with Ethan, we were only gone for about an hour," Andrew said, raising his hands trying to calm Michelle down.

Ethan watched the two, he could see their mouths move but he couldn't make out the words. His eyes watered up. His lips quivered out of anger, but, as he had always done, he bottled his emotions, keeping them locked deep inside, and turned around to walk away.

Ethan's first choice would've been to run forward and knock Michelle right off the side of the boat. He smiled at the idea of her paddling in the Pacific, screaming her lungs out at his father for breathing the wrong way or some other stupid, petty thing.

Instead of doing that, Ethan settled for walking around the boat, taking in the sights of the awesome ship. He must have walked for hours because by the time he came full circle it *was already dark out. He walked into the arcade, sat down at the Star Wars game and stared*

at the screen. He didn't put in any quarters; he just sat there and stared.

"What's up, buddy," Ethan's father said, crouching down next to the game. "You need

some quarters?"

Ethan shook his head, "I have quarters."

Andrew crouched there, not thinking the whole situation was a big deal, probably

because he couldn't stop thinking about himself.

"Look buddy sometimes adults fight. It's a part of life, but now everything's fine."

Ethan's head was about to explode. He didn't know much about relationships, but what he did

know was this couldn't be right. This definitely couldn't be how things in the world should be.

"Tomorrow is going to be awesome, Booka Man," Andrew said squeezing Ethan's shoulder.

"We signed you up to go to this cool club. You're gunna play video games, I think they're even

having a tournament...it looks great."

Ethan turned his head, looking at his father. 'You just put me into day care,' he thought

to himself. 'You just put me into day care on the Disney Cruise on our "family" vacation.' The

anger boiled again, it was like a friend of his now. He spent more time with his anger than he

did with his own father.

"Come back to the room when you're done, take this," Andrew said, handing Ethan a

couple of twenties.

Ethan watched his father walk away, laughing to himself. How many times had he seen

this one? The quick exchange of presents for mental brutality and destruction. Andrew had no idea. He had absolutely no clue how his actions would be oh so detrimental to the future of his

son.

Ethan sat up in the Charger, watching out the window as the snow fell slowly. He thought about the cruise, remembering everything that had happened, laughing at how miniscule that was compared to the hundreds of horrible things Andrew would go on to do.

"The killer, he…or she…definitely came from a broken household," Ethan said. "It really is an epidemic, Chris. We've both seen it first hand, adults destroying their kid's mentality, carelessly abusing their kid's innocence. This killer obviously just had enough."

"I still wouldn't wish what he's done on my worst enemy…I'm disgusted with my mother more than anything," Chris said, his face blank of emotion. "What she did to my family is irreparable…but still I would never want to see her in a bathtub like that…that was horrible."

Ethan lied back, thinking about the letter, dissecting every word, every sentence, trying to make some sense out of it.

"I guess you're right," Ethan said.

Chapter 26

Riddles

Ethan felt like he hadn't sat at his work desk in years. He actually missed Porter's shit

talking. He smiled as the angry agent took stabs at him.

"You guys have a good vacation? I always knew about you two, sneaking around

together," Porter said, sitting on top of Ethan's desk.

"What do you do here again?" Ethan said without taking his eyes off his computer.

Porter shook his head as he looked down at the agent.

"I know this may be news to you, but here, at the Federal Bureau of Investigation, we

fight crime and protect the rights of our fellow Americans," Porter said, saluting Ethan as he

jumped off his desk and strode away. "You should try it sometime!"

It felt good to break away from the drama, to come back down to reality even though he

knew the killer was still at large. Ethan stared at Chris who sat back in his chair, reading some

papers. He looked down, picking up his latest love letter, and realized that he still had

absolutely no idea what it meant.

'Out of many, I am one. I wouldn't mind adding a two.'

"You get anywhere," Chris asked, pulling up a chair and sitting next to Ethan's desk. He

held a copy of the letter in his hands.

"I know this line's there for a reason. 'Out of many, I am one. I wouldn't mind adding a

two.' It's not grammatically correct and the killer's smart. It's killing me how familiar it sounds.

I'd *like* to throw the rest of the letter out but you never know...we could be missing something important," Ethan took notes on the letter, shaking his head in frustration. "Anything on your end?"

Chris shook his head, "I can't pick up on any recurring pattern," he said laughing. "I have nothing either. One plus two equals three…the number two comes after one…I don't know. I've Googled everything I could think of, no matches. You realize what we have to do, right?"

"What do we have to do?" Ethan asked.

"Time to break out those old school yearbooks because Mr. J.A. has to be someone you know. That's all I come up with unless you've got something better," Chris said, nodding his head and nudging Ethan's arm. "Let's see what hormone crazy Ethan looked like."

Ethan laughed thinking about his high school yearbooks. He was definitely much different back then, who wasn't different in high school?

"I guess we should start now," Ethan said. "We have some time but we can't think that way. It's December 30th, we only have ten…eleven hours before it's gunna hit," Ethan got up, grabbing all of his paperwork. "Let's get to work."

The two agents walked out of the office, paying little attention to the critical eyes around them, and headed to Ethan's apartment. Ethan was sure they were being scrutinized, possibly even questioned in regards to their handling of the case. He could care less what they all thought, he would continue to handle this the way he knew best…the way he wanted to.

"I haven't seen a J. let alone a J.A.," Chris said as he flipped through Ethan's yearbooks. "I have another mystery for us to solve, though. What were you think with this hairstyle."

Chris pointed down to a picture of Ethan in freshman year. His hair was neatly split down the middle and combed to the sides, his smiling barring a mouthful of metal.

"That guy right there? That is a sexy, sexy man," Ethan said, smiling and winking back.

Ethan had a yearbook opened on his lap but couldn't stop thinking about that sentence. "Out of many, I am one. I wouldn't mind adding a two." He felt like he had heard it before. He hated the feeling of having something on the tip of your tongue and not being able to get it out. It was even worse when people's lives were on the line. They had a little more than eight hours to solve this riddle and save someone from being brutally murdered. At this point it seemed unlikely.

Hours went by of Chris and Ethan taking shifts, moving from the floor with all of the yearbooks to the desk with the laptop. The sunlight dimmed as the two relentlessly continued their search.

"It's almost seven, we should eat or something," Chris said, tossing Ethan's senior year yearbook on the ground. He looked worn out, the past few days had been so taxing.

"I'm gunna run down and grab a pie, any special requests?" Ethan said jumping off the floor, stretching his arms and legs.

"Doesn't matter to me," Chris replied. Ethan could hear the fatigue in his partner's voice. He could see the droopy eyes, the irritated head shakes, the side glances at the clock.

He walked out of his apartment, shutting the door behind him in relief. It felt great to finally be out of that prison.

"Burning the candle at both ends?" a voice called out. Ethan turned his head to see Luke locking his door, his little Schnauzer Roddick playfully jumping on his leg.

"I guess you could say that," Ethan responded, smiling as he shook Luke's hand.

"Ethan...you look like shit," Luke said, his light brown eyes piercing through Ethan's. Ethan could see himself reflected in Luke's glasses. He really did look like shit, so the doctor was right. "They're glasses, not a mirror you narcissist," Luke said as he started to walk down the hallway. "You give any thought to the party?"

"Yeah, put me down for two. My friend and his fiancé want to come also, you said it was ok, right?" Ethan said. He was unsure, but he was just so tired of saying no. He couldn't remember the last time he went out for New Years. T.V. Dinners and asleep by 11:00 was the usual agenda. He didn't like picking up girls on New Year's Eve because they always expected some fairy tale story to bloom, some fantastic midnight kiss.

"More the merrier, is Ethan Carey bringing a date?" Luke said laughing as he held the door open for Roddick and Ethan to step outside.

Ethan laughed back shaking his head. "It's nothing serious yet." Luke gave a sarcastic look and nodded his head back. "I wanted to ask you something in a patient-doctor light. I've been working a lot, so I'm sure that could be a reason, but I've been having...visions...lately."

The two stopped in front of Sal's Pizzeria. Luke stared at Ethan in a concerned, doctor manner. Ethan knew the look all too well. All the therapy sessions he had been forced to go to when he was younger resulted in this same look.

"It could be the lack of sleep. Why don't you stop in later or tomorrow, we'll talk about it," Luke said. "What are you seeing?"

Ethan hesitated for a few seconds. It all sounded so ridiculous, and he wasn't sure how far he could explain before the case made its way into the recounting. Obviously, he wouldn't be able to tell Luke anything regarding the case specifically. He needed to do something about the visions though, and Luke was such a reputable psychiatrist.

"My father. Clear, distinct images of him," Ethan said, watching Luke to see if there was any reaction. He didn't even flinch, but shrugged his shoulders instead.

"Common among people from a destructive household," Luke said looking down at Roddick who was sniffing everywhere. "Do the images talk to you?" Ethan laughed out loud to that.

"I'm not crazy, Doc...sometimes he smiles or laughs, but I've never heard any words."

"It doesn't mean you're out of your mind, perfectly sane people have visions. Actually, a large percentage of my patients do. Your father is still alive, right?" Luke said, still not showing any emotion. Ethan liked the fact that he wasn't being critical, that he wasn't stamping Ethan with the crazy label.

"I guess he's alive," Ethan said, looking through the pizza shop window and signaling to the man inside. The man nodded back and started to prepare Ethan's large pie.

"You've got resentment. I know you don't feel like talking about it right now...that's fine, but you really should come see me. The visions may be a combination of no sleep, aggravation, a buildup of emotions, stress...all that great stuff. A good way to rid yourself of it all is to simply talk about it with someone who can listen. Whether it's me...your new girlfriend..." Luke smiled as he inched away from Ethan. Ethan shook his head and smiled back. "Look, come see me if you want, if not, you have my number. I'll put you down for four for the party. You should really be worrying more about trying to beat me on the tennis court. I've been playing a little indoors, and I predict a 6-0, 6-0 win for our next match." Luke waved his hand as he walked across the street with the energetic Roddick still hopping everywhere.

Ethan appreciated Luke's friendship. The guy was an incredible doctor and a great friend. He knew exactly when to talk and when to listen.

"Thank God," Chris said as Ethan walked back into the apartment with the pizza. He ripped the box open and grabbed a slice. "I think I've Googled everything, even tried to translate the words to different languages."

The words shocked Ethan. He froze stiff as the last few words revolved in his head. "What languages?" Ethan asked, still frozen trying to think. It was right there, the answer to the puzzle was right in front of him. "Don't talk."

Chris had opened his mouth to answer the question but stopped, holding his mouth open as he watched Ethan think.

"When is it attacking?" Ethan asked, closing his eyes, struggling to find the answer.

Chris looked down at his watch, "Its 7:45, it's attacking in four hours and fifteen minutes."

"E Pluribus Unum," Ethan said, a chill coming over his body. "E Pluribus Unum." Ethan shook his head, putting his hands on his head.

Chris moved his head slowly, his eyes widening. "You know who the killer is," he whispered. Ethan shook his head, catching the excitement in Chris' voice.

"I studied Latin at Fordham; I don't know how I didn't catch this right away," Ethan said, frustrated with himself. "It means 'One out of many'. It's a phrase that's used on the back of currency." Ethan still couldn't figure out the clue though. He knew this is what it had to have meant. The killer was zoning in on his education, his study of Latin.

"Ok, so what does that mean?" Chris asked. He looked even more confused than before. Ethan smiled back at him.

"It's a riddle within a riddle," Ethan said, amused at how clever this killer was. He grabbed a pad of paper and wrote the phrase down, 'E Pluribus Unum.' He reached into his pocket and pulled out the change he had gotten from the pizza shop. "Check your money; I'm looking for the phrase written on the currency. I thought it was the dollar."

Chris reached into his pocket as well, pulling out his wallet and filtering through his money. The dollar bill never seemed so detailed until that very moment. Ethan placed it an inch from his nose as he searched for the phrase. He knew perfectly well that he had no idea what he was looking for. Even when he found the phrase, what was next?

"There's nothing on the one, five, or ten," Chris said, putting his wallet back in his pants pocket.

"Check your coin too," Ethan said, examining his fifty and his hundred. He shook his head and dove into his pockets again, pulling out the couple of coins he had.

"The quarter!" Chris said excitedly. "It's on the back." Ethan didn't have time to laugh at Chris' boyish excitement. His heart was racing; he could feel the answer coming to him. Finally they had a step up on this thing. Six brutal murders and they were going to stop it right there. Ethan caught Chris' quarter, staring at it, trying to find some type of a clue. He grabbed his pad and wrote everything down.

'Quarter...E Pluribus Unum...Out of many I am one...twenty-five cents.'

"J.A..." Ethan hesitated for a moment, taking it all in before he said a word. "John Adams was Washington's vice president. I was an American History buff in high school, no real way for the killer to know that though...that's just a coincidence...I think. Don't stop me just let me talk," Ethan said, holding a hand up to Chris. Chris put his hands up in surrender, giving Ethan the floor. "John Adams was just a way for this thing to tell us we're on the right path...I think...it could also be some type of a plea for me to lead it. It already said it wants me to join, it needs a two...but I don't understand what it's trying to say now."

Ethan stopped, rewinding a little before he spoke again. "Chris, this thing is smart. We can't take anything for granted; I don't know if we solved this riddle, but what else do we have? Like I told you in the car, its blowing smoke in our faces...giving us some crumbs of the real thing."

Chris was paralyzed, staring at Ethan as though he had ten heads. "So let's get a handle on this," Chris said, almost asking Ethan in a way.

Ethan laughed. He knew this was becoming a giant web of confusion. He looked down at the paper. "225," Ethan said, staring up at Chris.

"Ok," Chris said, still hesitant if he should move or not.

"I lived at 225 East Mosholu Parkway for over twenty years. My childhood was there," Ethan said, still staring at his excited partner. "Add a two, twenty-five cents...add a two...225." Ethan breathed slowly, his heart still pounding. He felt his head pounding, his skin growing cold as the beads of sweat formed around the crown of his head. 'Could this be it?' he thought to himself. 'Could this be what the letter was pointing to?' Again he had solved a riddle laid out by the killer; the only difference was this time he had done it within the time limit. He should

have felt triumphant, like he had accomplished something, but instead he felt weary.

"Let's go," Chris said jumping up and grabbing his cell phone.

"Wait," Ethan said, staring down at the original letter. 'I'm second guessing it now, or

am I guessing at all…I solved the case…did I?' Ethan realized the killer was winning; he had him

flip flopping on his predictions…Second guessing his leads.

"Never-mind," Ethan said, jumping up and grabbing his coat.

The two sprinted out of the apartment. Chris barked over the phone to the field office,

as Ethan's thoughts raced through his head. 'This can't be it,' he thought as he flew down the

steps. 'I want to catch it, I definitely do, but this thing is way too smart, it couldn't have

underestimated me like this.'

"We have the chopper and a S.W.A.T. team on standby and ready to go for midnight,"

Chris said, hustling next to Ethan as the two made their way to the Charger. "Illames wants us

to station ourselves in the building, keep hidden, and wait for anything conspicuous. At

midnight when this killer is supposed to strike, we'll have a S.W.A.T. team and a chopper

backing us up."

Sitting in the Charger, Ethan watched as the scenery flew by. Chris shouted next to him,

his adrenaline so evident. He obviously thought this was the icing on the cake, the end of the

line for this psycho killer. Ethan squinted out the window, running through the letters in his

mind, trying to find the clue he was looking for, the real answer to this whole thing, but he couldn't come up with anything else. 'Maybe this is the right direction,' he thought to himself, as the exit for Mosholu Pkwy became visible on the Bronx River Pkwy.

"There's two sides to the building," Chris said, staring out the window as he pulled in front of the massive, gloomy building. Graffiti covered its golden bricks. An older woman with her dog and a young man were engaged in a conversation outside, both stopping to stare at the tinted, black Charger as it stopped in front.

"Park up there, don't stop here, it's gunna look weird," Ethan said, pointing ahead to an open spot. "We'll have to pick a side; I'll take the 225 side on the left. You can go into the 227 side on the right. Anything weird goes on contact me and vice versa."

"Remember the S.W.A.T. team arrives at midnight. They're coming in through the top and the ground floors. The 52nd Precinct down the block is gunna back us up at that time too," Chris added as he opened the chamber to his gun, double checking that the clip was fully loaded. "Don't take any risks; this thing is crazy, it'll do whatever it has to."

Chris held up his hand, looking at Ethan with a concerned look. "It ends here buddy. This thing fucked with the wrong agents. Let's do work."

Ethan looked back at his partner, reaching up to grab his hand, squeezing it as he looked into his confident eyes. He and Chris had been through so much, locked away so many bad people, but right now felt so different. Ethan couldn't put a finger on it, on which aspect made this feel unique, there was just something about this case that made it seem like the finish line had been reached. Like this was the last hurrah.

He opened the door, moving swiftly through the parked cars and pressing his body against his old building's wall. He took account of the people around him, watching them stare him down like he didn't belong. Ethan was wearing blue jeans, sneakers, and a black t-shirt

that hung over his Glock which was nothing too conspicuous, but in a neighborhood where

crime was common, Ethan resembled a cop.

He reached down pretending to tie his shoe as a group of teens passed by, not taking

any notice to Ethan as they screamed and cursed. He could see Chris on the other side of the

building, walking nonchalantly towards the garbage room door, stopping in front of it with his

hands behind his back. After taking a quick glance around, Ethan took out his wallet,

pretending to look through it for something, and stopped at a thin, long plastic stick.

The air was cool tonight, the wind blowing Ethan's hair lightly. It wasn't nearly as bad

outside as it was up in Lake George. Ethan surveyed his old block under the streetlights; it

looked exactly as it had eight years ago with the line of apartment buildings overlooking a lawn

spotted with trees and benches. Parking was still shit. It was miraculous they had found a spot

so quickly. In a way he actually missed it. He missed that care-free lifestyle with no bills to pay

and no women to give him headaches.   Back then all he and his friends did was play baseball

and run around all day, even in the winter. Now here he was breaking into the garbage room

so he could hide in his old building and wait for a psycho to show his face.

The thin piece of plastic scratched against the lock, popping it open. Ethan turned

around with his keys in his hand and pretended to open the door the correct way, pushing it

open and walking inside. The walkway was narrow and dark as Ethan stood staring down the

long path cautiously. The horrendous stink of garbage burned his nose. He remembered all the

times he had to come down here, how he would throw the garbage in the can and run back

upstairs because he was afraid of the rats. He wasn't afraid now, but he was weary.

One foot in front of the other, Ethan walked down the walkway, one hand close to his gun. He could see the light up ahead from the small square opening where the garbage was kept. The doorway to the building's basement stood closely nearby. The smell of the garbage grew worse with every inch, his heart pounding faster the more he moved.

He entered the opening, looking around quickly and took in the sight of the garbage and dirt all around him. Up ahead he could see a small white and orange striped cat perched at the far end of another, long walkway. The cat sat motionless, staring at Ethan from afar, giving him a slight chill down his spine. Suddenly, a sharp crunching noise erupted from the corner of the garbage area. Ethan spun around to come face to face with a grizzly, savage looking man. He rose from the garbage, his toothless mouth open wide as he let out a yawn like noise. Ethan held his hand over his gun, watching the man toss and turn in the garbage. A rat popped out of one of the bags and scurried across the floor, hopping into a neighboring bag.

Ethan backed up, moving away from the homeless man and swung the door to the elevator room open, quickly moving inside and closing the door behind him. 'I guess that's why I was so afraid to come down here,' he thought to himself. He glanced around the large storage area; it was fairly empty except for a few boxes and bikes here and there. The room was dark with only a small, weak light bulb dangling from the middle. From around the corner he heard the elevator arrive and the faint sound of two pairs of feet walking towards him. He straightened up and walked forward acting normally.

Two men in about their mid-thirties walked around the corner, stopping instantly as they saw Ethan. They were both around six feet tall, massive, muscular thugs. Ethan could make out a couple of tattoos on both of them. The taller of the two sported a navy Yankee hat, but it was too dark to make out any more detail. As he got closer, he saw the two gangsters were staring at him, smiling widely, as the bigger of the two walked out in front of Ethan.

"Your wallet," he said as he whipped out a switchblade about five inches in length. His friend lifted his shirt, revealing a small firearm tucked into his jeans. Ethan staggered, pretending to be drunk, as he squinted at the men, fumbling to take out his wallet.

"The elevator working yet?" Ethan stuttered, pretending to burp between words as he surveyed the playing field and his odds.

The taller man with the switch blade laughed as he walked forward to confront the drunken idiot. Ethan stumbled closer to the man with the gun, watching as the two laughed, thrilled they were about to make some easy money. For many years Ethan had to endure being mugged, being jumped, being ridiculed. He'd have some vengeance now.

In one quick motion, Ethan flung his wallet at the man with the switch blade while planting his fist squarely into the gunman's stomach. The wallet smacked the man in the middle of his eyes, knocking him back a little. The gunman planted his feet, taking a sloppy swing that Ethan easily deflected. He grabbed the man's arm, twisting it around his back and stabbed him fiercely with his palm. The man's bones cracked loudly as he let out a shrill cry, dropping down to one knee as Ethan fluidly grabbed the man's firearm, dismantling it and tossing it away. The gunman rolled over, crying lightly as he gingerly gripped his mangled arm.

"Who the fuck are you?" screamed the man with the switch blade. He crouched in a ready position, his knife held out in front of him awaiting Ethan's next move. The man on the floor continued to cry as Ethan brought his foot firmly down on his temple, knocking him out cold. He stared at the remaining thief, watching him squirm, the fear emanating from his body.

Ethan walked towards the shaking assailant, waiting for him to lunge, ready to send him off with his friend. The man made his attempt, lunging forward with his knife poised in front of him. The lethal blade swam through the air, set to penetrate Ethan right beneath his rib cage. Ethan quickly stepped aside, tapping into his years and years of Krav Maga training to knock the blade cleanly from the man's grasp. His palm struck the man squarely in his chest, sending him back a few feet as the lowlife clutched at his shirt, struggling to catch his breath. He dove forward, attempting another futile attack at Ethan. His fist flew past Ethan's ear and his next punch was dodged just as easily, sailing by Ethan and leaving the man open and vulnerable. Ethan brought his knee up, pounding it into the man's side, and followed with a brutal cross hook to the chin. The man flopped into the wall of the basement, wincing in pain as he gained his composure once again, his partner still lying with his mouth wide open on the dirty, garbage dotted basement floor. He set himself up again, stepping in like a boxer would at a huge match, throwing another weak, sloppy punch at Ethan's face. Ethan grabbed the man's hand firmly, pulling him closer as he adeptly planted his right fist into the middle of the man's face. The bones in the man's nose collided with Ethan's knuckle, and blood, gushed from both nostrils, soaking his shirt and spilling to the floor. Ethan watched the man crumble, knocked out cold like his friend.

He dragged the two thieves to a small alcove by the elevator, leaving them piled on the ground as though they were sleeping peacefully. He wasn't here for petty, weapon wielding robbers. He was here to catch a raging lunatic. He stepped onto the elevator, hesitating as he stared at the floor numbers. He wasn't sure where this killer would be, wasn't sure where it would strike. Actually, he wasn't even positive if the thing would show up at all. He moved his hand to press the first floor but hesitated, pressing the sixth floor instead. As the elevator rose, he leaned his back against the wall, trying to go over the letter in his mind, to find some type of a clue as to what this thing was trying to say.

The elevator doors opened, leaving Ethan in an empty hallway with apartment doors and very dim lighting. The number six hung from the wall, all tarnished and ripped, so could barely even make out what the floor number displayed. The marble floors were dirty and cracked, but under the grime, it was evident this building once had a time of elegance and sophistication. That was before the riff-raff came and destroyed it all. Ethan walked up the marble steps, heading up to the roof's door.

He had never been on the roof in all of his years living here. He wasn't the trouble making type back in the day; the simple "Warning- Do Not Enter" was enough to keep him from going up there. This time, however, he opened the door without hesitation, pushing it slowly so it wouldn't make any noise. He crept onto the loose boards that lined the floor, looking around for any sign of life. The dark, wintery moon shined down on the roof-top, giving it an ominous glow. It was 9:14 p.m. now, still two and a half hours from game time. Ethan checked around the roof until he found a good, concealed spot to stake out from. He sat with his back against the wall of the roof's entrance, looking out to the neighborhood he knew so well.

Despite the heaviness of the event, the few visible stars were beautiful. He could see Fordham, his old college that held so many memories, the college he almost didn't attend. 'Such a beautiful neighborhood, it's too bad it's wasting away,' he thought to himself.

Chapter 27

Shrink

Ethan sat there staring at the boring woman. The room was so colorful. There were flowers perched on every desk, nice flowery pictures hung from the walls, and there was an assortment of board games on the table. The woman stared at him with a huge smile on her face, showing him how concerned she was by leaning forward, placing a red flowery box of tissues on the table in front of him. She was a middle-aged woman, with short blonde hair and small wire framed glasses. She had straight, white teeth and a flowery dress on.

"So Ethan, would you like to play a game? I have Connect Four," she said in a polite, gentle tone of voice. She smiled softly, moving the game towards him. Ethan stared at her blankly; he was absolutely miserable. He was an eighth grader, so no, he did not want to play Connect Four. His parents forced him to talk to Janice once a week because his anger started to worsen. They told him therapy was "very normal" and that it would help him "get better". He couldn't see the connection between the two; Ethan was the common case of a child refusing to speak. A child who sat in a therapist's office wasting his parents' money.

"Do you have kids, Janice?" Ethan asked. He was only twelve, but he had a good sense for detecting bullshit. He knew this woman was speaking out of her ass, and he knew she had never experienced anything like this first hand.

"That's a personal question Ethan, I don't feel comfortable answering that," she answered, shifting her weight to the other side of her chair. Ethan reached down picking up the crayons and piece of paper on the table. As he did that, she asked, "Why don't you draw me a picture of how you feel?"

There was something about those words that struck a chord. He emptied the box, letting the crayons roll on to the table as he searched for the black crayon. Janice leaned forward watching the young boy go to work, dragging the crayons all over the white piece of computer paper. Ethan finished coloring, dropping the crayon back on to the table as he sat back on the flowery couch, looking up at Janice, curious of how her expertise in this field would guide her interpretation of his drawing.

"Who is that?" Janice asked, pointing at Ethan's picture.

"Aiden," Ethan answered. He looked down at his own picture, frustrated with himself. Why had he even bothered drawing it, he thought. What's the point?

Janice sat back, placing her hand over her mouth, rubbing it as she widened her eyes. She took her glasses off, placing them on the table as she picked up the picture to hold it close.

"And this?" she asked.

"My dad," Ethan said, shuddering as the words left his mouth. He didn't know if it was right to call him dad at this point.

Janice nodded her head, her squinting eyes glaring over the paper. Every now and then they widened a little.

"Ethan, can you explain it to me?" she asked, placing the picture back on the table. She leaned forward; her face seemed more serious now. The kindness had been subdued by Ethan's Picasso-like talent.

He looked back down at the picture. He, his mother, and Rex were on the left side. Little stick figures portrayed them, and Rex the dog had a smiley face. Ethan also drew a sun and an apartment building behind them. At least that's what he had meant it to be. He drew another stick figure with a sad face and tears falling from its face. He put this figure next to himself. This was meant to be Aiden. He drew a line down the middle of the paper with his black crayon, sketching one stick figure on the other side. The stick figure had a happy face, a poorly drawn car, and a house with it.

"This is the reality world," Ethan said pointing to the left side of his picture. "This is the fantasy world my dad lives in," he said as he pointed to the other side.

"Why is he in the fantasy world?" Janice asked, taking notes in her notebook.

"Because he left," Ethan said. Janice sat back in her chair, watching Ethan with her critical eyes. "He has his new family now. A nice house, a nice car, a new dog...he has everything he didn't have before." Ethan could feel the burn inside, the anger—the resentment. "He left us. I barely see him now. He always tells me we're gunna do stuff and just doesn't show. He's a coward. Aiden needs help; my dad is too busy with his new world to realize it."

Janice reached forward, handing Ethan the tissue box. He hadn't even noticed the tears falling from his face.

"Do you want to tell me more about Aiden?" Janice asked. Ethan shook his head in response. He didn't want to talk at all at this point. The damn tears annoyed him. "Maybe we can try and get your father in here?"

Ethan laughed out loud, "He won't come. He has more important things to do. I wanna go home." Ethan got up; he didn't want to stay here talking to this woman anymore.

"Ethan, do you ever think about hurting yourself?" Janice asked, leaning back in her seat as she stared at a fuming Ethan.

"Yeah," Ethan said. He opened the door; Eileen looked up surprised, checking her watch to make sure she wasn't wrong.

"What's wrong?" she asked nervously, dropping her magazine back onto the navy cushioned seat. Ethan sat down, crossing his arms and staring down at his feet.

"Can we talk, Eileen?" Janice asked, motioning Ethan's mother inside.

"Sure. I'll be right back," she said, rubbing Ethan's head as she walked into the therapy room, the door closing behind her.

Ethan wanted to scream. He wanted to just scream at the top of his lungs because he was so frustrated. He looked up, finally noticing that he wasn't alone in the room. Across from him sat a woman who looked to be about his mother's age, and next to her sat a young girl. The girl was holding her mother's hand as she looked at Ethan smiling. It was at that moment Ethan realized he wasn't alone. There were others who felt his pain.

Chapter 28

Present

The pen graced across the clean sheet of loose-leaf, the horrible, inhumane, well thought out words appearing slowly across each line. Its smile curled across its face. Its hand grasped the pen, its current weapon of choice, as it knowingly wrote its message. The room was empty; the television set in the corner of the room was tuned to the popular sitcom *The Office*. The lighting in the room was excellent. Very bright, vibrant lighting reached every inch of the small office. It stopped, bringing the pen to its lips, still smiling cynically as it meditated its next few words.

It laughed loudly as it signed the bottom of the letter, leaning back in its chair and putting its feet up on top of the table. On the wall across from it was a picture of Ethan. It was a candid picture taken of him as he sat next to Sammy, the girl Chris had introduced him to on the recent blind date. Ethan was circled a bunch of times, the ink darkened around his head. Next to the picture was a giant map of the Westchester/Bronx area. There were circles all over the map, triangles here and there, and a few thumbtacks stuck into various spots. A few of the spots were colored in, pictures accompanying them of the victims who had been brutally killed.

It walked out of the office, making its way down a hallway, entering a sumptuously decorated bathroom. It washed its hands, still snickering to itself as it scrubbed the dirt from its filthy skin. It walked back to its office, taking down the map, the pictures, and the tacks, folding them all neatly and tucking them away in a small vault. Next to the vault sat a gift wrapped elegantly in beautiful red and gold wrapping paper. A huge, red bow was knotted neatly on top.

It picked the box up, placing it on the table and sat back to admire it for a few seconds. Slowly it pulled one of the ribbon's ends, causing the bow to collapse atop the box in an untangled mess. It tore at the wrapping slowly, pulling the ornate paper off the gift. The object sat there, naked now, as the room's inhabitant sat back admiring it. A smile spread across its face as it picked the object up, placing it back beneath its desk. It rose from its seat, still smiling as it shut the light off, leaving the room looking as normal as could be.

Chapter 29

The End

Ethan checked his watch. It was a quarter to midnight now. This was the one part of the job he really couldn't stand: the boring nature of a stakeout. He unholstered his gun, cocking the barrel back, preparing himself for whatever might happen. Taking a deep breath, Ethan threw his head left and right, feeling the bones crack and his muscles loosen.

He slowly maneuvered his way to the edge of the roof, peeking down to the ground below to see if there was anything peculiar. There was no one in front of the building, no car double parked, and nobody idling at the hydrant. It was a strangely dead Friday night on Mosholu Parkway.

Ethan took his time to survey the building, checking to see any shade flicker, any slight movement, but still he couldn't find anything. He moved back to his position, placing his back against the wall and crouched low, cautious to stay unnoticed and out of any unforeseen danger. The seconds felt like hours as his adrenaline pumped harder. A sense of hope began to build with the exhilarating possibility that this could be the end of the line.

The hour hand struck the twelve on Ethan's wrist watch, the silver band around his wrist laid steadily against his motionless, cool skin. Not a movement, not a noise, not a single word. Ethan pressed his back against the wall, breathing as slowly as possible, straining his ears for any sign of life. He closed his eyes, squeezing his lids shut as his heart beat against his chest. The anxiety was starting to get to him. The faint noise of a helicopter could be heard now. Then the very dim noise of its blades swinging in circles grew louder as the chopper approached. Ethan imagined the S.W.A.T. team and the police officers on the ground below making their way up the stairs, expecting to assist in an arrest, yet here he was still pressed against a wall on a roof looking like a fool. 'I fucking knew it,' he thought to himself.

Across the courtyard, on the roof of the 227 side, Ethan watched as the rooftop door swung open. A man emerged from its doorway, backing up onto the roof, a small firearm visible in his hand. Ethan aimed his gun, crouching down as he watched the man move slowly towards the center of the roof, still facing the doorway. He had no idea Ethan was aiming at him. Ethan estimated that from about two hundred yards away he had a very small chance of actually hitting his target.

The man stumbled back, the tears rolling down his bloody cheeks. He shook his head, squeezing his hair with his free hand as he hit himself with the butt of his gun. "NO," he screamed, still backing up as he shook his head more violently. "No," he whimpered uncontrollably, his knees occasionally buckling as the tears escalated to full blown hysterics.

Chris popped out of the doorway, three S.W.A.T. officers and two uniformed police officers following behind him. "Put the gun down!" Chris screamed, his gun held out in front of him, steadily, ready to fire at a moment's notice.

The man screamed out at the top his lungs, throwing his head back in agony. He threw his gun to the ground, kicking it over to the advancing team of law enforcers. Ethan watched from the opposite roof, confused. He had purposely asked Chris to take that side of the building because he figured the killer wouldn't be there. He had lived on the 225 side his whole life, apartment 1B, yet the action was on the opposite side. The chances of this crying mess being the killer they had hoped to find were slim. Ethan shook his head, holstering his gun and made his way back into the building.

"Wait—" Chris yelled. Ethan swung his attention back to the roof in time to see the man freefalling, plummeting to the ground, followed by the momentary sound of his body hitting the concrete. The group could only stare as the body lay motionless on the ground, six floors beneath them. The flood light from the helicopter above shined on the mess as police officers rushed to the scene to cover the sight.

Ethan shook his head, not believing what he had just seen. So many questions flooded his mind, all the letters still plagued him, and he felt like he was going to explode from the stress of it all.

"Ethan," Chris called from across the rooftops. "I'll meet you downstairs." His partner rushed away, disappearing into the doorway as Ethan stood there staring up at the sky. There was no matching clue in that letter. If this was a bust, then what did he have left to go on?

Ethan walked back inside and headed down the steps. His spirit was crushed by another defeat. He had no idea why a man had just fallen six floors to his death, and he had just spent almost three hours crouching on a roof. Here he was yet again, a step behind, another death added to the total, and another wasted night. As Ethan jogged down the steps, he tried to come up with an explanation for it all. *5th floor.* A reason behind his hunch, his abstract, crazy hint of a suspicion. *4th floor.* If he couldn't get this under control, then why even wear the badge? *3rd floor.* 'What's next,' Ethan thought to himself as he jumped down the stairs to the second floor.

He froze as his feet hit the platform, staring up at where the floor marker should have been. The number was removed. The *2* that should have been posted at the top of the wall was gone, but an empty exceptionally clean spot remained. 'You're fucking kidding me,' he thought to himself, still standing there staring at the spot. He looked around the empty hallway, seeing nothing peculiar or out of the ordinary.

"Ethan," Chris called, sounding irritated. His partner trudged up the steps, sighing heavily as he reached his partner. "What are you doing man?" he asked while putting his hands out and shaking his head slowly.

"I think there's a clue here...the..." Ethan started to say before Chris cut in.

"Ethan!" Chris said, shaking his head as he laughed lightly. "Ethan what's going on man...?" Chris walked forward, leaning against the wall as the officers of the 52nd precinct's voices bounced off the walls. "You're not yourself...you're losing your nerve, your edge."

Ethan could feel his skin crawl. Of course he felt hurt by his partner's doubt, by his suspicions, but deep inside it was his own insecurities that made him upset.

They stood in silence with the tension clouding the air as Ethan stood embarrassed and ashamed of himself. He was dragging his partner, the only person he really trusted, his best friend, on a wild goose chase. So far Chris had almost been shot, drove over ten hours round trip into a blizzard, and put his reputation on the line by placing his trust in Ethan, and Ethan knew Chris was right. He just didn't feel the same. This whole case was really getting to him, bringing up things he just didn't want to remember. Chris grabbed Ethan's shoulder, squeezing it tightly as he exhaled deeply.

"Ethan...I'm sorry. This case's been hell," Chris said, sounding regretful. He stared at the floor, still holding Ethan's shoulder. "We're gunna figure this out...you're not quitting on me. I'm not quitting on you."

This was new to Ethan. He had never felt this way before. He felt so defeated. He just needed to snap out of it. There was so much he wanted to say to Chris. He wanted him to know he was his best friend, his confidant, his brother. Unfortunately he just couldn't get it out. He wanted to tell Chris the real reason as to why he felt so depleted.

"Thank you," he said, glancing at Chris. "I'll be alright." Ethan didn't believe his own words. This feeling of helplessness was hard for him to swallow. He refused to believe this thing could be smarter than him. He needed to tap into his reserves, spark up the fire he usually had, and bust this case open. The clue was there, and he dealt with crazy killers before. He just had to figure out how to clear his mind and dismantle the clues one by one.

Ethan looked around the hallway, searching for anything he could use, anything out of the ordinary.

"The whole building's falling apart, you really think there's a clue here?" Chris asked, looking around the filthy hallway. The noise from the helicopters and police running through the building caused a few people to open their doors. A few residents looked out at the agents suspiciously. Ethan walked around the hallway, skimming each door trying to find a clue. Chris joined him, searching in the opposite direction. Chris muttered, "There's shit broken and ripped apart everywhere. It could just be a coincidence."

Ethan ignored his partner, knowing it was no coincidence. Chris' doubt was agitating him. He knew he was on to something. Yes, it was hard to believe and he couldn't understand what significance this had to him, other than the fact they were in his old home, but he could easily tell that number had been recently peeled off. As he walked the hallway, he stopped in front of 2G, staring down at the apartment's floor mat. He felt sick to his stomach as he stared down at the mat's design. Two Beagle puppies with their tongues hanging out were stitched into the carpet with the word 'Welcome' embroidered underneath. Chris joined Ethan, staring

down at the mat and then back at his partner.

"You owned a Beagle, no?" Chris asked, crouching down and lifting the mat. Beneath

the mat sat a small envelope. "What bullshit."

Chapter 30

Man's Best Friend

There was one thing Ethan could always count on, one thing he knew would never leave his side, never abandon him, and never pull an Andrew Alosi. Rex was more than a dog, and he was more than the family pet. He was Ethan's best friend. Ethan lay on the floor, holding Rex as the dog sat still, allowing Ethan to squeeze him tightly. Yet another day his father decided he couldn't spare some precious time for the boy he helped create.

Ethan couldn't understand it. He had remembered many great times with his father. They used to do everything together: Yankee games, the movies, baseball practice. Now all of a sudden, a new family had moved into the picture. They stole his father from right under his nose. Ethan contemplated if it was something he had done. Maybe he messed up somewhere along the road. He had been crying a lot lately.

Rex licked his hand. Rex's wet, warm tongue felt comforting. "I don't get it," he said to the dog. Rex stared at him, its tongue hanging from its mouth as it panted heavily. He petted the dog's head gently, smiling at how funny it looked. The dog had no idea that Andrew was gone, that he abandoned both of them. It had been Andrew's idea to get a dog in the first place. Like so many other responsibilities, Ethan and his mother inherited Rex through his father's disregard of responsibility.

Ethan let go of Rex and climbed into his bed, turning over onto his side to look out at the night sky. He was only eleven years old, but he had enough sense to wonder if his father saw the same sky. Did his father see things the same way, or was he so high and mighty? Was his vision so skewed that Ethan was correct in believing they saw different skies?

Ethan awoke to his mother calling his name. He could hear her standing in the doorway repeating his name over and over. The sun shone through his eyelids as he carefully tried to open them, the burning sensation piercing his body.

"Five more minutes," he muttered. He knew it was Saturday, and that there was no real reason to wake up early. His mother continued to call his name, but this time he realized she was whimpering. Panic took over as he spun around, seeing his mother standing in his doorway crying. "What happened?" he screamed. He jumped out of the bed sprinting to her, sliding down the hallway as he made his way to her room. He flew into her doorway as fear, panic, anger, and despair filled his body.

Ethan's knees hit the floor hard, his knees were bruising from the fall, but he didn't feel a thing. He opened his mouth wide, gasping for air, tears swelling in his eyes and bursting onto his face. He never felt the pain so bad before, his heart stabbed his chest repeatedly, his throat closed, not letting him scream let alone talk.

His mother walked into the room, still crying as she put her hand on his back. Ethan quickly shrugged it off, he didn't want anyone to touch him, and he didn't want to speak. He lost the energy to do anything. He felt like his soul was ripped away, like he had no life left inside. He stared down at his best friend, the dog he loved so much, as he lay on the rug motionless, his small tongue hanging from his mouth.

Ethan crawled forward, placing his hand on his dog's stiff body, the tears bursting from both eyes as he began sobbing. "No," he screamed. "No!" He felt the anger boiling inside as he placed his forehead on the floor. 'How can this happen right now?' he thought. His mother covered the dog with a towel, and the rest of the procedure was a blur. His best friend was buried in his aunt's backyard. Ethan wasn't present for the burial. He lay in his bed crying, unable to eat, sleep, or even talk. No one could understand why Ethan was as upset as he was. To them, the dog was just an animal. The dog was a part of the small family. It was visible that Ethan was devastated, completely torn apart by Rex's death.

Ethan knew the dog as a friend, as a pet, but most importantly the dog served as the last remaining evidence that his father existed in the family. Ethan could remember great memories of himself and his father playing with Rex, teaching him tricks, and just enjoying each other's company. Since his father vanished, Rex was all Ethan had to remind him of what was once a conventional household. Ethan would come to realize—many years from that moment—that a conventional household was no longer defined as a father, a mother, a son, a daughter, and a little dog all happily living each day together. The white picket fence and the happy morning goodbyes just don't exist. There is no Brady Bunch in the world today, and if you know a family that happy, well then God bless them. The bottom line, Ethan realized, is this world, the families in it, and parents from this generation are generally fucked up.

Chapter 31

Intricacy

Chris emptied the envelope, the tiny key sliding out onto his open hand. It wasn't the typical envelope they were so accustomed to. The agents looked at each other in the dimly lit hallway, both wondering if it could be a clue, or if it was just simply a comfortable resident leaving a spare key under the door mat.

Chris stood back up, still holding the envelope in his hand as he knocked on the apartment door. They stood there for a few seconds before Chris knocked again a little louder. "No one home," he said, as he twirled the envelope around in his fingers. "Should I?" Ethan widened his eyes and nodded his head. As Chris emptied the key back on to his hand, the door opened, revealing a tiny, old woman with a white linen nightdress on.

"Do you know the time?" she snarled angrily. She looked down at Chris' hand, reaching out to snatch the envelope from him. "That's not yours!" she screamed at him. "Were you raised by wolves? Can I help you?" She grabbed the envelope from Chris' hands, staring at them angrily.

"I'm very sorry ma'am," Ethan said. "I'm Agent Carey and this is Agent Hawkins. We're just here investigating a case, we're sorry to bother you."

"You're here about my son then," the woman said, laughing as she turned to walk back into her home. "My Desmond...," the woman said as she strolled down her hallway. The two agents glanced at each other before they followed her into the apartment. There were pictures covering every inch of the old apartment, and the smell of mothballs and cinnamon filled the air.

Ethan's heart sunk as he walked down the hallway. Each picture showed what looked like a mother with her son, both smiling cheerfully in every picture. He swallowed, feeling his stomach getting queasy as he remembered his own mother, his beautiful mother, who used to have so many similar pictures on her walls.

"I'm sorry to intrude ma'am, these are beautiful pictures," Ethan said, nodding at her as he pointed around him. The woman let out a giant smile.

"Me and my baby Desmond," she said softly as she walked forward, standing next to Ethan. "My poor boy...are you looking for him, Officer?" The woman walked into a dimly lit living room where the mahogany coffee table was cluttered with magazines and newspapers some of which had spilled onto her floor. Her tiny, old fashioned television set displayed a fuzzy, distorted picture. She sat down on a creaky, wooden chair, throwing a knitted quilt over her legs.

Ethan walked into the living room, observing his surroundings, attempting to find a tipoff to whatever it was the killer might want to say. He couldn't help but realize that this may easily be a coincidence, but he didn't believe it was.

"There's been a homicide over at 227, we were just wondering if you heard anything out of the ordinary," Ethan said, noticing the unopened mail scattered over the woman's table.

"Sir, in this neighborhood," the woman started to say, leaning into him. "Murder is ordinary." She stared into Ethan's eyes, the wrinkles on her face crumpling together as her face expanded into a smile. "Carey...are you related to the Carey family in this neighborhood?"

Ethan had tried to remember if he knew this woman, if he had ever met her son, Desmond. He could tell from the look of her apartment that she had been settled here for quite some time.

"No, I'm sorry," Ethan lied. He wasn't here to socialize; he had already found what he was meant to see. "Can you tell me a little about your son?"

Ethan noticed Chris was still standing in the hallway, still staring at all the pictures on the wall, carefully scanning his eyes over every last inch. Ethan couldn't see the pain in Chris' eyes, but he knew his partner was hurting. The thought of the mother he never had was draped over every inch of this apartment.

"My baby Desmond," the woman said, the smile crawling back across her face. "My Desmond is such a good, good boy. Are you sure I don't know you from somewhere?"

Ethan shook his head impatiently. "No ma'am. I'm sorry, I didn't grow up in the Bronx," he lied again.

The woman shook her head, seemingly annoyed by how familiar Ethan appeared. "I haven't seen my Desmond in years. He never comes by anymore."

Ethan leaned into the woman, watching her face change from happy to sad instantly. "Why doesn't he come by? If you don't mind me asking," Ethan said. He could easily tell the woman didn't talk to many people. By the look of her house she didn't take too much consideration in her own well-being.

"Desmond was always a good boy," she said shaking her head. "I love my boy, but he grew rotten." She looked up at Ethan, her eyes were clear of emotion as she stared into Ethan's. "His father was never around, always out with the boys...he'd come around the house for Christmas, maybe Easter, but otherwise he wasn't a father. He'd beat Desmond, I'd try to stop him but what could I do? I did my best, it just wasn't enough."

Ethan sat still, staring at the woman. Chris was now standing in the living room, his arms crossed as he watched, the pain still evident on his face. His eyes showed agony as the thoughts swirled in his head. His childhood memories were erupting back into reality.

"We won't take any more of your time, I'm sorry to hear about your son," Ethan said, standing up, picking up a newspaper off the woman's table as he rose. He stared down at the paper before he tossed it back down, giving the woman a wave as he turned to exit the apartment.

"Is there something else officer?" the woman asked, turning her head to look up at Chris. Chris' eyes were watery; he stood there struggling to hold back the tears. He smiled, he laughed, he made jokes, but inside Chris was tormented. He struggled every day to battle his emotions, to strive towards a happier mindset, to believe in the chastity of marriage. But there were moments like these when anger won the fight. His mother did exactly what Desmond's father had done, she ran away.

"I don't know you ma'am, but from what I see you're a fine mother. You'll see your Desmond again," Chris said, not making eye contact with the woman. He felt choked up, like his throat was swollen from the pain.

The woman laughed out loud, slapping the arm of her chair. "I'm sure your mother did a fine job also, you look like you did fine for yourself, sir."

Chris smiled, shaking his head slowly. He looked down at the woman, nodding at her as he walked towards the door. "Don't forget to lock the door ma'am, and I wouldn't leave that key under your mat." Chris walked out the front door with dry eyes and a smile on his face, this time taking care to not look at any of the pictures.

"You alright?" Ethan asked, staring at his partner, concerned. He was a little worried by the nature of that interrogation, he was well aware of how it felt to be haunted by a dark past, of how it could come back so quickly to disrupt even the best mood.

"Yeah," Chris said smiling. "Why wouldn't I be?" he said tapping Ethan on the arm and shrugging it off.

Ethan held out his hand, holding a stamped envelope up to Chris' eyes. The envelope was addressed to Special Agent Ethan Carey. Chris stared at it confused.

"Where'd you get that?" Chris said, reaching out to grab the envelope. The envelope was addressed to the woman's apartment, but Ethan's name was the recipient.

"It was on her table, mixed in with the rest of her mail," Ethan smiled as he watched Chris shake his head.

"What the fuck, man. What the hell are we dealing with?" Chris' eyes squinted as he tried to comprehend it all. "You could have taken the elevator, she could have put that envelope in a drawer, she could have thrown it out, she could have been lazy and not gotten the mail...it's not playing fair."

Chris was one hundred percent correct. Ethan didn't have an explanation for it; he could just hope there was something of use in the envelope. He ripped it open, pulling out the letter inside.

My favorite agent,

It's not always so clear is it? It's not like we asked for it, it's not like we provoked it, it's not like we made it happen, sometimes events unfold against our wishes. Clear, no, it's never clear Ethan. It's never laid out right in front of you, someone is always bending the truth, someone is always hiding the truth. You know who I am, Ethan. Everything isn't so clear, but this one truth is...you know who I am. You can join me, I'm asking you to join me. You can't stop me. January 2nd, Midnight. I'll be waiting for you. My plan will not diverge, I will prevail, my message, in stone, will be written. I know what it's like to get your hopes up, to expect one thing and receive another even after you've worked so hard. The truth is a beautiful thing; we've been lied to enough. The dead man knew who I was; You're the only one who knows me. Don't forget Ethan. Miles Davis once said, "A legend is an old man with a cane known for what he used to do..." Look up the rest.

See you soon

"...*I'm* still doing it," Ethan said, finishing the quote and looking up at Chris.

Ethan's phone vibrated in his pocket. He reached down, picking it up to see a text message from Rachel. 'I'm really happy we bumped into each other. I'm sure you're busy, I know we were supposed to go out tonight but if you're tied up it's fine. Can't wait for the party!' The message made Ethan smile, clearing his mind of all his troubles as he stood in the middle of the second floor hallway. He wanted to see her; an hour wasn't enough. He wished she was with him now, he wished he could see her beautiful eyes, feel her soft hair, hear her talk, but instead he was stuck in this shitty, old apartment building dealing with this lunatic.

"Surprisingly, I have no idea," Chris said, waving his arms around in a mocking, fed up manner.

"You've never heard me say this before, but we definitely need sleep," Ethan said, checking the time to see it was now a little after one. He was tired, he couldn't even remember the last time he had a decent night's sleep. "I said it before; it blows a lot of smoke. We won't be able to figure anything out on no sleep."

Chris leaned against the wall, sighing heavily as he leaned forward, placing his hands on his knees. The whole ordeal was overwhelming; it was taking a huge toll on them both emotionally and physically. Chris looked up, sucking his teeth and shaking his head.

"I guess so," he said, exhaling loudly. Chris looked more tired than defeated, and the thoughts of Desmond's mother's apartment clearly still haunted him. He felt the pain inside. The anger was still bubbling, but it was beginning to subside.

The two agents walked out of the building together, the crowd had grown significantly since they pulled up at nine. There were hundreds of people standing around, cop cars covered the street and the park. An ambulance, which was most likely useless at this point, sat by the hydrant, and police officers and FBI agents scrambled all over the building, barking orders left and right.

"What happened in there?" Illames' voice screamed out over the crowd. Their commissioner maneuvered his way through the crowd of agents and police officers, and his face looked like it was about to explode. "Keep moving!" he said staring at a rookie cop with a disgusted face. "What happened?" Illames stood in front of the two agents with his hands on his hips, staring at them wide eyed.

Ethan stared back at Illames, glanced sideways at Chris who also looked at a loss for words, and then decided to take the initiative. "It lied; it never planned on being here," Ethan said, bracing himself for Illames' response. He decided to keep going and see how far he could get before his head was taken off. "It's very smart. It's staying out of the water but somehow making huge waves."

Illames' mouth opened and closed repeatedly as he chewed on a massive wad of bubblegum. He stared into Ethan's eyes, and then turned his attention to Chris.

"That's a terrible analogy. What do you say?" he asked calmly. Ethan was very surprised at how he was taking this. There were news teams everywhere and the big boss wasn't breaking much of a sweat.

"I agree with Ethan, sir," Chris said, seeming to be just as surprised as Ethan was and continued, "whoever this killer may be, it definitely wants to get this message across." Chris stopped talking, looking over at Ethan. He was probably wondering if Ethan had anything more to say, anything left to input before they ran out of there.

Through the crowd Ethan could see the mess, the scattered blood and skin poured over the sidewalk. "Do we have an I.D.?" he asked, nodding his head towards the forensics teams and paramedics. Illames turned his body, scoffing at the center of attention, the focus of the media.

There wasn't much left to see. The mess didn't turn Ethan's stomach as badly as Lake George had, not as bad as St. Brendan's either, but, nevertheless, it was a horrible sight.

"I saw him pacing the stairway on the 227 side, I tried to approach him and he flashed his gun at me," Chris said, staring at the body heaped on the concrete. "He took off once I engaged him, crying."

Illames looked from Chris to the body. "He might have gotten scared," Illames said, making a confused face and shrugging his shoulders. "We'll figure it out, though. He had a few things with his name on it in his wallet. Ran a quick background check and found this guy has a lot of shit on him. Desmond Massaro. He actually used to live right there on the 225 side. You know this guy?" Illames looked at Ethan who was staring at Chris. "You lived here for a while, no?"

Ethan looked at Illames, so many thoughts running through his head as he stared at his commissioner. "Did you check up on my background?" Ethan asked.

"I have a serial killer on my hands, Ethan, and it's only targeting you...what do you think?" Illames asked, annoyed. "Is this a problem with you, Ethan, or should I confer with you before I do my job? Let me remind you that I'm the assistant director of the field office you work in. I know the ins and outs of all my agents."

As much as Ethan didn't like the idea of Illames checking up on him, he knew it was the obvious move. He felt edgy right now; he knew the lack of sleep was getting to him. It made him feel a little more aggravated than normal.

"I'm sorry, we just really need some sleep," Ethan said. He could tell that Illames knew he was withdrawing, bowing out of a battle he would have never won anyway. Illames glared at him, a tiny smirk forming out of the corner of his mouth before he waved them away. Ethan and Chris walked away from the crime scene, walking through the crowd of civilians that had formed to witness the spectacle.

Ethan was well aware that the man who had just fallen to his concrete grave was the little old woman's son, Desmond. He was pretty sure this wasn't a coincidence and he knew it wasn't the time or the place to mention anything to Illames. Even Illames himself seemed to understand that he had to figure Ethan out before he could figure the case out. It would just be a waste of valuable time to go over all the many, many details with him. Despite all that, Ethan had learned over his many years of experience that it was sometimes more efficient to not get too many people involved on one particular case. Sometimes two views on a situation shined more light on a case than the collaboration of twenty people's views.

As the two agents drove down Mosholu Parkway, Chris turned his head to stare at Ethan.

"Desmond...are you kidding me?" he sneered as he turned his attention back to the road. "I think me and you are in for a realllllly big vacation at the end of this one."

Ethan could barely keep his eyes open. He had just brawled with two lowlifes, sat on a roof for almost three hours, and then found a letter addressed to him in the apartment of a strange woman whose son had just fallen six feet to his death. Not to mention all the other bullshit he and his partner had just endured over the last few days.

"Sleep sounds like the perfect vacation right now," Ethan said, scrolling through his cellphone to the name he couldn't stop thinking about. Through all the death, through all the confusion, Rachel still occupied his mind. At 12:45 AM there was a pretty slim chance she was actually awake, but he figured he'd give it a try. 'Still awake? Wanna go for a ride?' As soon as he hit send, he wished he could have it back. 'Too fast,' he thought as he threw his head back against the headrest. He hated to be alone, that was true, but what he felt now was different. He felt sick to his stomach. He was so fed up with this case of dead ends.

Outside the car, he could see the gangsters who plagued the Bronx's streets. The menacing natives stared at the Charger as it drove by, their dark business concealed by the night sky. He could remember the many nights he would come home late, planning out the walking path to reach his apartment safely with all of his money intact.

Ethan's phone vibrated in his hand, jolting him awake. He rubbed his eyes and looked down at his phone to read Rachel's text.

Chapter 32

Home Sweet Home

Ethan packed his suitcase carefully, making sure he tucked the snow globe in between his clothes, buffering the box from any harm that might befall it. He stood back, staring at the suitcase, making sure his gift was in the safest position, before he zipped the bag up, placing it gently next to his father's stuff.

The cruise was alright. There was, of course, the hours that he spent in day care while his father performed his specialty trait: selfishness. Other than his father being manhandled and whipped like a rag doll, other than sitting in day care playing Super Mario Kart with some kid from Texas, and other than the fact that he couldn't stand Ray or Michelle and neither had fallen off the side of the boat, he would agree that the Disney Cruise was indeed magical.

"You ready to go buddy," Andrew said, walking into the hotel room with a smile on his face. He grabbed his son, hugging him tightly. "It was a good vacation, huh?"

"Yeah dad it was awesome," Ethan said, half faking his enthusiasm. Any kid would be thrilled to have been on the Disney Cruise, and Ethan was thrilled, he just couldn't help but remember the crap he had to endure during it. It always seemed to be this way. Something great would happen or be proposed, and then something else would interrupt. His father would tell him they were going to get some ice cream at Carvel, but then Michelle would be waiting at Carvel. His father would say they were going to a Yankee game, but then Ray would be there with them. Ethan wondered if his father had a brain or eyes.

"I need to go to the bathroom before we go," Ethan said, breaking the hug and walking to the bathroom.

He couldn't stop thinking about his mother's reaction. She was going to flip when she saw the snow globe. Ethan smiled from ear to ear as they sat in the cab on the way to the airport. Michelle sulked in the backseat, visibly upset about something. Ethan wasn't sure if she was ever truly happy. She always had to bitch about something, always had a sour puss on her face even on what should have been the happiest days.

The plane ride back was so long compared to the ride there. Ethan could barely sit still as he anticipated finally being back home. His father and Michelle sat beside him and Ray, they were arguing as usual, and Ray was showing Ethan his new Nintendo DS game. Ethan was actually being more friendly than usual, his mood was much happier now that they were so close to home.

As they arrived at the airport, Michelle stormed off away from Andrew, shaking her head in disgust. Ethan didn't bother paying attention to their petty squabbles; he was closer now than ever. Just a short car ride and he would see his mother's giant smile. Ethan had never been more proud of a gift in his life, this one was just so perfect he couldn't help but feel ecstatic.

"Dad, where's Michelle and Ray going?" Ethan asked, watching the two walking off to the parking garage. "Where are we going?"

"We're gunna jump in a cab buddy, why?" his father said, looking down at him confused.

This was another one of those moments where the master manipulator was at work. He made Ethan feel like the most unusual action was actually very normal. The fact that they were going to cab it to the Bronx and then Andrew would cab it alone to Yorktown was supposed to be no big deal, nothing to speculate over. Even at eleven years old Ethan knew this wasn't the truth. What had actually happened had gone something like this.

"Does Ethan's mother know what time we land?" Michelle asked, staring out the window of the jumbo jet.

"I'm not sure, why?" Andrew asked, not seeing the connection.

"Because she's picking him up," Michelle whispered to Andrew, staring at him curiously.

He sank a little in his seat as he stared back at Michelle confused. He licked his lips as his Adam's apple bulged a little.

"Honey, I thought we'd just drop him off on the way home?" Andrew asked curiously.

Michelle's face sunk, her expression growing nastier with each passing millisecond. She stared at him like he had just smacked her across the face.

"I hope to God you don't think I'm going anywhere near that shithole," she whispered angrily. Her face was shaking and started to turn red.

Andrew's mind raced, he had to find a way to pacify the situation, and quickly, before Michelle exploded.

"You take the car and I'll take a cab with Ethan," he said, hoping this would diffuse the ticking time bomb next to him.

Ethan didn't know this was the case. He didn't know his father was so weak, such a coward, such a poster boy for deadbeat fathers worldwide. His father had been doing it for years. He could give away an empty envelope but make it out to look like a brand new Mercedes. Ethan's true feelings for Andrew would never be revealed, never be muttered, and never be spoken in real words until Ethan grew up.

The cab pulled up to 225 East Mosholu Parkway, where the building shone brightly in the sun. The grass was green and lively, the walls were graffiti free, and the skies were beautiful, this day just felt so perfect.

"Here you go," Andrew said as he passed his money to the cabbie. "Can you wait here, I'm gunna run in and out. I'm going to 35 Charles St. in York Town Heights."

The cabbie turned around to face the backseat, letting out a soft chuckle as he stared at Andrew.

"No way, sir. I don't go that far," he said laughing.

"I'm sorry, but I'll pay extra if you can," Andrew said, dreading the thought of having to see his ex-wife face to face.

The cabbie shook his head annoyed, "Dude, I don't go that far, have a nice day." He nodded his head at the door and popped the trunk.

Andrew and Ethan hopped out of the car. Andrew pulled both of the suitcases out and watched the cab drive away. He glanced up at the corner windows of the building's first floor, the windows he had looked out of so often once upon a time. He turned around, praying for a cab he could wave down, but nothing came.

Ethan stared up at his father curious as to what the delay was. He was finally there, so close to giving his mother his gift.

"Dad, come on," Ethan said impatiently.

He ran through the courtyard, jumped up the steps, and rang 1B repeatedly. The buzzer rang, like the sound at the start of a race, and Ethan flew through the door, jumping up the soft, worn marble stairs in the hallway as he made his way toward his apartment. Andrew followed

behind him holding the luggage, his heart rate increasing steadily with every step.

Ethan's mother opened the door with a huge smile on her beautiful face. She placed

her head on top of her son's as the two hugged each other, squeezing each other tightly,

completely ignoring the fact that Andrew stood there idly.

"Mom, I can't wait to show you what I got!" Ethan said excitedly, running through the

front door, stopping briefly to pet an elated, jittery Rex. He darted to his room, jumping up

onto his bed as he waited for his father to bring his luggage.

His room was spotless; his mother had cleaned it while he was gone. There were

Yankees posters hanging all over his walls. His baseball equipment sat by the side of his door,

and his bike rested in the corner. He was so happy to finally be back.

"Dad, come on!" Ethan yelled, waiting for the suitcase so he could finally give his

mother what he had been dying to give her all week. His father appeared from around the

corner, walking out of the living room and down the hallway to Ethan's bedroom, carrying

Ethan's luggage in his hands.

"What's up buddy?" he asked, still sporting that stupid, curious look on his face.

Ethan's mother walked into his room, joining Ethan and his father, crossing her arms

and still holding on to her smile.

"Mom, you're going to love it," Ethan said, jumping off of his bed and unzipping his bag

as quickly as he could.

He tossed a couple of shirts and pants on to his floor, his mother reaching out one arm

to try and stop him, but decided to just let the boy go instead. It was obvious he was excited about something. Ethan shifted things around, lifted his toiletries, threw out more clothes, but he couldn't find a snow globe. His heart beat faster as panic seized his demeanor; he swallowed heavily, flipping the suitcase upside down as he searched all over his bedroom floor, desperately trying to find the snow globe.

"Where is it," he screamed. His parents stared down at him, clueless as to what was going on. "Where is it!" he screamed again. He looked up at his dad who stared back at him with a puzzled look.

"Buddy, what are you looking for?" he asked, kneeling down to pick up some of the thrown clothes.

Ethan couldn't believe his ears; he just couldn't believe what was happening.

"The snow globe," he said, tears starting to form in his eyes. He fought hard to suppress them, fought hard to keep them from coming, but this was killing him. His stomach churned as he folded over, so afraid that this really wasn't a joke, that the snow globe really wasn't there.

"Buddy," Ethan's father said, crouching next to him. "What are you talking about?"

Ethan's ears were on fire, his face felt like it was about to melt. His tears burst out, streaming down his cheeks as his mother came rushing over, placing her hands over his shoulders.

"Baby, what's wrong?" she asked worriedly. She stared at his father with piercing eyes, furious that her son was hysterically crying.

"I bought you a present," Ethan said through his panic. He could barely get the words out he was crying so hard. He slammed his hand on the floor as the anger, his new friend, started to knock on the door. He could feel it surging through his veins, bursting in every part of him, viciously bouncing off the walls of his body.

"What are you talking about, buddy?" Andrew stared at the boy with a dumbfounded look.

Eileen stood up; her face reflected of disgust as she stared at Andrew.

"Get out of my house," she said, pointing her finger at the doorway. "Get out!" she screamed.

Andrew stood up, taking a deep breath as he stared at Eileen.

"Eileen, you know how Ethan's imagination is," Andrew said, smirking and shaking his head.

Eileen walked out of Ethan's bed room, picking up the house phone in the living room.

"You're not welcome in my house. Get out or I'll call the cops," she said, holding the receiver to her ear. Andrew laughed and walked down the hallway; he grabbed his luggage and stormed out of the apartment, his work here was finished.

Ethan lay on the floor of his bedroom, and he felt so incredibly disappointed. He wanted to see his mother smile, to see her light up when she saw that present, and now he just felt crazy. He tried to remember, to think back to that day at the gift shop, and he tried to remember if he had even gone to the gift shop at all.

Eileen stood in the doorway, the tears slowly falling down her cheeks as she stared down at her son. She couldn't understand why anyone would do such a thing, why any man would intentionally hurt his son or daughter this way, but all she knew was the man who had just left was as close to the devil as any one person could get. It pained her more than anything to see her son this distraught.

Ethan got up from the floor, jumping up into his bed.

"Can you turn the A.C. on, Mom," he asked, throwing the comforter over himself. He didn't feel like doing anything, he just wanted to sleep. He was so upset, so confused by what had just happened. He waited what felt like months to give his mother the perfect gift and his thoughts were shattered.

Ethan would never forget that day. Andrew forgot only a few hours later.

Chapter 33

Stranger

'I'm awake, do you want to pick me up?' Rachel's text message read. Ethan felt the warmth cover his body. He was worried he might have jumped the gun a little, and he didn't want to push her away. This was all new to him, he hadn't felt this way for a girl since the last time he was with Rachel, and even back then he cowered away from the commitment.

"You can drive to your place, I'll take the Charger," Ethan said, putting his phone back in his pocket. Chris looked over at him surprised.

"You sure?" Chris said. He looked at Ethan, seeing the more passive look on his face and instantly knew what was going on. "Booty call?" Chris said laughing. He nudged Ethan's arm, shaking his head as he turned his attention back to the road.

Ethan smiled back at his partner; it was nice to see Chris smiling for once. "It's not like that this time. I'm feeling a little restless right now, can you blame me?"

"Of course not, bro," Chris said, nodding his head in agreement. "I'm all for it, we both just need to unwind right now. At least we have that party tomorrow. Dana's pregnant. She is crazy, man. Do you understand how pent up I am right now? I mean, the extent of our romance right now is when I bring her home some Italian ices. She craves that shit. I bring her an Italian ice and maybe—just maybe—I get a little relief. I'm probably more attracted to her than I've ever been in our entire time knowing each other, but Ethan, I am telling you man. She is crazy. I breathe the wrong way or look the wrong way and it's all, 'What the fuck are you looking at!'" Chris looked over at Ethan who couldn't look less interested. "You don't give a shit about this, huh? Well, like I said, the party should be good. We deserve a bit of fun, don't

we?"

Ethan had completely forgotten about Luke's holiday party. Maybe the party was a

good idea after all.

"We do. I'm not sure about it though," Ethan said, trying not to be too irresponsible.

He didn't want to take too much time off from the case, especially now that they seemed to be

at the end of the race.

Chris rolled his eyes, laughing, "Ethan, one day off man. Not even one day, just a few

hours. We can go take a load off, do some dancing, socialize with some rich doctors...I wanna

see some of those Carey dance moves." Chris started dancing around in the driver's seat.

Ethan smiled at his partner, nodding his head.

"You can't keep up with these dance moves, these two left feet command all dance

floors," he said, laughing at his partner who was still dancing around. Ethan couldn't remember

the last time he had been genuinely happy like this. He was laughing with his partner, had a

party to go to for New Year's Eve, and was about to pick up a gorgeous girl he actually had

feelings for. Things were looking up despite the lunatic terrorizing them with its letters and

murders.

Chris and Ethan swapped places, shaking hands before Chris jogged up to his apartment

building, happy to finally see his fiancé again. He waved back to Ethan as he disappeared

behind the apartment door, leaving Ethan sitting alone in the driver's seat.

He could faintly remember where Rachel lived, trying to retrace his steps the night of

their "first" date. The only thing he had really seen that night long ago was her. This time he pulled up in front of her small apartment building, and looked up at the three floor, red brick building, trying to remember if this was hers or not. The neighborhood was spotless, and the building was clean with beautifully arranged shrubbery outside of it. It was about two o'clock in the morning and the street was dead quiet. Ethan pulled out his phone, texting her to let her know he was outside. He sat back wondering if he was doing the right thing. He didn't know if he was ready for something like this since he had dangerous feelings for this girl. To have her come over so late could be a mistake. He took a deep breath, exhaling loudly as he flirted with driving away and never looking back. He reached forward, putting his hand on the keys, but reconsidered and sat back instead.

He looked up at the building, not a single movement could be seen. His phone remained still also. 'Maybe she fell asleep,' he thought. He stared up at the wooden doorway, and then it cracked open. Rachel came out, holding a small bag in one hand. She skipped to the car, smiling widely, as she opened the door, placing her bag in the backseat. Ethan couldn't help but wonder if the bag meant she planned on staying over.

"Hey," she said. "Long night?" She smiled as she sat down in the passenger's seat. She was wearing a nice pair of sweatpants and a cute, pink T-shirt shirt with a sweater over it. "It's freezing out," she said. Ethan smiled back at her, and she was even more beautiful than he remembered.

"It is definitely cold out, yes," he said laughing as she shivered next to him. He reached forward turning the heat on, then put his eyes right back on her. Her hair looked so silky, so soft as it draped over her shoulders. Her face was what he believed to be perfect, so smooth and vibrant. He couldn't take his eyes off of her, he didn't want to, but then the fear hit him again. He couldn't get this drawn in; he couldn't make himself so vulnerable. She stared at him; her beautiful brown eyes gleamed in the moonlight. All he could think about was kissing her, it's all he wanted to do, but he just couldn't.

"Are you alright?" she asked, her face was serious as she stared back at him. Her throat bulged as she swallowed, her skin showed goose bumps as her body convulsed from the cold. "I got chills."

"Are you still cold?" Ethan asked, reaching forward to turn the heat up some more. Rachel reached out, grabbing his hand. Her soft touch was shocking. Surprisingly, her hand was warm. It made the muscles in his arm stiffen; his body relaxed, the tension that shrouded him seemed like nothing more than a distant, stupid predicament.

"I'm fine," Rachel said, smiling awkwardly. "I'm honestly just nervous." Ethan could hear her breathing in and out as she looked out the window, still smiling. He turned the engine on, slowly driving down the block, still barely able to take his eyes off of her. He didn't know what was happening and in all honesty, at that very moment when her hand touched his, he simply didn't care.

"Do you wanna go for a ride?" Ethan asked. He couldn't believe he had just asked that. It was his thing; he loved getting in his car late at night and driving to his special spot. It relaxed him, helped him unwind from the rough days, it simply reset the anger.

Rachel sat next to Ethan, the surprise apparent in her eyes. She knew Ethan took these rides, but she had never been a part of one. She knew it was Ethan's secret thing. She had no idea where he went, no idea what he did, but she did know she wanted to be a part of this.

"Where do you want to go?" she asked, the anticipation building.

"I'd rather just show you," Ethan responded, still questioning if it was a smart thing to do or not. He had told Rachel absolutely everything about himself over the course of their relationship. She knew the ins and the outs of Ethan Carey, she was but one of a select few who did. Ethan couldn't put a finger on it; he wasn't sure what it was that made him so comfortable, so ready to open himself. Maybe it was the second chance, the ability to fix the mess he had once created. Whatever it was he didn't really care. He was too tired, too fed up with all the shit going on to even think about it at this point.

Rachel nodded back to him, staring into Ethan's bright, light brown eyes. She had never noticed how vibrant his face looked; even in the dark Charger he looked so alive, so beautiful. His skin radiated such a positive aurora, such a confident, strong presence that she wanted to embrace forever. She wasn't sure what it was that made it so different now, but she felt so passionate about being by his side. The one man she had ever met who could share in her life's horror, who could relate to her own terrifying, troubling childhood.

Ethan merged on to the Taconic North, and the highway was eerily dead. There were no cars on the side of the road. He took a deep breath as the car flew down the parkway, still contemplating turning around. He looked over at Rachel who looked confused, staring out the window trying to figure out where they were going. He had never told her about this place, never taken her there, never even acknowledged the fact that he went on these rides. Instead, he simply erased it from his mind.

The car crossed over the Amvets Bridge, a bridge spanning over the Croton River that brought the road to Yorktown Heights. Rachel finally realized where they were going as she saw the signs for Yorktown Heights come into view. She looked over at Ethan even more perplexed. She had absolutely no idea why he would be coming to Yorktown; there was nothing but mad memories there.

Ethan knew Rachel guessed it by now, yet she probably had no idea why exactly he was doing it. For the past ten years he had been driving up to Yorktown and parking his car in a spot near the woods. When he got there he would lie across the back windshield, staring at the beautiful night sky. It was so peacefully quiet, so beautiful, the sky was so clear in that area.

He got off the exit for Yorktown Heights, driving his car through a few side streets. The enormous, beautiful houses along the side of the road were dark and quiet. He drove down a long, wide hill, nothing but grass and grain surrounded them as he made his way to an intersection. To the right there was nothing but trees and dark, a few mansions could be seen in the distance but other than that there was just wilderness. Ethan turned the car onto the dark road, driving slowly so he wouldn't crash into any wandering deer.

"Oh my God," Rachel gasped, staring out the window at a family of deer on the side of the road. Ethan and Rachel were city folk. They were used to pigeons, water bugs, and rats not coyotes, deer, and foxes. She grabbed Ethan's shoulder, her mouth wide in shock as she pointed the family out to Ethan. Ethan laughed at Rachel's astonishment because he was the same way twenty years ago, when his father had first moved there. He came to another intersection; this one had houses lined along the right hand side and straight ahead. To the left and backwards was nothing but greenery shrouded in darkness.

Ethan drove the car up onto the curb, parking it in the grass to the left of the intersection, turning the lights and the engine off. He looked over at Rachel who looked back at him, confused.

"I know it's freezing so we don't have to get out," he said, opening the moon roof and putting his seat back. "Usually I lie on the car and just stare up at the sky."

The stars were so bright tonight, the moon just a small sliver in the night's sky. Rachel put her seat back as well, smiling at the beauty before her. Her smile made Ethan even more relaxed, he was hoping she wouldn't get nervous, or think it was stupid.

"Ethan." Rachel looked down at her lap. She appeared to be thinking of the words to say. "I never got a chance to talk to you at the wake. I know how much your mother meant to you, and I'm so sorry. I wanted to call you so many times, I really did, but I didn't want to—I'm not even sure what to say."

"Thank you," Ethan said. He could still remember seeing Rachel at the wake and the funeral. He had only given her a quick hug that day. He didn't talk to anyone. He was completely distraught.

"Why do you come here?" she asked, staring at Ethan cautiously and trying to change the subject.

There he was, staring at the moon, his mind already feeling so much lighter than it had before. He still couldn't figure out who was terrorizing so many innocent people. He still couldn't figure out who was cleverly staying fifty feet ahead of the F.B.I., but as he lay there he started to gain some of his notorious confidence back. He wasn't afraid to tell Rachel why he came here; he was going to tell her the truth.

"I come here to relive the past. I face my fears and I try and embrace them," Ethan said, turning his head to look into Rachel's gorgeous eyes. He resisted the unimaginable urge to kiss those perfect lips. "Facing it helps me beat it."

"This is where you've always come, even back in the day?" Rachel asked, still staring into Ethan's eyes.

"Yeah…If I hold it in too long I explode, and I hate losing control." Ethan turned his head, staring up at the moon again. He looked out the front windshield, staring off into the dark, staring at the stop sign in the intersection he had just turned from. He fought hard to tell Rachel the rest because he wanted to. He finally had someone with him, someone real that he could talk to, but still he was too much of a coward. He concealed his anxiety and his anger of feeling so cowardly.

"What's wrong?" Rachel asked. She could see right through him, she had been there before. "Just tell me Ethan, you can talk to me."

Ethan felt a tiny burst of anger. Could he talk to her? He hadn't seen Rachel in about seven years before she popped up unexpectedly. He closed his eyes and counted to five, a technique he used often when he wanted to simmer down.

"That house right there," he said pointing at a giant white house up ahead. The house was barely visible. The landscaping was exquisite, a very nice touch to an already beautiful home. In the driveway sat a brand new BMW sedan and a clean, white fence separated the house from the wooded area around it. "That's where Andrew lives."

Rachel stared ahead, looking at the house in amazement. She had never met Ethan's father let alone see his house. She was shocked to see they were sitting only a block away since she wouldn't have guessed Ethan would want to be so close.

Sitting there in the driver's seat, Ethan smiled. He knew exactly what she was thinking, and he was tired of holding it in. "I don't know Rachel, but when I'm here…" He stopped talking, trying to put the words together in his head before he came out with it. He had only ever said it to himself, in his own head not even out loud. Rachel sat still, not moving a muscle as she awaited his explanation. Ethan appreciated the fact that she wasn't trying to touch him; she remembered how much he hated being touched when he was in an uncomfortable spot.

"It makes me feel better when I'm here." Ethan stopped talking as he smiled widely, shaking his head. "I hate him...I hate him more than anything, Rachel. I think about him, and I seriously try and figure out what he is. How could a human do this to his child? How could a human being just abandon his own flesh and blood? Just walk away from everything and not look back?" Ethan felt furious, his fists clenched tightly by his sides.

Rachel lay quietly next to Ethan, not daring to touch him. She still knew he hated being touched him while he felt vulnerable. She completely understood him, though.

"I don't know why I sit here. I just do." Ethan felt hurt inside. He wished he could just take it back. Drive back to the city, go to his apartment, sleep with Rachel and never call her again. The demons raged inside his head, banging hard against his skull creating a splitting headache. "This was a mistake...I shouldn't have brought you here."

He sat up, turning the car on and throwing it into drive. Rachel also sat up, feeling slightly hurt by Ethan's words.

"Ethan," she said as Ethan drove back down the long dark path.

He kept his eyes straight and on the road, his face straight with no emotion, but inside he felt horrible. 'Why,' he thought to himself. 'Why can't I just talk?' He could feel her eyes on him, burning through him as she read all of his emotions, all of his troubles. 'If only she knew about the case I was on,' he thought to himself.

"I know how hard it is. You know everything about me, everything," she stared at Ethan, hoping for some sign of emotion. Ethan knew how terrible her past was. It had been a much different agony for her, something he could never relate to. "I don't want you to force it out. I like being with you, I like being next to you, it's okay if you feel like you can't tell me things. I just want to be here with you, I want to see what happens, where this goes. I don't want it to end up like last time."

Ethan appreciated her words more than she could ever know. He looked over at her, the Charger roaring down the Taconic, and he smiled.

"Thank you," he said. "You're the only one to ever see what I just showed you."

Rachel leaned back in her seat. The stars were so bright outside the car window, the moon still as incredible as it shone down on the trees, an ominous white glow appearing at their tops. They both sat in the car, smiling slightly as Ethan drove to his apartment. He couldn't believe what he was about to do. He couldn't recall ever doing it before. He would spend a night with a woman he genuinely liked, and he wouldn't try anything.

Chapter 34

Loyalty

The park lights illuminated the clear sky of the cool October night. The happy sounds danced around Ethan, Andrew, Michelle, Ray, and Aiden as they walked through the crowd at the Yorktown Heights' Annual Autumn Celebration. There were a lot more people at this thing than Ethan had expected. It was unusually packed for a city fair. There were small children running all over the place, screaming and laughing as they enjoyed their youth. People lined up along an assortment of colorful trailers, playing different carnival games with big stuffed prizes hanging there with toothy grins, waiting to be taken by the lucky winners.

The carnival was decked out with some incredible rides. They weren't all stupid kiddy rides, but some actual close-your-eyes-and-scream rides. Ethan had his eye set on one ride in particular: The Lightning Streak. He could see the majestic, enormous roller coaster up ahead, towering above everything else. Its candy red and bright yellow tracks intertwined around each other as a long, thin car filled with screaming passengers flew over it. Ethan couldn't take his eyes off the beast. He needed to be on it.

"Dad, you see that roller coaster?" he asked, pointing to the masterpiece. "We have to ride that!"

"Definitely buddy," his father said, holding his hand out for a high five. Ethan smacked his hand, smiling to himself as he stared at the roller coaster.

He looked over at Aiden, seeing that his cousin was much quieter than usual. He seemed upset about something; he wasn't smiling as much as normal. Something was different. Ethan walked over to his cousin, putting his arm around Aiden's shoulders.

"What's wrong?" he asked, seeing his cousin wince in pain as Ethan's arm landed across Aiden's back. Ethan could see a small welt on the side of Aiden's head and some red streaking at the bottom of his T-shirt.

"Let's go this way," Aiden said, pointing towards the haunted house out on the right side of the carnival. Ethan was taken aback by his abrupt response.

"Alright, hold on," Ethan said, turning to tell his father. Aiden grabbed Ethan's hand, shaking his head in disapproval.

"No," he said. "Come on, hurry up."

Ethan walked away from the group, staring worriedly at his cousin. He couldn't understand what his problem was. Ethan didn't think anything was really wrong. The roller coaster stood menacingly, taunting him as he walked away from it. All he really wanted was to have a good time with his father. But as badly as he wanted to have some fun, he could easily tell his cousin was upset about something. Though he wasn't completely comfortable about walking away from the group, he wasn't about to leave Aiden alone.

He stood there, staring his cousin in the eyes. Aiden stared back at him looking confident, like he knew exactly what he wanted. He was measuring Ethan up, the two may have only been about eleven but Aiden and Ethan were being forced to grow up at an alarmingly fast rate. They didn't know it, because to them this was life, it was normal.

"I'm leaving, Ethan," Aiden said. There was no doubt in his tone of voice, his mind was made up and his course of action was well planned. "This isn't how it should be."

Ethan stared at his cousin like he was crazy. He had never heard Aiden sound this way. He knew things were horrible at Aiden's house, but he never anticipated this. He never realized how bad Aiden actually had it.

"Isn't how what should be," Ethan answered, knowing exactly what Aiden was talking about. He wanted to hear what his cousin had to say, yet he wanted to postpone the inevitable.

Aiden shook his head, rubbing it while he winced. "I was thrown aside yesterday trying to get between my mom and James." Aiden parted his hair, showing Ethan his battle scar. "I'm tired of it, Ethan, I know this isn't how things should be. Don't you hear them at school? No one else deals with this."

Bouncing back and forth was different. Seeing Dad every Wednesday and every other weekend wasn't normal…but maybe it was. Ethan couldn't figure it out, he hadn't seen enough, but all he knew was Aiden was planning something drastic and he couldn't let that happen.

"I know but why don't you just tell my dad?" Ethan said. He knew he didn't want to leave with Aiden. Where would they go? How would they survive? They were still so young. "You can't run away Aiden, where are you gunna go?"

Aiden shook his head again, angry at his cousin's misunderstanding and resistance. He stared back at Ethan confused.

"Ethan, does it matter? All I know is I'm running away, I'm not coming back," Aiden said staring at Ethan with his eyes wide. Ethan knew exactly what he was about to ask next. "Are you coming?"

The fear was finally evident in his cousin's eyes. Aiden was scared. He didn't want to go alone; he wanted his cousin, his idol, with him.

"Aiden, we can't...just let me talk to my dad," Ethan said, looking around to see if his father was anywhere in sight.

Aiden disgustedly looked at Ethan. He was shocked at his cousin's decision, in his mind he believed Ethan was breaking his loyalty, choosing to walk away rather than stick by him.

"You never helped me!" Aiden yelled. He lunged forward, pushing Ethan hard, both of his hands planting firmly into Ethan's chest. Ethan stumbled back a few steps before he hit the ground hard. He let out a small groan as the back of his head hit against the floor. Quickly he reached up, rubbing it to soothe the pain. He stared up at his cousin who still looked so dejected, so disgusted. "You're always afraid...you're a little bitch."

A crowd of people had stopped nearby, staring at the two boys. A woman walked over to help pick Ethan up as Andrew, Michelle, and Ray rushed over.

"Ethan!" his father yelled. "Why would you run off like that?" His father held Ethan by the shoulders, looking back at Aiden who was still furious. Andrew could see the anger in his nephew; he could see there had been a fight. "Let's go."

Ethan's father held him by the arm with one hand and held Aiden with the other as the group marched out of the festival, away from the small crowd of people who stared judgingly. The people of Yorktown had hundreds of skeletons in their own closets, but they all loved to believe their shit didn't stink. They judged, they criticized, and they mocked each other to no end, the phoniest of the phony.

Their disapproving stares and their repulsion followed the group right to their car, but Ethan could care less what they thought. He hated them all; they were exactly what his father wanted to be. Andrew Alosi wanted to live amongst the phoniest of the phony. He wanted the *friendship of those who were loyal to your face and worst enemies when you walked away. He wanted the lifestyle of the rich and the famous.*

He couldn't believe Aiden had just cursed at him. He looked over at his cousin; the look of defeat in his eyes was too blatant. 'What did he want me to do,' Ethan thought to himself. 'Did he really want me to just run off blindly? That's crazy.'

As they made their way out of the parking lot, in the car humming along as quiet as could be, Ethan stared out at The Lightning Streak which zoomed along its track high above the rest of the fair. That coaster was so awesome. 'It just never works out,' he thought to himself.

Chapter 35

Inevitable

The room was icy cold as the winter air poured through an open window, and the bright light shone from the TV. ESPN echoed off the walls as Ethan tossed and turned, sweat trickling down off his forehead. His face was distorted. He murmured here and there as he rocked the bed. Suddenly he jumped up right in time to hear a knock at the door. He stared panting, rubbing his face with his hands trying to shake off the grogginess and confusion.

The knock sounded again, this time a little louder than the last. Ethan continued to stare at his front door. It was clearly visible through his bedroom doorway. He looked over to the left seeing Rachel was fast asleep, breathing lightly and looking even more angelic than usual. He couldn't take his eyes off of her, but the grogginess was slowly wearing off and confusion was settling in. He couldn't imagine who would be visiting him so late.

Before he could figure it out, the knocking sounded again, this time even louder. Ethan jumped out of his bed, grabbing his gun off his dresser as he slowly walked over to the front door. Step by step, Ethan inched his way to the gray door, holding his breath as he tried to hear anything from the other side.

Again the knocking sounded, this time it was a light tapping. Ethan looked back, making sure that Rachel was still asleep, but Rachel was suddenly gone. His body loosened up as he stared in disbelief. The bed was empty. There was definitely nobody else in that room. Ethan looked back at the front door, seeing that it was now wide open. He ran his hand through his hair as he looked from his bedroom to his front doorway, now revealing the mysterious living room he kept seeing.

"Rachel!" Ethan screamed. He screamed it at the top of his lungs. "Rachel!" He screamed her name again, running back into his empty bedroom. He checked his ammo, seeing a full clip of bullets, and then turned back to his front door.

He hadn't even realized he wasn't wearing a shirt. His skin was bare and freezing as he stood there in his apartment, completely freaked out.

"Ethan!" a voice screamed from outside of his apartment. "Ethan!" The blood curdling scream echoed through his apartment, rattling Ethan's nerves. The voice wasn't normal. The voice was full of desperation and agony. Ethan walked slowly down his hallway, walking towards what sounded like a whimpering, whining small boy.

"Is someone there?" Ethan called out, his gun ready as he slowly made his way through the doorway. Ethan's eyes widened. His gun dropped to his side as he rushed into the room, his eyes peeled as he took in the surroundings. He dropped his gun to the floor and dropped down to his knees in front of his cousin Aiden. Aiden knelt in the middle of the room holding his head and moaning. "Aiden—It's me, Ethan. Buddy, what's wrong?" Ethan said, worried.

Aiden was shaking and rocking back and forth as he continued to cry uncontrollably. Ethan put his hands on his cousin's shoulders, staring at him confused. Aiden removed his hands from his head, revealing a huge gash across his forehead, the blood seeping from it profusely. His eyes were bloodshot red and veiny, and tears poured out on to his cheeks as he stared up at Ethan.

"Why?" he said, his words stumbling out through the whimpering and tears. He sniffed up violently as he shook his head, placing his hands on his thighs. "Why!" he screamed as he started to punch himself viciously. Ethan fell back startled, staring at his cousin with wide eyes.

He checked around the room, noticing a knitted quilt draped over a couch against the wall, and jumped up to retrieve it. He needed something to stop the bleeding. The crying grew louder and louder as Ethan jumped over to the couch, grabbed the quilt and spun around to help his cousin. As he turned back around, he saw that Aiden was gone.

The room had grown quiet instantly, and the sound of the moaning and the tears stopped abruptly. Ethan stood still, the quilt still in his hand as he stared around the room confused again.

"Aiden!" he yelled. He quickly picked his gun back up, loading it as he noticed the wall unit in the corner of the room. The giant, wooden antique sat there alone, nothing else but the unadorned couch next to it. Ethan quickly glanced around again, still seeing nothing, as he turned his attention back to the wall unit. It looked so familiar to him, that stupid wooden piece of furniture. He had seen that same exact one before.

The top of the wall unit had a glass pane most likely to fashionably display the decorations inside. Ethan walked forward trying to get a better look. He could see there was something there, but the glare from the light was making it hard to see. As he stood in front of the wall unit, he saw that the display shelf was empty, and then the lights went out.

Ethan crouched down, getting as low to the floor as he could, and held his breath. He listened carefully for any sign of life. He had a feeling he wasn't alone. He closed his eyes lightly, straining his ears to hear, but there was nothing to be heard. The room was dead.

Suddenly, the lights flashed back on. Almost instantly, a loud piercing scream erupted, sending sharp pains through Ethan's body. He cringed, his body twisting distortedly. He could see a small object out of the corner of his eye. It looked to be a person but he couldn't turn to see, the pain was so excruciating he could barely move at all. Ethan let out a loud scream as he grabbed his hair, his muscles contracting painfully.

Ethan jerked awake in his bed, sweat covering his body. He panted heavily, desperately trying to catch his breath. Just another bad dream on a different night. He sat there, attempting to control his breathing as he looked around the room. Rachel wasn't lying next to him.

The light knock at the door shot déjà vu at Ethan. He stared at the door, contemplating if he was imagining things, as he struggled to remember everything in his dream. He lay back down, staring at the empty space next to him, trying to remember what had happened to Rachel but he kept drawing a blank. Rachel had surely fallen asleep next to him, at least he thought she did, yet here he was in an empty bedroom. A knock sounded at his front door again, this one louder than the first.

Ethan sat up again, rubbing his eyes as he stared at his door. It was almost 6:00 a.m. on Saturday morning, who could possibly be at his door so early in the morning? Ethan threw his sheet aside and jumped out of the bed, walking over to the door to find out who the nuisance was. As he approached it, the knock sounded again, but this time accompanied by a low voice.

"Ethan, it's me," Rachel said, sounding irritated. Ethan looked through his peep hole seeing the girl standing in the middle of his hallway. She was dressed in her pajamas and staring around the hallway as she reached her hand out to knock again. Ethan couldn't remember why she had gone out; he couldn't even remember falling asleep next to her, all he knew was he was happy to see her there.

He opened the door, smiling as he looked on to see the most beautiful girl in the world, but instead he was sent flying backwards, his body hitting the floor hard as he slid back gasping to catch his breath.

The foot had struck him square in his midsection, right between the chest and the abdomen, knocking the wind out of him. He let out an angry groan as he regained his composure, staring up at the barrel of a gun. He wheezed in pain, squeezing his eyes shut as he endured the sharp agony still coursing through his body. The kick was hard and shocking. He wasn't ready for such a vicious attack.

The assailant had already closed the door, advancing in on the defenseless Ethan as he staggered on the ground trying to gain his footing. He knew he was done, he had let his guard down and now it was all over. He had never gotten close to a girl and now as he took on a high profile case he decided to take on a relationship. He decided to tear the walls down and let someone in, and now his inanity had him staring down the barrel of an enemy's firearm.

"You were never there for me," the voice said. Ethan held his stomach as he stared beyond the gun into his cousin's eyes.

"Aiden?" he said, surprised to see his cousin in his apartment. "What are you doing?" He still felt queasy from the kick to his body as he got to his feet.

Aiden stood his ground, his gun still pointed squarely at Ethan's chest as he suddenly pulled the trigger. Ethan let out a scream of agony as he fell back again, grabbing his chest as the blood poured over his hands. He stared up at Aiden wide eyed as his knees hit the floor, he could feel his breath shortening. He closed his eyes; the pain was so sharp, almost unbearable. All he could do was clench his teeth.

"You were never there for me," Aiden repeated. Ethan felt himself spacing out, and it felt like the floor underneath him felt like it was falling apart. He stared up at Aiden, but he was no longer there.

"You can't," a voice said from the side of his room. Ethan lay on the floor, tears falling from his eyes as he looked over to see his father leaning against his dresser. "You don't have it in you." His father smiled down at him, his black hair neatly combed to the side.

"Ethan!" Rachel's voice screamed out. Ethan looked around but he couldn't see anything as he dropped his head down to the floor. The room was spinning now. His father's face was taunting him, still smiling as the blood continued to gush from his chest. His hands were caked in his own blood as he let go of his wound, placing his lifeless hands by his sides.

"Ethan!" Rachel screamed again. Ethan jumped out of his bed, sweat dripping from his forehead as he gasped for breath. He grabbed at his naked chest, feeling for the hole, looking around to see that his sheets were clean of blood and his front door was closed and locked. He stared around in a panic as Rachel reached out to touch his shoulder.

"Get off of me!" Ethan screamed, smacking her hand away. Rachel gasped in surprise, jumping off the bed to get away from him. He sat there alone, his sheets thrown off of him as he panted, sweat still covering his face. Rachel watched him terrified, not sure of what to do.

"I'm sorry," Ethan said, still panting heavily as he relived the dream over and over in his head. He looked over at Rachel who still stared at him cautiously. He didn't know what to say, he didn't know what to make of it himself, so he just lay down again speechless. Rachel lay in the bed with him, leaning up on her elbow, still staring cautiously while hoping for an explanation.

They had a great night together. It was the first time he could remember that there had been a female in his bedroom without any sexual activity. They stayed up together talking about old times, reliving the good moments as well as the bad, and watching TV until they finally knocked out.

Ethan now lay still, still trying to catch his breath as he tried to come up with some words to break the awkward silence. Rachel acted first.

"What was it about?" she asked, lying on her side as she stared at Ethan worried. He looked down at her, staring into her worried eyes, but he couldn't come up with anything to say. He just wanted to ignore it had ever happened, the way he would if he were alone. 'This is why I can't do this. I can't be with someone,' he thought to himself.

"It was nothing," he said back. "Just a bad dream." She looked at him critically, scrutinizing him before she rolled onto her back, visibly annoyed.

'What did she expect?' Ethan thought. 'I meet her again for the first time in almost nine years and she already wants my deep, dark secrets?' As much as Ethan tried to come up with excuses, he felt something he had never felt before. He looked at Rachel, and he saw things he didn't see in any other girl. He wanted the best for her, he wanted her to be safe, and he wanted to hear her voice, to see her smile, to smell her scent. He felt more than comfortable with her, he felt correct.

"My cousin shot me," Ethan said. He knew he couldn't reveal too much. He couldn't get into the details of the case. "It felt so real, I felt the bullet go through my body, I could feel the thickness of my blood on my hands, the room spin…it was one of those dreams."

"When's the last time you saw your cousin?" Rachel asked, turning back onto her side to face him.

"Probably around when my cousin John-David passed away, a little before I started to date you," he said, trying to remember if Rachel had ever met his cousin.

Ethan didn't see the need to elaborate on his dream, he figured that was enough. He was sure Rachel could figure out he was withholding some of the dream, but at least he had told her some of it.

The one thing Ethan knew was what he had been juggling in his mind for some time now. It was inevitable, something Ethan had to face. He had to man up and get it done. He would have to go retrieve a warrant to raid the house on Hull Ave. He would need to arrest his cousin under suspicion of murder.

Chapter 36

Unique

The two spent the rest of the day enjoying themselves. They had breakfast at a nice diner on Lexington, Ron Black's, and then took a long walk around the city popping into a few stores here and there. Ethan had completely forgotten about the case, he had forgotten about his cousin, about his dream, about murders and puzzles. He was happy, he was smiling, he was laughing, and he was holding someone's hand who meant something to him.

"What time is that party again?" Rachel asked as they strolled down 79th Street. She was wearing a pair of jeans, a long sleeved, pink shirt, and an unzipped, white winter jacket. Her long brunette hair draped over her jacket elegantly. Even when she hadn't done anything with herself cosmetically, the woman looked perfect.

"It's starting around seven, I think," Ethan answered. He was wearing his typical white t-shirt, blue jeans, and leather jacket. "You want a ride home so you can get ready?"

Ethan glanced at his watch and realized it was already almost 3:00 in the afternoon, and they were about ten long blocks from his car. He knew how Rachel was about getting ready for special occasions. He could still remember all the times he had to wait outside of her house while she ran around getting dressed, doing her makeup, and filling her purse. If that's what she was like for regular date nights, he figured New Year's Eve warranted some serious primping time.

"Yeah, wow," Rachel said, looking down at her wrist watch. "I didn't realize how late it was." The two walked back to the Charger, holding hands and talking the entire way.

It was a beautiful winter day in New York City. The wind wasn't too cold, the sky was clear and blue, and the sun was warm. Ethan would have loved to go to a movie and dinner, maybe even go check out the tree at Rockefeller Center, but he had committed to the party and he was sure that was a great invite. He couldn't believe he was even thinking this way at all.

Ethan dropped Rachel off at her house. The two stared at each other for a few seconds before Rachel opened the door and hopped out. He had just gone on a date with a girl, held her hand, and didn't kiss her. As he drove back to his apartment he felt a little disappointed with himself. He had really wanted to kiss Rachel again after all these years, knowing there was absolutely nothing wrong with an innocent kiss, yet he found himself too nervous.

His phone started to vibrate as he pulled into a spot. He was wondering when Chris was going to call. He assumed his partner would want to hear what had happened.

"What's going on," Ethan asked, picking up the phone with a smile.

"Oh yeah, Ethan Carey," Chris responded laughing. "How'd it go man?"

"Not too bad, she's a great woman," Ethan said. He waited a little to hear if Chris would say anything, but realized his partner was waiting for a more elaborate recount. "We hung out, I didn't want to take it to the next level…she's the same great girl I knew before. I'm just trying not to get too crazy."

Ethan trudged up the nineteen flights of steps until he got to his floor. The stairs were a little more taxing than usual today, probably because of all the walking he had done with Rachel.

"Ethan, you're not getting crazy, don't even think like that. That's all awesome news though, I'm happy for you," Chris said. Ethan didn't want to make a big deal out of it, and he knew Chris didn't either. In the back of their minds was the inevitable: a killer on the loose who was targeting both Ethan and the world of deadbeat parents. As Ethan turned to enter his apartment, he was abruptly stopped.

"Ethan!" a voice screamed out. Ethan had just arrived in front of his door as he spun to see Ed excitedly running towards him, with Roddick keeping up alongside him. Any thoughts that had popped into Ethan's head were immediately disrupted. "Ethan! I was about to ring your bell!"

"Hey, let me let you go, I'm about to walk into my apartment. I'll see you around 7:00," Ethan said into the phone, putting up a finger and nodding at Ed.

"No problem, I'll see you later," Chris said, as Ethan closed his phone, and put it back into his pants pocket.

"What's up, dude?" Ethan said as he put out his hand. Ed fervently slapped it.

"Ethan, please can you take me to the park! All of my friends are sleigh riding, and I really wanna go! Please! Please! Please!" Ed put up his hands as though he was praying...his tiny face glistened with hope.

Ethan looked down at the boy nervously. He wasn't the biggest fan of children, he was extremely tired and had hoped to take a quick nap before the party, and he definitely felt a little awkward taking the kid sleigh riding. He was close friends with Luke, but he had never been alone with Ed or Laura for a long enough time to grow a bond. The kid hopped back and forth, his hands still held up in prayer, as thoughts began to form in Ethan's mind.

"Is your dad around?" Ethan said as he looked at his neighbor's door.

"My dad's busy in his study and my mom hates the winter. She didn't even want to walk Roddick because of how cold it is." Ed pointed down to his ecstatic dog. Ethan had never seen such a lively dog before. "I'll only be there for an hour. Everyone's leaving by 5:00." Ethan put his head back for a second. 'How could I say no to this?' he thought as he looked back down at the beggar.

"Just let your dad and mom know, I'll go inside and get changed."

"YEAH!" Ed screamed. The scream actually shocked Ethan as the kid darted off towards his apartment. Before Ethan could even get his key in the door, Luke popped his head into the hallway.

"You sure, Ethan?" he asked. Even from yards away Ethan could read the confusion on his friend's face.

"Yeah, it's fine. We'll be back by 5:00."

"Alright, great—I'll send him over when he's ready."

Ethan barely had time to grab a scarf and some winter gloves before he heard the bell ring.

"One minute!" he screamed as he took his gun off and locked it in his drawer. He grabbed a hat off of his dresser and put it on before checking himself out in the mirror. 'Calm down, Ethan. The kid just wants to go sleigh riding...it's not a big deal.'

The two walked down the lively streets, making their short trip to Central Park. Ed was nearly skipping, his face beaming with happiness as he dragged his old fashioned, wooden sled behind him. Ethan picked the sled up, examining it as they continued to the park.

"You know I had a sled like this, too," Ethan said as he put the sleigh back on the snowy ground. "My father used to take me sleigh riding every winter." Ethan laughed as he thought back to one particular memory. "One year I nearly broke every bone in my body."

"How?" Ed asked. Ethan was surprised to see he was actually interested. He didn't even think the kid was listening.

"The snow was icy and thin. I flew down the hill by my house and nearly crashed head-on into a tree. I jumped off in time…the sled crashed though… it didn't break but it did chip a lot." Ethan looked down at Ed's sled. "This one is pretty messed up too, don't you want another one?"

"No way," Ed said, shaking his head. "My dad gave me this sled; I've had it my whole life." Ethan chuckled at Ed's reference to his whole seven years of living.

"Well you wouldn't want to get rid of such an antique. It has sentimental value."

Central Park was absolutely gorgeous in the winter. Ethan stood at the top of a fairly steep hill, looking out at the beautiful scenery. The children's laughter in the background, the happy families all smiling peacefully, the snow perfectly draped across each tree branch creating a winter wonderland…it was like something out of a fairy tale. Ethan watched Ed as he fooled around with his school friends, throwing snowballs and building forts...they were kids just being kids.

Ethan didn't even care, at that point, about all the years he had sat around waiting for his father to pick him up. All the times he had been promised a day in the snow with his idol. All the times he had sat on his front step waiting pointlessly. Ethan smiled as he watched Ed laugh. He didn't feel jealousy. He didn't feel envy of his friend Luke for having this family. He wasn't sure if it was the emergence of Rachel in his life, if it was the storybook scene he was staring at, or if it was the lack of sleep that had him feeling soft. For once Ethan was hopeful and optimistic about his own future.

"Is he yours?" a woman said, walking over to stand by Ethan. She was a pretty woman with blonde hair flowing down her brown jacket. She also had her make-up done nicely.

'Uh oh,' Ethan thought.

Ethan pointed at Ed. "No, no he's a friend's," Ethan said laughing. "They were busy so I lent them a hand."

"That's really nice of you," the woman said, smiling and touching Ethan's arm. "Do you live nearby?"

'Oh boy,' Ethan said to himself.

"I actually do. I'm sorry but I have to get him home now. He has a New Year's Eve party to go to in an hour."

"Oh, that's too bad. Are you doing anything for New Years? This is the first year I have no plans. Jayden's father left us a few months ago," she said, still keeping her eyes directly on Ethan.

'And there it is…' he thought.

"I'm really sorry. I just started seeing someone— hey Ed—time to go," Ethan waved down at the boy who sprinted back up the hill. "Maybe I'll see you around?"

Without a word the woman gave Ethan a nasty look and walked away.

"Did you see me hit that guy?" Ed exclaimed. His smile stretched from ear to ear.

"Yes I did, sir. Did you have fun?"

"Yeah!"

The two walked back to the apartment and hopped onto the elevator. Ethan held the sled in front of him, smiling as he was reminded of his own. As soon as the elevator doors opened, Ed darted down the hallway.

'Kid is just like his dog,' Ethan thought. As he approached his doorway, Ed jumped towards Ethan, embracing him tightly as the FBI Agent looked down stunned.

"Thanks a lot Ethan, you're the best," Ed said as he let Ethan go. He ran back down the hall and knocked on his door. Luke opened it and laughed as Ed flew through the doorway.

"Thank you Ethan," Luke said.

Ethan had been meaning to talk to Luke since the night before in front of Sal's. 'Since I'm trying new things, I might as well give the doctor a shot,' Ethan thought. The dreams were getting out of control, these visions of his father were messing with his head, and he needed to solve this problem before he could solve any others.

"What's up doc, do you have a minute?" Ethan said. Luke laughed back at Ethan's question as he walked out into the hallway.

"Minute?" Luke said surprised as he inviting Ethan inside. "Come in Ethan, we have more than a minute before we have to get ready."

Ethan felt bad because he knew how much it sucked to have your job follow you everywhere you went. He felt like he was cornering the guy, but he really couldn't push it off anymore. Ethan walked into the doctor's beautiful apartment and was almost instantly greeted by Roddick. The little dog jumped all over Ethan, he could barely take a step without nearly stepping on him.

He knelt down to pet the dog as Ed ran in. Robert Edward was such a small, scrawny boy for his age. The boy had a huge heart, the biggest reason why Ethan liked the kid; he just never lost his giant smile. Ethan still felt good from when he was called "the best."

"Ethan!" Ed screamed. "I can't wait for the party!" Ed had a huge smile from ear to ear as he ran up to Ethan, slapping him a high five. "Mom and Dad found out I didn't finish my English homework. Do you think you can help me?"

Before Ethan had a chance to answer the little guy, he had already run off to his room to get his homework. Ethan laughed as he looked over at Luke who smiled back shaking his head.

"He's excited about the party," Luke said laughing. "You know he tried out for the Babe Ruth League the other day? He made the first cut too. We might have the future face of the Yankees in front of us. I think it's ridiculous that they start the kids so early...I mean it's December...but he likes it so what can I do?" Ethan nodded his head in agreement as Ed came sprinting back into the hallway. "Robert, leave Ethan alone, Daddy and Ethan have to talk inside for a little while."

"Don't worry about it, I can take a quick look," Ethan said, looking at Luke to see if it was alright. Luke shook his head and walked over to Ed, picking up the notebook to examine the child's work. It was very easy to tell that Ed hadn't done what the directions had indicated. Luke handed the notebook back to Ed and put his hands on his hips as he stared down at the boy.

"Alright, I'm sorry," Ed said, putting his head back and sighing as he marched back to his room.

Luke nodded his head towards a doorway near the front door, ushering Ethan inside to a study. Had Ethan not known Luke was a psychiatrist he could have easily guessed it by just looking at this room. It was lined with books and fancy furniture. The floor was carpeted in a nice burgundy rug, with gold lining running through it. Ethan sat down on a plush velour couch, putting his feet up on the matching ottoman as Luke sat down behind his desk, opening a notebook in front of him. Ethan was all too familiar with the practice of psychiatry. The note taking, the couches, the peaceful setting—it was like Psychiatry 101.

"Same homework since Monday," Luke said, shaking his head. "I told him to finish it a couple of days ago, the kid just doesn't listen. Teacher has them doing some injudicious winter holiday assignment on the foundation of America." Luke shook his head and rolled his eyes. "I don't know why they become teachers; they don't give a shit whether these kids acquire knowledge just as long as the summer comes."

Ethan shrugged his shoulders. He didn't know what it was like to have a kid, nor did he really want to know about it just yet.

"You taking notes on me?" Ethan asked smiling. "Not my first time being a patient."

Luke laughed. "I want to help a friend out in the best way I can. Would you rather me not?" Ethan shook his head, gesturing for Luke to continue his note taking. "To be honest I've been given all these awards and I'd probably have none of them if it weren't for this," Luke said as he pointed around the room at all of his plaques and then back down at his notebook. "I'm sure you feel the same as me, it's better to let things settle sometimes...you don't always see everything right off the bat."

Ethan stared at Luke, chuckling to himself. 'If you only knew,' he thought. Ethan looked around the office, seeing the doctor's diploma from Loyola College and his Master's from Pace. He could see all the pictures of him with different people, seemingly "big wigs" from the Psychiatry community. Ethan thought for a second about the possibility he had never thought of. What if Luke Lianessa could actually fix him? What if this decorated doctor could actually crack the thick shell so many had given up on? Ethan realized he had come to the guy with the wrong intentions. He never even expected to get fixed.

Luke stared at Ethan confused. "So...what's up?" he said, leaning forward and removing his glasses, polishing them with a piece of cloth from his desk.

Ethan shook his head and shrugged his shoulders. "I've been having...very real dreams. I've also been seeing my father...while I'm awake. Like in a mirror or a quick flash of him when I turn a corner, doesn't really matter where I am." Ethan had played tennis with Luke, he had eaten dinner with him and his wife, but never had he said a single word to him about his father. He had never told Luke a single thing about his personal life.

The door to the study opened and Laura, Luke's wife, came walking in holding two pairs of shoes in her hands. "Honey, which one..." she stopped short as she saw Ethan sitting on the couch. "Oh my God, I'm so sorry; I didn't know you were here, Ethan."

Ethan smiled as he jumped up, hugging the woman. He liked Laura a lot, she was a great mother. Laura was beautiful also. She was about 5'5'' and had long curly blonde hair and blue eyes. She was the typical southern belle except nowhere near ditsy. She was one smart cookie. Ethan had watched countless debates at the dinner table over politics or religion. All the debates always ended with, "I'm so sorry Ethan, that's so rude of us...But you would agree with me, right?"

"It's not a problem," Ethan said, sitting back down as Laura backed up to the door.

"Sorry, sorry, sorry, i'll leave you guys alone," she said as she scampered back out of the room.

"The left one!" Luke yelled as she closed the door. He laughed and looked back at Ethan, leaning back in his chair. "Continue please, I'm sorry about that."

Even the slightest distraction had Ethan second guessing what he was doing. This situation was putting him way out of his comfort zone. He shrugged his shoulders and continued.

"I'm not sure what the problem is…lately it's been getting worse." Ethan looked up at Luke, he knew a few guys in the field office who had seen therapists. He wasn't sure what the rule on revealing confidential material was when it came to a shrink, and he definitely didn't want anyone at work to know his business. Ethan knew what the next question was going to be.

"Can you tell me more about your father?" Luke asked, still sitting up straight, listening attentively. Ethan was shocked. He was sure the next question would be directed at what was going on lately but Luke took a different turn. "How do you feel when you see him?"

"I get angry," Ethan said, feeling the anger bubble inside. "Just the thought of him can get me going, but I deal with it."

"What makes you angry?" Luke asked calmly, writing a few things down in his notebook.

"My father's a coward…he's a piece of shit in my eyes," Ethan said, shaking his head at his choice of words. When it came to his father, there was so much to say that he couldn't figure out the perfect way to summarize it. It would take far too much time to give the full, complete reason as to why he hated his father, but when asked to give it all in a nutshell he was stumped. "My father taught me one thing in life."

"What would that be?" Luke asked curiously.

"He taught me how to be a man," Ethan said, smiling wryly, knowing how weird it sounded. He couldn't help but think about that one time, that one memorable phone call he had in his 1984 Buick Regal.

Luke leaned forward, scribbling a few things into his notebook and staring at Ethan curiously.

"You said you think your father is still with us, right? Have you ever thought about reaching out to him? It might do you good if we could get him in here for a group session," Luke said, still scribbling in his notebook. Ethan shook his head in response, which Luke immediately acknowledged.

"It's been like this for a long time now, I have nightmares, I have visions, I wake up violently, I have commitment issues…like I'm seriously scared to settle down…I tense up, a hundred reasons flash in my head of why I should run the other way. I try hard to swallow it, to push forward and be normal."

"Ethan, there's nothing wrong with you; this is all normal behavior for someone as hurt as you are. I understand you don't want to talk to me about your father right now; you don't want to get into specifics, so let's just talk about anything else. In time you'll come to open up, you don't have to force yourself. You don't have to be the macho guy you think you have to be."

"I'm not trying to be a macho guy…" Ethan put his head in his hands, closing his eyes to try and reset…unwind a little. He looked at Luke who leaned back so calmly. Ethan felt like a wimp, like a coward. He felt like he was sitting here like a drama queen while there were millions of people in the same exact boat as him not being as pathetic. Maybe they all didn't have a psycho blowing them kisses, but they all had their own problems. "What makes me different?"

Luke shook his head slowly, "I'm sorry?"

"Why am I here? What makes me different from everyone else, from Rachel, from Chris, from the million other children whose parents quit?"

"Is Rachel your date?" Luke asked, scribbling even faster now.

"Yes. Luke...I want to talk, I want to explode," Ethan said laughing to himself, shaking his head in frustration. "I just can't. I try to get the words out and I feel like my throat closes. I feel like if I just forget about it all, I'll be alright, but then I fall asleep and my world is rocked. Then I turn a corner and I see him standing there." Ethan realized how pathetic he looked now. He was pleading to Luke, praying that this man, this doctor, could save him.

Luke nodded his head and closed his notebook, taking a look at his wristwatch.

"What you did right now is great. We're done for today and I definitely want to see you again," Luke said as he got up, placing his notebook in his drawer and locking it. He sat on the edge of his desk, taking off his glasses and placing them down next to him. Luke was a handsome man, he was well kept, his hair freshly trimmed, combed perfectly, his facial hair neatly shaven and almost nonexistent. "You have about two hours to get ready for the best New Year's Party you'll ever go to."

Ethan got up from the comfortable arm chair, still thinking about the session, noting that he wasn't angry. He made his way to the front door with Luke, waving good bye to Laura as he exited their apartment. 'Could it really work?' he thought to himself. 'Could a couple of pow-wows with Dr. Luke be all I need? Would he even want to see me if he knew there was a killer in close pursuit? Should I let him know that his safety, Laura's safety, Ed's safety, could possibly be in jeopardy?'

"Ethan," Luke said, as he followed him into the hallway. "I've seen hundreds of people and it's always that same question, 'Why am I different?' You sat in that office, they didn't.

You're trying to get a grasp on something that's bothering you. You're doing the right thing...We'll work these problems out."

Ethan didn't say anything back; he just nodded his head and went into his apartment. He threw his clothes off and hopped into the shower. He didn't want think about anything just then, so he just stood there under the water, letting it pour over him. There was one moment Ethan would never forget. Not to say that it trumped others, but it was one particular moment he had always remembered, one he had always pushed aside. He dreaded it, he ran from it, but now, after his first session to recovering, he wanted to face it.

Chapter 37

Decent

Christmas was Ethan's favorite holiday. He loved everything: the decorations, the snow, the Christmas trees, the happy faces. Most of all, he loved spending it with his mother. This year was different than others; he had always spent Christmas with his parents at his grandmother's house—his grandmother on his mother's side of the family. This year he was being forced to leave his tiny apartment on Mosholu Pkwy to go up to his Father's beautiful house in Yorktown Heights.

Anyone who knew the two areas knew the differences were easily distinguishable. It didn't take a Master's Degree in geology to know that Yorktown Heights was safer, nicer, and richer than Mosholu Pkwy in the Bronx. For Andrew Alosi, however, the differences weren't so palpable.

"Buddy, what's the big deal about this house? It's just a house, no different from the apartment," he would tell Ethan.

Ethan and his mother had started to troop it everywhere they had to go. Ethan didn't mind though, he enjoyed the long walks with his mother. He got tremendous power in his legs from all the long walks. All the grappling and submission moves he mastered in the Academy came from the years of marching all over the Bronx. Ethan had always wondered why his father drove around in a brand new Honda Civic.

"It's not my car buddy, it's a friend's," Andrew would say. "I'm just borrowing it for now." This would be the excuse he always got. Ethan, much to Andrew's surprise, had two eyes

and could easily see that this "friend" who owned this Honda was actually his future wife, Michelle.

Ethan also didn't have his own room there. As big as the house was, he didn't have his own bed. He was forced to share a pullout in Ray's room.

"Buddy, you have a room, what are you talking about," Andrew would insist. Ethan felt like his head could explode. He was positive there was no room in that house for him. His father was so selfish that he couldn't even see this simple fact.

These were all reasons as to why Ethan despised going near his father's house. He remembered how awesome it had been when his dad lived nearby, when he had first left. They went to the movies, played ball, played video games, and completed homework, but then suddenly it all vanished. In its place stood Michelle, and with Michelle came the nice furniture, the nice car, and, of course, the beautiful, tremendous home. Going to his father's house made Ethan feel like he was visiting the enemy. Like he was visiting all the things that were better than what he had back on Mosholu.

Christmas was a time Ethan enjoyed spending at his grandmother's with his mother's side of the family. It had always been this way: Christmas Eve with dad's side and Christmas Day at mom's. Ethan wasn't particularly fond of Michelle at the moment, nor was he happy with his father after the recent episode on the Disney Cruise. Unfortunately for him, his father had claimed the right to display his trophy son at his new house for Christmas this year.

Ethan sat in the living room of his apartment, listening to his mother go over with him the different things he could do if he felt uncomfortable.

"Just call me, Ethan. Alright?" she said as she knelt in front of him. He nodded his head back in response. He hated how things had to be different. How his father could just forget to come pick him up countless times, but now that it was Christmas and he wanted to save face with the family, Ethan had to go with him. 'What about baseball?' Ethan thought. 'What about sleigh riding a few weeks ago?'

His father had promised him they would go sleigh riding just two weeks before Christmas when he suddenly broke off the plans. Ethan couldn't even remember what the excuse had been this time. He didn't cry, for once he actually didn't cry. He sucked it up and moved on.

The doorbell finally rang, 4:00 PM on the dot, one of the few times his father had ever been on time. There he stood at the front door, Rex jumping on him wildly, as he knelt down to pet the dog. Rex had no idea that this man had been the brains behind the whole "let's get a dog" operation and then escaped about two years after. How could this man kneel there and pet that dog, grinning from ear to ear as the animal licked him and barked in excitement, and not think about how terrible of a human being he was?

Ethan hugged his mother tightly, so sad to have to leave her on their favorite holiday, and walked out of the apartment with his duffel bag in his hand.

"You ready, Booka Man?" his father said, grabbing his son's shoulder as they walked out of the apartment building together. "I heard on the news that Santa was already seen flying over China."

It was freezing outside; some flakes of snow fell from the sky to the already covered ground. It had been snowing so much that year, and most people wondered if they'd ever see grass again. Mosholu Parkway might have been in a dangerous neighborhood, but God was it beautiful during winter time. The snow covered the many, many trees making the area look like some kind of winter wonderland. There was so much wildlife around the neighborhood, so many trees, bushes, and patches of grass. There were so many places for thieves and gang bangers to hide, but also so much beauty to absorb.

Ethan hopped into his dad's Honda, putting his seatbelt on as his father got into the driver's seat. As the two pulled away, Ethan could see his beautiful mother waving from his corner window, smiling at her son as he drove away to live through one of his most terrifying memories.

Chapter 38

No Vacancy

The steam billowed through the bathroom, fogging the mirrors and seeping under the doorway. Ethan remained under the water, feeling the steaming hot water smack against his skin, as his phone rang out loudly. He ignored it, his eyes closed tightly as he remembered that Christmas Eve. It was a memory Ethan had never relived before, but maybe now was the time to confront it.

Ethan thought about what Luke had told him, how he would come to eventually discuss his father, and he knew he didn't have to rush himself. This was something Ethan had feared for so long, something that even trumped the drug dealers, the mobsters, the hostage situations; it was far beyond that level of fear. If he was going to confront his problems, if he was going to fix these inner demons, then he would have to do exactly what Luke had said and not rush.

Ethan took a deep breath, turning the shower off and stepping out to see who had called. 'Illames' showed on his display screen, the only name he didn't want to see on a Saturday afternoon. He wanted to enjoy New Year's Eve, to go out and have a good time with close friends, so he was trying his best to detach himself from the case for a day.

"Ethan," Illames said, no hello, no how are you. "We got the confirmation on the other bodies from Lake George, but still nothing that stands out. Same goes for this guy Desmond, no connections anywhere. No prints were found, of course."

"I don't even have anything off the top of my head, I have no idea what its trying to say," Ethan said truthfully. He couldn't even reach for something abstract; he had no clue what so ever. Just another puzzle piece that didn't fit. "While I have you on the phone I have a request. I want a warrant for a crack house on Hull Avenue in the Bronx. 333 Hull Ave."

"You have a lead?" Illames asked, his interest shining.

"I might, I have reason to believe a suspect may have been or is living there, my cousin Aiden Moore," Ethan said, bracing himself for Illames' response.

"Your cousin?" Illames said, taken aback by the request.

"The killer knows me well, I have reason to suspect my cousin from my father's side," Ethan said, as his head started to hurt him from the confusion. "We used to be close a long time ago…he comes from a broken household, he knows my childhood well…" Ethan hesitated before continuing anymore. "He's a little unstable, too."

Ethan hated to think of his cousin as the killer, especially because it still pained him that he was never able to help him. The thought of failing his cousin and now accusing him of manslaughter irked him. He couldn't imagine him doing such a horrible thing. Ever since he had seen Aiden outside that house, he had denied it, but what he couldn't deny were Aiden's qualifications as a suspect. Keeping the personal life out of a case was rule number one for many agents. Special Agent 101: Don't bang your informants. Don't get comfortable with suspects. Unfortunately for Ethan, there was no way around getting personal with this one.

"52nd Precinct has jurisdiction over there. What's your plan?" Illames asked, knowing

what had happened the last time Ethan had ordered a S.W.A.T. team.

Ethan was on the money with the 225 East Mosholu Parkway raid. Yes the killer hadn't

showed up, but nevertheless, he was accurate.

"Just me and Chris won't cut it, the place is gunna be flooded with drug addicts. I don't

need S.W.A.T., but I need a team of professionals. Four guys should be enough."

"Porter and Anthony then." Ethan put the phone to his head, shaking it in disapproval.

He couldn't stand Porter.

"That's fine. We'll go in early Monday morning...January 2nd, the same day the killer says

it will strike...I think that would be the best time. I haven't seen my cousin since I was about

eighteen. We've got some homework to do," Ethan said, trying to calculate the timing in his

head. The killer had set the next date for Monday night. Any time before then would suffice.

He needed some time to scope the place out, to try and dig up whatever he could find on his

cousin.

"Stay sharp, Ethan," Illames said, hanging up on Ethan before he could respond.

Ethan put his phone back down on his sink, rubbing the fog off the mirror in front of

him. He stared at himself, wondering if what he was doing was right. There were a lot of

people close to him in his life, a good handful of people who knew him well enough to say the

things in these letters, but Aiden did stand out as the front runner. Aiden had gone through a

ridiculously tough childhood, ridden with abuse of both the mental and physical nature. Ethan didn't want to picture his cousin at the helm of these brutal murders but, placing bias aside, it made sense. Mens rea was present; he knew Aiden had reason enough to commit the deeds. It was proving he actually did them that would be the difficult part.

Ethan shook his head, as crazy as it seemed at the moment; he knew it would all come together in the end. It was the same with most psychopaths, nothing made much sense, but eventually they would slip up and that's when Ethan stepped in.

He got dressed, cleaned his guns, and made his bed before he finally sat down to watch some Sports Center. He was actually excited for the party. He felt restless as he sat there awaiting a phone call from someone, since he was dying to get out of the apartment. He turned the TV off and sat there in silence, thinking about the night ahead of him. He couldn't wait to see Rachel again, even though they had just parted a few hours ago. 'Is it corny that our first kiss might be at midnight on New Year's?' he thought to himself. He didn't want to be like one of those stupid romantic comedies. 'It's not that big of a deal," he thought, and then, 'Yeah it definitely is…that's so tacky.'

Ethan's phone rang out through the silence, causing him to jump out of his seat and run over to it.

"Oh, come on," Ethan said, seeing that it was Illames again.

"Hello?" he said, wondering what else there could be.

"Ethan, breakthrough in your case," Illames said, sounding excited. Ethan's heart jumped at the sound of his boss' voice. "We found a calling card on each victim."

Chapter 39

New Year

"A peace sign etched into a random section of skin. A very light etching, it's the branch with a light circle around it. Like the hippie peace symbol," Illames said, sounding slightly excited to have this new piece of junk evidence. Nothing made sense.

Ethan stood still with his folder of evidence in front of him. He shook his head as he looked at all the pieces to this puzzle. He was starting to feel like he was given one piece from several different puzzles and then given a time limit to make them all fit together. 'You have to be kidding me,' he thought as he rubbed his eyes.

"The symbol is found on each body, the coroner made a note and took pictures. Anything click for you?" Illames said. Ethan shook his head, trying to make some sense out of it.

"No," Ethan answered simply.

"Happy New Year, Ethan," Illames said before he hung up.

"Yeah, Happy New Year," Ethan said out loud to his empty room.

'A peace sign?' he thought. 'What the hell does that mean?' He paced around his room with his hands on his head, trying to search back into his past, looking for anything that could be of help. 'A peace sign in the skin…peace…love…happiness…the sixties?' Ethan had no idea what he was looking for as he spread all of his paperwork out on his desk. Each victim had been a deadbeat parent, a failure in some child's life.

Ethan sat back on his arm chair thinking to himself about his own experiences. He could still remember his mother throwing plates across the kitchen, as she caught his father and his adulteress-wife-to-be. He could still remember when she found Michelle's credit card in the car, could still remember the times his mother had cried her eyes out in disbelief and agony, could still remember all the games his father played at his expense.

He put his head in his hands as he leaned forward onto his nice black dress pants. He was wearing a casual suit: a regular white dress shirt, black tie, black suit jacket, and some black dress pants. He couldn't wait to see what Rachel would be wearing. The girl was perfection in sweat pants and a T-shirt, let alone in a dress.

'I'm going to do this,' Ethan thought to himself. 'I'll pull out of this alright.'

His phone rang again, this time Chris was on the receiving end.

"I'm ready when you are," Chris said. "I hope you wore a nice suit, I don't want to make you look too out of place."

Ethan laughed, "I'll show up with a wetsuit on and look better."

"Ahaha, I just need a beer man. I've been waiting an hour for Dana to put an earring on. You ever watch a woman 6 months pregnant get ready for a fancy party?" Chris said, and then Dana's voice sounded in the background.

"I hear you. Iliames called. We'll have the warrant and Porter and Anthony for back-up tomorrow. He told me the coroner found a calling card, he said there's a peace sign etched on the bodies."

"Like the two fingers?"

"He said it's the hippie symbol," Ethan said as he bundled up all of his paperwork, placing it all into his drawer. He grabbed his jacket and locked the door, making his way to the stairs.

"What the hell does that mean?" Chris said sounding a little irritated.

"Let's just go out tonight and enjoy ourselves. We'll study tomorrow," Ethan said, jogging down the steps.

"Call me when you're outside."

Ethan jumped into the Charger, as he scrolled to Rachel's name in his phone. He pulled up in front of her house, hopping out of the car to ring her bell. He leaned against his car; the anticipation of seeing this angel open that door was building. He felt his hands getting clammy, his stomach get queasy, and he was so unsure about himself. 'What if she doesn't feel the same way?' he thought. 'She must feel something if she agreed to spend New Year's Eve with me. Maybe she's not sure, though.' Ethan shook his head and smiled at how weird he was being. He remembered the last time a girl made him feel this way, and his current situation happened to be extremely similar.

All doubt, all questions, all worries were long gone the second Rachel stepped out of the front door. There was nothing else that mattered; Ethan knew it for a fact as soon as he saw her. She walked down the steps, smiling widely and blushing. She was wearing a tight, black dress that came down below her knees. Her dark hair, with the hint of blonde streaks was curled and fell across her shoulders. She had a small amount of make-up on, and wore a set of long, dangling silver earrings and a beautiful silver necklace.

Ethan had no words to describe what he saw; he could only just stare helplessly. She stood in front of him, staring up into his eyes, and shrugged her shoulders, making a face as she waited for Ethan to say something. Her building could have crumbled to the ground. Every car alarm on the block could have went off at the same time, and Ethan wouldn't have noticed.

Peace signs in dead skin, riddles and early morning raids. With such a treasure in his life, nothing could bother him.

Rachel opened her mouth to speak, but Ethan stopped her, putting his hand on the side of her face. He felt the warmth of her skin under his fingertips. He couldn't contain himself; there was nothing in the world that could stop him in that moment. He leaned in, placing his lips on Rachel's, feeling her soft lips under his and then he pulled away, staring into the woman's eyes.

Rachel burst out in laughter, bending over as she cracked up hysterically. Ethan laughed with her, staring at her like she was crazy. He shook his head smiling, watching Rachel as she continued to laugh.

"It's about time," she said, still giggling. "It didn't take you that long ten years ago." She stood in front of Ethan with her hands on her hips, nodding her head. "You tried to kiss me the first day you met me, remember that? It wasn't that good ten years ago, though."

"To be honest with you, I just really didn't want to do it at midnight," Ethan said laughing.

"I was so worried that's what you were waiting for; I thought you might have gotten cornier over the years," she said laughing. Ethan reached forward again, kissing Rachel one more time before he turned around to open her door. The two drove away much more relaxed than they had been.

"I can't believe you're an FBI agent...I mean I believed you could be one but I've never known someone in the F.B.I.," Rachel said as they pulled up in front of Chris' house. Chris walked towards the street with his arms outstretched, doing a little turn to show off his Armani

suit. He nodded his head, a huge smile stretching across his face as he pointed at Rachel.

"Is he pointing at me?" Rachel asked, laughing next to Ethan.

"Yeah, let me introduce you three," Ethan said, hopping out of the car. Before he could

say any introductions, Chris had already moved into hug Rachel.

"It's so nice to meet you Rachel, I've heard so many good things about you," Chris said,

letting Rachel go and shaking her hand. "You look beautiful."

Ethan loved how Chris carried himself; he was so well-mannered and always had the

right thing to say.

"Dana, you look incredible also," Ethan said, leaning into kiss Dana on the cheek. She

was wearing a nice red dress with dangly earrings and a diamond necklace hanging around her

neck. On her left hand sat the rock that Chris had given her. Ethan still remembered that day in

Atlantic City. He proposed to her right in the middle of the casino, telling her that he had hit

the jackpot when he found her. She had laughed hysterically in front of him, crying her eyes

out as she said yes.

"Thank you Ethan...you look smashing yourself," she said sarcastically. Ethan laughed as

he got back in the car.

"The party's on Lexington at some hall between 77th and 78th street," Ethan said, turning

the Charger onto Lexington Avenue. It was easy to tell where they had to go once they made

their way down the block.

Ethan parked the Charger and the two couples followed the groups of sophisticated

looking people into a large, grotesque looking building. There was nothing glamorous about the place, but Ethan had realized so long ago that this was the case with many spots in Manhattan. So many of the most popular hotspots didn't appear to be the most well-kept establishments from the outside, but once you entered, once you had walked through that front door, it was like stepping into Narnia. Ethan's theory held true tonight as well.

The couples walked through the revolting steel doors, stepping onto a plush carpet covering the floor of a stunning lobby. Marble pillars surrounded the room, the walls were painted a light, gold like color, and a sophisticated chandelier hung from the middle of the ceiling. The four stood there in amazement, their mouths almost hitting the floor as they stood amongst the rich and the famous. There were men and women scattered across the room, enjoying cocktails and hors d'oeuvres. There was a small bar in the corner of the room with a bartender who was dressed in a fine tuxedo as he stood straight with his hands behind his back. The whole picture reminded Ethan of something out of an old movie.

"Ethan!" Luke called from over the crowd. Luke, Laura, and Ed wound through the couples, making their way to the four outsiders. "I'm glad you came...you must be Rachel." Luke turned his attention to Rachel, reaching out his hand. The shock on Luke's face probably matched the shock they had been in when they arrived. Ed could care less as he took off to play with some of the other children.

"Luke," he said as he shook her hand. Ethan liked the fact that he didn't always introduce himself as Dr. Lianessa. Luke was very personable and not some stuck up rich prick. He walked up to Chris and Dana, introducing himself to both of them as well.

"Have you guys had a drink yet? Let's go into the main hall," Luke said, taking Laura's hand as he started to walk towards the giant archway at the end of the room.

The gigantic marble pillars towered up to the top of the entranceway as the six walked into the enormous banquet hall. It was equivalent to the transition they had just experienced. The transformation from city streets to incredible lobby was easily trumped by incredible lobby to magical, unbelievable ballroom.

"Psychiatrist New Year's Eve party?" Ethan said, as Luke laughed back at the four's amazement.

The cathedral ceilings were decorated with unimaginable paintings of clouds and stars. Giant, inconceivably expensive chandeliers hung down from the heavenly ceiling, generating a bright light that stretched across the room. The marble floor was spotless, the many tables were garnished with beautiful assortments of roses, and there was a giant stage at the end of the room with what looked like a screen from a movie theatre on it.

"Wow…" Rachel said, looking at Ethan with wide eyes. "Are you serious? I don't even feel like we should be here."

"Nonsense, it's paid for by a couple of retired entrepreneurs out of the psychiatry field. Very nice men…as you can tell…" Luke said laughing. "We only know a handful of people here; it's just such a remarkable party we couldn't say no."

"They don't even check people in at the door," Ethan said. But, at that moment, Luke held out four cards.

'Thank you for attending the 36th annual Geoffrey Ruggeri New Year's Eve Party'

"If anyone questions you, just flash this," Luke said as everyone took one. "There won't be a problem though. Every year we get a group of yuppies sneaking in, but they have some good security here. Four hours until the ball drops." Luke nodded up to the stage; the screen was on and showing Times Square.

The party was incredible, the best Ethan had ever seen hands down. He scanned the room as he waited for his Budweiser and Rachel's Long Island, looking at all the people as they laughed and chatted amongst each other. He was, of course, still thinking about the peace symbol. The killer had etched it into the skin of all his victims, maybe as a symbol that they were at peace, maybe as a symbol that those they hurt were at peace. But Ethan couldn't figure it out. He had never been this stumped before, but he had also never encountered such an erratic, sporadic killer. The only pattern they saw so far was the quickness of the whole thing: it was obviously well planned out. The history of each victim was similar also; they had all been failures as parents. The only one who wasn't was Desmond. Something was up with this guy Desmond.

"Don't tell me you're doing homework at this party…dude…there are chandeliers more expensive than everything you own put together…and you still can't take off for four hours. Even 'it' took off for a few days to enjoy itself!" Chris said as he joined Ethan at the bar.

"It's out there right now just planning its next step," Ethan said, smiling at the exaggerated look of surprise on Chris' face. "You're right." Ethan looked back at Rachel and Dana; the two were talking and laughing together. Luke and Laura had gone off to make their rounds and say hello to their fellow psychiatrist friends. Ethan still couldn't believe how beautiful Rachel was tonight.

"We'll get cracking first thing tomorrow, without a doubt we'll have whoever it is in cuffs Monday," Chris said, grabbing his Yuengling off the bar. "You know that." Chris raised his beer to Ethan. "Happy New Year, brother."

The music was great, the drinks were boundless, and the energy was electric. 'Whoever Geoff Ruggeri is he really knows how to party right,' Ethan thought to himself. Ethan had never danced so much, and he wasn't much of a dancer, but tonight he was Patrick Swayze. He moved around the dance floor, had an incredible chicken parmesan dinner, and met some interesting people.

"Thanks for taking me," Rachel said as she came over to sit next to Ethan who had just taken a break from his excellent dancing.

"Yeah no problem, you don't have to thank me," Ethan said. "Thanks for coming." The two looked around the room; the countdown to midnight was now at only eight minutes.

Ethan searched his mind for the right thing to say but nothing came to him. He was open to this new trait, this speechless veil that fell over him whenever Rachel was near. He was growing more accustomed to it now.

"There's a lot going on right now, in my life," Ethan started to say. He felt like this moment was the best time to say what he had to say. "I know you're very busy with your journalism career." Ethan moved his chair closer to Rachel, looking out to the dance floor to see Chris and Dana and Laura and Luke dancing with each other. "Ever since ten years ago I've never settled down with anyone, but you're just amazing. Your smile is a miracle." That same smile was vibrantly displayed across Rachel's face at that moment. "I wasn't ready then, I had so much growing up to do, but…" Ethan felt the words in the pit of his stomach. It was hard to get them out.

"You're perfect," Rachel said. "For me at least. I know your flaws and I accept them, I always have. I've always understood what you were going through, you tried your best to understand me, I know you tried. There's just always been something about you."

Ethan was well aware that he could possibly be the luckiest guy in the world. He had the most attractive woman in the building on his arm, telling him that he was perfect for her. Ethan smiled at Rachel, reaching out his hand to touch hers.

"Our lives are complicated outside of our careers…even more-so in them…but I want to see where it goes, if you want to," Ethan said, staring into Rachel's giant light brown eyes.

Ethan knew about Rachel's past. He knew the terrible, atrocious events that had unfolded; he knew the long, tiring road she had to travel to come to where she was now. He respected her, and he had at one time tried to comfort her, but back then he was too juvenile. He was ready for it now.

"Seeing you at that bar was the highlight of 2011," Rachel said laughing. "Do you remember that guy I was supposed to be with?" She shook her head laughing.

"You have no idea how happy I am that I actually showed up that night. You know I stood outside and almost went home?" Ethan said, recalling the night.

"You guys," Chris said, pointing up to the countdown, only thirty more seconds until the New Year. Ethan got up, taking Rachel's hand as they moved over to the rest of the group. Times had been rough lately, his past had been eating away at him, but right now Ethan looked forward to his future.

The clock struck midnight, the New Year arrived, and Ethan already loved it. As the couples walked out of the ballroom, a young man in the crowd caught Ethan's attention. The man stood on his toes, waving frantically with a big smile across his face. Ethan continued to walk to the door, still staring at the man, watching him as he put the peace sign up.

Ethan had a drop dead, bombshell, smoking hot woman who had a killer personality around his arm, and he was as rattled as he had ever been in his life. He wanted to take Rachel to his apartment, to kiss her all night, to never let go, but he couldn't function like this. He didn't want to be a paranoid, nervous wreck their first night back together. Ethan got even more nervous suddenly. He had just had another incredible night with Rachel where there was no sex involved. He looked down at his dazzling date, her smile enchanting anyone who laid eyes on her, and he smiled back. He couldn't wait for the case to end.

Chapter 40

Mansion

The Honda Civic pulled into the stone driveway. Outside the car's window, Ethan could

see the beautiful landscaping, the healthy, green grass, the flowery bushes, the stone's

artistically placed around the edges of the greenery. It was a work of art.

Ethan could see his father's dog, Lucy, jumping up, stretching its head out to see past the

white picket fence she was locked behind. She wasn't a bad dog, Lucy, but she wasn't Rex.

Ethan watched as his father unlocked the gate, letting her run out and jump all over him. His

father had told Ethan that he had "found" Lucy while he was at work. All Ethan saw was a

sham. He saw a loveless, artificial life, and a bogus excuse for happiness and satisfaction.

Michelle opened the door, waving and smiling widely as she jogged down the stone

steps, down to the driveway to give Ethan a big hug. 'Just some more phoniness,' Ethan

thought to himself. 'Pour it on baby…what happened to the yelling, screaming, and sour pusses

like on the Disney Cruise?'

Ethan walked up the steps and into his father's house, leaving the two idiots outside to

mingle with each other. This was the last place he wanted to be, but here he was being his

father's son for the weekend before he would be back to his chopped liver status. The front of

the house was very nice. The living room sported a fancy looking Christmas tree with neatly

arranged ornaments, and a fireplace with four stockings. 'Lucy has a stocking and I don't,'

Ethan thought to himself. He shook his head in frustration before he noticed the gifts under the

tree. He walked forward, and his eyes focused on one in particular, a rectangular, medium sized

present. Dropping his bag, Ethan reached for the gift, holding it in his hands to measure the weight of the object. He shook it a little, placing his ear next to the wrapping to hear what was inside. He was tempted to open the gift, to just tear the wrapping a little bit, but his father was already walking in with Michelle. Ethan placed the gift back under the tree, and picked his bag up, walking past Michelle and Andrew without saying a word.

He went upstairs to his "bedroom", which was more commonly known as Ray's bedroom with the addition of a pullout mattress, and threw his bag down by the night stand. Ray was laid out on his bed playing X-Box, which had actually been Ethan's when Andrew had first moved out. That's right; they basically stole the X-Box from Ethan. The boy's room was nice and roomy, with nice wooden furniture scattered around the room, a small television set, and a full bed that had a compartment on the bottom which pulled out another mattress.

Ethan realized after a few visits to his father's new home that a lot of what was in his old apartment had appeared in this one. It had occurred to Ethan that this was obviously very suspicious. He heard a lot but most of the time he didn't entertain the slip-ups because he just didn't feel like dealing with it, but he did hear some of the lies untangle. Little things like seeing that the Honda was registered under Michelle's name. It all bothered Ethan so much, but he found it was easier to just put it aside and forget about it.

"What's up," Ray said, not taking his eyes off the TV. "You wanna play?"

"I'll just watch for now," Ethan said, sitting on the edge of "his" pullout. "You wanna go outside in the snow after?"

"Yeah definitely," Ray said, looking over at Ethan approvingly. "We went to this awesome hill the other day, I have to show you."

Ethan didn't say a word; he just sat there staring ahead at the TV. He had waited for his father to take him sleigh riding just a few weeks ago. He waited with his gloves on, with his scarf on, with his snow boots on, but his father never showed up. He called an hour late to tell Ethan he couldn't make it, that something had come up. Now here Ethan was listening to how his father had gone sleigh riding with his new family.

Ethan jumped up, walking downstairs to the kitchen to grab a drink. The kitchen was beautiful. There was a small bar section as well as a nice, big oven surrounded by marble counter tops. From the kitchen the patio area was visible. The gas grill and patio furniture looked almost brand new, and there were a few coolers set up for the Christmas party.

Ethan picked his brain, trying desperately to come up with some escape plan, some way he could get out of there before it was too late. He could see it now, his whole father's side of the family rushing into the house like a phony mob hugging and kissing him like they even knew who he was. He hadn't received a birthday card from these people since his father left, yet now they're going to act like he's part of the family?

"What's up buddy, you hungry?" Andrew said, walking into the kitchen and checking the fridge. Ethan stared up at his father, still furious from hearing that they had gone out in the snow. He tried to bottle it up, to hold it in but he couldn't help it.

"I thought you were too busy to come down and play in the snow?" Ethan asked, his father turning to stare at him. "You told me you got caught up."

"I did," his father said, staring at him disconcertedly. This was his signature move, the whole make you feel like a crazy person routine.

"But you had time to go out with Ray and Michelle," Ethan said. He knew as soon as he said it that he didn't sound very confident. The truth of the matter was he was scared, he was afraid to go up against his father, he felt weak and stupid next to him.

"Ethan...I wasn't busy when we went out, so I went out for a few minutes, what do you expect me to stay inside when you're not around?" His father looked at him, scrunching his face up to make himself look confused.

Ethan walked past his father, not saying another word as he strode up the steps back to Ray's room. He knew better. He knew it wasn't a good idea to try and say something. No matter what, it would always be his fault. His father was always right. Ethan doubted there would ever be a day his father would confess to his wrongdoings, since he didn't think he had any.

Chapter 41

Puzzle Solving

Ethan lay awake in his dark, freezing bedroom, staring up at his ceiling. 'This is it,' he thought to himself. 'Aiden is the killer.' There was no other explanation. Ethan could still remember that Christmas Eve so clearly, when he had confronted his father about the sleigh riding. It wasn't so much the sleigh riding; it was more the humiliation of his father choosing other people over him. Aiden was there that year. He had been there for that Christmas. Ethan closed his eyes, shaking his head to move past that topic.

That peace symbol was still bothering him. He had hoped the answer would fall on his lap, but still nothing had clicked. He looked over at his desk, the folders of evidence and files were sprayed out over the wooden top, his guns sitting idly next to them. Ethan didn't want to get up, and he didn't really feel like moving at all. It wasn't the laziness, it was just the headache that this case was causing him.

Ethan jumped out of bed, jumped up on to his pull-up bar and started his morning routine. It was crunch time, this was it, there was no mistakes allowed now. The killer laid it all out in front of them, put calling signs on his victims, and even wrote Ethan personalized letters. Ethan knew he had to keep his wits about him and stay sharp.

He finished his workout, watched some SportsCenter, took a quick shower, and jumped out right on time to answer his partner's call.

"You here?" Ethan asked as he picked up.

"I'm at Nikita's, you want anything?" Chris said, the noise from the coffee shop deafening in the background. Sunday mornings were crazy at almost any diner or coffee shop in the city.

Ethan hated breakfast. Not dislike, not tolerate, he absolutely hated breakfast foods. Something told him that today would be a taxing day mentally and Chris obviously knew this too. Ethan knew Chris would never normally ask him if he wanted something to eat so early in the morning.

"Bacon, egg, and cheese on a toasted bagel with salt and pepper," Ethan said, smiling to himself. "Might as well throw in a chocolate milk too."

"You sure dairy is a good idea?" Chris teased.

"I'll see you soon, I'll get everything organized," Ethan said, tossing his phone on to his bed and pulling out some clothes.

He got dressed and sat at his desk, looking at all of his paperwork as a whole. He still hadn't seen this peace symbol Illames had told him about. According to his boss, the symbol hadn't appeared in one particular spot, the killer had placed the symbol anywhere it felt like. He sorted all of the papers out, putting each crime report with the matching evidence and pictures. He sorted out the letters in chronological order, reading over each chilling sentence carefully before placing it on his desk.

Chris finally joined him, knocking on the door with the bag of breakfast. Ethan eagerly grabbed his sandwich, forcing it down quickly without saying a word. Chris stared at him curiously since he had never seen Ethan eat breakfast, let alone act as though the food was the best he ever had. Ethan felt invigorated, he felt ready to take this case on for once, but in the back of his mind he knew what was really going on.

Ethan finished his food, popped open his chocolate milk, and picked up the pictures of the first three victims. Seeing the man with the ax sticking out of his head did nothing to his stomach. He stared closely at the backdrop to each picture, trying to see some type of reflection, signal, anything that could give him an ounce of a hint as to who the killer was.

"We're still going on Aiden being the lead suspect, right?" Chris said, staring at Ethan sideways. He was studying the pictures of the other victims, but Ethan saw the glances here and there.

"Yeah, I just have this feeling," Ethan said, not taking his eyes off the pictures as he sipped his chocolate milk.

Ethan didn't think Aiden was the killer. It made sense logically but he just had a hunch it wasn't him. In the world of law enforcement, a hunch didn't go so far in the boss' eyes. Ethan knew who Aiden was. He still remembered his cousin from so long ago and couldn't picture him doing all the things he was looking at now. Clipping a woman's eyelids off, slamming an ax through a man's head, electrocuting a woman in a bathtub. But the evidence pointed to Aiden.

"Did Aiden visit Lake George with you at all?" Chris asked.

Ethan hesitated before answering. He knew all these questions would come up, and he also knew the answers would point even more to Aiden being guilty.

"Yeah he came up a few times, this is when we were very young," Ethan said, staring at Chris to see what his reaction would be. "We were still in grammar school. It was before my father left."

"You said you saw him after that though, like at your cousin's funeral," Chris said, staring up at Ethan.

Ethan knew Chris wasn't interrogating him. He could tell Chris was being as cautious as possible and didn't want Ethan to feel cornered. So Ethan couldn't figure out why he felt cornered, why he felt so defensive. He hadn't seen his cousin in about ten years yet he felt like he had to defend him. For all he knew, this guy had gone off the deep end.

"I did but we barely spoke," Ethan answered, thinking back to that day. "I told you before. He was just upset that I wasn't around."

Ethan placed the pictures back on his desk, rubbing his mouth as he looked at Chris. He figured he might as well spill the beans on everything being he was going to be asked anyway.

"Look, Aiden was unstable. He wasn't a straight arrow but he went through a lot, there's no way you could come out of what he did without some bolts loose. I decided to work for the Bureau to put the right people behind bars; I don't feel like this is right."

Chris sat back in Ethan's arm chair, biting the side of his mouth as he stared at Ethan.

"I know what it looks like, Chris," Ethan said, before his partner said anything.

"I don't know how it feels, I've never been in your position but seriously Ethan, I know you see the facts."

"I see that he is a suspect and we need to apprehend him, but I don't see any clear evidence that he's done anything. He has no record in the system; he has no ties to any gangs other than us seeing him on that porch."

"Honestly, Ethan, seeing him on that porch at that time of the day is enough for me," Chris said, leaning back into grab his orange juice. He picked up the killer's first letter and sat back in his seat. "I hear what you're saying...I'll keep looking with you but at some point we have to get over to Hull and map the place out."

Ethan picked up the second letter, skimming through it for something that popped out. Hours went by that the two sat there and read, trying to figure something out, throwing out absurd theories here and there.

"Each of these quotes," Ethan said. He grabbed a notebook and a pen and started to jot down the different quotes the killer used. "It makes reference to where we end up in this letter." Ethan got up, walking to his closet door to grab his leather jacket off the handle. Chris followed him, grabbing his jacket and walking out the front door.

"It is a weird group of people to pull quotes from," Chris said as he got into the elevator. He saw Ethan reach for the staircase's door, but he just laughed and kept walking to the elevator. "They're from all different eras. I'm pretty sure this killer isn't doing random shit. It's got a plan and it's sticking to it. It's been banking on you to figure everything out."

"We have until tomorrow night, unless it strays from that plan again like last time," Ethan said as the two agents walked out of the building. "Why would the killer go through all of this trouble just to hand itself over tomorrow? It's really smart, we can't forget that."

Chris nodded his head, stopping as they walked down the block to point at Sal's Pizzeria. Ethan nodded back in approval and the two went inside, sitting down to have a bite to eat. Ethan loved Sal's. He loved how serene the environment was, how great the food tasted, and how friendly the guys working there were. The walls were painted beautifully to illustrate the streets of Italy, the tables were always clean and decorated with nice placemats, and there was never a bug in sight. People always thought of New York City as a dirty city. Ethan had experienced this perception whenever a case took him out of state. New York pizza is the best. The end. It isn't a myth, it isn't overrated. Its just the best.

"What time were you thinking?" Chris asked, hopping into the passenger's seat.

"You mean for the raid?"

"Yeah, I was thinking early would be better, get them when they least expect it," Chris said.

"That's what I was thinking; the killer won't be doped up though. It wouldn't make sense for him to mess with his inhibitions but it would make sense for him to hideout in a place like that," Ethan said, looking over at Chris who gave him a "that's what I'm saying" look. "I'm still not sold on Aiden."

Chris looked away shaking his head. "I know you aren't but just don't block it out completely."

The Charger rolled off the Major Deegan at the Van Cortlandt exit. The streets were infested for a stunning Sunday morning. It was only a few days after the holidays and people were all rushing to get back to where they came from or return unwanted gifts.

Ethan couldn't even remember if he had received any gifts for Christmas. He couldn't even remember what he had done. This case was dominating his life.

The Charger rolled down the day-lit Mosholu Parkway. It was a crisp day on the tree-lined street, and a group of happy kids enjoyed a pick-up game of football on the grass in the middle of the parkway. A realtor could easily trick someone into moving here under these conditions.

Ethan made his way to Hull Avenue, parking the car at the same hydrant they had sat at a few days ago. The yellow brick house was sandwiched between two others, stretching two floors with a thin window visible at the base of the house indicating a basement. There was no air conditioner in any of the windows. Each one was shut and the blinds were all drawn. The porch was worn down, there were holes visible in the wooden steps leading to the front door, and old, rickety metal chairs were messily arranged around the porch. The door was a solid wooden slab with two locks along the side.

"Looks dead now and it's past 2:00 PM," Chris said, jotting some things down on a pad. "You wanna check?"

Ethan looked over at Chris, looking to see if he was completely serious.

"What do you think?" he said laughing.

Chris laughed back, putting his hands up and shaking his head.

Ethan nodded back and got out of the Charger, walking up the block a little before crossing the street on to the crack house's side. Chris followed him, staying close behind and looking all around to make sure they were all right. There were a few people on their porches talking, playing cards, and drinking, but none of them paid any attention to the two agents. Lucky for them it was a pretty cold day, so that must have been keeping a lot of people indoors.

They crept through the front gate, watching closely to make sure none of the shades flickered. Chris carefully closed the gate behind them as they slowly made their way to the building's side. Still no one had noticed the two and even if they had they probably wouldn't say anything. It's not like it wasn't common for two strangers to walk into this house.

Ethan didn't like the location at all. There were too many openings, too many avenues for an attack. They walked along the side of the house, ducking under the first window and slowly moving across the array of twigs and garbage on the floor. It was absolutely disgusting with broken bottles, syringes, pills littered everywhere along the dirt path that led to the backyard. Across from them was the neighboring building, however their windows were all open and the shades were all drawn. Chris kept his eyes peeled, making sure no one spotted them and making sure they weren't caught by surprise from behind.

Ethan's hand floated gently by his pistol's handle as he quietly moved forward. He controlled his breathing, making sure he didn't make too much noise; the neighborhood was so quiet that anything could sound an alarm. He ducked under another window, moving quickly past it as he came to the edge of the house. He wasn't able to peak into any of the windows because they were all closed and concealed. Ethan slowly put his hand over his gun as he prepared to glance around the corner.

Chris grabbed Ethan's arm, tugging him back towards him. He stared at Ethan and then straight ahead, looking towards the window across from them. Ethan watched as a Hispanic man walked into view, his back turned as he fiddled with something. The man was about six feet tall wearing a white tank top and a yellow bandana. He had tattoos covering his arm and a strong, muscular build.

Ethan glanced at Chris who glanced back, his hand moving down towards his weapon. Ethan realized they were in a very sticky position. This block was a heavy drug and gang area, so should they be spotted they would surely be fired on. They had no right being where they were. Ethan watched the man as he turned to his side, his face visible now as the two agents

stood like deer in headlights against the wall of the crack house.

The man had a box of Lucky Charms in his hand which he poured out into a bowl. He

turned again, this time completely facing the agents as he reached for what must have been the

fridge. The grotesque scar that stretched across the left side of his face was now visible and

ominous. Ethan could feel Chris' arm tense as he closed his fingers around his gun, letting out a

very light exhale. Neither of them moved a muscle as they stared at the scarred, cereal making

brute.

The man finished making his cereal and put the milk back into his fridge. He still faced

the two agents, but finally turned around and walked out of the kitchen. Ethan and Chris

looked relieved at each other before continuing their dangerous reconnaissance. Ethan

stopped quickly, throwing his arm out to knock Chris back as the two fell against the building

again.

Ethan shook his head as he glanced over at Chris, then he slowly peaked around the

corner. There was a man laid out on a set of wooden steps, his mouth opened wide and a

bottle of Jameson lay on its' side next to him. The man was wearing weathered clothes, and it

was visible that he had lost a few of his teeth.

Ethan just wanted to case the backyard, to make sure there was an opening and to see

what the area looked like. He didn't want to go into the raid without a good idea of what this

place looked like, especially with pricks like Anthony and Porter tagging along. Ethan stared

across the yard, taking a mental picture, and then pointed to the front of the house indicating

for Chris to continue.

The back entrance was a prime spot to break in from. Ethan could envision the four agents splitting up and sandwiching the house, Ethan and Chris would take the upstairs and Porter and Anthony would make their way down. It wouldn't be the first time they had raided a druggie hive and each time was different. There were times where the people scattered, attempting to run out of the house. There were also the few occasions when they put up a fight. Ethan wasn't sure how this would end up, but at least they had the 52nd Precinct down the block.

As they made their way under the windows and back out to the front of the house, Ethan noticed the shade had been drawn at the top window. He stared up at it, still moving forward as he checked to see if someone was watching. Through the window he could only see a dark room, plain white walls and a corroded ceiling. There was no sign of life, but it still made Ethan feel uneasy. He pointed it out to Chris, but his partner just shrugged his shoulders. Even as Ethan made his way to the Charger, he couldn't see anyone in the window.

"You have to be kidding me," Chris said. Ethan turned his attention to the car to see Chris reaching towards the windshield. "A ticket…" Chris said as he held up the orange envelope. He shook his head, staring at it as he cursed under his breath.

Ethan laughed to himself; he had gotten so many of those when he lived on Mosholu. The reaction was still the same though, whether an FBI agent or not, nobody liked a nice New York City ticket.

"Two in the back, two in the front?" Chris said as they drove away.

"I was thinking Porter and Ant through the back and they make their way downstairs. Me and you through the front and upstairs. I might have a picture of my cousin at my house, if not I'm sure there's one in my mother's old stuff," Ethan said. He had put a few boxes of his

mother's old things into a storage area in his building's basement. Nothing too valuable, just

some old pictures and a few old articles of clothes.

"Do you think he'll run?" Chris asked, looking out the window as they got back on the

Major Deegan.

"I have no idea—if he sees me, he might not."

Ethan wasn't sure what Aiden's reaction would be when he saw him. He hoped to be

the first one to make contact; he had hoped to see the reaction on Aiden's face so he could

determine if he was really the killer. If Aiden was the killer, and this was where he lived, then

there had to be some evidence there in relation to the case.

The Charger drove by Yankee Stadium, the majestic castle in the Bronx. The two agents

always goggled at it like small children. The Stadium was gorgeous with its white, dazzling walls

stretching by 161st Street, brightening the cold, dark streets and giving them meaning. There

wasn't a single person who didn't take a second to notice it, even if they had seen it a million

times.

Ethan had loved the Yankees his whole life. His father had introduced him to them and

brought him to his first game. He made a lifestyle of loving them and watching every game.

The Yankees were one of the few things that Ethan still greatly appreciated despite his

shattered memories of time spent with his father. He could still remember the time his father

had gone to game 6 of the 1996 World Series, Yankees vs. Braves. He had two tickets, but

decided not to take Ethan. The Yankees won the World Series in that game too. His father's haunting memory never stopped him from relishing nights out at Rambling House enjoying

some incredible games with Chris and Luke.

Ethan and Chris looked at each other and it was at that moment that Ethan realized

Chris might see things his way.

"What if we had never seen Aiden that day?" Ethan asked. "Would he be a suspect

still? If Aiden was the killer then why would he even be near the scene of a crime…it really

doesn't make sense."

"You're reaching too much," Chris said. "I learned a while ago not to look for that one

piece of evidence that just makes it all click. Sometimes it's just nonexistent, you know that."

Ethan wasn't looking for the clicking piece of evidence; he was just looking for the piece

that made Aiden free from suspicion.

"I mean if you look at it that way, then you would also be a suspect here," Ethan said,

glancing over quickly to see what Chris' reaction was.

"Are you serious?" Chris said, staring back at Ethan with a look of disgust. "You've been

my partner for about seven years now, and you think I'd do some of this stuff. How would that

even be possible, I was with you the entire time?"

"I know, I know. I'm just saying—just because Aiden knows me and just because he was

there that night doesn't make him a cold blooded, psychopathic killer," Ethan said feeling bad

about the accusation. "I'm sorry though."

"I get you, it's a touchy subject…I'm trying my best to go about it the right way but it's

tough. Tomorrow might get dicey, and its gunna be tough on you. I know you're a strong guy but this sorta thing would be tough on anyone. Don't take this the wrong way, but I hope you're ready."

The day was a success for the most part. They were able to get a good idea of the layout of the house and the neighboring houses. They saw the backyard, scoped out the back entrance, and made it out unnoticed. The operation should run smoothly but there were always unexpected complications.

Unfortunately tensions were high. Ethan realized there was some animosity growing, some impatience present, but hopefully the case would be resolved soon. They appeared to be on the brink of solving it. The murders would end, the letters would stop, and Ethan hoped it would be the last time he had such a big fan in the psycho community.

The two pulled in front of Chris' apartment building, and the awkward silence in the car was unnerving. Chris didn't budge. He just sat there staring out the car window. Ethan hoped he wouldn't say anything because he just wanted to go home and scream and watch the Jets alone.

"Let's go watch the Jets game," Chris said, looking over at Ethan. "I don't wanna get out of the car like this man, I'm sorry I said that shit."

"It's not a big deal, don't worry about it," Ethan said. "Not every day you deal with a case like this." He actually was a little offended, but he knew he could be overly sensitive sometimes

"It is a big deal man," Chris said shaking his head. "Don't think I don't care about you. I just want it all to stop."

Ethan pulled away from Chris' apartment.

"Rambling?" Ethan said. Chris nodded his head back, the awkward silence slowly melted away as the two began discussing football.

Ethan knew Chris was on his side, he knew there was no way Chris would see things entirely the same, but he did understand that Chris was more than a co-worker.

Chapter 42

Careful

The wind blew fiercely through Ethan's open window. The cold air circulated through the room, blowing past the TV which displayed highlights from the Jets' win over the Pats, it blew under the bathroom doorway, and over Ethan's rigid, conscious body. He lay on top of his sheets feeling the cold run over his bare skin, staring up at the dark, dull ceiling. He had wanted to spend the night with Rachel but he thought it was wiser they wait until after the raid.

Next to Ethan sat the folders of evidence, the photos of the victims, and his notebook of logic and sense making. The notebook was fairly empty. He was so sick of looking through it all, he practically had it all memorized. It was already after 5AM. The raid would take place in two hours and Ethan was terrified. He was more worried than he had ever been during a case. It wasn't the raid that scared him, and it wasn't his cousin being the top suspect either. Ethan was petrified they might be way off.

"You ready, buddy?" Chris asked. He strapped his bullet proof vest on as he watched Ethan. They were gearing up in full SWAT attire. They wouldn't be playing games at such a crucial point in the case. They didn't want to rush into anything without being fully prepared, especially when they would be coming face to face with such a desperate, ruthless killer.

Ethan strapped on a 3A Kevlar vest, fastened his knee pads, and fastened his Glock to his waist and his pistol to his thigh. He was prepared physically and had more than enough training and experience to pull off a small raid such as this one, but he just hoped he was mentally ready.

He could see the glances he was getting from Chris and the nods from Porter and Anthony, but he blocked them all out. It was another day at the office. He was going into that house, he was pulling Aiden out, and that was the end of it. It didn't matter what the victims had done. The bottom line was these people were brutally murdered. They were murdered in cold blood. The killer had to be put away.

Ethan stood in front of his three counterparts, staring them down as they stared back up at him. He watched them carefully, critically examining their composures to see if they doubted him, to see if they showed any concern.

"You all know my personal connections with this raid. Let there be no misunderstanding, my intention is to apprehend Aiden Moore and bring him in for interrogation," Ethan began, staring down the line at each individual. "There's nothing personal about today...I'm done talking about it." Ethan reached forward, passing out a sheet of paper to the three agents. "This is Aiden Moore, the picture was taken about ten years ago but I can assure you not much has changed."

Porter laughed out loud as he stuffed the picture into his chest pocket. He shook his head as he looked back and forth between Anthony and Chris.

"Are you kidding me right now? You wanna go bust up a crack house, grab a highly dangerous suspect, and you hand out his baby picture," Porter said, shaking his head with a look of disgust. "You're joking right."

Ethan swallowed hard, doing his best to keep his composure as he stared daggers through Porter.

"Aiden Moore is 5'6'', Caucasian, about 158 lbs., dark brown hair, and light brown eyes. We have enough reason to believe he's there now. Aiden has been seen at this house, and we have eyewitness confirmation that this man lives there. Porter and Anthony, you'll both go in from the front, you'll wait ten seconds before breaking in, give Chris and me enough time to position ourselves in the back. We're dealing with drug addicts and alcoholics, but this isn't anyone's first crack house so I'm expecting a complete success."

Porter shook his head more, ripping the picture back out of his chest pocket to take another long stare.

"The 52nd Precinct will be backing us up. They'll secure the area and give us the added presence we'll need to ensure a safe operation. The use of deadly force is strictly limited to absolutely necessary situations. I have full confidence in all of us. I know we'll be successful."

Ethan looked down at the picture of Aiden, wondering if his cousin had any clue they were coming. This killer was so smart. Therefore, if it was Aiden, wouldn't he have already prepared for this?

"Be very careful, watch your step, and don't underestimate what we're up against. This killer is highly intelligent, highly dangerous, and from what we've seen so far there's no limit to what it'll do."

Ethan was slightly worried about the operation. It wasn't a big deal, the whole thing was very routine, but when Ethan thought about what the killer had done thus far and where they were intending to go now, he got goose bumps.

The four agents jumped into the Charger, and they didn't want to look conspicuous as they rolled down Hull Avenue. They didn't speak a word as they roared along the Major

Deegan, staring out at the Hudson River as they rolled by. The sun was beaming off the water, casting a glare across it, giving it a metallic look. Ethan felt butterflies forming in the pit of his stomach, but it didn't worry him. Nerves were a part of the job. However, it was dealing with the nerves that set a good agent apart from a dead one.

He knew Chris would be pissed if he knew what he was thinking about. He went over each of the letters, skimming them for some type of sign that would tell him to turn around. Any sign that would indicate it wasn't his cousin.

He stopped at the light on the corner of Bainbridge and 204th Street, only a block away from Hull Ave. They watched around them as the people went about their normal daily activities, no idea of what was about to go on right down the block. Ethan looked up in his rearview mirror, his body jolting at the sight of his father sitting there in the middle seat. His stomach rumbled and his heart beat a little faster as he squeezed his eyes shut, wishing the vision away.

'Not right now,' Ethan thought to himself. He opened his eyes again, this time just seeing Porter and Anthony staring out their windows. No one had noticed anything. Ethan took a deep breath, trying to relax his mind, to clear his thoughts and prepare himself to take care of business. It was weird for him to look around and see the neighborhood he had grown up in. To see the McDonalds he had gone to so often, to walk through the park he had played at, even to see the spots where he had been jumped. He did feel a little nostalgic. He loved the neighborhood; overall, he really had enjoyed his time there.

He parked the Charger down the block from the house, putting his police sign in the window this time. Chris looked over at him and gave him a nod and thumbs up. The four filtered out of the car and slipped across the street, staying close to each other as they moved slowly towards the house. This time was a little different than yesterday: people were stopping in the street to watch. Some of them ran, some poked back into their houses, and some braver, dumber stragglers leaned against parked cars to watch as if it was a movie.

Ethan stared at the house, watching it carefully to make sure there was nothing off. It looked exactly the same as it had yesterday. All the windows were closed, all the shades were drawn, and it looked as though no one lived there. The front gate was open and motionless.

Ethan moved forward, nodding for the others to follow him. Up ahead Ethan could see the 52nd Precinct blocking off the bottom of the road and as he turned, he saw they had also blocked off the top. They were doing their part. He continued to move into the front yard still keeping his eyes fixed on the windows, making sure no one spotted them as they advanced on the unsuspecting occupants. On the killer. Ethan flicked his hand to the side, quickly looking towards Anthony and Porter, and then made his way with Chris to the side of the house.

Porter and Anthony positioned themselves on top of the porch. Porter put up his two hands, signaling to Ethan that they would move in ten seconds. Porter picked his gun out of his holster, Anthony following suit, and the two propped themselves lightly against opposite sides of the front door.

It was amazing how slow ten seconds moves when you're anxious. The time ticked down gradually, beating what felt like once every minute. Ethan and Chris quickly shuffled down the side of the house, ducking under each window as they made their way to the back door. Ethan pressed up against the house, quickly poked his head around the bend, and then moved into the yard carefully, pulling his Glock out and into a ready position in front of him. He stared around, carefully inspecting every nook and every cranny as the two prepared to kick the flimsy wooden door open. Chris loaded his chamber, sending one lethal bullet into position and ready to scream out of the barrel and ripping through whatever stood in its way.

Ethan breathed slowly, looking down at his partner who looked back up at him. *3.* The killer was only a few feet away. The source of the letters, the person who fired on them in Lake George, the person who had killed so many in such a gruesome manner. *2.* Just seconds away from grabbing his cousin, from putting an end to his tirade, to his "mission". *1.* Just one second away from proving Ethan wrong, from reversing all of his doubts, from confirming what Chris believed: that Aiden was in fact guilty.

Ethan turned his body, placing himself squarely in front of the back door, and then jerked his body back, driving all of his force through the door. The door burst open, shattering against the wall next to it, as Ethan and Chris dashed through the opening, their guns pointed in front of them. From across the house they could hear Porter and Anthony smash through the front. The two agents stood in the hallway, their mouths opened in confusion. They looked at each other, unsure, mystified by what was before them. This is something they didn't expect.

Chapter 43

Presents

Christmas morning at last. Ethan jumped out of the pullout, excited beyond belief that the weekend was almost over. This was his favorite day of the year, but this Christmas he didn't have his mother with him. He had, instead, the man who barely showed he cared the other 364 days of the year. Just a few more hours and he could leave.

Ethan walked down the hallway to the upstairs bathroom, ignoring Ray's voice from downstairs.

"I really wanted that!" Ray screamed. Ethan shook his head as he washed his hands and his face, preparing himself for what awaited him downstairs. He didn't know at that moment that there was nothing that could prepare the eleven year old for what was to come.

"Booka Man!" his father screamed, running over to his son to give him a big hug. "Merry Christmas buddy!" Michelle also gave Ethan a hug and a "Merry Christmas". There were a bunch of gifts under the tree, including the box that Ethan had eyed the day before. He had never forgotten about the snow globe. He still firmly believed that it had been in his bag. His eyes scanned the box; it looked to be the same size, the same weight, but it just couldn't be.

"This one's for Michelle," Andrew said, picking up that very box and handing it to Michelle. Ethan watched their expressions as Michelle slowly pulled away the wrapping paper. All eyes were on Michelle as she smiled widely, laughing as she looked at Andrew and then back at the box. She raised it to her ear and gave it a little shake. She continued to pull the wrapping away, completely tearing the paper off of it as she stared in shock.

Ethan felt the rage build inside as he stared at the object, and he felt his body shake uncontrollably as he jumped forward. He reached out, grabbing the box, and Michelle and Andrew both stared at him in confusion.

"Ethan what's wrong?" Andrew said. Ethan looked down at the box in his hand, realizing that he was holding on to the new clock radio they kept advertising on TV.

"I'm sorry, I don't know, I guess I'm still asleep," Ethan said with a laugh, handing the gift back over to Michelle. Everyone else laughed with him, brushing off the outburst as just an act of being tired and delusional.

He didn't know how to move past it. He didn't know how to let it roll off his shoulders. He was only eleven, after all. He sat in the living room, opening his gifts with a smile on his face. Ethan wasn't ungrateful; he understood how fortunate he was, but was it too much to wish that he could have his mother there too? Was it being a spoiled, rotten brat that he wished his father cared the rest of the days of the year, and not just when it looked good in front of the family? The conflict hurt Ethan's head. The doubt and uncertainty of how he should act was overwhelming. Did his father love him?

Chapter 44

Slowly

Ethan quickly dove back out of the door, coughing roughly as he spit on the backyard. Chris did the same, leaning over the railing as he shook his head erratically, gagging as he jogged further away from the door. The smell was vial. By far the worst, most pungent smell Ethan had ever had to endure. He could hear Porter and Anthony coughing around the side of the house also as some officers from the 52nd stared at them cautiously.

"Shit!" Chris sputtered. "Oh my God, what the hell?"

Ethan stared at the open doorway, feeling the array of emotions overcoming him. He was annoyed, he was confused, he was fed up, and he wasn't surprised. As much as he wished he was, he just wasn't surprised. He had thought about it the whole way to the raid, he thought about it before he even kicked the door open. He knew the killer wasn't stupid and part of him knew they'd be expected.

"Gas," Ethan said, shaking his head as he cursed to himself. "I need everyone away from this house, shut the door, start evacuating the nearby residents, and call in the emergency crews to contain this shit."

Ethan stormed back down the alley to the front of the house. Chris jogged around him to let the rest of the guys know the situation. They had seen bodies on the floor inside the house, more people victim to this psycho. Another operation spiraling out of control, a crack house filled with gas in a highly populated area. It was a miracle this house hadn't blown out of the state.

Chris and the others moved the bystanders back, knocking on the neighbors' doors to issue the evacuation warnings. Ethan stood with them, but his mind was gone. He knew he had to hold it together but at this point he didn't know what was right anymore. 'Another loss,' he thought as he pushed some bystanders back. You would think they'd run back knowing that a simple electric spark could blow the whole house sky high.

Ethan leaned against the Charger, watching as the emergency teams worked to contain the leak in the house. Chris, Porter, and Anthony stood nearby, chatting amongst each other, shaking their heads periodically and looking over at the house in disbelief. Ethan felt like he was waiting for hours before the emergency crew finally gave them the all clear to move back into the vicinity.

He didn't have time to soak it all in. He didn't have the chance to feel uneasy from the smell of the dead, to feel nauseous from the bodies that shrouded the floor, to piece together the puzzle that was Aiden Moore, the killer behind all the letters. He walked straight through the front door, past the forensics teams that dusted the room down for any sign of the criminal behind this sabotage.

The house was a ruin of drugs and disease. The filth that scourged its floors were despicable low lives, nuisances to society who would have ended up this way ultimately. There was cocaine on the tables; marijuana floating around all over, pills and needles piled messily, the house was a drug safe-house, a source of business for the power hungry criminals in the neighborhood.

Ethan took one step at a time, slowly making his way closer to the top floor. He wanted to investigate the room he had looked at the day before, the room with the open window. As he stepped up the final step, he could easily tell there was something wrong. He stared from forensics scientist to police officer, watching as they stared at him warily, backing away and muttering amongst each other.

"What's the problem?" Ethan said, tired of the weird glances and whispering.

"Look inside," Captain said quietly, the nerves in his voice were blatant. Ethan hadn't seen him in the group. He looked at him, watching him as he nervously shuffled around in his place. Captain shook his head, looking down at the floor, and pointed to the doorway behind him. Ethan's heart raced, he wasn't sure what he would see beyond that doorway. This whole case was so unpredictable, but at this point it seemed certain who the culprit was.

Ethan walked towards the entrance, breathing deeply as he anticipated what stood ahead. He stepped into the room, the small, hot, grotesque box of a room. The paint had almost completely chipped away from the dull white walls. The destroyed, metal bed post was broken and distorted, the worn-out, thin mattress was shredded and hanging off to the side. A small desk stood against the wall on the side, one of the drawers was missing and the other was halfway out and chipped all over.

Ethan stood in the middle of the room, looking from side to side as his heart beat faster and faster. He could feel his body shaking slightly, his lip quivering. He closed his eyes, doing his best to calm down. He could feel the room start to spin around him, his legs were getting shaky as he took a deep breath. He had to pull it together, this wouldn't do any good. He had to fight through this.

"Holy shit," Chris said, joining Ethan. Porter and Anthony stepped in for a second, taking a quick glance around before they stepped back out. Ethan could hear Chris taking deep breaths. He was convulsing just as bad as Ethan had. He looked over at Ethan, who looked back with a blank stare. There weren't words to describe what was in that room. The two agents just stood still, their bodies and minds completely in shock as they stared at the hundreds of pictures of Ethan hung all over the room.

The pictures were all candid shots, pictures taken of Ethan as he went about his normal daily routines. There was a picture of him at Sal's, a picture of him at Rambling House, a picture of him getting into the Charger. Ethan walked around the room taking a look at each picture.

"This was like three months ago," Chris said, glancing at one of the pictures. "We were on our way to the Yanks, Red Sox game."

There were pictures thrown everywhere. The floor was almost covered in them. Ethan stared at himself everywhere he looked, at his unaware poses. It was unnerving, the thought of his cousin watching him for so long, taking snap shots of him everywhere he went. It was disturbing.

Ethan noticed it sticking out of the drawer, the white paper catching his eye as he still stared around the room in disbelief. It was the proof they needed, the easy distinction that told them Ethan was wrong and Chris was on the money. Ethan reached into the drawer, pulling out the paper and began to read.

To my clueless friend,

The road is over. Each obstacle has been hurdled, each painful memory has been realized, and now, my friend, you can free yourself. So many in this world do not deserve a place, but I'm sure I need not tell you this, the path I've lead you on has shined enough light. You know what must be done, as do I, and as tough as this realization may be, I accept it. It's justice, after all, and justice, and the truth, is what we strive to obtain. You know where to find what you're looking for. You know where to find me. I'll be there at Midnight on the 2nd. I'll show you justice. I'll show you undeniable truth.

I'm always yours

Scattered around the room Ethan could see there were more copies of the letter. He folded the letter up gently, placed it in his chest pocket, and took a seat on the beat up, torn apart bed. Chris read through one of the letters' copies, folding it and putting it inside his pocket as he stared down at his distressed partner. He sighed deeply, still standing there like an idiot, he had no idea what to say or do. None of the typical, cheesy lines seemed like a right fit at a time like this. "Come on buddy, we'll make it through this." "We'll get this guy, I'm positive. Let's do it." None of it seemed right.

Ethan looked forward, staring blankly through the doorway. He was trying to gather his thoughts, to put together what the next step was, what the next move in this insane chess game was, but he came up blank.

"What can we do?" Ethan said, breaking the awkward silence in the room. He sat there, right in the middle of all of his pictures. It looked like some sick photo shoot. "We're doing everything we can…no?" Chris nodded his head back. Ethan was wondering if he was losing it, if he was losing his touch, his edge. He and Chris had a reputation, a great one, and here they were facing about ten or so dead bodies and an assortment of ridiculous letters.

Ethan got up from the bed and began to walk out of the room before stopping abruptly. Chris stopped close behind him, backing up a little as he stared on to see what his partner would do. Ethan clenched his fists tight, turning slowly to take the whole scene in one last time, and then he screamed. He screamed at the top of his lungs, scaring some of the people outside the doorway. Porter and Anthony both poked their heads around the corner, staring into the room startled by the loud noise. Chris didn't flinch, he just stood still and watched his partner, letting him unleash the built-up stress. Ethan put his hands on his face, rubbing it fiercely as he shook his head in aggravation.

"What do you see in this room?" Ethan said, looking over at Chris. Chris jumped a little; he seemed almost surprised that he was being spoken to. He knelt down, picking up a few of the pictures and turned them over examining them head to toe.

"We have some prints, Ethan," Captain said as he came walking back into the room, cautiously stepping around some of the evidence on the floor. "We found a bunch of prints but it could be anyone's. We have a head count of twenty-five."

Ethan's heart almost stopped beating. He stared back at Captain, his face showing a plethora of disgust.

"What?" he stammered.

"Twenty-five found dead, we have I.D.'s on about half of them," Captain said, looking down at a clipboard he carried in his arms. "All criminals and druggies, all have records for robbery, armed robbery, kidnapping, drug trafficking, possession of an illegal firearm, the list goes on." Captain looked up at Ethan as he put his clip board back under his arm. "No Aiden Moore found."

Ethan shook his head as he looked down at the floor, staring directly into his own eyes. He remembered the day in the picture he was looking at, it was Chris' birthday about a year back. He had a huge smile on his face and a Bud Light in his hand, the picture only focused on him, which is the same way the rest were. They were at a bar called The Playwright in the city on that day. Nice little bar, real great bartenders too. One of them was actually his own uncle, Joe Carey.

"Tonight at midnight," Ethan said, turning and walking out of the room. Chris followed close behind. Ethan jogged down the steps and walked in between two forensics scientists who hovered over one of the bodies. He knelt down low, examining the body closely, scouring over it inch by inch. The man was probably in his late thirties, very thin, and it was evident by the marks on his body that he was an avid drug abuser. The needle marks could still be visible, some of them obviously fresh.

"The gas leak killed all of them from what we can tell, but we're still investigating," one of the women said.

"Have you noticed any markings that stand out?" Ethan asked.

"Markings on the body?"

"A peace sign in particular, yeah," Ethan said as he squinted, trying to see past all of the scarring and needle punctures.

"Haven't seen any. We'll have the reports faxed straight to you though," the women said, staring at Ethan confused.

Ethan handed her one of his business card and walked out of the house. He was furious, he was embarrassed, and he was nervous. He didn't know what the next step for him and Chris was, but he did know "the end" would take place tonight at midnight and they had to get ready for it.

Ethan jumped into the Charger, followed by Chris, Porter, and Anthony, and roared off, putting his sirens on as the car tore down the road. Inside the car they remained silent, letting the blaring sounds of sirens make all the noise. The agents all sat uneasily, glancing briefly over at Ethan every so often, but none of them had anything to say. Even Porter, the biggest wiseass in the Bureau, sat quietly, staring out his window at the cars whipping by on the other side of the highway.

"Let us know if you guys need anything, if you guys need someone for tonight, you know where to find us," Porter said as he got out of the Charger.

Ethan appreciated the offer, but he knew what he was going to do. He already had it in his mind, this case was personal, no ifs—no ands—no buts. Chris sat quietly next to Ethan, and he could easily tell by the look of certainty in Ethan's eyes that he had some of his fire back.

"I'll let Illames know," Chris said, leaning back in his seat and checking his Glock again. He popped the clip out and punched it back in, his superstitious quick check. "I have your back."

Ethan already knew Chris would be there. He knew he didn't have to bother asking. They had developed a bond over the years, and it wouldn't break because of this. Ethan raced back the way they had come, heading straight back to his old neighborhood. He wasn't playing games anymore. He was going to take the offensive.

"We're working around the clock on this, doing everything we can," Chris said, looking over at Ethan as he spoke to Illames. "He's fine, just a little stressed, but nothing unusual."

Ethan figured Illames would be concerned. No one, Illames especially, wanted any agents going haywire and losing their cool. Ethan understood this better than anyone since keeping one's anger under control was a huge part of being a successful and safe agent. He had a lot of practice in this field.

Chris didn't ask Ethan anything. He knew the answer to all of his questions already. He wasn't sure where Ethan was going, though, as he looked out the window at Mosholu Parkway. Ethan was never more certain during this case than at this very moment.

Ethan parked the car at the hydrant in front of his old apartment building, jumping out quickly as he ran through the courtyard to the metal front door. He looked through the names on the buzzers until he found the one he was looking for.

MASSARO

He rang the bell repeatedly until the door buzzed, rushed inside, and jumped up two steps at a time. The little old woman's door was already open when Ethan turned the corner. She stood in the doorway looking rattled and confused, but Ethan had no time for explanations.

"Ms. Massaro, I met with you a few days ago," Ethan said, reaching into his pocket as he rummaged around for what he was looking for.

"Yes, yes, I remember…" she began before she was cut off.

"Do you know this man," Ethan asked, holding up the picture of Aiden as his heart began to pick up speed. The woman stared at the picture for a few seconds, squinting to make out the face of Ethan's cousin. "Have you ever seen this man?"

"I believe so…" she started again before Ethan cut her off once more.

"Aiden Moore. Do you know Aiden Moore and have you seen him lately."

The woman stared blankly at Ethan and then suddenly her composure shifted.

"Yes, yes, yes I know Aiden. He was good friends…" she started before she stopped, tears welling up in her eyes.

"I'm sorry Ms. Massaro. I'm so sorry for your loss, but I need you to help me right now. I need to find this man before more people get hurt."

"I haven't seen him in some time. He's very familiar in the neighborhood though." She was more solemn now.

Ethan needed to find Aiden now. As far as he was concerned, the time limit for midnight was a bunch of crap. He needed him in custody as soon as possible. He turned away from the woman, running back down the steps as he dashed out to the Charger. He roared back up Mosholu Parkway, blasting the sirens as he flew towards the Oval Park, Chris sitting next to him still curious as to what they were trying to accomplish.

The huge stone archway that stood in front of the oval park was empty as Ethan continued to speed towards it. The sirens still screamed loudly as people stopped to watch the car fly by.

"Ethan," Chris said, staring from Ethan to the park's entrance. "Ethan," he said again. The entrance way was narrow, but it wasn't not fitting that worried Chris, it was the chance of some unsuspecting resident trying to exit the park only to find a Charger roaring towards him. "Ethan—," he yelled but Ethan paid him no mind as he drove the Charger straight through the entrance way.

The car screeched into the park, sliding as it turned towards the basketball courts. Ethan had hoped the same guys from days ago would be there. He could see the usual gangsters jumping up off the benches, some of them running away as the cop car, sirens ripping

apart the silent park, flew across the emptying park heading straight for them.

Ethan drove the Charger straight onto the basketball courts, speeding towards the now

much smaller group, and screeched to a stop before jumping out. He stormed towards the

group, spotting the short, stocky "leader" he had spoken to that other day. The Spanish

gangster walked out towards Ethan, his facial expression more shocked than angry.

Behind him there were only about three of his "friends" left. Ethan studied them

quickly as he made his way to meet with the little leader. They looked more petrified than

anything.   Probably wasn't every day they saw a black undercover car come screeching through

the park's entrance.

"What the fuck are you…," the man started before Ethan lunged forward sending a right

hook directly into his chin. Chris quickly grabbed his gun, pointing it at the man's three

counterparts.

"Don't move! Don't move!" Chris screamed, keeping his eyes on them as he glanced

around, making sure none of the cowards grew backbones and came running back.

Ethan dodged the man's counter attack, mercilessly throwing him to the concrete and

swinging him around.

"Listen to me—Listen to me—" Ethan implored as his left hand grabbed his firearm and

placed it against the man's head. The man squirmed uncomfortably, letting out moans of pain

in between trying to catch his breath and trying to understand what was happening. "I can take

you in and question you in prison. I have all fucking day. We could do this right here, right now

and be done in five minutes. Where is Aiden Moore?!"

Ethan saw the tattoo on the dead body back on Hull Avenue. He saw the spider web on his hand. He knew it was the marking of Lucky's gang. If Aiden was affiliated with that gang in any way, then the low life Ethan had in his hands had to know something. The man shook his head painfully, hiding his fear as he stared into Ethan's eyes.

"Ethan, come on man!" Chris screamed, still watching the man's friends who were starting to get over their initial shock. "My finger bends, asshole," he said, staring at one of the men.

"I won't ask again. I sped in to question you, you attacked me, I ended your fucking life." Ethan leaned in close to the man, pushing the barrel of his Glock so far into the man's head that the tip was concealed under his fat. "Where—is—Aiden—Moore?" Ethan's finger rested heavily on the gun's trigger. He squeezed it, putting his pressure on the metal piece as the man moved his eyes to watch. Sweat trickled across his forehead as his teeth started to chatter.

"He's been weird," the man exhaled. His fear was at its peak. "Been bouncing all over, acting crazy and shit...we ain't bother with him no more, not since he moved to Hull..." The man clenched his teeth, squeezing his eyes together as his body shook. "Used to be bad-ass...not no more."

"Why?" Ethan said, pushing the gun further. Chris stood motionless by his side, the man's three friends frozen solid next to each other.

The man let out another whimper, some blood began to drip from where Ethan hit him. He looked up at Ethan, his eyes widening.

"You think that motherfucker's my boy? Fuck him," the man sputtered, the blood still flowing across the side of his face. "Last seen him last night."

Ethan finally pulled the gun away, releasing the man and letting him spit his blood on to the concrete. He got up, walked back to the Charger and got in, leaving the four men on the court to watch him as he drove away. Chris sat next to him, his gun still firmly in his grasp as he stared at his partner in disbelief. Chris took a deep breath and looked forward, still wide-eyed in shock.

"I'm not sure what scared me more today," he said, still looking forward.

Ethan shrugged his shoulders. "I think the room filled with my pictures did it for me."

Chris looked at his partner, straight faced, and shook his head.

"What's next…" he whispered, his heart still racing.

Chapter 45

Rubik's Cube

Ethan sorted through his bundle of letters. He didn't even read anything. He just shuffled through them staring aimlessly. Chris sat across from him, staring at the crime reports and the pictures of the dead victims. He also stared aimlessly, unsure as to what he was exactly looking for.

"This is all coming down to you," Chris said, taking a sip of iced tea. "I hate to say it man, but it is what it is. You know where your cousin is buried. That's where I think we have to go. You said Aiden idolized him, right? He's made reference to 'where we all end up' so it has to be there."

Ethan laughed whimsically, "You realize this is bullshit?" He got up, walking back and forth as he shook his head. "I have no idea. I don't know. All I can think about is how this is gunna kill me, kill you too as far as our reputations go. Why would Aiden tell us where he'll be, it makes no sense, Chris. He would have just stayed in that house if it was really him."

"Who gives a shit about that, man?" Chris said, leaning forward and putting his head in his hands. "We're on the hunt for Aiden Moore. It's not the first time we've looked for someone. You're still trying to figure out who the killer is when we already have him. It's plain as day, sometimes it's just that easy."

"How do you know it's him, there's…" Ethan stopped, throwing his head back in frustration. He slammed his fist down on his desk, letting the pain course through his body as he shut his eyes tight. "Then it's Aiden."

"Ethan...come on man, isn't it obvious?" Chris said, placing one hand on Ethan's shoulder. "Listen, I'm gunna run out." Chris picked up his jacket, sorting through his pockets looking for his phone. "Have to pick up a few things before I lose my fiancé. I'll be back in a while with some coffee...gunna be a long night, but this case ends soon." Chris walked out of the apartment, waving behind him as Ethan closed his door.

Ethan sank down into his armchair, staring at his dull white door as the time on the clock ticked by. He went through the letters quietly by himself, reading them over and over again, envisioning the dead bodies as he read. He spoke the words out loud, he read through each crime report thoroughly, but still nothing popped out.

Hours went by. Chris returned with pizza. Later they drank coffee. Still the agents sat dumbfounded. They swapped paperwork, each analyzing everything four, five, six times before finally placing it all down.

"What similarities are there?" Ethan asked, while standing up as his phone rang out. He saw Rachel's name displayed across the screen, hesitating before he decided to answer it.

"Hey, what's up?" Rachel said, sounding cheerful and wide awake. "How was work today?"

"Work was fantastic," Ethan said, looking at Chris who looked back up at him with a perplexed face. "I'm actually still working with Chris, burning the candle on both ends."

"Fantastic?!" Chris exclaimed. He laughed loudly.

"Oh I'm sorry, I'll let you go then. Tell Chris I said hi," Rachel said, sounding less cheerful then she had. "Give me a call when you're less busy."

Ethan loved his job, he loved the psychos, he loved the gangsters, and he loved the raids. Ethan loved the puzzles, he loved the thrill of the chase, but at this particular moment, he wished he could put it all on pause.

"You know what, why don't I pick you up and we can go grab some dessert or something to eat if you're hungry. Maybe catch a movie if you want?" Ethan wanted to say, but the fact of the matter was he didn't have that option.

"I want to talk, but we're just at the tail end of this case," Ethan said, staring down at the pictures of the dead bodies. "It should be over soon, we're just making sure we have all of our ducks in a row. How about Wednesday night? The case will definitely be over by then." He made sure not to look at Chris, since he was sure his partner was making some kind of a face.

"Yeah that sounds fine," Rachel said, her voice sounding a little happier. "I guess just call me and let me know."

"I'll talk to you later," Ethan said, hanging the phone up and placing it down on his desk. He leaned forward, his head hanging as he stared at the bodies.

"Hey…if she's gunna be with me then she'll have to accept me for who I am and what I do," Ethan said, looking over at Chris who shrugged his shoulders. Ethan didn't completely agree with his own words. He knew he had something good with Rachel and he wanted to do this right. He wanted to devote to her the time she deserved. He wanted to enjoy her company and treat her like a princess. Right now just wasn't a great time.

"Anyway, what are the similarities," Ethan resumed aloud, spreading out the letters across his table.

"Look, this is what I've gathered so far," Chris said. "Each victim was last seen leaving work...mysteriously they all vanished after that. There was no sign of funny business, no sign of forced entry. They just disappeared...which is impossible. We do have video evidence of Walter Veteri and Naomi Cotroneo who were both last seen leaving their jobs. They're believed to have left for home, and they weren't seen until this video was made. They were obviously knocked unconscious...I mean me and you both took the ride to Lake George, there's no way you can get someone there against their will unless you knock them out..."

Ethan shook his head, "We're both assuming that there must be a clue here leading us to the right spot, right? We see that there's this peace sign etched into each of the victims. Each letter has a different quote. We need to analyze these letters more."

"I think we have our location, we have our motive, and we have our killer—but if you want to keep analyzing we have time before we'd have to leave," Chris said, sounding slightly annoyed.

The clock ticked on as the time crawled precariously closer to their midnight deadline. Silently the two moved about, studying, reading, typing away on their laptops as they researched different leads on the internet. They took turns making coffee and Monster energy drink runs, keeping themselves fresh and their minds keen, but their lethargy eventually had them both snoozing away.

Chapter 46

Don't Close Your Eyes

Ethan was aware of where he was. He was sure he was in the hell he remembered so clearly, the nightmare he lived through. He stood in the middle of his father's living room, staring straight at the elaborate, sophisticated Christmas tree that stood in the room's corner. He remembered the beautifully decorated, strikingly festive tree so well.

"Ethan! I can't believe you got it!" a boy's voice screamed. The boy came flying into the room, running right through Ethan as he stood there watching his cousin Aiden laughing riotously, the smile across his face seeming to be permanent. Ethan stood in shock as he watched himself run into the living room, jumping up on to the couch as his cousin did a dance around the table. Ethan shook his head, shaking off the grogginess that eroded him. There was no escaping the fact that little Ethan had just run into the living room.

He watched the two boys chatter amongst each other, rambling on and on about some new video game system Ethan had just gotten. Ethan walked out of the room, leaving his younger self to revel in his glory. He had just realized exactly where and *when* he was. Ethan walked around the corner, entering the dining room area where most of his family sat discussing random politics and their newest accomplishments in the world of the rich and the famous.

Ethan's eyes watered as he saw one person in particular, his cousin John-David. Ethan watched as his beautiful, talented cousin laughed and played around with his younger cousin, Louis.

Isn't that always the case? Something so beautiful, something so wonderful and loved, has to be stripped from us without a moment's notice. John-David had been 'cool' in Ethan's eyes back then. He played the guitar, he loved the Jets, and he was a skilled athlete and a great husband who would soon be an incredible father to a baby boy. He wouldn't be giving himself that opportunity though.

Ethan moved from the dining area to the entertainment room—yes there was an entertainment room—where he saw him. His father sat in the room, laughing and making giant arm gestures as he amused his guests. Michelle sat near him laughing heartily as her eyes gleamed in excitement.

Ethan stared around the room. He knew what day it was, and he knew what would happen. It was one of the moments in his life he had blocked out for so long, but here he was standing strong. Ethan remembered what Luke had said to him, he knew he had to face this. As he watched the memory unfold, Ethan could feel his emotions begin to surface. He wasn't angry, he wasn't resentful. Instead, he was feeling a new feeling, one he had barely felt before.

He looked at the doorway, seeing his younger self still smiling widely while he played with his cousin. He knew there was nothing he could do to alter what would happen. No matter what, he would go through this day unknowingly. Ethan stood watching helplessly, wishing he could do something, as his younger form walked into hell.

Chapter 47

Where We'll All Be

Ethan slowly opened his eyes, drifting back into reality. Chris was knocked out, lying across Ethan's bed with some paperwork underneath him in a messy heap. His mouth was wide open and some drool poured from it onto Ethan's already dirty floor.

He looked over to his bedside table, staring at the picture of his mother over Chris' sleeping body. He wished she was here, he knew she'd have helped him through.

Ethan got up, grabbed a Monster out of the fridge, and placed the drink to his lips. The sugary taste gave him chills as the drink poured down his throat. "Let's do this," Ethan said out loud, staring over at the clock that read 8:15 p.m.. 'Alright,' Ethan thought to himself. 'We have about four hours before we need to make a move. I should give Illames a call.'

Ethan picked up his cellphone, briefly thought of calling his mom since it was a kneejerk thought anytime he picked up his phone even since she passed, and then scrolled to Illames in his phone. It rang for a while, but Ethan knew his boss wouldn't ignore the call.

"Talk to me," Illames said, picking up the phone sounding wide awake. Ethan sometimes wondered how he could always be so refreshed.

"I've been up most of the day analyzing this evidence, I think we'll have our minds made soon. We believe the location may be St. Raymond's Cemetery in the Bronx," Ethan said, gathering all the evidence together to organize himself for round two.

There was a long pause after Ethan spoke. It made him feel a little uneasy. His boss was never at a loss for words. The one thing Ethan didn't want was to lose this case, so he really hoped Illames wouldn't pull him.

"Midnight, right? Call me when you're positive," Illames said. Ethan couldn't hear any emotion from the tone of his voice.

"You know we will."

"Ethan…I'm not gunna get cheesy on you, but I will say I don't doubt you. I know who you are," Illames said, hanging up before Ethan could say anything back.

'Do you know who I am,' Ethan thought. He sorted through the evidence, organizing himself before he took another stab at the whole thing.

"If this killer…if Aiden took the time to scout out Lucky, to take pictures of those kids, to be sick enough to abduct all of these people and torture them…kill them so horribly, than this shouldn't be easy to figure out."

Ethan stood up, pacing the room as he thought out loud, walking around Chris who still snored lightly on the bed. Ethan thought about waking him up, but he realized what Chris was doing was smart. 'We've barely had any sleep lately…we'll need to be well rested,' Ethan thought.

"Everything's been a puzzle so far, from small ones like the school gym, to bigger ones like my old apartment. It's playing games with us. It doesn't wanna get caught, but it is banking on us to run in the opposite direction. Some shit doesn't make sense. Was that the killer in Lake George, and why was it there? Why would it turn the gas on in the house? That's risky, it could have blown that whole thing up…I wouldn't have said it was a big risk taker until I saw the gas. The peace sign doesn't make much sense either. It doesn't mention it at all in any of the letters."

Ethan plopped back down in his chair, looking at Chris who turned to look back at him.

"What a fucking case!" Chris yelled, as he jumped up from the bed and made his way to the bathroom. "WHAT A CASE!"

Ethan cracked a smile as he dove back into his research. Everyone thought that being a special agent for the Federal Bureau of Investigation was all about the high speed chases and the gigantic gun fights. Little did they know that most of the job consisted of just this—paperwork, paperwork, and some more paperwork.

For hours they had labored, slaving over their laptops and the now beat-up pages of evidence, and now they only had hours left before this killer would kill another innocent person under their watch.

"This guy at the park mentioned that Aiden was darker…I can't remember what he exactly said, but he thought Aiden seemed different lately," Chris said, tossing some paperwork on to Ethan's table. "Yeah, this guy could be anywhere. We were on the money the last few times…I really think this guy's letting us see what he wants. If you asked me, Aiden Moore doesn't want to be caught tonight. Maybe you're right, Ethan. He's got something in store for us." Ethan had that same feeling, like they were being toyed with, like Aiden was showing them exactly what he wanted, and withholding exactly what he wanted also.

He stared out at the miserable city streets below. It was a freezing, rainy, dark day in New York City. Ethan could see the cluster of umbrellas below, quickly scattering around as their owners tried to make it to their destinations dry. The sound of thunder rattled the air. The streak of lightning scarred the night sky. It was just an all-around miserable, gloomy day.

As the nasty weather tormented the New Yorkers below, Ethan suddenly felt a revelation hit home. All the hours he had spent reading the countless pages of evidence, over and over, and over again, had instilled each word into his brain. He could recite each letter backwards at this point.

"Every letter he says something about where we all end up," Ethan said, spinning around and running back to his desk. He sounded so repetitive but he could feel he was getting somewhere now. "You see, he refers to it in some capacity in each letter." Ethan felt the excitement building. Chris had even straightened his posture and become more attentive. Chris nodded his head, staring at Ethan with wide eyes.

"Well in the end where do we all end up? We end up in a cemetery...other than me; Aiden's role model was our cousin John-David...John-David is buried in St. Raymond's cemetery on Tremont Ave."

Chris let out a loud laugh, a smile erupting across his face as he slapped Ethan on the back. "This is what I've been saying to you already. What else could it be?"

"No," Ethan said, his face still straight and emotionless. His brain was moving so fast he could hardly keep up. "I'm not going to fall into this trap again."

"What trap Ethan!? This took us nearly two days to figure out and about a hundred dollars in coffee," Chris said, his face looking surprised as he reached to grab his phone.

Ethan quickly grabbed Chris' hand, staring at him with a confused look on his face. Ethan shook his head slowly as he stared into Chris' worried eyes.

"It's not St. Raymond's," Ethan's heart felt like it was about to explode. He could feel his adrenaline pounding, slamming against his throat and his chest. He could barely breathe through the excitement. "Aiden wants us to go to St. Raymond's...I think...but he won't be there." Ethan ripped through the paperwork, looking for the letters. The thunder cracked outside the window, the loud clamor mixed with the heavy downpour rattled Ethan's shades. He jumped up to slam the window closed.

Ethan stood over his desk, his hands ripping at his hair as he read through each letter again. Chris sat quiet and still, doing his best to avoid interrupting his partner.

"This guy does nothing by chance…it's all done for a reason. One way or another it's all done for a reason," Ethan said, closing his eyes and shaking his head. It was killing him; there were so many miniscule twists, so many tiny, narrow discrepancies. "Ok…He made Lucky bring that envelope; we traced that back to him on Mosholu. He knew we wouldn't apprehend Lucky…he knew we'd follow him…knew we'd use him to find the main source. The dead body in the school turned out to lead us to Lake George. The letter in Lake George led us to Mosholu. Mosholu led us to Desmond who led us back to Aiden…" Ethan pounded his fists down on the desk, the anger building inside of him as he felt the frustration begin to seep in…and then it all became clear.

Ethan's phone started to ring, snapping him back into reality. He stared down, feeling the excitement creep back as the display screen showed 'work', the rollercoaster of emotions was driving him crazy.

"Hello?" Ethan said, putting the phone on speaker as he sat next to Chris.

"Ethan, I got some news for you man," Captain said, chuckling as he spoke. "Amazing how much forensics can show us nowadays. So the shooter at Lake George was Aiden." Ethan and Chris looked at each other quickly. "After analyzing the bullet and bullet casings found in Lake George to make sure it's rifling impressions pattern matched that of the gun's barrel that we found in Aiden's room, I'm more than positive you've got your guy…ballistic fingerprinting baby. He had to have been wearing gloves that day in Lake George because there were no fingerprints found on the handle. We did find fingerprints of an unknown subject within the house. The prints were all over your shrine room and also found all over the stove. Based on this and with Aiden suddenly missing...I'm no agent...but I'd say—"

Ethan cut Captain off, "—Thank you. Were there markings on the bodies?"

"I was about to tell you that there weren't markings, I mean that doesn't mean much though...the people in the house died from the carbon monoxide concentration...Ethan, the levels reached over 6,400 ppm. You guys are lucky you got out of the house when you did."

Ethan shook his head as he stared at Chris. "Thanks Cap, we're making moves soon, we'll keep in touch." Ethan tossed the phone on to his bed, crossing his arms as he delved back into deep thought.

"I guess the markings weren't there because of how he killed them...no real way of getting them on so many bodies if he couldn't stay in the house long enough," Ethan said.

"Nothing's done without reason, though," Chris said. The lighting cracked outside, the rain still hadn't given up.

It was already almost 10:30p.m.. The time was drawing nearer as Ethan sat at his laptop doing some last minute research. The time continued to trickle down. Both of the agents feverishly typed away on their computers, desperately racing to find the answer to their problems. Ethan kept one eye on the clock as he tried to put himself into his cousin's mind. He knew he had this, but now he had another difficult decision to make. He felt bad as he looked at his partner.

'"Have no fear of change as such and, on the other hand, no liking for it merely for its own sake." Robert Moses.' Ethan closed his eyes as he repeated the man's words.

'"We must make the best of those ills which cannot be avoided." Clarence Day.'

'Duke Ellington says, "You've got to find some way of saying it without saying it."' Ethan even reviewed the way Aiden introduced the quotes.

'"To the last, I grapple with thee; From Hell's heart, I stab at thee; For hate's sake, I spit my last breath at thee." Herman Melville.'

Ethan mulled over the final quote the most. '"A legend is an old man with a cane known for what he used to do. I'm still doing it." Miles Davis.'

Ethan had pounded every word he could into that computer and had prayed to God that with every click of the mouse he would receive a pop of enlightenment, that jolt of acknowledgment like when you have that one thing on the tip of your tongue and someone finally says it. Ethan knew Chris had already mapquested 'St. Raymond's Cemetery'. Ethan was getting frustrated at how close-minded his partner was being. It hit Ethan hard. He had told himself to stay calm and cool, but the revelation was breathtaking. He now had to wait until Chris was fed up with sitting around, until they finally made a move to head out. It seemed like hours before Ethan heard what he was waiting for.

"I'm not finding anything," Chris said, closing his laptop. "It has to be St. Raymond's and if it isn't than what does it matter anyway? We have nothing else. I know it seems almost too easy, but there hasn't been a puzzle this tough yet. Seriously they're like baby puzzles when you think about it."

"Yeah I thought about that before," Ethan said truthfully. "One thing I always remember though...don't get cocky." The killer had been a step ahead every time so far and it killed Ethan to admit it, but right now Ethan *knew* he had him. He figured it out, and he was excited. He looked at Chris, who jumped on the phone to relay the location. The wrong location. Ethan wasn't going to be taking Chris to St Raymond's cemetery.

"Alright, it's already after 11:00 p.m.," Chris said, checking his clip again. "You ready for this?"

Ethan watched his partner as he slowly ejected the clip of death out of his Glock and punched it back in, setting it up to kill. Chris wasn't thinking of it the way Ethan was, but Chris was carrying that weapon with the intention of using it on Aiden. Should Aiden resist, Chris planned on planting one of those shiny bullets inside Aiden's chest.

"Ethan?" Chris was standing right in front of Ethan, holding out his leather jacket and staring at him like he had three heads. Ethan felt queasy; he felt his stomach turning and his head getting light. He nodded his head at Chris, grabbed his jacket and his gun, and walked out with him. As they waited for the elevator, that one resonating thought continued to press Ethan's fears.

There were two people that boarded the elevator that night. One liked hip-hop, one preferred rock. One liked blondes, one fancied brunettes. Both faced astronomical hardship growing up, and both went on to fight crime. One thought he was heading to St. Raymond's, one knew he wasn't. One knew he was confronting a psychotic, sadistic murderer, but the other feared he wasn't.

Chapter 48

Confessions

The rain poured on the two agents as they hustled to the Charger. The thunder was at its loudest and the lighting streaked through the dark night sky. Ethan jumped into the driver's seat, not saying a word to his soaked, unsuspecting partner. This wasn't what Ethan had wanted, but he realized something crucial. This realization excited Ethan at first. It gave him a quick uplift, but then it also opened the door to another fact and introduced him to new terrors. He hadn't just uncovered a slip up. He had solved a puzzle embedded deeply in his cousin's words.

As the Charger roared down the slick, slippery road, Ethan's mind became focused. He could already see his partner was wary. Chris had begun looking around more frequently and it was only a matter of time before he realized they were off track. There was a lot that could happen, a lot that could go wrong, but Ethan held on to the hope that he'd make it.

"You shoulda got off there," Chris said, pointing a finger back to the last exit. The Tremont Avenue exit was long behind them now as the Charger continued to roar forward, heading back in the direction of Mosholu Parkway. Chris was now aware something was wrong.

"Ethan…what are you doing?" Chris said staring out the car window and trying to make out where they were. The rain was covering the glass, making it hard to see even with the wipers on full blast. Ethan saw Chris reach for his phone out of the corner of his eye.

"It's not St. Raymond's," Ethan said. "I know for a fact it isn't." Ethan exited the Major Deegan at the 233rd Street exit. He knew Chris was staring at him, but he didn't want to make eye contact. He didn't particularly enjoy lying at all, let alone to one of his closest friends and partner. Fact of the matter was Ethan had been lying the entire case because there were just some things that couldn't be spoken.

"What the fuck are you talking about Ethan…Where are you going?" Chris was flailing his arms around in a panic. He was well aware that at this point there was almost no way they could make it to St. Raymond's by midnight. The time was already a quarter to 12. No matter what, they were in deep shit at this point.

"Listen, just trust me," Ethan said. He had devised a plan during the car ride. Between the vicious storm, the short time limit, and the desperate search for a way out of this mess, Ethan was shocked he hadn't crashed. "I need you to call up Illames and tell him that we had it figured out wrong." Ethan slowed down as he came to a stoplight by Jerome Avenue, he didn't want to risk putting his sirens on so he had to take the red light and pray no one smacked into them.

"Holy shit Ethan!" Chris screamed as the car slid around the bend, skidding right through the red light and safely on to Jerome Avenue. "What are you talking about, you're losing it man!" Chris screamed. He threw himself back in his seat, putting his hands on his head in disbelief. Ethan could tell that he was contemplating what to do.

Finally Ethan pulled up to exactly where he wanted to be. He reached the finish line. He stared out his window, examining the nearby area to make sure the coast was clear. The time was now 11:54 p.m.

"Not a lot of time. I realized it while we were in the house, but I needed it to be just me and you. I need to know why this is happening Chris, so I don't need a hundred officers and agents swarming the place. That's why I couldn't tell you. I knew you'd call it in. It seemed like St. Raymond's was the right place, and honestly I don't know what would have happened if we went there, but we'll figure that out now." Ethan glanced at the clock quickly. "All the letters did have one thing in common. The killer doesn't say anything that is meaningless, every word matters. The killer referred to a place we all end up, yes that may be St. Raymond's, I know John-David is there, but I think it's too much of a coincidence that each person used for those quotes was buried right here at Woodlawn Cemetery. Miles Davis, Herman Melville, Robert Moses. Every one of them, they are all right here. Every single quotation was spoken by a dead body at this cemetery. I checked, Chris. I looked them all up on the internet, I saw the similarity. Do you think that's coincidence? That last letter said "Where will we end up," so he's mocking us. Aiden hasn't done anything by accident. Everything has a purpose. He wants us to go to St. Raymond's so that, yet again, he can laugh at us. Something is going down right here at the Woodlawn Cemetery." 11:59 p.m. Ethan's heart was racing. Time was moving so fast. Chris didn't hesitate for a second as he grabbed his phone, but he also saw the time and knew he had to act, not sit back mesmerized.

"Illames, we were wrong, we need everyone at Woodlawn Cemetery in the Bronx," Chris said, ripping the door open and diving out into the horrific storm. The two raced to the gate, the rain ripping across their bodies as they jumped the curb, sliding between the parked cars along the side of the cemetery gate. The gate was about 12 feet tall, and the spikes at the top were sharp to keep out any unwanted late night visitors. Ethan didn't even give it thought; he instantly jumped up to the top of the gate, grabbing hold of the metal, slick bars and threw himself over, landing softly on the grass inside the cemetery with Chris landing beside him.

The two began to run, finally realizing that they had not even an inkling of a clue as to where they were supposed to be running to. Woodlawn Cemetery was an enormous museum of tombstones, and at midnight in the middle of hurricane-like weather, finding one person was not a simple task. The words from that last letter revolved in Ethan's head, 'You know where I'll be.'

They both took out their weapons, Chris because he believed Aiden to be a dangerous killer, Ethan because he still held on to the hope that Aiden was innocent, that someone else was the killer all along. The cemetery was incredible, the rain, thunder, and lightning gave it an even more majestic, yet disturbing feel. The mausoleums were gigantic, beautifully decorated structures created from stone, marble, and brick. They stood in haunting splendor over the agents as they quietly crept through, running their eyes over the dark, silent grave yard.

The sporadic booming of the thunder annoyed Ethan as he peered around each grave stone and mausoleum. He knew he wouldn't have too much time before the backup arrived. And if it was his cousin he wanted to speak with him one on one, not a whole army on one, and not in an interrogation room.

Ethan slowly moved around a giant mausoleum, and he could feel Chris by his side as the two tried to stay low and out of sight. The mausoleum in front of them was enormous. The giant, bold letters across the top spelled ROBERT MOSES, accompanied by the dates 1888 - 1981. 'He was one of the first quotes,' Ethan thought. Standing in front of the structure's doors stood two Ancient Egyptian statues, both depicting figures with a man's body and a jackal's head. The building was exceptional. It was remarkable to think that someone took so much time and money to design their eternal resting spot.

Ethan felt his heart pound in his chest. He could feel his stomach flip inside as he stared ahead. He saw a man standing there, just standing in the open, no weapon in sight, no jacket on, no hat on. He just stood in front of a giant statue in the middle of the cemetery.

Before Ethan could do or say anything, Chris was already moving much faster, his gun pointed directly in front of him. "Don't move; put your arms in the air!" he screamed, skipping forward, still keeping low with his eyes peeled and focused. The rain was still falling heavily, but that wouldn't be enough to stop Chris…it wasn't as bad as Lake George. Chris was an exceptional marksman.

"Stop!" Ethan screamed, placing his gun back in its holster as he walked forward. He felt calmer now. He was just so confused, so torn up inside as he stared at his cousin. "What are you doing, Aiden?"

Aiden laughed as he stood motionless in front of the gravesite. The giant, green marble statue pointed straight up like the Washington Monument. A small angel stood on top, its wings spread wide as it stared down at Aiden. Ethan could barely make out the small lettering through the rain. He was having enough trouble seeing his cousin.

"Here you are…the hero," Aiden said, still not making a move. Ethan pointed at Chris, who still stood in a ready position, and he shook his head.

"Please," Ethan said. Chris looked back and forth between the two cousins before he finally put his gun down.

"I figured you'd show up," Aiden said. "I don't deserve jail, Ethan. I'm a monster."

Ethan couldn't believe what he was hearing. The whole case, the whole show was over. It was Aiden the entire time, his own cousin, the man who was once a boy who looked up to Ethan.

"I haven't seen you in...it's been about what...twelve? Maybe thirteen years?"

"It's been thirteen years," Ethan said, nodding his head at Chris who stood uneasily across from Ethan.

Aiden turned around, his eyes staring daggers through Ethan as the rain and the wind howled around them. Despite the conditions, Ethan felt like they were alone. He hadn't seen his cousin in so many years, but he still felt like he knew him well.

"I was never there before but..." Ethan began. He was quickly interrupted as Aiden whipped out a small 9mm pistol from the waist of his jeans. Chris quickly responded, whipping out his gun as well and pointing it at Aiden.

"Stop!" Ethan screamed, lifting one arm to point at Chris. His partner moved uneasily, taking a few steps in place as he licked his lips, his finger moving dangerously close to squeezing the trigger.

"Shut up!" Aiden screamed. "You need to just shut your mouth."

"Put the gun away Aiden...We haven't hit rock bottom yet..."

"We!" Aiden screamed, cutting Ethan off again. "Who's we? You don't know me Ethan. You have no idea what I've been going through."

Ethan stood still and quiet, he stared back at his cousin who still had the pistol pointed at him. Ethan knew that sooner or later Chris would have enough.

"I need to know why you did this," Ethan said quickly, wiping the rain from his face.

"Why? I'm a murderer, Ethan…that's what I am!" Aiden screamed. He sounded like he was in agony, like he had a massive headache that just wouldn't' stop.

"Who's grave is this?" Ethan asked, quickly changing the subject and pointing to the statue behind Aiden. Aiden shook his head, smiling widely as he stared at Ethan.

"All those people deserved to die," Aiden said, still seeming to fight with himself. "Not this one though."

Aiden kept his gun pointed at Ethan, and Chris kept his gun pointed at Aiden. The three stood in a triangle around each other in silence just feeling the rain fall over them.

Ethan stared ahead at his cousin. It broke his heart to see the man this way. He had been through so much with him, but when his parents had separated it was too difficult to keep up a relationship.

"I'll stick with you through it all. I won't walk away from you. I swear," Ethan said, he could feel his eyes burning.

"I'm not going to jail, Ethan…Can you still remember John-David's funeral?" Aiden said. The rain was heavy, but Ethan could still make out the stream of tears now covering his cousin's face.

"I'll never forget that day." Ethan could recall that entire day like it was yesterday. He remembered seeing his cousin and thinking of him as a stranger. He remembered how cruel it was to hear his cousin speak to him so maliciously.

"I always thought that was the worst day of my life," Aiden said, still smiling wryly as the rain and tears saturated his face. His gun's barrel was still pointed directly at Ethan, unwaveringly. "End of the road now, Ethan."

Ethan could see Chris' body shake. The words had jolted him back to reality, forcing his instincts to kick in. Ethan could see Chris' hand shaking, itching to grab his gun and pop one into Aiden. His face was tarnished with anger and distress, even worse than when he was informed they weren't going to St. Raymond's. Ethan hadn't even taken a second to realize that he was right in coming to Woodlawn Cemetery.

Before either of the three could say a word, a faint siren entered the air, the low wailing growing louder with each passing second.

"Aiden, I need to know why you did it," Ethan said again, not afraid of the 9mm pistol poised to draw his last breath. "Why?"

Aiden laughed in between loud cries. Ethan could see the pain in his face. This was exactly what they had thought the killer looked like. They had said the killer was most likely someone very distraught, someone who had come from a messed up family. Aiden most definitely fit that description right now.

Aiden shook his head, still fighting with the demons in his mind. Ethan whispered urgently, "Don't cry...don't feel bad...When we're older we won't be like them." The tears streamed down faster. Ethan remembered those words. They stunned him as he spoke them over in his head. He remembered the day his cousin spoke those words to him, although he had always tried to forget them.

The sirens were on top of them. Their loud, obnoxious wailing disrupted the serenity of the graveyard. Ethan could hear voices now, the sound of radios and shuffling coming closer to where they stood. They were stuck at a stalemate.

"You can drop the gun, and we can deal with this..."

After a moment of painful silence, Ethan watched as Aiden dropped the gun to his side. His cousin stared at him, and his eyes weren't as angry anymore, they looked sympathetic now.

This was what Ethan had dreaded as soon as he saw his cousin on that porch. He was afraid it could actually be him behind the whole thing. Ethan saw how he acted that day, the nervous jitters as he stood on the porch, looking everywhere before he walked away. They hadn't seen each other in so long, but as Ethan looked on he could still see the boy he used to know. The one he used to have so much fun with, the one he loved so much. Aiden had such a difficult life, filled with brief ups and corroded with downs, but Ethan still couldn't understand why.

"I love you, Ethan," Aiden said suddenly. Ethan's heart sank as his world crashed abruptly. He watched his cousin as he brought the gun up, the barrel staring Ethan in the eyes again. He took a deep breath, his body stiffening. He could see Chris bringing his gun up, trying as best as he could to protect his partner. The whole thing moved in slow motion. Aiden slowly turned the gun away from Ethan, placing it squarely against his own head.

"No!" Ethan screamed. He felt as though he had just jumped into ice cold water. His whole body shook, his breath was knocked out of him, his hand reached out for his cousin as his legs did their best to make it there in time. Ethan took a few steps, his eye exploding with tears as he screamed at the top of his lungs. Aiden stared back at him, smiling again, and then he pulled the trigger.

"NO! NO! Oh my God!" Ethan cried, his knees hitting the floor. He rolled forward, placing his arms out on the soaking wet grass as he tried to catch his breath. He crawled forward, crying hysterically, as he looked up at his cousin's lifeless body. "Oh my God," he whimpered. He stopped crawling, grabbing at his chest as his heart painfully, violently shook inside his chest. Ethan screamed loudly, unable to move as he rolled over on the wet ground, slapping at it pathetically. He had failed.

Chris holstered his gun, putting both of his hands on his head as he turned away from the horrid sight. He was in complete shock. He felt his knees wobble beneath him as he turned back to see his partner in agony, writhing in the puddles on the ground. He ran over to him, unsure of what to do, he had never seen anything like it in his time at the bureau. He had seen bullet wounds, he had seen shots to the head, but never had he seen a man take his own life this way. He stared down at the body, it was lying in a heap in front of the tombstone, quiet and still.

The agents and the cops swarmed the area, taping off the entire scene as though there were something more to find. Ethan stayed on the ground with his eyes closed, one hand resting on his cousin's arm. His cousin who had endured so much, who had been through hell and back, or actually just went to hell altogether. The guy never got a break. Never.

The noise around him was a distant buzz. He couldn't hear anything but that gun shot. He watched the image over and over in his mind. It was a wonder he kept from vomiting everywhere. Ethan opened his eyes, staring over at his cousin's blank eyes.

"We don't have to be them," Ethan said through the crying. Tears still streamed down his cheeks. "You weren't them, Aiden. It's not your fault." He cried heavily. FBI Agent Ethan Carey, the renowned grappling specialist, cried like a baby in front of a squadron of officers, agents, and forensics scientists.

Ethan looked up at the grave in front of him. The tall pointy statue with the baby angel sitting on top. The words on the grave opened Ethan's eyes.

John David Moore

September 25th, 2001 - April 4th, 2011

So beautiful, so innocent

We'll be together again, my son

'John David Moore…no hyphen…and that last name,' Ethan thought to himself. 'Aiden had a son.' Aiden had a son, and he named him after his cousin John-David.

Chapter 49

Two Months Later

"I won't force you to do anything you don't want to do, Ethan," Luke said, sitting back in his arm chair as he stared at his friend.

"I wanna tell you, Luke, but it hurts," Ethan said. "I've barely told anyone about it." Ethan was so sick and tired of the emotional bullshit. He was tired of sitting in Luke's study. He was tired of the "Are you alright's?"

"Look, I told you leave the macho at the door," Luke said, getting up to sit on the edge of his desk. "You have to want to get better. You need to want it yourself...for yourself."

Ethan closed his eyes. He could keep running, he had for so long as it was, but right now seemed like the time to come out with it. He could still feel the pain from the night at the cemetery, but he had to put it aside. The agony was killing him. It was affecting his everyday life.

"Just let me talk," he said, putting his head in his hands and keeping his eyes closed. Ethan began to retell the memory, placing himself back in that day.

Ethan stood there in the entertainment room of his father's house, watching as his father joked with the rest of his family. Everyone was so happy, and they were all smiling and laughing as he waved his arms around, saying something about a helmet and the pool at his friend's house. Ethan shook his head at the corny sense of humor.

"Let's play hide and seek!" a boy yelled from the kitchen. Ethan spun around and looked down at his cousin Aiden.

It pained him inside to look down at the boy, the innocent child who had nothing on his mind but PlayStation and cartoons. Ethan had no tears left as he watched the two roughhouse with each other. He knew what was coming and the apparition of the young boy in front of him didn't. He looked over at his father, the weak, whipped, small man who entertained his guests like he was some kind of rock star. Ethan felt the hatred inside, the fury tearing through his innards. He felt nothing but wrath as he looked on at the thing in front of him.

"Ethan! Go hide and I'll count!" Aiden screamed. Ethan could still remember how much fun he was having that day. He loved playing with his cousin and he hadn't seen him in so long because of the divorce.

This was it. Ethan had never gotten this far before. He hated the memory so much. He could still smell the roasted chicken in the oven, the sound of the laughter filling his ears, the bright Christmas lights in every corner of every room.

Ethan watched as his younger self ran about trying to find a hiding place. The smile on the boy's face looked like it would never go away. Ethan moved through the rooms, wishing there was some way he could stop him, any way he could just reach out and grab the kid, scream at the kid and tell him to go home. Just leave this place, don't look back, don't ever call again, you don't have a father. But he was forced to play spectator to this memory.

Ethan rushed ahead, standing at the opening to the living room, standing by the side of the fancy Christmas tree with its bright white lights gleaming. 'Why couldn't I just hide upstairs?' he thought. 'Why couldn't they have just gone downstairs and played PlayStation?'

But low and behold there was little Ethan, smiling away as he dipped in and out of doorways trying to find a good hiding place.

Ethan could feel his heart beating faster. His hands began to shake as the sweat formed across his crown. The anger was so intense. It was so Goddamn painful, and he felt it exploding in his veins, smashing against his skin. Ethan let out an enormous scream as he fell to his knees in the doorway. No one came to see what was wrong, no one could hear him. He grabbed hold of his head, punching the floor as hard as he could, this was it. This was it.

Little Ethan came skipping right through his older self. Ethan stretched his arms out, trying to stop him, but there was no stopping fate. This was meant to be. He couldn't even feel the boy as he ran through him, straight through his outstretched body. Ethan quickly jumped to his feet, spinning around to watch the boy look for a hiding spot.

"Buddy…what are you talking about?" Ethan whispered his dad's words, as he moved further into the room. "You know he has a crazy imagination, Eileen," he continued as he reached out a hand, passing it straight through his younger self.

Ethan didn't know it, but tears had begun to fall from his eyes. He wasn't sad, he wasn't angry anymore, but he couldn't stop tears.

"We never got it, remember?" Ethan said laughing in amazement.

Then he saw it. Ethan watched as the boy moved slowly towards the wall unit on the side of the room. Ethan felt like a lump had formed in his throat, it had suddenly become hard for him to breathe, but he knew he had to stay strong. He wasn't running.

The boy stood directly in front of the wall unit, his mouth opened and quivering. Slowly he opened the glass cabinet door, reaching up to pull down the peculiar object. The tears had already started to form on the boy's cheeks, and his legs and his arms shook. Ethan could still remember this particular moment, when he had first, truly met anger.

He held a beautiful decoration. A delicate, intricate piece of work. The object was the same exact Beauty and the Beast snow globe he had bought his mother on the Disney Cruise.

The boy broke down completely, falling to the ground as he screamed loudly. Tears streamed from his eyes as he stared through them at the snow globe, the incredible gift he had bought for his beautiful mother. Instantly, the whole family had come running to his aide, his father leading the pack. Ethan stared his father down, wanting nothing more than to choke the little 'man' out, but he let it go instead.

"Buddy, what's wrong?" his father asked nervously. He fell down to the floor, grabbing his son in a panic. The boy quickly threw his father's hands off of him. Ethan could see the fire in young Ethan's eyes, could see the rage that he knew so well. His teeth were clenched. His hands tightly squeezed the snow globe as his father finally noticed what was happening.

"I thought we never got it," the boy said through the crying and anger.

His father looked astounded. He moved back a little, looking tensely to Michelle and then back to his enraged son.

"Buddy, it's not..." he began but Ethan wanted no part of it.

"Don't!" Ethan yelled as he jumped up and ran away, weaving in and out of the countless Alosis standing around. Aiden quickly pursued him.

Ethan looked down at the snow globe. The whole room had frozen. He was never there to know what happened next, all he could see was Andrew's stupid, surprised expression. He could also see Michelle's satisfied, smug face. Ray looked confused and, like most of the others in the room, had not a clue what was happening.

Ethan walked through the room and down the steps to where young Ethan and his cousin had run to. He could hear the agonizing crying, the sound of a betrayed boy who knew he had just lost his father. He stood in the basement, staring down at the two. Aiden had one hand on Ethan's back, rubbing it slowly as he watched his cousin lay face down on a couch, shaking from the anger inside.

"Ethan," Aiden said. "Don't cry."

Ethan rolled over, wiping the tears from his face. "I'm not crying." Aiden looked at him understandingly. Crying was weakness and Ethan didn't want to appear weak. "I'm just mad."

"Why are you mad?" Aiden asked. The boy stared down at his hurting cousin with sympathy.

"He's my dad, he's not supposed to lie to me like that," Ethan said, the anger bursting through each word. "That's not how it should be." This was more than just a snow globe. It was more than just some stupid souvenir from a cruise. This was Ethan slowly realizing that his father was horrible. A man who would rather see himself profit before seeing his on happy.

Older Ethan shook his head as he stood there, staring at Aiden as the painful scars reopened in his heart. His cousin had a good heart and could have been such an extraordinary person, but all the bullshit that he had no control over acted like a paperweight on his goodness.

"Don't cry, don't feel bad. When we're older, we won't be like them," Aiden said.

The study was deathly quiet. Luke sat on his desk, his mouth closed as he held his glasses in his hand. He squinted down at Ethan, shaking his head in amazement.

"How do you feel, Ethan," Luke said, hopping down from the desk and walking back to his seat.

"I don't know," Ethan said, feeling a bit lighter but still in pain. "I've never spoken about it until now."

"Well that's very brave of you to speak about it today," Luke said nodding his head at Ethan. "No really, it is. I wish I had a dollar for each my patients who've had trouble doing what you just did."

"I'm still pissed off," Ethan said. He got up and stretched in his place as he walked towards the door. "Thank you, Luke."

Luke reached out, shaking Ethan's hand as the two stared at each other. Ethan could tell that Luke didn't want him to leave. Luke sighed heavily and pursed his lips, raising his eyebrows as he walked towards his study door.

"Ethan, you're a great guy...I know you're not miraculously healed, but my door isn't closed," Luke said, opening his front door.

"Bye, Ethan!" Laura called from down the hall.

"Bye, Ethan!" Ed yelled, waving ecstatically.

Ethan waved back, smiling widely. He felt indifferent. He knew he wasn't healed. However, Ethan was almost positive he was on the right road.

Chapter 50

Deception

"I really want to go to Six Flags. I don't care what else happens next week as long as we get there," Rachel said, laughing as she slurped her soup. Ethan smiled across from her, watching her as she carelessly burnt her tongue.

"You must be starving," Ethan said, watching Rachel painfully drink her soup. Rachel nodded fervently as she continued to bring spoonful after spoonful to her lips. 'Amazing,' Ethan thought. 'I wish I could eat like an animal and not gain a pound.'

"How's work going today?" Rachel asked, wiping her mouth and taking a breather.

Work had been interesting over the past few months. Since his cousin had killed himself, a lot of the guys had taken it easy on Ethan. Even Porter had cut down on the usual wisecracks and jabs.

"Work's different, but I'm sure it will go back to normal sooner or later. Were you busy today?"

Rachel nodded her head. "It's always crazy, there's always news to report. They're starting to give me more responsibility. Hopefully soon I'll be able to write full-blown articles. How about you, are they back to giving you any good cases, or are they still babying you?"

"I told Illames to give me the tough stuff. I definitely think I'm ready. I told him I'm seeing Luke about the grief issues, but they still want me on this drawn-out recuperation plan. It is what it is..." Ethan smiled reassuringly at Rachel.

It was tough going from a reputation of a known ace in the Bureau's operations to being a towel boy. This was the "procedure" according to the higher-ups. They didn't seem to care what Ethan said, or how he supposedly felt. They wanted to do things their way.

"I have to head out. I have to file some more paperwork before I get a time-out," Ethan said smiling sarcastically and dropping some money on the table.

Rachel laughed back at him. "Take your money, it's on me today. You pay all the time." Ethan winked at her, leaned in to kiss her lips, and walked out with his leather and his shades on.

He loved the fact that they could share lunch. He didn't mind working so close to her; he found it to be a nice release from the stress of everyday work. Ethan marched down the long Manhattan streets, glancing around as he noticed a young boy posing for a picture with his friend. The two were laughing as they put up the peace sign. Ethan stared at them, stopping in his tracks. The thoughts of the case rolled through his mind. It still bothered Ethan that Aiden had never told him what that peace sign meant, not to mention he couldn't figure it out himself.

"What up, Mr. Carey," Johnny greeted, as Ethan walked into 26 Federal Plaza. He loved that hallway, the shiny spotless marble floors, the clean, white walls, the waterfall display pushed up against the far wall. It felt so peaceful.

"What's up Johnny," Ethan said, waving as he jumped on the elevator. He wasn't in the mood for the long flights of steps.

Ethan had his vacation coming up. He had never been more excited for time off in his career at the bureau. Chris would be taking vacation the same week so they would be able to catch a Jets game and finally unwind the right way.

He hopped off the elevator, smiling as he walked down the aisle to the entourage of waves and nods. Half the agents in the department hadn't said a word to Ethan in the eight years he was there yet now they were so cheerful. Plopping himself down at his desk, he punched in his password to his computer and got to work.

He'd been working diligently since the funeral. He wasn't getting any taxing work from Illames, nothing he could go out and keep himself busy with. He'd been doing some average paperwork and surveillance. The kind of work he'd normally throw at the interns. He understood why they wanted him in the office, but he still hated it.

"Ethan, can you come in here for a minute?" Illames said. Ethan quickly minimized his screen and locked his computer.

"Yeah," he said curiously. 'Maybe they'll finally take the training wheels off,' he thought to himself.

Ethan sat down in the Chief's office, taking a quick glance around at all the Yankee stuff. He loved Illames' office.

"What's going on Ethan?" Illames said, sitting down across from him and staring him down.

Ethan shrugged his shoulders. "Same old boring paperwork. You have to get me out there, boss."

Illames nodded his head, pulling out a folder and tossing it in front of Ethan.

"Take a look at that and let me know what you think," Illames said, leaning back in his arm chair.

Ethan reached forward, grabbing the folder off the desk. He felt a lump in his stomach as soon as his eyes met the contents. Images of different files Ethan had been studying were compiled together, all the lists and documents he had been searching for the past month or so sat right in Illames' folder.

"You've got someone following me?" Ethan asked tossing the folder back on Illames' desk.

"I don't have to answer your questions, but you have to listen to me," Illames said standing up. His voice was stern. "We have background checks and searches dating back to two months ago. You've been doing this for two months, Ethan. You need to stop. If you value your career it has to end now. You've got a full investigation done on Andrew Alosi...your father right? Why are you looking into him when the case is closed? Aiden Moore is guilty...I really thought you were over this Ethan."

"Listen, I'm over it," Ethan said, shaking his head. "You've been giving me bullshit work to do so I have a lot of time on my hands." Illames picked up the stuffed folder and pretended to weigh it, widening his eyes at Ethan.

"This is extensive work here, Ethan," Illames said pointing at the folder.

"I've had *a lot* of time," Ethan said again.

"It ends now. The case is closed, move forward, and forget about it as hard as that may be to do. I can't relate to how you feel, but at some point we all deal with a case that strikes closer to home than we'd like—though maybe not as serious as yours."

"You're right," Ethan said. "Look I just need to be back out there. Sitting around all day is killing me, so I can't get my mind off things like that."

"Try. You're going to have to try. You're on vacation next week, right? Do something good," Illames said, staring as Ethan made his way out of the office. "Why don't you start a little early, get outta here."

"Thanks," Ethan said, skipping over to his desk to shut his computer down. Ethan was perfectly fine with hitting the road early. He had finished all his work for the day anyway. He took a quick glance around, trying to find Chris amongst the office of agents, but he wasn't going to stand around. Ethan gave Captain a quick wave and almost ran out of the building.

The New York City streets never looked better. Ethan marched through the Friday crowds with his head held high, happily free from the burden of work. As he neared his apartment building, he felt his phone start to vibrate inside his pocket. He reached in, seeing Chris' name displayed on the screen.

"And I'm on vacation!" Ethan said as he answered the call.

"Thank God," Chris said laughing. "I heard Illames spoke to you. I told you to cut the shit."

"Yeah but it's alright," Ethan said, feeling rejuvenated now that he was outside and on vacation. "Honestly the case is over. I swear. It's done."

Ethan slid through his apartment building's door, waving at the doormen as he made his way to the steps.

"That's good man, it's gotta be tough to let go of something like that. I'm here for you, you know that," Chris said as Ethan jogged up the steps, making his way quickly to the 19th floor.

3rd floor

"I'm really feeling a night out in Atlantic City," Chris said. "Just one night away from the girls…we can have a good time. Get some steaks, have some beers, do some gambling—get our minds off this the right way."

"Yeah that sounds great," Ethan said, hopping two steps at a time.

10th floor

"Rangers game Sunday, we should try a different place instead of Rambling," Ethan said as he hopped up another flight of steps.

"I was thinking about maybe going to Ron Blacks over on 1st Ave., I think it's a Rangers bar. Or we can even try to get tickets. They're playing the Penguins at the Garden tonight. What do you think?" Chris waited for a reply. "Hello?"

There was only silence on the other end.

"Ethan?" Chris said.

Still just silence.

Ethan stood at the bottom of the 19th floor's staircase staring up at the top. There was no emotion, his face was blank. He could feel time freeze. He felt a numbness devour his body.

"Ethan! I hear you breathing," Chris said. "Stop messing with me."

Ethan stood still at the bottom of the stairs. His phone dropped from his hand, breaking into pieces on the marble floor below. His eyes were clear; they were focused. His mouth slightly ajar. He couldn't move. He couldn't speak as he stared up at the Beauty and the Beast snow globe.

The inanimate object towered over him. It looked identical to the one from his past.

Ethan floated up the staircase; his stunned body wouldn't allow him to feel. He nearly fell over the ghastly snow globe, knocking the *thing* down the steps as he whipped the hallway door open. Nothing was there. Empty space, empty hallway. Nothing.

He turned his attention, his shocked, terrified expression, back to the stairwell and watched as the snow globe bounced, like a frigid, fragile slinky, down one step after another. Pieces chipped away as the globe rumbled faster, the loud noise ricocheting off the solid stairwell walls. The noise pounded in his head as he watched it fall. As the snow globe finally arrived at the platform, it smashed into the wall, shattering to pieces next to his already broken phone. Ethan stood watching in horror. His vacation was over.

He had no feeling as he walked down the stairs, the stairs he had walked down countless times.

He kept his eyes on the globe as he neared it. He could see the globe's glass shards glistening on the floor. His own reflection stared back at him through the tiny pieces. He slowly bent his knees, coming closer to the hellish object and turned the globe's base over to reveal a tiny, handwritten inscription.

Guess again